AZIMUTH SOUTH
Book 1
Malanda

*J*enifer Jones was born in Birmingham, England shortly after the end of World War II. Her family migrated to Australia in the early 1950s and she grew up in Far North Queensland where she was an inaugural student at Trinity Bay High School in Cairns. She left Australia in 1969 and travelled extensively in Europe and parts of South East Asia before returning in 1981 to Sydney, where she now lives. Whilst abroad, she worked in Papua New Guinea, and London where her only daughter was born. This is her first novel.

AZIMUTH SOUTH
Book 1
Malanda

by
Jenifer Jones

Cover design by Peter R. Jones

[Azimuth Publishing – 2012]

Published by Azimuth Publishing 2012
BN98616141

First published in Australia in 2012 by
Azimuth Publishing
3/40a Roslyn Gardens
Sydney 2011 Australia

www.azimuth-publishing.com

Telephone numbers, postal and email addresses for Azimuth Publishing can be found at
www.azimuth-publishing.com/contacts.htm

National Library of Australia Cataloguing-in-Publication entry:

Author: Jones, Jenifer.
Title: Azimuth South. Book 1, Malanda / by Jenifer Jones ; cover
                   design by Peter R. Jones.
ISBN: 9780987283504 (pbk.)
Subjects: British--Queensland--Fiction.
Dewey Number: A823.4

ISBN 978-0-9872835-0-4
Printed and bound by Lulu

For Mum and Dad - and the people of Malanda,
past, present and future.

When equipping the Endeavour Bark, which was to sail under his command from Plymouth on 25 August 1768, First Lieutenant James Cook requisitioned thus: 'Admiralty Office: Dr. Knight hath got an Azimuth Compass of an Improve'd construction which may prove to be of more general use than the old ones: pleased to move my Lords Commissioners of the Admiralty to order the Endeavour Bark under my command to be supplied with it.'

Table of Contents

Chapter 1
Homecoming
MALANDA – 1952

*H*ere he was again, grateful for the corrugated ceiling that separated him and his family from the outside world. At least the world beyond these tin walls was at peace; bore no resemblance to that beyond the corrugations of the bomb shelter in the family's back yard for all those years. He thought on his circumstances and relief far outweighed the apprehension coursing through him. Even so, the latter was sufficient to keep him awake, restless. Unable to sleep, he lost the battle to lie still, rolled over onto his back instead, and clasped his hands behind his head. His eyes remained closed which made not one iota of difference to the profundity of the pitch blackness in which he lay. Drawing in a deep breath, he filled his broad chest, but consciously controlled its exhalation, loath to disturb the peace. In this total absence of light his hearing was acute and he smiled at the rapid, untroubled breathing of his young daughters who slept like puppies on a makeshift mattress of clothes held together with one of the sheets the farmer had given them this afternoon. Next to him his wife, heavy with a child close to readiness, slept soundly, the pattern of her breath deep and regular - the occasional change of tempo hinting at some subconscious nocturnal escapade. He caught her daydreaming sometimes, when the faraway look in her pensive eyes stirred his protective instincts. It was so quiet he could almost hear the blood coursing through his veins, an awareness strangely exhilarating. His aural investigation spread further afield, picked up the susurration of soft leaves sweeping the external corrugations of the roof, a leafy besom wielded by a breeze too gentle to hear. An occasional skittering sound, as of skeletal creatures scampering across the roof, was probably loose or broken branches tossed about by stronger gusts of air. Beyond these sounds lay the utter, uncluttered silence of a world in repose. No road or highway, domestic motor, dog, cat, or passerby to sully the silence; just the singular, slumbering breath of his family and the gently breathing world.

3

He drew another deep breath. "*Bloody 'ell,*" he thought - and he thought it as he spoke it, "bloody" rhyming with "woody" – "*William Johnson, you can't lie here in this state. Move, man ....*"

The thought remained unfinished. No sooner had it arrived than he found himself at the door, clutching the torch the farmer had given him earlier, fiddling with it to find the "On" switch. "For any urgent calls during the night," his host had said, and was understood to be referring to calls of nature. He got the torch working, aimed its dull beam down as he passed through the door, closing it gently behind him, mindful of advice to keep the room closed up tightly whilst sleeping to prevent unwelcome nocturnal visitors. To his satisfaction, all the doors in the house worked well, this one especially so, having been oiled this afternoon from an old can they had found in the shed behind the house.

The layout of the house was a simple one with which he was already familiar. He pointed the weak beam of the torch in the direction of the front door, found it almost immediately. There was minimal furniture; nothing to bump into. His new home filled his nostrils with the organic smell of dirt, dust and leaf-mould. A rickety side table, to the right of the front door was where he had left his 'makings' on top, and his slippers underneath. Picking up the tobacco pouch, he put it in the breast pocket of his pyjama shirt before pulling on slippers which looked strangely out of place and citified here. He looked around for something to wedge between door and jamb to keep it shut but not locked after he'd gone out. The intense darkness surrounding the beam of the torch presented a challenge, but he found a wad of paper squares hanging limply on a loop of string from a nail above the side table and to the right, away from the door. He wondered at their originally intended purpose as he carefully, to be as quiet as possible, tore a few sheets and folded them into a wedge of sorts to fulfill his purpose.

Then he opened the door, lifting it slightly to ease its passage, stepped down onto the top step and turned to fix the wad of paper in the door. All this he achieved easily and when he turned to walk down the path to the gate he realized why – he was surrounded by a luminous light the like of which he had never experienced before. It was a twilight of sorts, the beam of the torch quenched, totally absorbed into it. He looked around him; the hairs on his forearms stood up, a quick intake of breath stopping him in his tracks – from the Stygian depths of the house he had emerged beneath a breathtaking sky alive with vibrant stars in crystal clear relief against a luminous background which seemed to stretch back beyond eternity.

The gentle valley and the folds in the low hills surrounding the homestead lay clearly visible beneath this extraordinary heaven in a peace unbroken by any visible intrusion of man, save the few modest farm buildings in the immediate vicinity that were to become his home. Pulling himself together, he made his way through the gate and across the freshly churned space in front of the house, a circular drive overgrown through lack of use, to the large tree stump he had noticed when they had arrived during the late afternoon. He sat down and gazed up for an indeterminate age at the awesome canopy of this southern night sky; a will-o-the-wisp floating freely above his human form, at one with this exquisite world of which he was a surreal inhabitant. With an uninhibited lightheartedness and optimism he had not felt in a very long time, he turned his attention earthward.

The air was fresh and he felt greater comfort than he had since arriving in this country he had adopted, sight unseen. Enjoying the sensual pleasure of the ambient temperature, he bent to the scrutiny of his immediate environment. The lie of the land was pleasing to the eye and seemed to afford the homestead, for want of any other description, the practical benefit of protection from some of nature's harsher manifestations; certainly from flood, being nice and high, and he thought probably from strong winds too, but only time would tell; and the advice, no doubt, of the locals would be rained upon him, obvious tyro that he was, though only time would tell on that score as well.

The house, he decided, was built with the back facing south and the front, at which he now looked, facing north. "Why would a subsistence farmer build his home in any other direction, given a choice?" he thought, "Surely the East and West of things is the same here as back home." He'd always had a good sense of direction and certain skills developed as a dispatch rider in England during the middle war years were genuinely useful now. Although he couldn't see it, he knew that the road back to the town of Malanda ran along the ridge which he could see above the house on its

Western side. There were a couple of quite large, gently rising fields between the house and the ridge.

The track from the house up to the road led back in a northerly direction, away from the township, to the perimeter of the neighbouring property. It came to the fence close to where the squatter's humpy occupied a bald rise of earth a short distance from a copse of trees in a large field under cultivation. The crop was an enigma to him and not like anything he'd seen before. He had a lot to learn about this farming lark, of that there was no doubt. At this point the track turned sharply to the left and skirted the fence dividing the two properties for about half a mile up to the road. After crossing the cattle grid, a left turn would take you to the township of Malanda. It was a solid bitumen road. The benefit of that was not lost on him, the amount of rain this area obviously got.

The names they'd seen on signposts came to him – Lakes Barrine and Eacham, Yungaburra, Kairi, Milaa Milaa, and more – but where a right turn out of the farm would lead eluded him. "There will be plenty of time for that," he thought, the future beckoning again with tantalizing promise. He looked back towards the house where his family slept. A vision of Dulcie's face suddenly came to mind, at the precise moment when Ray Watson, the farmer, pointed to the house by way of introduction to their new accommodation. She must have seen it, as they ground their way slowly towards the "homestead" in the ute. The farmer had kept slightly off the beaten track, riding ridges between entrenched ruts, avoiding pitfalls unprotected by the thick, unchecked grasses. He had taken it nice and easy, his patience evidence of a deep-rooted and natural respect for Dulcie's condition. She had obviously thought the house to be one of the working farm buildings, some repository for grain or livestock or carryings on to do with such things. Her astonishment when the farmer pointed it out robbed her of comment, struck dumb by innate good manners and the respect she afforded her fellow man. All the same, Bill knew she was rocked to the core by the manifestation of this crude dwelling that was to become home. If he was to be honest he would have to admit his own incredulity that the building being pointed out could have been erected for human habitation. There would have to be a few changes around here!

These thoughts led to his natural contemplation of the events of the day, a day probably almost at its end; if he could read the sky above him he would have a better idea of where exactly he was in this strange limbo between yesterday and tomorrow. 'Yesterday' had been an emotional roller-coaster, a day on which they had experienced high excitement, at departing on the last leg of a very long journey: a day on which the journey itself had been a source of sheer delight, by train from the coastal town of Cairns up the ranges and through a string of townships – he couldn't remember all of their names – to this small township of Malanda. Malanda – the name which had become a beacon of salvation to them over the many months during which they had worked their way through the formalities which would lead them to a new life, a life which offered real hope of a solid and happy future for them and the nippers; hope which had made their parting from their families bearable, and had been a guiding light during the subsequent weeks of travelling by train and ship and train.

But then, 'yesterday' had also been the day on which they had arrived at this source of hope, to learn that their "sponsor" was, indeed, a fraud, a squatter, in his own English sense of the word, and no more able to look after them than he was to look after himself in a conventional sense. But as it had transpired, their squatter was a resourceful and genuinely benevolent man with a not inconsiderable intellect, capable of finding solutions for himself which involved, in their realisation, solutions for others.

As events had unfolded, they were plucked from the depths of despair before ever consciously sliding into its dark pit. He sat gazing at the gentle valley before him, unable to staunch the memory of the day's events which flowed suddenly and overwhelmingly through him.

- 0 -

Cairns: 2 December 1952: After an early breakfast, they had set off from The Temperance Hotel at about 8 o'clock, the squabbling of the girls over the last of the Vegemite still ringing in their ears. Their preference for Vegemite over marmalade had started on the voyage, was now firmly entrenched. A packed lunch of sandwiches had been prepared for their trip –

cheese and chutney, corned beef, baked beans, tomato with vegemite, each individually wrapped in greaseproof paper. All perfectly satisfactory to Bill, so long as the others ate the corned beef, the taste for which war had knocked clean out of him. He preferred a jam sandwich any day. War, and its aftermath, had starved them all of sugar. He liked the way jam managed to crystallize into the bread after a bit, making a dry, crunchy confection reminiscent of a dessert his mother had used to make back in Birmingham, long before war had erupted, back when he was the eldest of five kids, not the current tally of ten, one of his Mam's eleven having been lost in wartime. Having been evacuated to the West Country with the rest of the youngsters, when Jerry was blitzing the major industrial cities nightly, hell bent on obliterating the place, Bill's young brother Johnny had been taken, ironically, when an outbreak of meningitis erupted in the otherwise safe haven to which he had been dispatched.

For their trip up to Malanda, Bill had ordered oranges and bananas as well, out of the pure pleasure of being able to do so. He'd no doubt this modest picnic would be supplemented with dried fruits, perhaps a wedge of Madeira cake, special treats for the girls who were not slow to make their tastes known in influential quarters - quarters they had seemed, throughout their travels, to identify with pure animal instinct. Their main luggage, all of their worldly possessions packed into a trunk and two large suitcases, had been taken ahead of them to the railway station by Joe, who had, during their short stay in Cairns, genuinely befriended them, been afforded the title "Uncle Joe" by the girls.

An Italian 'Giuseppe', Joe was a waiter at the hotel when he wasn't working on his Dad's cane farm, south of Cairns, out Edmonton way. He had caused quite a stir bringing the car into town. It was a rare occurrence, done only once before in fact, when he'd dropped Mama in to the Hydes Hotel over in Lake Street, for some special 'Senoras' reunion in the Palm Court, about a year ago. On that occasion he'd parked up on the Esplanade, wandered up to the "oyster man's" kiosk to buy a couple of dozen shucked oysters and sat to eat them on one of the benches overlooking the sea, enjoying the salty, slightly marshy smell of the high tide. That occasion had come clearly to mind as he'd organised the Johnson's baggage under the interested eye of staff and guests alike, the day before their departure.

Nowadays, the FX was not only Joe's means of recreational transport, but also, on account of his current lack of an all-encompassing romantic attachment, his main occupation during his time off. It was odd how the FX attracted the girls, and then somehow led to their departure. To him she lived. He loved her, simple as that. The care he lavished on her gleamed from her highly polished, latest, a-la-mode, green body, the light which zinged off the pristine chrome grill, front and rear bumpers, hubcaps, and the rest. Bill's spontaneous admiration on seeing the car had been genuinely gratifying, the more so coming from an obviously knowledgeable man, with more than just a passing interest in motors. An interested and thorough inspection of the interior had been accompanied by an enthusiastic running commentary on the upholstered leather bench seats front and back, 3 speed manual column gear shift, the proportions of the steering wheel and its substance, dashboard design, the sophistication of the car's gauges and meters; the crucifix hanging from the rear vision mirror got a mention, "Keeps Mama happy!", as did the lack of a nodding dog in the rear window, "No use to anyone."

They'd laughed together - the comments offered and taken in good humour. The manufacturers claimed that the FX would go from 0 to 60 mph in 20 seconds, which equated to covering 440 yards in 20.5 seconds. "Which is all well and good," Bill had said, "But you'd need to glide through your gear changes, no clutch mind – it'd all be in the timing. You've given her a workout have you?"

Joe's response had been easy, "Yeah course, first thing I did! Once she was run in of course. There's a good road between Gordonvale and Edmonton which is in pretty good nick in the middle of the road, and straight for long enough to see the road clear well ahead, and behind, so you can give it the lead foot without any worries. Right near home as it happens so I don't have to go out of my way," he'd laughed, but finished up by saying, "but you're right, you've got to be good at it to match their claims."

They had talked about her fuel efficiency and a few other things and Joe knew he'd found a fellow enthusiast. "Pity he's leaving tomorrow," he'd thought wryly, "but then, Malanda's not the end of the earth."

9

That had been yesterday. This morning Joe parked at 7.45 a.m. in Spence Street in one of the spaces reserved in front of the hotel for guests, ready to pick them up and take them to the station for this last leg of their gargantuan journey, a journey they'd undertaken in search of a new life, hope and succour. They had already promised to write and let him know their exact whereabouts as soon as they were settled, stressing that he was naturally welcome to come up and visit whenever he wanted to.

"Like as not we'll stand out like sore thumbs up there, Joe," said Bill, "so if you decide to come up before you hear from us, just enquire at the local pub, which I've heard tends to be the hub of rural communities out here. Not too different to back home, except that I think our - I suppose I should say their, eh? - rural communities are a bit different! Apparently the pub in Malanda dominates the town – big and prominently located I gather."

They all laughed, imagining the sensation the FX might cause in the farming community they were heading for, since even here in the big smoke she turned heads. Jess and Jilly laughed along with everyone, not having the vaguest idea what the joke was. Typical kids, they just hated feeling left out. Bill had settled the account the night before, leaving precious little of the forty pounds he'd had in the kitty to pay for their entertainment and incidentals during their migration and relocation - thirty saved and ten borrowed on the voyage - so they bid farewell to the waitress in the dining room, and to the staff on duty at the front desk and Joe installed them in the car, Dulcie and Bill in the front and Jess and Jilly in the back.

Cairns Central Station wasn't that far, the lift more a friendly parting gesture than a necessity, but they'd all agreed that arriving at the station in style was befitting for such an auspicious journey; "Like Lord and Lady Muck!" as Dulcie described their arrival to her brother Harvey in her first letter to him after they had settled in.

It was plain from the start that they weren't going straight to the station. Joe laughed at their puzzlement, "You didn't think I'd bring the car all this way just to drive you down the road and round the corner, did you? There's plenty of time. The train doesn't go until 9.00 and there's nothing to do at the station unless you want to sit and have another cup of tea which I thought hardly likely. Everything is fixed up with Selwyn; your luggage, seats,

10

everything, all organised. I thought a nice drive along the Esplanade, then up past the hospital and back would be a very pleasant way to say "see-ya-later" to the place. It won't take long. You couldn't ask for a better morning; nice to see the sun after all that rain. It'll be hot and sticky later on, but it's real nice now, so wha'd'ya reckon?"

He'd slowed to a virtual standstill, glanced left, meeting Dulcie's eyes which twinkled with unambiguous acceptance. Bill's concurrence was drowned out by the shrieks of excited approval from the back seat but Joe got the message. He navigated the turn onto the Esplanade immediately opposite to the little jetty which ran out into Trinity Inlet. Bill and Dulcie had wandered along the jetty a few times during their brief stay and recognised some of this morning's "usual suspects" whom they had observed fishing for hours on end from the same spot every day, some of them sitting on the edge with their legs dangling, nursing their reels and peering reflectively into the water below, whilst others would simply set up their lines along the railing and then come together in small groups to have a smoke and engage in the desultory conversation of men with no real demands on their time, much of which they spent in each other's company. This morning however, as they could see from the car, the waterline in the mangroves across the inlet was way down, and the distinctive smell of the exposed mudflat lingered in the air. So the "would be" fishermen had a wait on their hands before it would be worth throwing in a line. "Reckon they'll be heading down to The Barrier Reef soon as one of them notices it's after 10," said Joe, "what a life, eh!"

No one commented as they passed the point, driving past the larger pier on its north-western side. They all craned their necks, turning to look past the line of trees which ran the full length of the Esplanade, benches set neatly between them on the well-kept lawns running down to the paved pathway which ran along the sea wall. They peered out to sea, beyond the mud flat which lay exposed by low tide. The mud flat teemed with life, and had been the source of enormous fun and amusement for them during what seemed long periods of low tide, such as it was right now. It was a fresh, clear morning and the sun sparkled off the myriad small pools in its dimpled surface, glinting off the flashing backs of the tiny, soft- shelled crabs which slipped sideways between one bolt hole and another. Joe drove sedately, allowing plenty of time to take it all in.

A cooling breeze came in through the open windows, carrying with it the distinctive smell of salt, mud and rotting vegetation. They didn't mind the smell of the mudflat, liked it in fact, finding it an intrinsic and natural part of the exotic character of the place. The end of the Esplanade petered out into a sandy parking area where Joe pulled in and parked facing the sea. Looking back to the mountains on the other side of Trinity Bay, Bill pointed out to Dulcie and Joe the outline of a supine woman, gazing up into the heavens, an image he'd perceived in the two mountain ranges which ran along the spine of the promontory, overlaying one another with varying depths and shades of colour. After a few minutes scrutiny with more than a couple of questions about which mountains represented which parts of this mysterious woman's anatomy, Dulcie and Joe saw her too, almost simultaneously. Her pert little upturned breasts were the first to come into focus, with her flat stomach, prominent hipbones and long upturned thighs following in rapid succession. Once identified, she became an unmistakable part of the landscape – and an unforgettable one. The scene before them was beautiful in the clear morning light, but the heat of the day was already building. It promised to be a "real stinker". Joe got them mobile again, generating a breeze through the windows, for which Dulcie was especially grateful.

"Aye, these trees are lovely!" said Dulcie, as they drove back towards the station.

"Jacaranda and Poinciana," said Joe. "We've got 'em on the farm, near the house. Beaut colours aren't they, that lilac-blue and the orangey-red - almost like flame. They're pretty good on their own, but together they are something else, eh?"

The street was, indeed, a blaze of colour, with a lilac carpet stretching in irregular patches along the footpaths and the soft edges of the wide street, interspersed with flame coloured orange-yellow-red parasols under which the dense shade offered a welcome respite for passers-by from the harsh tropical sun.

"We've still got plenty of time," Joe said. "Do you mind if we stop? I'd like to show the girls how to make jacaranda necklaces. It'll only take a few minutes; I can see everything we need from here!"

A chorus of "Can-we-pleases" from the back seat almost drowned out Dulcie's positive response which she qualified with, "We shouldn't be too long, mind."

Joe pulled over beneath one of the jacaranda trees, opened the back door on the passenger side and the girls jumped down with glee, landing in the gentle lilac carpet of fallen flowers. He ushered them to the nearest house where, along the fence line where the lawn mower blades didn't reach, they found long stems of grass seeds growing out of the unchecked clumps of grass. One at a time, he firmly but gently pulled until a stem came away with a "pop!", one for each of the girls and one for himself. Then they trooped over to the jacaranda tree he had parked under and bent down to gather the best of the fallen trumpet blossoms. Jess and Jilly crouched down beside him as he showed them how to thread the blooms onto the grass stems end on end so that they settled slightly into one another and formed an unbroken strip of pure fragrant lilac. He was a patient teacher and they were willing learners. They soon got the hang of it and were happily engrossed in the occupation.

Bill and Dulcie hopped out of the car too, and walked along a little way to stand in the shade of the nearest Poinciana. On an impulse Bill plucked a small spray of its exotic flowers, "There were a lot of these in India you know, love; jacarandas too, but not so many. I know what Joe meant. Their colours go perfectly together; uplifting somehow."

"Aye, the colours are wonderful," Dulcie agreed, "and this shade's certainly a Godsend. Is it going to be this hot in Malanda do you think?"

Before Bill had the time to answer, their peaceful contemplation of the streetscape was suddenly interrupted by the excited shouts of the girls, who were calling out for attention as they ran towards them, their necks adorned with fragrant lilac necklaces, crudely tied on from behind. "Don't you two look gorgeous?" said Dulcie, "Did you say thank you to Joe for showing you how to make such lovely necklaces."

"Thank you, Uncle Joe," they clamoured, holding onto their mother's hands as they walked back to the car.

13

"OK," said Bill, "we'd better get cracking. I think it's time we headed for the station Joe - and don't spare the horses my friend!"

Back in the car Bill fixed the spray of flowers to Dulcie's blouse with magical effect. She had not set out today without some trepidation and was already starting to wilt in the heat. His attentions, as ever, gave her courage, strengthened her confidence, and in this particular instance, made her feel a part of this exotic landscape. His gesture somehow reaffirmed her place here, and in his life, he for whom she had left behind everything with which she was familiar; he for whom she had indeed come to what seemed the end of the earth. Surely, if the ship had just kept going they would have been homeward bound as soon as it had passed these shores! Suddenly, they all seemed lost in their thoughts and were, as a result, strangely subdued as Joe drove them the last few blocks to the station where the train stood at the platform with just 25 minutes until departure.

One of the benefits of arriving anywhere in a flash automobile - a fitting description for the FX without a doubt, even if only because she gleamed so - was that you didn't have to worry too much about finding the person you were meeting, who invariably came to you. They pulled over into an easy parking spot at the front of the station and Joe's friend materialised out of thin air at the front passenger door. Opening it smartly, he greeted Bill and Dulcie with a smile, "Selwyn Mitchell at your service. You must be the Johnsons."

Bill shook Selwyn's proffered hand, "Bill Johnson," he said, "and my wife, Dulcie; how do you do."

"And these are the girls, Jess and Jilly," said Joe, who had climbed smartly out from behind the wheel to look after them.

"Hullo," they said. "Are you taking us on the train?" Jess asked.

"No, not me," he responded, smiling, "The train driver will do that. I work here at the station, so I've arranged your seating for the journey; somewhere where you are sure to get a very nice view of the scenery. So, come along, let's get you settled in. Not long now before you set off!"

He turned to lead the way inside and through onto the departure platform. Turning back to Bill and Dulcie, he continued, "Your luggage is all stowed and ready to go. Joe tells me you have refreshments, which is good, it's quite a journey you have before you. As you probably know, you'll be climbing virtually all the way up to Kuranda so the air will cool down, Mrs. Johnson. You should have a very pleasant trip on a day like today."

He steered them smoothly through the bustling crowds of people making their way with their luggage to their allocated carriages. Some of the people crowding the platform just stood watching the action, clearly here to see someone off, to whom they occasionally waved or blew kisses towards the train. Selwyn had picked Jilly up with absolutely no complaint on her part, and Joe held Jess's hand as they made their way towards the front of the train where the big engine stood snorting, and letting off some of the steam being built up in readiness for its imminent departure, seemingly impatient to embark on yet another long haul up the mountain. After its laborious climb up to Kuranda it would enjoy the relatively easy run to Atherton, stopping on the way at places like Mareeba and Tolga, which is where Selwyn told Bill they were to alight the train to take the logging train to Malanda.

Bill was a bit startled by this news, "A logging train?" but Selwyn was quick to reassure him, "Don't look so worried," he said with a chuckle. "It's not unusual to take passengers on to Malanda with the loggers, especially during the wet, Gillies Highway being so unreliable. It's closed now as it happens. You'll be right. They'll hook up a passenger carriage of sorts so you won't be arriving like swaggies stowing away in a goods van! They're expecting you to make that connection at Tolga so you'll be right as rain, excuse the expression; likely as not you'll have a reception committee. They'll take good care of you. You just relax and enjoy the trip. It's pretty special by anyone's reckoning." After a pause, he resumed, "We put in a call to Malanda Station. They confirmed that they will let your contact there - Joe gave me his name - know the time of your arrival so they should be there to meet you. For your own info, you should get in at around 3 pm, give or take, so there will be plenty of daylight hours to get you set up wherever before dark. Ah, here we are," he said as they reached the first carriage. He opened the door, which was two-tone brick-red and white, white up - red down and carefully put Jilly down in the carriage at the top of the stairs. He asked her to move back a bit so Jess could come up next. After Jess was safely deposited next to Jilly, Selwyn climbed up to extend his hand to help Dulcie up. Bill was

15

shaking hands with Joe, patting Joe's right arm with his left hand, unable to find the words to sufficiently thank him for all he had done. Dulcie turned to blow him a kiss and the girls followed suit before Selwyn escorted them a short way down the corridor to their seats which in a special compartment reserved for their exclusive use. Bill boarded the train and Joe handed him up the picnic luncheon and their small overnight bag.

"See youse later, mate," Joe said with a broad smile. Selwyn shook hands too, wishing him all the best, clambered down from the carriage, and closed the door firmly. Then, with much huffing, puffing, ritual tooting, and the squealing cacophony of tortured metal on tortured metal as the wheels ground tenaciously into motion along the guiding tracks, the mighty engine slowly pulled the train out of the station spurting clouds of smoke and steam, and they were headed for home, excitedly waving farewell to Joe and Selwyn from the corridor outside their compartment.

Once clear of the station and its outbuildings they settled themselves in and prepared to enjoy the sights. The trunk and suitcases were strapped onto the metal luggage racks overhead and Bill found enough space to stow their overnight bag up there too. It was a handsome train, its deep burgundy and white carriages constructed mainly of wood; the compartment they had was comfortably, if simply furnished, with upholstered padding on the seats and the backrests and a semi-circular table of polished wood under the large window which had a filigree brass edging rising about an inch above the surface of the table to prevent anything placed on it from falling off whilst the train was in motion. Through the large, fixed window they had, initially, an excellent view of the wide streets of Cairns, graced with Jacarandas, Poinciana, mango, and palm trees. The residents' gardens were resplendent with lush bougainvillea and hibiscus of many colours, elegant palm trees, mango and occasionally banana trees, and a plethora of manifold ferns, crotons and coleus. The foliage was dense and one caught only rare glimpses of the dwellings themselves. Bill noticed that Selwyn had opened both of the smaller windows above the big viewing windows to ensure a good influx of refreshing air into the compartment. He slid the door back a little to ensure a good flow through the compartment and briefly inspected their opening and closing mechanisms so that he could react quickly to close them if the smoke from the stoker's fires became a problem, though they were so close it was hardly likely. Bill left the blind up on the door and pulled the side curtains back as far as possible too, to give them as clear a view out of the far windows in the corridor as possible.

"There, I think that does it. How are you doing, darling? And how about you two? Is everyone comfortable? Excited? Not too hot? This is all quite cosy, isn't it?" said Bill, thinking to himself of their indebtedness to Joe for the excellence of the arrangements. The "cane cocky's" son had demonstrated a bit of influence in this town. They'd found the Aussies to be a friendly lot all round, but apart from being a good friend, Joe now seemed a good friend to have! *"Reciprocation will be a pleasure,"* he thought. *"We'd best make the most of today's trip though; it could be our last for quite some time; time to put down roots once we get there, build up a bit of a nest egg once I see myself clear."*

They all nodded and smiled in approval of their current comfort.

"Good as gold," said Dulcie with a laugh, "Joe has done us proud and that breeze is just what the doctor ordered."

"And I love my new necklace," Jess piped up, stroking the jacaranda blossoms about her neck, adding as she did so to their darker, crushed patches and causing them to release their scent into the air. Jilly said not a word. She lay dozing with her head on the outer edge of her Mam's lap. Dulcie gently stroked her straight, brown hair back from her forehead to comfort and cool her.

"There are a few stations to go through before we start climbing the range," said Bill. "It won't be long before we're virtually in the bush, according to Joe. But there are a few new areas opening up and I think we'll be stopping at Freshwater and Redlynch, maybe not in that order, before we start the climb – we've been up since really early and it's going to be a long day. I think we should follow Jilly's example and have a bit of a rest for the next half hour or so. If you doze off I promise I'll wake you up when we're going up the range – I don't think any of us should miss that, eh, unless Jilly doesn't want to wake up."

The train had indeed, already passed through the town's north-western suburbs and after the first stop at Cairns North Station the view from the windows on either side quickly turned to one of unkempt bush land which, though lush and green, did little to elicit attention or excite the imagination. They'd been spoilt by the blaze of colour and carefully cultivated scenes of the township and were pleased to settle back and relax to the soporific rhythm of the carriage's steady movement as it bore them ever onwards but not yet upwards towards their destination.

As his family dozed around him, Bill's thoughts turned inwards, to a concern which had been niggling for the last few weeks and which he had borne alone. He didn't want to worry Dulcie unnecessarily at this time. She had rallied to every call during this long voyage, bolstered by her belief in the new life they were embarking on and the peace and prosperity it might bring. Before her present pregnancy she had lost a babe in its early stages, and her grief had been profound. He had wanted to protect her from unnecessary worry or hardship during this confinement and had forced himself to continue to trust in the plans which had been set in place for their future in this country.

His heart had lurched at Selwyn's parting words at Cairns Central, about having been in touch with Malanda Station to ensure that their "contact" would be there to meet them. This had had far more significance to him than the standard of their accommodation on the train or indeed, what form their transportation took, as he had neither had a single response to his telegrams to Athol Bernard Wadkins, nor an unsolicited message from him, since arriving in Australia. Consequently, his apprehension had grown exponentially about the strength or verity of the plans which had been laid for their future.

The miracle which had saved him from succumbing to despair, and indeed given him the impetus to carry their plans through, had been, and remained, the extraordinary friendships he had found in this country, and the fact that these new friends had aided and abetted his passage to the final destination of their journey, like Joe and through him Selwyn, and so on, back through the days since their arrival in Melbourne. *"Well,"* he thought, *"if Selwyn's co-worker mate in Malanda can get a message to Athol Bernard Wadkins, then at least he exists! I look forward to making his acquaintance in person, and hopefully our meeting will be an auspicious one."* He composed himself and, deciding to take Selwyn's advice to relax and enjoy the trip he suddenly remembered the

18

leaflet Joe had given him which gave a bit of the railway line's history and some of its statistics. He pulled down their overnight bag to retrieve it. Dulcie stirred and asked him dreamily what he was doing. "Just getting something to read, love," he said, "go back to sleep and I'll wake you after the next stop."

"I wasn't sleeping really, just drifting with the rocking of the train; in a pleasant hypnotic trance of sorts, you might say," she responded.

"Me too," said Jess, who was curled up on her side with her head on her hands, eyes still shut, and they all burst out laughing.

"Shush, shush, shush," said Dulcie, getting her laughter under control, "we'll wake Jilly up and she hasn't had enough sleep yet."

"Righto then, as we are none of us asleep, except for young madam, let's look over the course of our trip," said Bill. "According to this leaflet it's only about 21 miles up to Kuranda from Redlynch, but if you look at the timetable it's going to take about an hour and a half. Do you want to know why it takes that long?" he asked.

Dulcie indulged him with a smile, knowing he was going to tell her anyway, but Jess piped up with, "Why Daddy?"

Bill smoothed the leaflet out, "According to this, we will climb about 1,000 feet, go through 15 tunnels, cross more than 40 bridges and, we will also go through 98 bends – which is a lot of bends to fit into 21 miles!"

True enough, after pulling out of Redlynch they were soon climbing. The intimate landscape of the lush green rainforest opened up from time to time with glimpses of the land below and they saw the sheltered bowl in which Cairns and its outlying cane farms lay, like a random patchwork rippling in the wind, stained by the shadows of rain clouds building once again above the mountain ranges. Dulcie saw her immediately when Bill pointed out his lady of the mountains overlooking Trinity Bay, whose reclining form pointed heavenwards in which direction she appeared to gaze.

The scenery was breathtaking and held their rapt and thoroughly enchanted attention. They continued in this fashion for a long time, exchanging "oohhs" and "aahhhs" at the beautiful sights, and the amazing antics of the train as it flew across the bridges and burrowed through mountains via the 15 tunnels Bill had alerted them to. Dulcie suddenly said,

"How on earth did they build this railway line? I just can't imagine it! It's almost unbelievable – I only believe it because I'm actually traveling on it. You just couldn't describe this to anyone so that they would really understand, could you?"

"Took a long time, I believe," said Bill, "and there was a considerable human cost as well as a lot of money, I believe it cost more than a million pounds! The mind boggles, eh? But yes, I agree with you Dulce, it was an audacious undertaking, no mistake. And they did it! Just goes to show, eh?"

The subject was too big for immediate discussion. Each moment blossomed into a new experience as the wonders of the tropical rainforest gave the illusion of flashing past whilst they sat stationary. They smiled at one another and became absorbed once more in the sights. They had been travelling for some time, probably just over an hour when suddenly, Jess said, "What's that, Daddy?"

"What's what, darling?"

"What, Jess?" asked Jilly simultaneously.

"That noise? I feel like I can feel it too. It's like a giant humming! It's giving me goose bumps. But, there are some tinkly bits too. Can you hear it, Mummy?"

As they had been speaking, so the noise had grown louder. The train ran along the side of the mountain in a wide curve. A fine spray materialized in the compartment; Jess looked up and saw a host of little rainbows dancing in the dappled sunlight, and what happened next came back to her in various manifestations throughout her life, the vision triggered sometimes by rainbows, sometimes by music and once simply by a feeling of intense happiness. For a brief moment in time she was suspended, airborne, with the water falling all around her. The noise was intense now, and the sun flashed off the tiny droplets of water which leapt in all directions from a huge waterfall which created a veil over the whole side of the mountain before vanishing into a deep, deep gorge below them, from which rose a cloud of mist. The sun's rays played upon the myriad tiny airborne fragments, striking them cleanly to produce twinkling, tinkling notes so clear and charming as to eclipse all the other sounds and hold her spellbound in an all-encompassing kaleidoscope of light and sound.

It was over quickly like a passing dream, but it left all of them exhilarated, each with sublime images etched into the treasury of their memory. Afterwards, the air had a crisp invigorating freshness which sharpened their wits and thereby their appreciation of all that surrounded them.

"Wow!" said Bill, "That was certainly worth the price of admission! I think it must have been the Barron Falls!"

The magical qualities of the rainforest absorbed them again, and when Dulcie suggested they take a short walk during the half hour stop scheduled for Kuranda their excited anticipation was mutual. When they arrived nothing had prepared them for the station's simple beauty. It had been built with pride and foresight to be in complete harmony with its idyllic setting, the buildings styled along the lines of a Swiss chalet. Its gardens, potted plants and hanging baskets burgeoned with an amazing variety of ferns and colourful tropical flowers. There were many handsome tree ferns in the company of banana trees in between the two main buildings and the baskets hanging along the outer edges of the bull-nosed corrugated iron roofs over the platforms sported petunias of every colour imaginable, both plain and variegated. "Oooh, look, petunias!" said Dulcie, "Fancy that!" The buildings were painted in the same deep red as the train with cream trim and red tiled roofs. The overall effect was the epitome of picturesque, and they bubbled over with delight as Bill helped them all down from the carriage.

Their time in Kuranda passed in a flash, and the guard was soon blowing his whistle to signal all aboard. They climbed back on the train which set off soon afterwards, bound for Atherton with stops on the way at Mareeba and Tolga. Bill and Dulcie wondered afresh, and not without some trepidation, what awaited them in Malanda. Each determinedly eschewed these thoughts, individually acknowledging that it was a bit late now to get cold feet! The fresh air and their walk had made them all hungry and the girls clamoured for whatever fare the hotel had prepared for them. The scenery had changed, no longer holding them in its thrall. They turned their attention instead to lunch, after which the girls were willingly settled down for a rest. The train had continued to climb for a short while, but not nearly as steeply. Now the line ran on level ground in a more direct line to its destination which, although much further, would be reached more quickly. They expected to be in Tolga in well under two hours.

"Selwyn did say that we should arrive in Malanda around 3 pm, didn't he darling?" asked Dulcie, "So the trip from Tolga should only take about 45 minutes."

Bill agreed, "Yes, not long now, love, eh? I wonder how far we'll have to go from Malanda Station. I don't know where I got the idea from, but I seem to think it won't be far. I think it was something Joe said about there being a lot of small holdings around there, nothing too big. I think he said anything with a Malanda address would be quite close to the township."

"Ah, well, we'll see, darling. As you said, it won't be long now!"

The passing landscape wasn't as spectacular as it had been on the trip up the Kuranda Range, but Dulcie was inveigled by the ant hills which proliferated in the bush land in sprawling reddish brown colonies, with the occasional whitish ones, some of them quite large. For a time the bush tended towards scrub, with lots of young eucalyptus trees of various kinds, the occasional grey ghost or silver gum towering magnificently above its neighbours. The rail line traveled through several tobacco plantations as they neared Mareeba, and their pulses quickened as their ultimate destination grew rapidly closer. The stop in Mareeba was brief, and they arrived in Tolga just before two o'clock; true to Selwyn's word, they were expected. The guard on the train taking them to Malanda greeted them as they climbed down onto the platform, introducing himself as George Kinnear, and his accompanying co-worker as Harry Melvern, who, as they learnt later, was the fireman. These two brushed aside Bill's asserted intention of returning to their compartment to fetch their baggage, hopped up into the carriage in lively fashion and soon had the trunk and suitcases on a trolley on the platform, to which Bill added the small overnight bag which now bulged with the remains of their picnic lunch, and all the associated bits of paraphernalia. The first thing they all did was visit the toilets on the principle, developed during their travels, of never missing an opportunity. They then waited on the platform until the Cairns to Atherton train pulled out of the station revealing in a nearby siding the train on which they would finish their journey. Under the charge of an unknown driver, the logging train, comprising steam engine, 14 empty S wagons and a small four wheeled boxed Guards Van which had obviously provided many years of faithful service, was brought, via a series of shunting manoeuvres, alongside the platform. They then boarded the Guards Van with George Kinnear whilst Harry climbed aboard the tender to stoke the furnace which would fuel their trip to Malanda.

The S wagons were used for transporting logs, and brought to mind the exposed rib cages of massive prehistoric beasts which, having died on their backs, had been stripped of their flesh and their skeletal remains mounted on vast rolling, horizontal platforms. The girls' eyes were like saucers and they regarded this conveyance with suspicion. Indeed, its appearance transported them all into another, not entirely comfortable world, an evocation which was exacerbated by their finding themselves in the company of a gentleman of few words and even fewer social graces. These circumstances acted to subdue their mood, and create an air of introspection

Even so, before long they were installed in the Guards Van comfortably enough, together with their luggage and, of course, the Guard himself, the taciturn Mr. Kinnear. Jess and Jilly sat on a rug on the floor and amused themselves with some esoteric children's game of make believe whilst Dulcie and Bill settled into the seats indicated by the Guard. Dulcie clasped her hands in her lap whilst Bill, uncharacteristically, slouched with one forearm draped across his left thigh and held his chin cupped in his right hand, his elbow resting on the arm rest. They both mentally prepared themselves for their arrival, and their imminent meeting with their host and sponsor, on whom each of them wanted to make a good impression. Bill especially felt the importance of getting this relationship off to a cordial start with a good chance of a fruitful and mutually gratifying future.

Restricted though their view of the surrounding landscape was, they couldn't help but enjoy the transition into rolling hills and lush pastures. There was no scrubbiness here, everything seemed established and the countryside burgeoned with life and vitality. Any land clear of strong, vibrant trees had obviously been cleared for use though they saw no signs of current tree-felling. The main activity of the area seemed to be dairy farming as expected, but there were also quite a lot of corn fields and the unmistakable smell of silage assailed their nostrils once or twice, signalling the presence of pigs. Bill attempted to strike up conversation with their travelling companion more than once but the repeated monosyllabic responses achieved their purpose, and he ceased his attempts. He was, however, cognisant of, and grateful for, the generous manner in which George and Harry had actually looked after them, and indeed whoever else had been party to the organisation of this remarkable trip which had cost him nothing, being part of the sponsorship agreement. He fervently hoped that he wasn't heading for a township of socially self-sufficient inhabitants to whom the society and conversation of others was superfluous to life's needs. There was the sudden raucous screech of metal on metal as they drew into Malanda Station. *"This is it,"* he thought, *"Let's trust this is not another fine mess I've got us into!"* He'd taken one of Dulcie's hands in his at some point, and squeezed it now before letting go, to stand up and crane his neck out of the narrow window for a quick inspection of the people on the platform.

In addition to the one who appeared to be the Station Guard, there was one other.

The station itself comprised a crude concrete slab for a platform, a signal box which, unbeknownst to him, was a standing joke in the town as there was but one train providing travel in both directions which were known as IN and OUT or UP and DOWN, sidings used for maintenance, spare rolling stock and "juggling" carriages, and a corrugated iron hut which housed the Stationmaster's various clipboards - holding his manifests, time sheets, and schedules, et cetera - a small desk and a rickety chair, a mantel lamp hanging from a six inch nail driven into a piece of the 4 x 2 frame on which the corrugated iron was hung, and the all-important telephone which had replaced the old teletype some years back, performing as important a role as ever as a conduit between the community and the outside world. It was situated alongside the now silent sawmill whose produce it carried to Cairns from where it was distributed to the most lucrative markets identified by the company bosses both in Australia and abroad. As the train drew to a halt, George Kinnear gripped the rail on the left side of the step ladder with both hands and swung himself easily down onto the platform in a well-practiced manoeuvre which avoided any contact with the ladder itself. As he approached his colleague he asked, "Whose ute have you got organised,

Cecil? It'd be best if it could be brung around to the end of the platform, over there, if it's not too much trouble." He pointed superfluously to the end of the concrete slab closer to the Guards Van.

The other party on the platform spoke before Cecil could respond. "It's OK George; I'll take care of that, all in good time. My car's parked out the front and I'd just like to get Mrs. Johnson and the kiddies over to Mavis and take Mr. Johnson down to the hotel for a chat before we do anything else. Got to get our priorities right, George. The train's not going any further today, is she?"

George noted an unaccustomed formality in Reg Johnston's address and quickly responded in like fashion, "Sorry, Reg, just keen to get home to the missus, not thinking. Let me introduce you to the ….." at which point he turned to find Bill Johnson standing just a couple of feet away.

"Reg, did you say?" asked Bill, adding, "I was expecting an Athol, or Bernard, Wadkins, whatever he calls himself."

"Yes indeed, Mr. Johnson, Bill. Allow me to introduce myself; I'm Reg Johnston – unlike you, I have a silent "t" in my name," he smiled reassuringly. "Unfortunately, Mr. Wadkins couldn't be here, and the responsibility of meeting and welcoming you somehow fell to me, maybe on account of our sharing the same name, as near as damn it." He paused, "The real reason is more likely that I'm the foreman on the early shift at the local butter factory. Being married, I don't spend a great deal of time in the pub so meeting you at this time posed me no problem. You'll meet Mr. Wadkins before too long, and others besides. You and I need to talk about what we've arranged for you, but for now I think the best plan is for us to take Mrs. Johnson and the kiddies up to my place to freshen up after such a long journey. Then you and I will be free to go and sort a few things out. It's not far and my wife Mavis is expecting us any time now."

They had shaken hands during this speech, and started to move back towards the Guards Van where Dulcie and the girls were standing near the door, poking their heads out to see what was going on and trying to work out what was being said. Dulcie hated going up and down most stair cases but had no qualms about getting down the ladder to the platform when she could see the platform, so solid, so nice and close. Once it was clear that a plan had been agreed upon she descended from the carriage with a reasonable degree of ease and grace for a woman in late pregnancy. Bill covered the distance between them quickly, reaching out to steady her first, and then he reached up to hand his daughters down to the platform one by one. He introduced her to Reg Johnston, appraised her of the imminent visit to Reg's place to meet his wife, Mavis, thanked George Kinnear for looking after them, and they all walked down the wooden steps by the side of the stationmaster's hut to the front of the station where Reg Johnston's car, a Model T Ford, was parked. Bill, for one, hoped he looked more composed than he felt. His immediate future was in no way set in concrete, if his understanding of the brief conversation with Reg Johnston was correct.

The car fired up at the first turn of the key, and the short drive to Reg's place was a comfortable, if silent, one. In no time he was parking at the side of a wide street with soft edges outside a weatherboard cottage painted pale green with dark green trim. It had a corrugated iron roof off which the afternoon sun glinted. A set of four steps led up to the centre of a front verandah, opposite the front door. The front garden consisted mainly of large flowering bushes strategically placed either side of the steps and along the front of the verandah. The lush green lawn was broken only by the ubiquitous frangipani tree whose scent mingled with that of the creamy white flowers on the bushes to create an intoxicating tropical cocktail which assailed their nostrils as they piled out of the car. Reg indicated that they should take the path down the left side of the house, which was formed by regular squares of concrete separated by thin strips of carefully tended lawn. As they reached the back of the house, a thriving vegetable garden came into view, further evidence of the existence in the household of a "green fingers".

Mavis came down the back stairs which were similar to the front ones but leading to a covered verandah beyond which the eat-in kitchen was clearly visible through the door and two sash windows which were open to get the afternoon air. She greeted Dulcie cordially and bent down to welcome the girls. Her open, friendly manner won them over immediately. Reg informed the ladies that he and Bill had a couple of things to tend to and promised they wouldn't be too long. Bill quickly squeezed Dulcie's shoulder and gave her a reassuring smile as they turned to leave. Then Mavis ushered them upstairs with the promise of light refreshments whilst the men were doing their business.

"But first," she said to Dulcie and the girls collectively, "I am sure you would like to freshen up a bit after such a long journey. Oh, I'm sorry; I should have asked if anyone would like to use the toilet before we came up? No? You're sure? Lovely!" With which she led them a short way down a corridor to a bedroom where, on a pine dresser trimmed with blue and white ceramic tiles with matching knobs on the draws, there was a pitcher of water standing in a matching china basin beside which she had laid out a cake of soap, washers, and hand towels. The room was redolent of tea roses from the large bowl of pot-pourri on an occasional table in the corner of the room.

"Thank you so much, Mavis, you've gone to so much trouble and we really appreciate it," said Dulcie as she poured the water from the jug into the basin and proceeded to wipe Jilly's face and arms and the back of her neck with a damp face cloth. Jess dangled her hands into the water and patted her face, and then did it again because it felt so good. Dulcie wiped her face and the back of her neck with a cool cloth and they all dried off.

"It was no trouble, Dulcie, a pleasure more like – nice to have company, and someone to look after. Now, come along everyone, and we'll all have a nice drink, tea for the grown-ups and milk or lemonade for the young ladies. What do you think? I've made some fresh scones as well and a batch of the best Lamingtons you'll find on the Atherton Tablelands!"

"Yeah!! Yummy, yummy!" chorused the girls, as Dulcie tried to shush them down.

"Let them be," said Mavis to Dulcie, "they probably need to let off a bit of steam - it's a long and confining journey as I recall, and I've only ever done it as a grown up. Come along girls. What's it to be, milk or lemonade?"

With which they all trundled back into the kitchen which, as they had noticed on the way through, was bursting with the all-embracing smells of baking. As they sat themselves down at the table, they all felt thoroughly at home in Mavis's generous care.

Meanwhile, the conversation between Reg and Bill had gone very differently. As they pulled away, Reg concentrated on executing a U-turn to head back towards the pub which they had passed on the way from the station. Bill had an undisciplined battalion of questions going through his mind, which he strived to bring to order.

"OK," said Reg. "Thanks for taking my rather cryptic welcome so calmly mate. I think we shared the same aim of not upsetting the family unduly, right?"

"You can say that again. Thank you for your understanding, and your hospitality," said Bill. "I don't want to seem ungrateful, but this is us now, and I need to know what in blazes is going on. I've felt that something was seriously out of whack ever since we arrived here – in Australia, I mean. I've not had a single response to the telegrams I've been sending, not one, and no-one has contacted me off their own bat either. So where is our famous sponsor, Mr Athol Bernard Wadkins? It's been over a month now since we arrived in Perth and his lack of any sort of contact just hasn't felt right; but the papers are all in order, and everyone's been nothing but helpful and encouraging, so I've been telling myself I've been worrying over nothing. Now I'm here and he has failed to materialise I can definitely smell a rat. And, if you don't mind my saying so, you seem to be in charge of pest control around here, so, does my nose let me down, or what?"

"OK, OK, now, if you've finished!" said Reg pulling over to the side of the street just as the pub loomed into sight, "You're partly right. I need to tell you what's happened, but before I start I want you to know that you are welcome in this township. OK? We just need to sort out a few things but you won't find yourself ousted and you won't be on your uppers. There's a few of us in town who know what's happened and we will all be looking out for you. If you're happy with what we've set up for the moment, and make a go of it, I reckon things'll turn out pretty good for you."

"Right, thank you," said Bill, tight-lipped and drawing a deep breath, "So, tell me, what is it that I know nowt of, and what arrangements are you talking about?"

"It'll take time, but for starters you need to know that in this town, Mr Athol Bernard Wadkins is known as Old Bronc. His squat is up on a patch by one of Ray Watson's farms. OK, I know, I know! Please, let me finish – just listen to me. He's been here a while, much longer than me, good ten years or more. He's a bit of an oddball but he's become one of the

28

important townsfolk over the years. He's no bludger; generates his own livelihood his own way, curing pig, growing pineapples; no idea what his relationship with Ray Watson, the farmer, is but he has won the respect of folk around here over the years. Well, anyway, it seems he filled in all the papers'n that to sponsor you and your family. Ray knew nothing about it until the first of your telegrams arrived about five weeks ago. Old Bronc kept it up his sleeve until he knew you were in the country, it seems. And unfortunately, this afternoon Ray is up in Atherton – his missus is crook. Bad, we're thinking, but we hope we're wrong. He hoped to be back in time to meet you at the station but I'm sure you'll be sympathetic to his priorities at a time like this. So that's why you're sitting here with me."

Following his frustrated interjection at the "Old Bronc" revelation, Bill had reined himself in and listened intently to what Reg had to say. "So, correct me if I'm wrong, but what you're saying is that Ray Watson is prepared to take us on; take on the sponsor's role?" he now said.

"Yeah, that's exactly what I'm saying," said Reg, "but he hasn't had a lot of time to prepare for your arrival. A few of us have been pitching in to help but things aren't exactly as we'd've liked, and it wasn't until we heard from Selwyn Mitchell the other day that we knew anything about your two girls. Still, as I said earlier I reckon if you put your back into it you could make a real good go of things."

Bill let out a big, gusting sigh, "Whew! So we do have a home to go to then?"

"It's a bit rough and ready, mate" said Reg, "but, yeah, you do have a home to go to; and we'll all pitch in as best we can to help you settle in."
There was a tremor in Bill's voice as he said, nodding towards the pub up ahead, "I'd like to buy you a drink Reg, and that looks like just the place to do it!"
"Pleasure to accept, Bill" said Reg, the relief he felt at the outcome of their conversation clear on his face. He started the car and headed towards the vast wooden structure on the corner which was the pub, The Malanda Hotel. "Ray Watson said he'd meet us there just as soon as he could, and there're a few people there I'd like to introduce you to as well. I hope you're not too disappointed about how things have turned out."

"Disappointed?" Bill said, "My friend, I am over the moon!"

-- 0 --

He stirred, easing his buttocks on the hard stump on which he sat; as this same sentiment washed over him afresh he smiled at the conscious realisation of its total veracity. He was indeed, over the moon. Tomorrow was going to be a big day, but he made his way back to the house feeling calm and settled, sure that sleep would now come easily.

Chapter Two
The lie of the land ......

*H*e was woken by the unfamiliar sound of a ute buzzing in his head. As his feet touched the cold floor boards he shivered, shook sleep from his limbs and felt, to his pleasure, restored. It was still pitch dark in the room and he turned on the torch as he opened the door. Finding the front door quickly, he opened it wide to a gentle predawn light. Not much after five, he thought, watching the ute draw level with the milking sheds across the way, proceed slowly towards front gate. The sides of the tray were down, to accommodate an unwieldy load, strapped haphazardly in but secure nevertheless. *"Looks like this is it,"* he thought as he went back to the bedroom to grab his clothes. He changed quickly in the dim light of the outer room then left the house, closing the door gently behind him, hoping to reconnoitre and get a bit of a handle on the lie of the land before the girls woke up, and that included Dulcie.

The ute ground to a halt in front of the gate. Having anticipated the arrival of one of the men he'd met in the pub yesterday, he was surprised to be confronted by a young woman. She introduced herself quietly as Gladys Watson, Ray Watson's daughter, smiled warmly as she jumped down from behind the wheel.

"Bill Johnson, good to meet you," he said, returning the smile.

As if reading his mind, she said, "A couple of the boys will be over soon, once they've finished milking and the herd is back out to pasture. They'll move in this lot first," she nodded towards laden tray, "and then Dad wants 'em to check out a few things - milking shed, generator, windmill," she paused, "for starters."

"I expected it would be a busy day," he said.

"Yeah, the kind that's best handled with a good feed under the belt, Bill. I've brought over plenty of tucker 'n that. As a rule Mum'd have breakfast on the go back at home, so in the circumstances we'll be killing two birds with one stone." He expressed his condolences at her mother's illness. She thanked him, but made no further comment. She'd located a sack in the back of the ute as she'd been talking, opened it up and rummaged around to come up with a couple of tin mugs and a Thermos. "Thought a cuppa would go down well before we get cracking. Afraid it's white and it's sweet," she said matter-of-factly, pouring a cup as the sun heaved itself over the horizon.

"Just the way I like it," he said, after taking a tentative sip; privately rejoicing in the restorative qualities of both the tea and the sunrise, to whose low cutting rays they had automatically turned their backs. He savoured every mouthful, "first one in morning lubricates the eyeballs it does," he observed appreciatively. He excused himself briefly and popped back inside to get his makings, build his first rollie of the day. He got it going and rejoined her near the tray of the ute, leaving the front door open to let the light in for the girls when they woke.

They drank their tea in a companionable silence, adjusting to the new day, taking pleasure in the landscape coming to life under the golden wash of early sunlight. Her tea finished she said, "I think we might build a camp fire over there in your front garden," chuckling as she surveyed the overgrown wilderness beyond the path in front of the house. "That log will be useful to sit on at any rate. How about you get a fire going and I'll unpack a few essentials. The boys won't be too long and I wouldn't mind betting your little uns'll be up any minute now."

Though not exactly scout master material he could build a decent camp fire, and didn't leave the occasion wanting. Plenty of kindling lay around, small rocks and heavier fire wood all close at hand. By the time the girls woke up, the 'boys' had arrived, a couple of whom Bill recognised as Curly and Bruce, from his visit to the pub the previous afternoon. A big surprise was the third 'boy', George Kinnear, the Guard on their train from Tolga yesterday, a memorable trip prematurely relegated by the ongoing tide of events.

By 7 o'clock breakfast was well under way and a big billy of water was coming to the boil in the side of the fire. The smell of sizzling bacon was tantalising. Gladys, Glad for short, was frying eggs for everyone except Jilly and Jess who were a bit overawed by all the activity and wanting only vegemite on toast. They watched curiously as Bill toasted them a healthy dodger of bread each, spiking the bread on sticks, holding it in front of the hot coals. Dulcie had cut old-fashioned 'doorstops' from one of the loaves Mavis Johnston had insisted they take with them yesterday. With Marg Watson's legendary butter it was a treat with or without the vegemite.

"It's won the regional CWA award you know, Marg's butter," Curly informed Dulcie on the QT, "more than once."

"The CWA?"

"Yeah - the Country Women's Association."

"Ah," said Dulcie, still wondering.

Curly ask Glad after her Mum's health – his enquiry acknowledged, but eliciting a noncommittal response.

Though everyday fare to the others, this cornucopia overwhelmed Bill and Dulcie, their experience having been gotten elsewhere.

"Mmmm, Old Bronc's bacon's best there is," observed Bruce through a mouthful, his mention of their aberrant 'sponsor' creating a brief self-consciousness in the group. They all tucked in with healthy appetites regardless, the result of early and hard work for the men, the freshness of the air and the good, wholesome quality of the fare for the Johnsons. Whilst they ate, Gladys Watson talked them through the day's schedule, a task she was obviously used to. The boys were comfortable with the day's agenda and a few important priorities were set. She made a point of ensuring personal time with Dulcie first, keen to introduce her more thoroughly to the domestic arrangements.

Her own main tasks for the day were to help with the not inconsiderable chores of checking the tank, cleaning the kitchen, getting the wood stove going and making sure the flue was drawing efficiently. They'd need to organise a supply of wood for the stove and the copper too. Apart from these practical achievements, she was keen to instill in this doughty English woman some sense of personal custodianship, inherent in which lay her right to genuinely make this house, and indeed this place, her home. If they stayed, and Gladys thought it was *a pretty big if*, Bill was going to be a busy bloke, he would need a contented and committed wife if they were to survive on the land and build a happy life here.

37

Bruce and George finished breakfast first, and Bill soon joined them to dismantle the furniture strapped to the back of the ute; a double bed, for which the mattress eventually turned up, a kitchen table and two bench seats, a carver and a rocking chair, all of which had seen better days but were in solid nick with years of service still left in them. Boxes contained all manner of things: enameled tin plates and pannikins, eating irons, cooking pots and pans, an old Bakelite radio which Glad was delighted about having unearthed. "It's still in perfect working order. We got this for Mervyn when he first moved down here. It's battery operated," she informed them with satisfaction. "The batteries seem to be alright but I bought a couple of spares which are in one of the bags, just to be on the safe side. Don't know whether you're interested in the cricket, Bill, but the first test match in the series against South Africa starts at the Gabba day after tomorrow."

"The Gabba?" asked Bill.

"Yeah, Woolloongabba — the cricket ground in Brisbane. They're having the first test there this series." She paused, "I've also thrown in last Saturday's paper too, somewhere. The North Queensland Register, our local paper. Every Saturday it has the weekly radio program inside, near the back. Makes a good back up for dunny paper if you run out too," she finished, grinning.

Her final comment went right over their heads and Dulcie's delighted response was, "They're sure to have music programmes," as visions of the beautiful old upright piano they'd sold before leaving England flashed through her mind, "and there'll be some kiddies' programmes, too. Speaking of kiddies," she looked around, "they're a bit quiet, aren't they? Where could they be? They were here a minute ago."

"They're round here with me," said Curly from round the side of the house.

Bill went back to unloading the ute as Glad and Dulcie joined Curly and the girls. "I'm teaching 'em how to make slops for the pigs," Curly said, scraping the left over bits from another of the enamel plates into an old 4 gallon drum with a wire handle. "You can save any old scraps, whatever they are it doesn't matter – left over food, drink, it's all the same to the pigs – mix

38

it all up and it turns into their favourite tucker - some people call it Swill, but we call it Slops," he explained proudly to his attentive juvenile audience.

"Pigs?" said Dulcie, as an aside to Glad.

"Yeah, pigs," laughed Glad. "Dad wants the place stocked up as a fully-fledged mixed farm; give you a better chance of making a go of it. By the time we've finished you'll have 40 to 60 cows, chickens, ducks and turkeys, pigs of course and all your working animals of course - a coupla horses, dogs, cats. You'll end up growing corn on land and veggies in back garden; just you wait and see. But don't worry Dulcie; it won't all happen in a day and you will have help – in fact Old Bronc will help out with the pigs, no fear. He's your nearest neighbour, you know, and he used to spend quite a bit of time down here with Mervyn. He doesn't say much, but I think he needs company if not conversation. Once everything's been got back in working order and you're all stocked up it'll keep you busy, but you look after it and it'll look after you, honestly. I expect it will all be a bit of an adventure for your girls and the little un in time."

Dulcie was conscious of the mention, yet again, of the enigmatic Athol.........., Old Bronc as they called him, but retorted, "Yes, and they're not the only ones. We're city folk, Glad. I thought Cairns was a country town, and not the kind I'm used to at that. But don't worry; I'm looking forward to it. It's a nice spot, this, if a bit remote, and good food certainly seems abundant." She paused reflectively, "Things have been a bit grim back home; end of the war wasn't the end of our troubles by any means. Sorry, I didn't mean to mention war; rather hoping to forget it really." She paused to compose herself, "The girls are as happy as Larry here, and Bill's getting the old twinkle back in his eyes, but I must say it's not at all what I expected. I'll be glad when I know how things work in the house here, I'm in the dark in more ways than one, and that's a fact; and how I'm supposed to do the grocery shopping, and where, indeed how, will the kids go to school?" She pulled herself up and apologised to Glad, "I don't want to seem ungrateful. I expect I'll get the hang of it all sooner or later but at the moment it's all double Dutch to me." As an afterthought, she asked quite seriously, "Did you ever wonder who the heck Larry was?" Gladys looked a bit baffled for a second and then laughed out loud.

39

She wasn't however, distracted from the seriousness of Dulcie's concerns. "Don't worry Dulcie, I hear you plainly enough," she said, "but I reckon you'll feel differently when we get the place ship shape and you've had time to settle in," she paused, looking over towards Curly and the girls who were washing up. "I just want a quick word with Curly, Dulcie, and then I'll give you a guided tour of the house and garden?"

"Garden?" Dulcie smiled to soften the disbelief in her tone.

Gladys walked over to ask Curly, out of earshot of the others, "Is Nancy off duty today Curly, and at home? I don't want to impose, but it would be really useful if the girls could go over to play with your brood for a few hours while I try to give Dulcie and Bill a better handle on things around here, how certain basics work 'n that, you know?"

"Yeah, as it happens Glad, Nance's in the middle of a few days off at the moment - doesn't go back to work til Saturday, and you've just beaten me to the draw. We talked about it last night when I got home after meeting Bill at the pub and I was gunna suggest the very same thing myself. We thought maybe Bill and Dulcie might like to come over for tea later this arvo too. I can take the kids over in the ute now."

"So where do you want this stuff, Glad?" called Bruce.

"OK, I'm coming, I'm coming," responded Glad, simultaneously turning to Curly with the thumbs up for his plan of action. "That's a beaut idea, Curly," she said. "I'll just run it past the Johnsons, eh? And there are a few things you could pick up on your way back too."

"Move the bed in first, eh boys?" she yelled, "Front room to the left! And open all the windows while you're at it, eh, please? Let's throw a bit of light on things."

"Windows?" thought Dulcie.

Bruce, George and Bill unloaded the ute and moved everything into the house, generally managing under their own steam, only yelling for directions every now and then. Curly set off with Jilly and Jess; after having a wipe down and cleaning their teeth out of a basin of the remaining boiled water, they'd had their hair brushed and put on fresh clothes, socks and sandals. The prospect of meeting Curly's children was all that had been needed to get their enthusiastic agreement to their planned outing.

"I think I just found out what a hot potato feels like," observed Dulcie philosophically, as she stood with Bill and Glad in the turnabout waving goodbye to the girls whose beaming faces peered out through the back window of the ute's cabin. They both waved energetically back while Curly took their departure over the rutted track nice and steady. The three of them turned back towards the house when, as if on cue, the air was rent by a tremendous creaking of wood and metal, the tortured sound accompanied by a series of muffled curses, as a section of the corrugated iron wall facing them suddenly lifted outwards and upwards to form an awning above an opening which framed the sheepish, sweaty faces of Bruce and George; faces sheepish at finding their coarsely expressed frustrations public rather than private, and sweaty because, as George now bluntly put it, "Bloody rust! We'll have to oil these bloody hinges or someone's going to end up with a hernia!"

"It's a rum looking house, if you don't mind me saying," said Dulcie to Glad. "I haven't got it worked out at all."

"If it's any consolation to you Dulcie, we all thought so too at first. But oddly enough, it grows on you, and more importantly, it works. It's better from the inside looking out, believe me. I've had lots of good times over here with Mervyn – my younger brother; he built it – out of 'leftovers'." The two of them stood gazing at it. It was a patchy corrugated-iron box with no apparent redeeming features. It sat on concrete stumps that were quite short at the front – just two shallow steps to the front door - and diminishing in height towards the back where there appeared to be an extension of sorts. It had a pitched corrugated-iron roof. The patchy look was suddenly and simply explained by the "window" which Bruce and George had opened, of which there appeared to be several. Dulcie imagined it would look like a big seaside kiosk with all these iron shutters up, smiled wryly to herself at the thought. "A good lick of paint would make the world of difference," she mused. The top of a water tank could be seen at the back, on the right, not far from a tall pole the purpose of which was lost on her.

Bill had taken his cue from George and gone promptly round the back to get the oil can he'd found the night before. As the girls walked in the front door a second window went up with miraculous cooperation. A

41

transformation was taking place; from the inside, the house now felt quite different, now there was light and air, and a view of the farm which was easy on the eye, restful.

The layout was simple. To the left of the big main room which you entered from the front door there were two side rooms. These were to be their bedrooms. Dulcie gathered the bed things to make up the double bed which was now in the girls' bedroom. As they stood on opposite sides of the bed to make it up, Gladys warned Dulcie about the noise on the tin roof when it rained.

"Can be deafening during a storm - might scare the kids at first," she warned. "The best thing is to open one of the doors at least to show them the rain, and let them hear the outside noise of the storm which is quite different. That's what Mum and Dad did with us when we were nippers, and I don't think any of us have ever been too worried about it. In fact, I remember us showing off and screeching at the top of our lungs under the cover of the noise which we would've never got away with otherwise."

"Don't worry," said Dulcie, "We had a couple of real doozies of storms in Cairns and The Temperance Hotel had a tin roof so I know exactly what you mean – couldn't hear yourself think! I'll do as you suggest, Glad. Might help me too!" she added ruefully.

From the living room, there were a couple of steps down into the kitchen which stretched almost the full width of the house. The left hand end was taken up by a large walk-in pantry cum larder with a grouted brick floor, a mixture of solid and slatted shelves, several large hooks hanging from the ceiling and a row of wooden pegs on a board on the back of the door.

"Mervyn used to keep his ice box in here too," said Glad, "Over there. He said the ice lasted longer. I don't know what he used, but he insulated the pantry to keep it cool. The lack of a window calls for a lantern if you've a bit to do in here; best not to use one of the big mantel lamps for any length of time though; way too hot. Tilley lamp's the idea, or a candle."

They'd had gas lighting at home for as long as she could remember and Dulcie didn't have a clue about mantel lamps. Still, she had no doubt she would work it out, and related immediately to the benefit of a gentle light, having made many evening rounds of the wards lit just so. She looked around

42

and was impressed - domestic arrangements of an acceptable standard had materialized as if by magic; her mind shifted in a positive direction; maybe she could make something of things here - this kitchen, this house, this opportunity. She sighed.

Back in the kitchen the earthen floor screamed for attention. "*We'll have to do something about that!*" she thought, visions of a child learning to propel itself from one place to another on such a surface unsettling her. She took in the wood stove in its "cubby hole" at the end of the room, its brick floor, and the chimney disappearing through the low, slanting ceiling. To the right of the alcove she was flabbergasted to see a window; a conventional glazed window through which one looked back along the track to the road. Gladys saw the expression of astonishment on her face and laughed. "You know, there was a reason for that," she said, "and for the one in the laundry which you haven't seen yet."

They sat down on the bench seats the boys had brought in, facing each other across the table. "I hope you'll meet Mervyn one day," said Glad. "As I said he built this place. It cost him next to nothing, which fact might provide you with a lot of answers. He was, and no doubt still is, an independent thinker. He's down in Victoria, has been for the past six months, was in the Philippines for a couple of months before that. Too long a story for now, but in short he went to the Philippines for a holiday, met an Australian girl from a farm in Victoria who was there on holiday with her family and fell in love. You wouldn't read about it, eh? He's as good a bloke as you'd want to meet, but until now he's been a bit skittish, not real sure of himself. Where this place is concerned but, everything he did had its purpose."

She paused and turned towards the window, "For example, you can see the lights of home through that come evening. Kept him company he reckoned. No doubt you will be able to do the same – the old homestead hasn't moved. I have the feeling it was no accident. I can't remember the story behind the laundry window, but it would have had a reason too." She paused, taking a deep breath. "But anyway, I can tell you from experience, it's nice to look out over the garden when you're wrestling with getting the sheets through the wringer on washing day." She smiled, "Come on; I'd best get on with things. I'll start at the top," she cast her eyes upwards to the cobwebbed ceiling and walls, "and, when I've finished, we can work our way round here together," she concluded, taking in the oven and bench top along the wall adjoining the laundry.

"How old was your Mervyn?"

"17 when he started building this place, 19 by the time he finished, well, just stopped really."

"Just a boy really," Dulcie observed, thinking how different Mervyn's life had been to Bill's. She chased these thoughts away. "I might just go and reconnoitre out back while you do that ceiling," she said, rising to leave. The result was that by the time Gladys had finished cleaning ceiling and walls, Dulcie had a list of questions a mile long, about the outhouse, the water tank, the 'empty' pole, the vines growing over the big shed down the back, the purpose of the shed itself, the huge tree stump near the wood-stack, what plants constituted remains of the garden and so on and so forth, as her Dad was wont to say. Gladys gave her as much instruction as possible whilst they worked together on cleaning rest of the kitchen, getting the stove going, storing the kitchenware away on the shelves under the work top – by lunchtime when the boys came in from the milking sheds, the kitchen was a going concern. There was a big kettle simmering away on the stove and the tea was drawing in a no nonsense pot before the boys crossed the threshold.

A second loaf of Mavis's bread was on chopping board in the middle of the table, in the company of hard boiled eggs, tomatoes, sliced cucumber, and a large block of cheddar. A tray containing the accompaniments left over from breakfast - butter, lemon butter, vegemite, strawberry jam all in good condition from Mervyn's pantry - and a pot of ETA Peanut Butter which Glad had come across whilst they were unpacking the kitchen stuff was also on hand on the work bench. As with breakfast, healthy appetites overcame any bashfulness about breaking bread together; Dulcie played Mum and sliced the bread to order, otherwise everybody helped themselves. While they ate George gave the girls his account of their morning's progress. Between them they had: flushed out the lines of the milking machine, given the motor a rudimentary service but hadn't turned her over yet, inspected the cow bails and made a list of what they needed for repairs and to patch up a piece of the roof which had either been blown off or ripped off some other way. All in all the milking shed was in pretty good nick, Mervyn had put things to bed neatly before he'd left but there was no sign of the suction cups and leads.

"Sorry George, I should've remembered, they're up at the homestead, Dad thought it best at the time, it comes back to me. I'll get one of the lads to check them over tomorrow, bring them down."

The plan was that when Curly returned with the ute, Bruce would head off to pick up the stuff they needed from the homestead while Bill and he were "gunna" inspect chicken coop, barn and wind mill.

"We reckon we'll need a couple, well probably three more full days before stocking up, except maybe for the poultry. That's right, isn't it mate?" Bruce nodded his head, un-diverted from the important occupation of eating. "One thing I'm pleased to report, Bill's no newcomer to hammer and nails; real handy with the motor too; wouldn't've got her sorted so quickly otherwise. It was a pretty good suggestion not to turn her over until tomorrow, too mate, after checking all the levels 'n that. Good thinking. I reckon you're gunna be orright mate!" concluded George, punctuating his comment with a light punch to Bill's right shoulder. George Kinnear had just said more in one mouthful than anyone knew he had the ability to string together. Bill smiled in appreciation of this vote of confidence, surprised too by George's latent loquacity.

"Speaking of Curly," said Dulcie, "I think this might be him now," as the thrum of the cattle grid and the unmistakable drone of the ute reached their ears.

"Bit more unloading to do before anything else," said Glad, heading for the front door. She pulled up before leaving the room and turned back to Dulcie. "I'll be back in a minute Dulce, to help clear up in here. Then I think you should relax, have a bit of a lie down maybe before youse go over to tea with Curly and Nancy. Good idea, don't you reckon? Once the boys have moved in this load, that is."

There was a sudden exodus, except for Bill who lingered and slid his arms around Dulcie, kissing her resoundingly on the lips, asking how things were. True to form she gave a positive account of the morning's achievements. "Gladys is a marvel, darling! I like her so much; she gives me

45

confidence. I mean there's still plenty to learn. I'm not what you'd call on top of things at all, but it's not such a bad house you know, really." She giggled. "I can't believe I just said that." She rested her head on his shoulder, "I am a bit tired now actually – probably relief, more than anything, eh? How about you?"

"Mmmm," he said, nuzzling her neck, "Exactly! Relief!" he concurred.

"I'd best go and join them, love, still a lot to do. Lie down and have a rest, it'll do you good." He felt their child pressing against him as he gave Dulcie a hug. Letting his hands drop softly over her buttocks, he kissed her lightly on the lips, released her from his embrace and left. The contents of the ute on this trip comprised the all-important ice box, an iron bathtub, a number of mantel lamps, half a can of kerosene, a copper stick, an iron, a red and white checked oilskin tablecloth for the kitchen table, etcetera, etcetera.

- 0 -

"An iron?" laughed Dulcie, "Are you kidding me?" as she and Bill walked through the field on the south side of the house towards Neville, a.k.a. Curly, and Nancy Coughlin's place.

"No love, no, I kid you not," he chuckled, "Maybe it's the harbinger of a prosperous future – you know, in which we'll need to get ourselves up; meet the sartorial standards of a higher station, perhaps; I had a quick look at it. It's a bit of a monster. Exhibits all the properties of a jet propelled doorstop, ask me. But I think we owe it respect all the same."

They paused in their journey, sharing their amusement. He put his arms around her, cradling her from behind as they stood to take stock of their surroundings, a valley of smooth contours with no outstanding or dramatic features, the land rising and falling gently. It was a different kind of green to the English countryside, and the sky, though it was close to nightfall, was still a vivid blue. From where they stood they couldn't see their house, or the Coughlin's, or anyone else's, creating the illusion of being in a world of their own. The late sun cast long shadows across the landscape, of trees and boulders, the undulations themselves. They sighed as one, taking in the peaceful beauty of the early evening.

Then they continued down the side of the gently sloping hill.

"Curly brought me down to show me the way this afternoon, when you were having a nap. There's a little stream down here, one of many, he reckons, that flow into the South Johnstone River. It's beautiful – wouldn't mind tracing it up and down and getting to know it a bit; must come from a spring. It's crystal clear and icy cold – you'll see."

It wasn't long before they came to the place where crossing was easiest. It burbled irrepressibly, drew them in. They paused in their journey. Dulcie sat down on a rock at the edge of the bank and watched Bill as he straddled the narrow channel through which the stream flowed at this point and bent to harvest a handful of green leaves growing near the banks. It was but a rill. But it ran with energy, and supported a lot of different kinds of aquatic plant life including masses of watercress which was what had caught Bill's eye. It had a sharp tangy flavour – "That's good cress darling - be marvelous with a nice bit of beef," said Dulcie as she nibbled a bit. The clear, cold water swept down over the smooth pale rocks, or was sucked into tiny caves formed in the soft earthy banks. In places the edge of the stream, which was never more than three or four feet wide for as far as they could see, got caught up in lazy spawning pools where tadpoles teemed and water spiders made ripples on the surface with their hairy legs.

"The girls are going to love this," said Dulcie. "And they wouldn't be in harm's way down here, would they? Couldn't be too deep anywhere could it? I suppose we really should check it out to see first."

"No question," agreed Bill, "but there'll be cows in this paddock, love, so they might not be inclined to treat it as their playground."

"Paddock?" said Dulcie.

He laughed, "Bruce was quick to point out to me today that they don't have fields over here. They have paddocks. Come on, we'd best get moving. Nancy will have tea ready, and to tell you the truth, I could eat a horse." He helped her to her feet and across the stream and they made their way towards a regimented stand of trees a little way down in a gully, hoop pines. "Their place is surprisingly close – down the bottom there, just around the side of that hill." And suddenly, as they emerged from the tangy redolence of pine needles, there it was, and the high-pitched voices of the children playing carried to them across the paddock, what little remained of it before the fence dividing the two properties. Curly was working in his garden, had been keeping an eye out for them. He now came across to the fence to help them with the gate. Nancy walked out onto the front verandah, wiping her hands on her apron, called to the children to come in and wash their hands ready for tea. Jilly and Jess hadn't caught sight of them yet and turned with the other three to do as they were told. To Dulcie's keen eye Curly's offspring looked older than either of their two, but not by that much. It suddenly occurred to Dulcie that the girls had been totally deprived of the company of other children since they'd left the ship in Brisbane. It was good to see them playing boisterously, uninhibitedly engrossed in their game, lost in that special world which only children inhabit. The freedom afforded them by this wide open space, the lack of a road within sight or earshot, and the continuing warmth of the sun even at this late hour was something they had rare experience of; occasionally in the local park back home on an exceptional summer's day, where they'd shared little space with a lot of other youngsters. This was a new experience for them and they were clearly taking to it like ducks to water.

The house was a timber plank bungalow, battleship grey with a creamy white trim. It had a large verandah at the front with a bull nose corrugated iron roof, an abundance of windows, and the ubiquitous rainwater tank could be seen at the back. Dulcie took it all in with a twinge of envy. Curly gave them a quick tour of his garden before they went inside; a flourishing and well-used vegetable patch, roses and a colourful variety of annuals. A mixed bunch of cut flowers adorned the kitchen sideboard, near where Nancy was in the process of serving their evening meal when they came in the back door. She greeted Dulcie warmly as Bill introduced her, and had everyone sit down with no further ado. It was a satisfying meal of steak, fried onions, mashed potatoes, sliced carrot and silver beet. Salt, pepper and mustard were available in the cruet set in the middle of the table next to which was a large bottle of Heinz Tomato Ketchup. "The children are having sausages and mash," she said, "out on the verandah. Bit more peaceful in here that way," she smiled.

The little conversation they engaged in whilst they ate their meal was accompanied by a deafening cacophony of insects, cicadas apparently, a daily occurrence at sunset according to Curly. To Dulcie's amazement the Coughlins seemed hardly to notice it. When they'd all finished Dulcie helped clear the table. Nancy made a pot of tea from the kettle simmering on the stove, and, while it was brewing, went out to tell the girls to come and say goodnight to Mummy and Daddy because it was time for bed. Once the children were settled, or at least pretending to be, Curly popularly suggested a game of cards, "Do you play that new game, Canasta?" It so happened that they all turned out to be keen players, and he took the requisite two full packs of well-thumbed playing cards from the dresser while Nancy spread a wide strip of thick green felt, produced as if out of thin air, down the middle of the table on which to play. They were clearly keen, and obviously experienced players. The conversation flowed comfortably around the requirements of the game, the stridency of cicadas having abated though its echo still rang in their ears.

Old Bronc's 'aberration' came up and Nancy and Curly explained the dilemma he'd created, and how the situation was exacerbated by Marge Watson's illness. Apparently the few whose support Ray Watson had garnered to find a workable solution were all relative newcomers - "including us," said Nancy - meaning they'd been here for less than thirty odd years. "We had a big influx of strangers in the Tablelands during the war, mostly soldiers," Curly said, "and some of the business people up here did very well out of it, but the local farmers tend to keep to themselves. Apart from anything else, it's a full time job, and bloody hard work - beg pardon - keeping a farm going I suppose, so there's not a lot of time for socialising. Shopkeepers and small businessmen in town are orright, and you're under Ray Watson's wing now, which is not a bad place to be…. and that's me out," Curly finished, laying his last cards on the table.

"It's good to have someone living up on the farm again. We've missed young Mervyn this past year. Marvelous with the children, he was, a natural family man," said Nancy, "Graham, my eldest really missed him when he left, but my lot have had a good time with your two young uns today,

Dulcie. It's good to see them in company more their own age. I hope to see them become friends," to which Dulcie agreed wholeheartedly.

After a time, with the scores at Nancy and Curly 2850, and Dulcie and Bill 2270, Nancy suggested a pause in proceedings for a cup of tea and a spot of supper. It was a welcome suggestion. She rose from the table to prepare their supper smiling warmly at Dulcie and commenting how well she looked, "Especially with having two little nippers to look after and another one on the way!"

Bill turned towards Dulcie and saw the sun's touch of honey mingling with her naturally glowing peaches and cream complexion. He said, "Nancy's right love, you look wonderful; completely recovered."

"You haven't been ill have you? I'd no idea," said Nancy.

"Not ill, in that sense, no," said Dulcie, "just sick. Sea sick! For what seemed like a life time, although it was only really bad for a couple of weeks. I don't remember exactly how I eventually overcame it, I tried so many so called remedies; it was something Bill eventually found at the pharmacy on board that worked. That and the fact that the weather calmed down, I think. It was diabolical Nancy - when the ship left Southampton we'd hardly left port before we were hit by bad weather. The waves were gigantic, terrifyingly so. The ship rocked, she rolled, she pitched, she tossed, she almost did somersaults – oh Lord, it makes me feel queasy just thinking about it. I was worried. About me, about the baby, you know, what with not feeling like eating, and then not being able to keep anything down anyway. But I kept my fluids up and soon recovered my appetite when Bill found the wonder remedy."

Nancy had poured the tea and was cutting a nice piece of fruit cake for everyone, "Here Dulcie, have a piece of this. It's one of my own, or there're some nice fresh Anzacs too, if you'd prefer something lighter."

Dulcie accepted the cake with pleasure, reassuring Nancy as she did that she'd had plenty to eat and this was pure indulgence.

"You know, I hadn't thought about the trip itself at all. You've had quite an adventure really; traveled half way around the world – you must tell us about it - it must have been real interesting – sea sickness aside, that is!" Curly found the turn of conversation stimulating.

50

"She was horrible green about the gills, Curly, I kid you not," Bill confirmed, stroking his wife's hand where it lay on the table. "But I was fine. So were the girls, thankfully. Still, we all laid low until we sailed into the Mediterranean – the Straits of Gibraltar were especially bad. We came out on the SS New Australia, nice ship, interesting history."

"Bill is fascinated by all methods of transportation – motorbike, motorcar, boat, plane, train, submarine –you name it."

"And they had plenty of information about her on board too, photographs, reading material; it was interesting. The ship was the Monarch of Bermuda in a previous incarnation, sailing between New York and Bermuda – I liked that, it had a romantic ring to it. She was a big ship you know – over 20,000 tons. They used her during the war as a troopship but there was a bad fire on board not long after the war ended and she had to be completely rebuilt; in Liverpool if I recall correctly. So everything was fairly new, nicely finished like. She was handsome, no doubt about that, a black and white steamer, single funnel, 580 ft. long, 84 ft. across, that much I do remember, and with a working speed of 18.3 knots."

"See what I mean?"

Bill smiled as he warmed to his subject, "She was capable of carrying more than 1,500 passengers and I think the crew was around 500. I reckon she was carrying close on her full complement on our voyage and there weren't half some complaints – families being split up so that all the berths were occupied. We did alright though, eh Dulcie?"

"Well you'd expect to in First Class wouldn't you? He spoils me he does," she addressed her comment to Nancy, "I felt right sorry for passengers on lower decks though. The heat in the tropics, sailing between Aden and Colombo, was awful, like being in a steam bath most of the time wherever you were, and the ship with no air-conditioning. I know I'd've made a limp rag look crisp, most of the time."

"It were bad, that," agreed Bill. "The ship has a punka-louvre system. I don't know whether you're familiar with it," both Coughlins shook their heads, "Well, it's supposed to force the circulation of draught air. To be honest it worked quite well where we were but, Dulcie's right, it was no match for the tropical heat we copped day after day – unremitting it was!"

"A lot of people ended up sleeping out on boat deck," said Dulcie, "so you had to be quick in the morning to bags a shady spot to sit and relax out in the open air. Still, I suppose beggars can't be choosers, can they, as the saying goes; and I wouldn't mind betting the majority of us were on assisted passages, so we were all very lucky really."

"I'll say," said Bill. "If you'd seen the way they transported troops about, strung up in hammocks like so many salamis in a Polish charcuterie, and with another layer packed in beneath 'em like sardines. They really had something to complain about, and many of them did of course, regardless of the consequences. If you're being transported to the front line, what worse could the brass throw at you, eh?"

They all "Mmm'd" and nodded, shifted in their seats, none of them wanting to visit that particular scene.

"So what did you during the trip – I mean, how did you pass the time?" asked Curly.

"There were all sorts to do, really. There was more than one heated swimming pool. The girls don't swim but they loved the shallow end, so we bathed a lot. We joined in games on deck too, deck quoits, other games I don't know the name of. The girls made friends and joined some of the activities organised especially for the nippers. Once Dulcie gained her sea legs, we made a couple of friends too, didn't we darlin'? Had plenty of card nights – that's where we learned Canasta, on the boat. Back home we played a lot of Gin Rummy, Cribbage, just the two of us."

"Yes, and they had some good evening entertainment – remember the fancy dress ball, Bill. That's where we met Don and Ruth – well it's where I met them, anyway." She paused briefly but resumed before anyone could speak, "And there were several concerts – variety concerts, like – they were a bit of fun," she tailed off.

Curly and Nancy were engrossed.

Bill continued, "Ah, but the trip itself; it was a cracker, with the passing parade of new places. We were all still getting our sea legs during the Mediterranean part of the voyage and the weather was still pretty awful. The Suez Canal was quite a busy waterway, flanked by such arid, empty land it was surreal; like being all at sea in the middle of a desert. Port Suez was our

52

first really exotic, populated experience; you know what I mean, although we didn't go ashore. Those Arab dhows, lovely, graceful looking boats they are, and the buildings on shore were straight out of Arabian Nights. The girls' eyes were out on stalks watching the Arab merchants running baskets of wares up to the different decks, and all the shouting and bartering," he laughed. "It's a pity you missed it love," he smiled at Dulcie. "But," he resumed, "the real show stopper was the spectacle of the young Arab boys, begging and diving for the coins which were tossed overboard to them. The water was so clear and they swam like fish! Wonderful piece of theatre really! I wonder if they'll remember it – the girls I mean."

He sighed, Dulcie said, "I hope they do," and Nancy and Curly urged him to continue.

"There's no doubt we had the best times in port. It's over 1,200 miles down the Red Sea from Port Suez to Aden and a good five days of full steam ahead. I can't remember much of what we did in that time, but I won't forget arriving in Aden. It was a glorious day and Aden was beautiful, though we only saw it from the ship. The girls loved it; they thought it was straight out of a storybook. We didn't go ashore because it was actually quite expensive to get one of the motor launches in to the port to spend the day; over two shillings each return I seem to remember, and only Jilly was half price. But apart from the expense, Dulcie's get up and go had well and truly got up and left at that stage, no sign on the horizon!"

"Oh Lord, don't remind me! Thank heavens I did come good soon after that. I'm really pleased I could struggle up to the boat deck on that next leg in that stinking heat. I enjoyed that part of the trip though, down to Colombo; it was suddenly like being on holiday! How long did that take, Bill? It was a good few days, wasn't it?"

"Must have been eight or nine days, darling – it was over 2,000 miles."

"So did you go ashore there?" asked Nancy.

"We most certainly did," said Bill, smiling with remembered pleasure.

"And what an experience," said Dulcie. "It was irresistible! A beautiful harbour, and the island is just exactly what you'd imagine of a tropical paradise – lots of blue and green and golden light. We caught the motor launch from the ship and it landed us at the Passenger Jetty, right next to the Colombo Fort shopping centre. Well, you've no idea the beautiful things they had in that market; such delicate carvings, beautiful jewelry which must have taken such a long time to make it was such intricate work though many pieces were really very cheap by our standards. Before we left to go back to the ship Bill bought me a little carved rosewood elephant as a keepsake which I will treasure forever, and we couldn't resist a beautiful ivory letter opener either. But Nancy, you should've seen the Kandy silver-work, it was exquisite! Absolutely exquisite! It was more costly, but still a huge bargain, I'd say. They say Kandy itself, up in the mountains, is a very beautiful place."

"Mmm, I thought Colombo was beautiful too, in its way," Bill again took up the narrative. "It's a surprisingly large city; lots of fine buildings, though many languished in seedy company. What was most noticeable to us, and an unexpected comfort - there wasn't a single bomb site – the city was completely unscathed. First time Dulcie and I had spent any time at all together in a place visibly untouched by the war. It was a revelation, wasn't it Dulce?" to which Dulcie nodded, and clasped his hand. He pulled back from the unexpected intimacy of his narrative and continued, "But you know, the contrasting architecture of the city is reflected in the contrasting fortunes of the people who live there too. It didn't affect me so much; I think I became inured to extremes of wealth and poverty on the streets during the years I spent in New Delhi. I took Dulcie and the girls for a tour around the town and we traveled in a couple of rickshaws. Dulcie was shocked at the state of the men pulling the rickshaws – skinny to the point emaciation. I didn't realise it at the time but we've talked about it since, and, when you think of it, it is one hell of a way to make a living. But they vie for your custom, and the chances are that the alternatives for eking out a living for themselves and their families are probably worse. What is one to think, do?"

"It was an amazing experience all the same, darling," said Dulcie, "I'll never forget it. The heat and the humidity, the rickshaws, the water buffalo pulling those enormous covered wagons, the people, my goodness the people, the shopping, all those amazing tropical plants, the colour, the heat, the tea, and what about the Kulfi we had in that cafe, Bill, you know the

Indian ice-cream which the girls loved too do you remember, that's what it was, wasn't it – Kulfi? I wasn't brave enough to have a curry or anything," Dulcie added by way of explanation, "so we both had tea and ice-cream!"

"It all sounds so exotic," said Nancy, "I've never been further south than Brisbane, or further north than Cooktown! Did you take any photographs?"

"We did take a few but we haven't had them developed yet," said Bill. "But when we do, if they're any good you'll be the first to see them."

"Blimey, is that the time," said Bill, catching sight of the clock on the dresser. "We've been getting a bit carried away. I hope we haven't been keeping you up! It's time we made a move; Glad will be over again in the morning, and before sun up if I know her. I think we're going to have to get used to these early starts, somehow."

"I've really enjoyed this evening; thank you both ever so much," Dulcie said to their hosts who had stood up to clear away the remnants of supper. "It's been lovely having a nice long chat. You'll have to come over to us when we've got ourselves settled in, so that we can repay your kindness."

"Plenty of time for that," said Nancy. "Curly is going to drive you all back home now and we'll be expecting you over tomorrow night at about the same time. We still haven't finished that game of Canasta remember. What do you think we should do with your girls? They are very welcome to stay here if you think they will be alright in the morning - or would it be best to take them home and Curly can bring them back tomorrow."

"What do you think, Bill? Maybe it's best we take them now, eh, just to be on the safe side? I don't want them thinking we've deserted them! It's wonderful of you to have them, and thanks for the offer of picking them up Nancy, but I can walk them over in the morning after they've had breakfast. I'd enjoy that, so long as it's not pouring down."

And so they roused the girls and left with Curly, all fitted very snugly into the cabin of his ute, Jess snoozing on Bill's lap, and Jilly snuggled down beside her mum and using what little of Dulcie's lap was still accessible to rest her head on.

"We've got a big day planned for tomorrow, darling," said Bill as they took off, driving slowly past Curly's pig sties before coming out on the tarred road, "including, according to Glad, a nice trip into town for you to stock up the larder."

"Goodness, I won't know myself! I'll have to get all the makings of a nice steak and kidney pudding then, eh love? And just hope I remember how!"

"The way to a man's heart, eh, Curly?" laughed Bill, and Curly smiled with him in appreciation. "Yeah," he said.

Curly had been right about the time the trip took by road – it really was the long way around, but they drove with the windows down and the cool night air was invigorating. Their ears perked up to the steady shushing of the Malanda Falls as they crossed the South Johnstone River and its ambient vapors drifted in a cool cloud into the cabin.

The girls barely opened their eyes when they carried them indoors by the light of the torch and tucked them up in their own bed in the front room. After a quick visit to the laundry they tip toed to their own room where their eyes too were shut, almost before their heads hit the pillow and exotic dreams of a faraway tropical island drifted lazily through Dulcie's sleep bringing a warm feeling of pleasure and contentment with them. Bill's excitement had lost its nervous edge and he too slept deeply and sweetly, experiencing the uninterrupted, unconscious revitalisation of absolute repose.

Thursday was different. Bill and Dulcie each had "things" in their mind to do. They woke simultaneously. Bill's arm was draped over Dulce's hip and as they stirred he murmured, "Morning, love. Mmm, you feel so cool and smooth. You slept soundly, didn't you?"

She rolled over to face him, stroking his face and smiling sleepily in the dark, "Mmm, lovely."

"Wonder what woke us up? Probably something Glad's up to, like as not, though I can't hear anything? I'm going to get up and get the stove going, I'm sure it's time – we'll have breakfast in the kitchen today, eh? Fancy a cuppa?"

"Silly question," she murmured, "but before you go could you show me how to get these windows up? They're not going to wake the girls are they? It'd be nice to have some light and see the day coming to life."

He rose from the bed and turned on the torch.

"They were as good as gold when I put them down before we went over to Curly's place yesterday. Here, you hold the torch - look, it's easy. They are propped up by this rod. It's just a wooden stick, secured by a chain to the sill. Here, see what I mean. It is secured so if you drop it it's easy to retrieve. But you can move it about quite freely, see. So, now that the hinges have been lubricated it's easy to just push the window out, like this, stick the top end of the rod, which is the free end, in this socket here, see what I mean," he said pointing to a hole drilled into the bottom of the frame to which the corrugated iron was fixed, and then use the rod to push it all the way out until you can put the bottom end of the rod in this socket down here," he finished by showing Dulcie where the rod slotted into a hole drilled into the window sill. Not only was it a good lesson, but the resulting view of the predawn light over the paddock leading down to Curly and Nancy's place was uplifting in its peaceful serenity.

"Thank you, darling, I can look after the other one. I'll join you in the kitchen; getting the stove going early is a good idea. I wonder what the time is. Do you think we could have a nice basin of warm water for a good wash before anyone gets here?" She kissed him lightly on the shoulder as he turned to head out to the kitchen, promising to satisfy her needs with no further ado.

Before getting the stove going Bill filled up the copper and set a fire under it. When he eventually took the iron tub down from its hook on the wall in the laundry, he created such a din it had Dulcie running in to investigate and the girls yelling from their room. The cause of the din, and the prospect of a bath, brought both relief and excitement and they hurried off to fetch towels from the trunk and to pick out their clothes for the day. Then the order of proceedings was set. Dulcie enjoyed the privilege of first tub, Bill next and then the girls leapt in together, splashed around and had their hair washed. Jess helped Jilly to get dressed and they were both looking forward to going over to Curly and Nancy's place for the day. Dulcie laid the table and made the beds. She gave the girls a big glass of milk each from the thermos Glad had left for them and some bread and vegemite before walking them over to the Coughlin's as arranged. By the time she returned Glad had arrived with breakfast supplies and the three of them shared a pot of tea. By the time the lads arrived Bill had things under control in the alcove with a big pot of tea brewing and the hotplates ready to meet all challenges. They were all starving and ate with the healthy appetite of people who did demanding physical work. Whilst Bill had been on cooking detail Dulcie had had her mind firmly set on writing a shopping list but not having familiar suppliers to visit she was discombobulated. "I don't know whether I'm Arthur or Martha," she thought with chagrin. Common sense saved her; she decided to await further developments.

Apart from all the makings of another resoundingly good breakfast, this morning Glad had also brought over a couple of new workers; cats. "The girls will be excited," thought Dulcie, until Glad opened the cardboard boxes she had brought them in and the cats escaped in yowling complaint and "shot through", as Glad described their introduction to the place to Bruce a little while later. His reaction was to head out towards the back shed with a saucer of milk and a bowl of water. In her innocence Dulcie was touched by this response, intuitively thinking him a kind-hearted lover of animals. She had a lot to learn about the relationship between farm animals and their masters, which was generally an entirely practical one.

But then, if Dulcie had a lot to learn about farm life, she also had a lot to rediscover simply about living. An opportunity was all she really needed to blossom; to come to life, take it by the scruff of the neck; to work hard to achieve the pleasures and the rewards of it; the real, solid, conscious reward being the hearth hewn to support the rude good health of her family, their happiness and humour, and, at the centre of it all, William Johnson, her Bill, who shone like the sun itself. Without him the life blood of her world would drain away.

- 0 -

They held hands as they stepped out once more towards the Coughlin's place. Dulcie had unpacked some of their things during the day and was wearing a skirt - let out to maximum capacity - and a top he particularly liked. She had a crocheted cotton shawl draped over her

58

shoulders. It was surprisingly cool in the late afternoon which was perfectly satisfactory as far as they were concerned. It had been a good day, though not without its hiccups – the trip into town had been cancelled, not that Dulcie had seemed to mind much Bill thought, and the boys had had to reschedule the reparations to the milking bails in favour of preparing the chicken coop for immediate occupation. The shopping expedition had been cancelled because the only available ute had been detailed, at the last minute, to pick up a clutch of chooks from a Tumoulin resident with whom Ray Watson had done a mutually beneficial deal. The change in plans really didn't matter – but it did bring a new and immediate responsibility with it.

"So, who's to feed the chooks, with what and when," asked Dulcie, the latter half of her question seeming to assume the answer to the first.

"I think they only need feeding once a day, in the morning, early. The general advice from all of 'em was that hens lay their best eggs on a regular serving of special feed mix, a bag of which George brought over with the chooks, augmented by raw vegetable scraps, from the kitchen or the garden, and, very importantly, their water troughs have to be kept topped up. None of which is too difficult. There's a food bin up near their pen and the hose on the tap at the end of the milking shed reaches the pen easily. I wouldn't mind betting looking after them is something the girls will be able to do. There'll be the eggs to collect, you know, and they'd love that, wouldn't they? I reckon whoever feeds 'em will always be welcome. Has to be a law of nature, eh – so it makes sense really, doesn't it, that they do both? Don't you think?"

"Yes, it's a good idea. It'll be good for them to have some responsibilities and I can see the mornings are going to be busy. If you're going to be milking at four o'clock I'll need to get things happening in the kitchen bright and early so it would be a big help too. I don't suppose it matters much when the scraps are thrown over the fence if they have their feed and fresh water nice and early. Glad was absolutely right when she said it would be a big adventure for them. Let's see how they take to the idea, eh? I don't think they'll have a problem with the hens – just not sure how they'll get on with that rooster!"

59

This time Jilly spotted them immediately they came through the trees and greeted them excitedly, running up to Dulcie and throwing her arms about her legs. Jess was quick to follow suit and the four of them walked up onto the front verandah as Nancy came out, greeting them warmly and suggesting to the girls that they go and wash their hands ready for their tea. And so the pattern of their previous evening was repeated, except Bill and Dulcie, after beating Curly and Nancy to the target of 5000 points to win their first of what was to be many games of Canasta, declined the offer of supper and opted for a sensibly early night. Having decided Jilly and Jess were to stay over, they set off to walk back home together by the luminous light of the moon accompanied solely by the sound of their own progress, footsteps swishing in the grass, puffing breath punctuating their steady climb up the hill. Even the few trips they had made this way had already worn a clear passage between the two houses. They relished once again the sense of having the world to themselves.

As they reached the top of the rise they could see through the trees the dim yellow glow of the Tilley lamp they had left in the laundry, an unnecessary beacon as it happened but an inviting one all the same. They came through the gate into what was to become the veggie garden and as Bill helped Dulcie up onto the concrete slab floor of the laundry she remarked, "Those cats are obviously around though I've had neither sight nor sound of them. See, they've had all that milk I left out for them."

Bill picked up the Tilley lamp, using the cloth he had left nearby to grip the handle, opened the back door and led the way in. The red and white checked tablecloth greeted him cheerfully. He put the lamp on the table and went to stoke the fire in the stove, "Quick cuppa before bed love?"

"Mmmm, yes please, as fire's still going. And we can have a couple of Nancy's Anzacs." Dulcie sat down on the bench seat, facing the back door and looked out through the house's only glazed window. Sure enough, there was a light glowing out in the distance although she couldn't tell whether it was from the homestead or a lantern burning outside Old Bronc's place, the humpy, as everyone called it. She absentmindedly drew her shawl closer about her, opened the jar of biscuits and started to nibble on one. "Mmmm, these are good," she said.

Bill sat down on the bench beside her, putting his arm around her shoulders. They sat quietly with their heads leaning together, enjoying the peace of their joint solitude, for the first time in what seemed like ages. When the tea was brewed, Bill put a spot of milk and sugar into two mugs and poured. "To the farming life, eh?" he said as he passed a mug over to Dulcie.

"Yes, my love, yes indeed - nothing like jumping in at the deep end, eh? You'll be teaching me how to ride a horse next!"

"Now that might not be such a bad idea," he said laughing, "but I think you'll have your hands full with the nippers, and keeping the home fires burning. Anyhow, that's something I have to master myself yet, so I'd best not get too cocky! Anytime you want to learn anything you just tell me, love."

"We'd best get to bed soon I reckon," he continued. "Tomorrow will be another big day. I think we're in for more poultry, namely ducks and turkeys - and don't ask, darling, because I have no idea why. And I had a chat with Glad about the shopping… she'll talk to you about it in the morning, but be prepared - it's not your ordinary shopping list, love. Ray Watson popped over this afternoon too and we had a bit of a chat about things. He sent his regards to you, by the way, was pleased to hear you're settling in. And just so that you know, darling, the arrangement we agreed upon is that in return for running the farm we get to live here, all found and he'll pay me a small stipend on top of that, probably monthly, the actual sum to be determined when he sees what income we generate out of the farm. It's going to be up to me to keep an account of things and he and I will go through things on a monthly basis. He'll inspect both the books and the farm itself is how I understand it, which is fair enough. Until then he'll pay us twenty pounds a month and he'll pay that in the middle of every month. So for the moment, and until this arrangement changes for any reason, whatever we purchase, for ourselves, within reason of course, or the farm, we just put it on his account at whatever establishment we purchase it from and make a note of it in the books. He has accounts everywhere he reckons. I seem to recall from the other night when I met him up at the pub that he has an account there as well. It seems that's the way they do business around here. Not that we're likely to be putting anything on the tick at The Malanda Hotel, eh?" he chuckled. "He seems to be a fair man, and he certainly has the respect of the townsfolk. I'm happy, and relieved, with the way things have turned out. What do you think?"

"Well it all sounds fair enough to me, and I'm sure you will come to a good understanding with him, darling. We have a lot to thank him for really, in the circumstances; could have found ourselves on streets, when all's said. Thanks for letting me know though, it's good to know how we stand."

Bill quickly rinsed the tea things in the laundry and left them to drain on a cloth. He closed the back door, picked up the Tilley lamp and carried it into the bedroom whilst they prepared for bed. When he eventually turned it off, they were plunged first into a Stygian darkness and then into a deep sleep.

- 0 -

Cock-a-doodle, doooooo!!!!!!!!!!!!

"Hells, bells and buckets of blood," Bill mumbled as he was dredged up from the depths of sweet oblivion, "Glad's put a deputy in!"

Dulcie giggled sleepily, "I wonder what the time is?" she murmured, yawning. Bill was out of bed, pulling on his trousers which were on the chair by the bed, and pushing open one of the windows in a trice. His brief inspection of the outside world revealed the merest lightening of the eastern sky, "probably about the right time to be rounding up the cows for milking," he said. "Funny that! Well I'm up now, and I'm going to have to get used to it sooner or later so I might as well stay up. You take it easy, darling, and I'll bring you a nice cup of tea as soon as it's brewed." He'd turned the torch on, located the Tilley lamp and took it with him into the kitchen to get it going. A gentle golden glow falling suddenly through the open doorway signified his success and he came back in to put his long sleeved shirt on. "I'll tell you what, love; I don't know how we'd manage without that torch. Maybe we should put batteries on the shopping list. I'll make a note of what they are and how many it takes."

"Mmmm, good idea," she yawned again, stretching.

"Go on, you go back to sleep. I'll go up and feed the chooks and do a few chores before I make a pot of tea. I'll wake you up in about an hour or so if you're not already up by then." With which he set off to fulfill his side of the bargain and she rolled over, luxuriating in fulfilling hers.

When he came back, arms laden with more firewood, he found her already up and performing her ablutions in the laundry. The stove was giving off good heat and the kettle rapidly coming to the boil. "I didn't expect to see you up, darling. You looked as if you were settling back into a nice cosy snooze."

"It was the predawn chorus, I'm afraid," she said. "I couldn't shut out that bloody rooster's crowing, pardon my French. To be honest though, I feel fine, not tired at all now that I'm up."

"I'm going to make a slice of toast to have with tea. I'm ravenous, how about you?"

"I'll just wet leaves then and cut a couple of slices. But how are you going to toast them?"

"I thought I'd just open the stove door and hold the bread on a stick or a long fork if we've got one, in front of the fire. That should do the trick. Won't take long."

And he was right; it didn't take long at all. They took their tea and toast out front and sat on log waiting for the dawn to break.

"Have you any idea what those shrubs by the steps are, love?" Dulcie asked.

"As it happens, I do. But only because Glad made a comment about how sad it was to see them so neglected. There used to be several, all along the front of the house. She says the rest were probably eaten by the goats which were left here for a while after Mervyn went away. They're hydrangeas, love. Apparently they are gorgeous, given half a chance. The flowers are white, blue or pink depending on the constituents in the soil.'

"Well I'll have to give them a good pruning, see if I can propagate them by cutting. Find out what their preferences are," said Dulcie, "they would really give the house a lift, wouldn't they. Much as I've not done such things before, I've seen others no more capable than me do 'em often enough. I reckon Mavis would know. I thought I'd like to pop in to see her if we go in to town today. That'd be alright, wouldn't it?"

"I also thought I'd like to take the girls in with me," she rambled on. "I think they'd enjoy it, and I'd like to find out where the school is. Go and have a look, you know, although I know they're all on holidays at the moment. Are you coming in to town with us, or am I just going in with Glad?"

"You'll probably end up going in with Glad, I'd say darling," he said, stroking her back. "I think Curly's working at the butter factory today so I'll like as not be tied up helping George and Bruce to finish off the cow bails, and the pig sty needs a bit of attention too."

"Speaking of Curly, I told Nancy I'd be over to pick the girls up at around 11 o'clock so if you come over to the house and I'm gone you'll know where I am."

Talk of the day's activity compelled them both to action and they rose as one, she to go inside to make the bed, set the table, and make preparations for breakfast, and he to move the tools and materials from the shed over to the bails. Almost simultaneously and right on time they heard the familiar sound of Glad's ute thrumming over the cattle grid, and threw one another a parting smile.

Shortly afterwards Glad walked in to the kitchen carrying a large, shiny stainless steel container with a lid, a handle rather like that on a bucket plus a handle on each side. Swapping morning greetings, Glad swung the container up onto the table and said, "I've brought you a milk churn, Dulcie, for domestic use. When Bill starts milking, probably sometime early next week, he'll bring you about half a churn of fresh milk every afternoon, around four o'clock. It needs to go straight on the stove and you should bring it fairly quickly to boiling point. Just as it reaches boiling point the idea is to take it off the heat quickly before it foams over everywhere and, as you know, it'll settle immediately. Then you just cover it with a tea towel or something and put it somewhere to cool right down before you put the lid on – on the work bench is probably as good a place as any. Leave it in the pantry in the cool overnight and you won't believe the cream you will be having with your breakfast in the morning – so thick you'll have to slice it with a knife. It's really important to sterilize the milk this way. We all do it religiously – cows are healthy but it's best to be on the safe side."

"Thanks Glad, sounds as if it would be just the thing to have on a good bowl of porridge in the morning. Bit of a family favourite is porridge."

"We're having a bit of a change for breakfast this morning as it happens. Not porridge I'm afraid. I'm going to do scrambled eggs and sausages – how does that sound?"

"I can't get used to all this food," Dulcie paused, "we've been on rations for so long. I'm looking forward to our shopping expedition today Glad. Bill said you'd have a bit of advice about what I need to stock up on, where to shop of course." They had unpacked the breakfast provisions as they had been talking and there was still some time before they expected the boys to turn up.

"What about a cup of tea, and we'll write a list while we're at it," said Glad, "Oh, and by the way, Friday's the day the ice man comes, so the timing is perfect for buying a few days' supply of meat."

"Oh, that's marvelous. I've been wondering about that. I gave the pantry and the ice box a good scrubbing down yesterday in preparation for a good stock up," said Dulcie as she put two fresh mugs of sweet white tea down on the table, hers next to a small note pad on which Bill had written in his precise but fluid hand, the details of the torch batteries. She picked up the pencil, "So, where do we start?"

- 0 -

Just before 11 o'clock, Dulcie set down two saucers of milk in the same place in the laundry, and embarked on the walk down to the Coughlin's to pick up the girls. The highlight of the morning had been the arrival of the ice man with his huge gauntlets and massive ice hooks, and blocks of ice big enough apiece to satisfy the cavity in the bottom of the ice box. By the time they returned with the shopping the temperature in the food compartment would be ideal. Glad had introduced Dulcie as the lady of the house and indicated that a delivery each Friday and Tuesday, same as up at the homestead, was to be put on the account of Ray Watson.

She could hear the staccato din of hammering coming from the cow bails but couldn't see Bill or either of the lads when she turned to look back in that direction. It was a lovely morning, but hotter and more humid somehow. Although the clouds were only gathering over towards the coast the atmosphere seemed heavier today. The clear water cascading down the rill was cold as ever and she paused to splash her forearms and pat her face. Invigorated she resumed her walk and soon came through the hoop pines to where she could see the children sitting on the verandah. Nancy, with good-neighbourly thoughtfulness, had obviously given them all an early lunch.

Their cries of greeting brought Nancy to the door with a big smile on her face and the welcoming suggestion of a nice cup of tea before heading back. Dulcie happily accepted and the children turned back to their lunch as she followed Nancy into the sitting room where the tea was set out, accompanied by a couple of slices of Madeira cake. Over tea Dulcie told Nancy excitedly about the plan to shop this afternoon for provisions and asked her about the usual cuts of meat sold by the butcher. She was reassured to learn that the butcher presented a fine display of his produce in the very latest of refrigerated display cases. "His name's Arthur," Nancy said, "Arthur Grubb – English as your luck would have it and he's an excellent butcher. You'll find him very accommodating. He sells Old Bronc's bacon by the way," she added as a final reassurance of the excellence of his fare.

Dulcie thanked Nancy again as she and the girls prepared to leave. "You've been marvelous, Nancy. Your kindness has made such a difference. I look forward to having you over to our place." Dulcie kissed Nancy impulsively on the cheek which, judging by Nancy's taken-aback-ness was not common local practice. But she smiled warmly in response nevertheless, and wished the three of them good luck and waved them goodbye as they set off.

The girls were full of their games and adventures and chirruped like birds at sunrise. Then, at Dulcie's mention of a shopping expedition, they were equally excited about that. "Can we have an ice-cream, Mummy?" was Jilly's first question and Jess wanted to know if there'd be any comic books in town to look at. "We'll just have to wait and see, won't we? I haven't been to any of the shops myself yet, don't forget. If we can find you a treat then we will, but only if you promise to be good girls, and remember," She stressed, "promises are only any good if you keep them."

"We know, we know," they chorused, "and yes, we promise," said Jess with Jilly nodding her agreement. By now they were up near the rill, and they all stopped before crossing over at the special narrow bit, to listen to its gurgling passage down the hillside towards the big river. Dulcie moved them on quite quickly, conscious of the fact that neither she nor Bill had had time yet to have a thorough look at the little water course to assess the true benevolence of its character.

Just as they reached the top of the rise they saw Bruce heading towards the shed. He spotted them and waved casually in recognition as he proceeded on his way. They were soon at the back gate and Dulcie opened the latch to let the girls in before her. "Ooh, look, Mummy, what are they?" said Jess, looking towards the laundry. Dulcie followed her gaze, caught sight of a number of sinuous black creatures of varying lengths, supping from the saucers of milk she had put down in the laundry. "Well I never," she said. "I'm not entirely sure," she paused, "but one thing I do know is that it is not wise to disturb a wild animal when it is feeding," she finished quietly, almost to herself. "Right, let's walk around and go in the front," she decided, taking their hands and leading them up the side of the house to the front, giving the laundry a wide berth. Once inside, they went straight to the back door, opened it a fraction, and peered through the crack at the strange scene in the laundry.

"They're squiggly, wriggly like big black worms, aren't they, Mummy?" observed Jess.

"They're funny," said Jilly, giggling.

"They're snakes," said Dulcie, "I think. But they seem harmless enough to me!" She opened the door and they all three advanced down the steps into the laundry to get a closer look at this strange spectacle.

At that very moment Bruce came out of the shed having found what he was after, and glanced towards the house. "Jesus Christ!" he gasped, stepping back into the shed so quickly he trod on the wrong end of a rake causing the handle to lift suddenly and wallop him in the back of the head. "Fark'n hell!" he gasped, rubbing his head in exasperation and rubbing his eyes in utter disbelief. "*I don't believe this. That crazy English woman is feeding bloody snakes. Is she a screw loose or what? What'll I do?*" he thought, in exasperation and frustration. "*I can't disturb them, Christ knows what'd bloody happen. Should I tell Bill? He wouldn't know what to do and George'd be bloody useless?*

Fark'n hell!' He took a couple of deep breaths to steady himself. The resultant flow of oxygen to his brain led him to renewed respect for discretion being the better part of valour. He departed from the shed in the other direction, skirted around the back, and raced to the ute. Throwing himself behind the wheel, he got her going without a moment's hesitation before shooting off down the track and heading with all speed to the homestead which housed not only Ray Watson, but also an arsenal to meet any challenge this country could throw at them.

Chapter Three

Pseudechis porphyriacus......

Glad saw Bruce shoot out between the gateposts and fishtail up the road a ways towards her before getting the ute back under control. He flashed past without acknowledgement, his obvious destination the homestead. "Wonder what's eating him?" she thought, bemused. She'd been up to Atherton to spend a couple of hours with Denis. In a perfect world she would have stayed longer, overnight maybe. Her pulse quickened, but she dragged her thoughts back to the here and now as she turned into Mervyn's place, changing down into first gear to drive over the cattle grid then nursing the ute along the rutted track in second. She looked over towards the house and farm buildings and saw Dulcie heading across the turnabout towards the milking shed with the two girls. She found herself looking forward to their shopping expedition. She liked Dulcie – she was a down to earth character, didn't bung it on the way some city girls did – but she still had her doubts about the Johnsons staying on. She turned her attention back to negotiating the track and waved to Old Bronc who looked up from his stooped occupation in the pineapple patch, shook a fist of weeds in acknowledgement.

Meanwhile Dulcie had found Bill and George in the cow shed, having a smoke, yarning about where Bruce had gone in such an almighty hurry. They were obviously surprised to see her – "Everything alright love?" Bill asked.

"Yes, fine," Dulcie responded, smiling, "go on girls, you've been wanting to explore in here so now's your chance." She patted Jilly on the head as the two of them raced away into a nearby cow bail. A deep breath brought with it the almost sweet smell of long dried cow dung, the molasses cured wood of the feeding troughs. She saw the dust motes swirling in a needle of sunlight which penetrated a tiny ragged hole in the corrugated iron roof to pin its own luminous puddle of existence to the concrete floor just beyond the first cow bail. In so doing it pricked her subconscious where fragmentary motes of past inquisitions and interrogations stirred fleetingly before resettling below the memory line.

The men waited patiently for her attention.

She sensed their tension, "We've just seen the strangest thing. I thought I'd best come and tell you." She drew a deep breath to help put her thoughts in order and addressed Bill, "You know I put milk out for them cats last night love, and it was all gone when we got home?"

Bill grunted in the affirmative, wondering where this might be leading.

"Well, I put more out this morning before I went down to pick up the girls." She paused, drew a deep breath. "We've not long been back and well, when we did get back there were these strange creatures drinking the milk. There were a number of them. Different lengths, mainly black I think, though not all. We didn't disturb them mind – they were in the laundry, you know where I put the milk down. So we came in the front door and went back through the house to have a look at them more closely. It made me feel a bit uneasy somehow and I thought I should come straight over to tell you."

George was clearly agitated by her revelations, "Wha'd'ya mean by lengths, and by ALL, for that matter?" he asked, his eyes starting to bulge.

"Well, as I said there were quite a few of them and they were on the concrete; lying on the concrete; they were long – not tall. You know what I mean. To be honest, although I've never seen a snake, I've got an idea that's what they might have been. Snakes."

"Shit!" said George with commendable restraint.

"What?" Dulcie

"What?" Bill

"Snakes, the bastards," he was almost gulping for air, and then something visibly clicked, in his head. "Bruce saw them, didn't he Dulcie?"

"Well he certainly could've done. He was going over into far shed just as we came up the hill on the last stretch home. I know he saw us because we waved to one another," said Dulcie.

"Well, that explains it," he said to Bill, "he's probably gone over to Ray's to get a couple of guns, more than likely. It would've been a shock to his system, I'll tell ya. Shit!" he said again in exasperation, "Sounds like an infestation. They must've settled in under the house. Can't say as I'm too confident Bruce's universal solution will work either."

"What are you talking about? Guns?"

"I'm talking about getting rid of the bastards mate. They are seriously inhospitable – not on, no way; poisonous, some more deadly than others." It was obviously taking George an enormous effort to keep his voice down, "One bite could be enough to see off either of your little uns," he tilted his head in the girls' direction. "The snakes around here are not generally your aggressive types, but you can rile them easy enough and they definitely bite. Anyone with any sense hates the mongrels. They give me the creeps."

"Bloody Norah," Bill shouted in a whisper.

"Bill – language," Dulcie said, automatically.

They heard a vehicle pull up outside and reached the doorway as Glad jumped down from the cabin and came towards them asking what Bruce was in such a hell-bent hurry about. George was quietly filling her in on what was happening, the Kelpie snuffling around his ankles, when they heard Bruce coming back over the cattle grid. By then Glad had a fair grasp of the situation.

"OK, Dad was at home, and if I know Dad, he'll be with him too," she said; "Dulcie, the boys can take care of this. We'll go on into town as planned; no point in us hanging around here."

Dulcie walked back into the cowshed and called to the girls to come and go "ta tas"; they quickly extricated themselves from a hanging-upside-down contest and raced past her and out of the cow shed, whooping in excitement as they headed for the ute. Jess climbed up into the cabin, determinedly unassisted, and Bill was just lifting Jilly up when Ray Watson and Bruce pulled up beside them. Ray Watson greeted them with, "G'day Mrs. Johnson, Bill - you've got visitors, I hear."

"Seems that way," said Bill.

"Yeah, well," interrupted Glad, "I was just heading into town with Dulcie and the girls, Dad; thought we'd leave you to it."

"Hello, Mr. Watson, how are you?" said Dulcie.

"Good idea, Glad. Nice to see you Mrs. Johnson, be seeing you later then."

With which the two women climbed up into the ute, Glad behind the wheel and Dulcie settling Jess in the middle, with Jilly perched on her ever-diminishing lap, little hands braced firmly against the dashboard.

Dulcie looked towards Glad and their eyes met in tacit agreement to avoid any talk of their slippery problem until they were out of the range of young ears. Looking down at Jess, Dulcie said, "So what's on our shopping list today, do you think Jess?"

"Ice-cream," said Jilly without missing a beat.

"Yeah!" said Jilly and Jess in unison.

"Silly question, really," said Dulcie, grinning at Glad.

The ute bumped along towards Old Bronc's paddock. "The list is in the glove box, under the dash there Dulcie, and you'll see I've written down the other things you want to do as a reminder too. Probably won't get it all done today, but we will just do the best we can, eh. But I can tell you young ladies right now that we can't get an ice-cream until later, and I thought you might like to spend a bit of time with Mavis while your Mum and I do all the boring things first. She said she'd love to see you again." Slowing almost to a stop, Glad turned left and headed towards the cattle grid.

"Who's Mavis?" asked Jess, scrunching up her nose. Jilly looked back, expectantly.

"We stayed with her after we got off the train, remember? Before we came out here to the farm," said Dulcie.

"You mean the lady with the beautiful red hair. The one who gave us those square cakes with runny chocolate and white stuff on them?" said Jess.

"They were nice cakes, I merember," said Jilly.

"That was Mavis alright. I knew she'd won you both over with her Lamingtons. I knew you would RE-MEMBER them Jilly!"

- 0 -

Bruce had parked his ute over in front of the house and he and Ray Watson climbed out, turning to watch the ladies' lurching departure down the track. The farmer turned to Bill, "Quite a woman you've got there, Bill. She's been here two days at most and she's already caused young Bruce here to move faster than I'd ever have believed possible. Goin' off like a frog in a sock he was when he got to my place."

He chuckled. Bruce hung his head, grinning sheepishly.

"Apart from which, if he's not been suffering from hallucinations, she's also managed something else I'd never have believed possible. He reckons your missus has a nest of snakes drinking milk out of saucers in the laundry out back?"

"Well yeah, that's what it sounded like," said George, cutting in. "She came over to tell us. Didn't even really know what they were; had no idea that the bastards can kill ya."

"True enough George," said Bill, a bit on the defensive. "But, as she said, she didn't put milk out for snakes. She put milk out for those cats Glad brought over yesterday morning. We've seen neither hide nor hair of them since they scarpered and I think she was taking Bruce's lead."

"Yeah, well they're over in the barn," said Bruce glancing down past the cow shed, "Saw 'em this morning. Cat heaven over there – rolling in vermin."

"Thanks, I'll let her know." Bill turned back to Ray Watson, "But George is right Ray; Dulcie came over to tell us fairly prompt like, give her her due. She said she thought they might have been snakes. You might not be aware, but we don't have many snakes back home, and none of them are poisonous. Most people would have no experience of them at all and I reckon she'd count in their number. All the same I think maybe they roused an intuitive discomfort in her."

"Well, I don't underrate intuition, and I've a lot of time for a level head which she certainly seems to have," said Ray Watson. "Can be real friends out here, place like this. But I reckon a bit of an education might be a good idea too. I'll get Glad on to it as far as Mrs. Johnson goes, but I leave Bill to you George – to fill him in on, well, you know, anything of an unfriendly or pestilent nature - animals, birds, insects, spiders, plants, the elements, strange characters passing through, or hanging around which is usually worse, cantankerous neighbours." He paused in this deliberate enumeration of potentially unfriendly agencies and sucked his teeth, his face awry, "Yeah, anything that might come back to bite him on the bum one way or another if he doesn't pay due respects, take proper precautions. There's plenty to be wary of," he paused, lifted the tarpaulin covering the rifles in the back of the ute and started to distribute them. "Used one of these before?" he asked as he passed Bill a rifle.

Bill took the gun, weighing it in his hands, "Blimey, it's been a while since I had one of these in my hands" he said tucking the end of the stock into his left shoulder with fluid familiarity. He held the barrel horizontal with his right hand as his left index finger slipped easily around the trigger. He peered down the barrel and focused through the rear sights to line up one of the two tall smooth-trunked slender trees in the paddock to the left of the house, adjacent to the laundry. The marksman in him instinctively wished there was a more testing target to zero in on.

"Well I take it that's a yes," observed Ray Watson. "So how does that one suit a Southpaw?"

"She feels comfortable, seems to sight well but hard to say without a bit of real target practice. Any rate, could always make a few adjustments. I'd say this unit is unloaded; without the bayonet it's hard to say," he finished in a murmur. He paused and inspected the gun more closely. "Bolt action's the same - mastered that gammy handed way back," with which he gripped the mechanism with his right hand to manipulate the bolt, "smooth as a baby's bottom," he congratulated himself, pleased with his speed and dexterity. He'd been right. The chamber was empty, and the drum expelled no spent cartridges in the process.

He grinned at the trio of men watching his performance. "You couldn't have given me a better weapon than a .303, Ray. It's an old friend. I'm not off the land like you men, but I've had plenty of experience with the .303 in different circumstances. Is this one for me to keep here on the property?"

"Yeah, she's all yours Bill. I reckon you'll be pleased to have her over time, if you stay on. Especially when George here finishes pointing out the potential dangers to life or profit you could be in for. You'll find a bracket for her on the wall to the left of the front door as you go in; it's a good spot, well out of reach of your nippers. You'll have to decide for yourself where you keep the ammo, no need to point out the obvious," he finished, handing over a small, weighty, cardboard box.

"Thanks."

Bill hesitated.

"You don't have to worry about our intentions, Ray. I know you're going to a lot of trouble for us here. We appreciate it, and we certainly mean to stay on alright. But I must say I'll be a lot happier to get the place a bit more comfortable, make it safe." His words brought everyone back to the task in hand. "So, how's a rifle going to help rid us of snakes?"

"No saying it will," said Ray Watson, turning towards the laundry, "they provide a bit of reassurance in these sorts of situations but. To be honest, I'm pretty sure we've missed any opportunity to deal with 'em today. So let's just try to get a handle on what's going on, work out a plan of attack. Yeah, and I do mean attack, it's gotta be dealt with, and dealt with quickly, no question."

"I don't suppose I need to tell any of you Galahs to watch how you go in the long grass, eh?" he added as they trooped along behind him.

George rolled his eyes and grunted. It was an open secret amongst his mates that George Kinnear feared and hated snakes. His mates didn't wear their fear on their sleeve the way he did, but most of them were the same way inclined, and Bruce was no exception.

They halted, in line with, but about seven or eight feet from, the edge of the concrete slab floor of the laundry. They peered in, breathing fast and shallow into fear-tightened chests. These sorts of challenges came along often enough. They'd all had experience, learnt to manage their fear, still the trembling hand, control the sphinctre.

Nevertheless, they sighed in unison as Ray Watson's conjecture became reality. "Eu-bloody-reka!" Not a snake in sight. They stood and absorbed with heightened awareness the minutiae of this imminent arena.

The crude nature of his domestic arrangements confronted Bill with bleak and startling clarity; the blanket he and Dulcie had hooked up across the back section of the laundry to afford their makeshift privy some privacy; in the gap between the bottom of the blanket and the concrete floor he could see the base of the bucket they'd been using; the girls' commode against the wall on the far side of the steps leading up into the kitchen. *"Oh, Dulcie, it will get better, love."*

Ray Watson studied the back steps, the neat fit of the back door; he saw with satisfaction that his son had built a good house – or at least one which appeared sound, safe from reptilian invasion provided they continued to close up properly at night and didn't get sloppy. *"Bit of a baptism by fire this,"* he thought, *"One they'll not forget in a hurry."* "Best inspect the rest of the place," he said for the benefit of the boys.

George thanked his lucky stars that the problem had gone away, even if it might be only a temporary reprieve. Though they couldn't be seen, his flesh crawled at the thought of their proximity. Bruce just scratched his head and pointed out that the two saucers were empty, still convincing himself of what he had seen with his very own eyes.

Bill suggested he put the kettle on, so they could mull things over with a bit of bread and cheese and a good strong cup of tea.

"No chance of a bit of rum in it eh, Bill?" asked George, only half joking.

Necessity had once again rewritten the day's agenda. By the time Ray Watson and the boys left they had laid a plan for the following day. Between now and the appointed hour the boys would track down a couple of characters who might be useful, and they would also alert Curly to the fact that the girls would be at his place tomorrow with Dulcie joining them at around eleven thirty for lunch. Fixing the cow bails and the pig sty would have to keep.

- 0 -

Bill came out of the house to meet the girls as Glad pulled up out front in the long shadow cast by the house in the late afternoon sun. He kissed Dulcie on the cheek as she climbed down from the cabin, took Jilly in the crook of his left arm and smiled in greeting to Glad as he leaned down to help Jess down with his free hand.

"So how're things?"

"Not bad," he said. "Lindsay Hassett won the toss and opted to bat. Australia was 240 odd for 6 last I heard. South African bowler by the name of Watkins has been making a bit of a name for himself."

"Oh, wonderful, you got the radio working," said Dulcie, laughing.

"Thanks for the commentary," said Glad, "but what about………"

"Not exactly sorted yet but there's a plan for tomorrow. And, you don't have to worry Glad; we'll make good and sure all the hatches are battened down tonight. I've had it drummed into me."

"So is it…..?" Dulcie inclined her head towards the house.

"Sorry love, yes, of course it is. I'll go first but there's nothing to worry about, honestly. There's a lamp on in the kitchen and another in the girls' room. Come on, let's get you two inside so your Mom can get you ready for bed, you look worn out," he said to his daughters, "and then I'll unpack this lot. Serious shopping expedition you've had by the look of it, eh?" he finished.

"Will you stay for a cup of tea, Glad?"

"Lovely, ta. If you just take the meat Dulcie, I'll give Bill a hand with this lot. We should be all done by time tea's brewed."

It was a while before they sat down to discuss tomorrow's plan of attack over a cup of tea. Dulcie put the meat in the ice box and got the girls off to bed, and then oversaw the appropriate stowing of her provisions. The first thing she spotted on going into the kitchen was a bowl on the table holding 5 eggs, one of them sporting a tiny, scruffy feather stuck on with what could only be chicken shit. She was suddenly overcome with emotion and gulped down a lump in her throat, "Our very own eggs!" She had forgotten all about the hens, but Bill obviously hadn't. She bit a wobbly bottom lip as "this lot," as Glad had called it, proceeded to appear through the door at a fair clip, comprising:

a 50lb sack of plain flour,

a 20 lb. sack each of tea and rolled oats,

a quarter, or 28 lbs. of sugar - "…rations for half of Birmingham!"

dried yeast, bicarbonate of soda, custard powder, mixed dried herbs,

salt, pepper, mustard, tomato sauce,

vegemite, peanut butter, marmalade, plum jam, honey,

"a block of cheddar and a whole pound of butter, can you believe?"
potatoes, pumpkin, brown onions, carrots, a large cabbage,
a nice piece of braising steak and a pair of kidneys, 4 plump beef
sausages, and a pound of mince, "to make a nice meat loaf" were
already languishing in the ice box with a nice quantity of suet,
Dettol, a packet of Aspros, Calamine Lotion (suggested by Glad),
Vaseline, a big tin of Nivea Cream, a small bottle of Faulding's Olive
Oil, 6 cakes of pure soap - Sunlight, 2 tubes of toothpaste
half a dozen candles, a carton of matches, 1 gallon of paraffin,
4 torch batteries, what looked like a small, short-handled netting
umbrella, several different-sized, circular pieces of netting with beads
sewn decoratively around their circumference, 6 tea towels, 2 fly
strips, a bag of lime – "*whatever's that for?*"
and from Mavis, 2 more fresh loaves, her recipe for the very same
and a banana cake which she said would make a nice supper

The day had taken its toll, but though tired she had the presence of
mind to take the little Tilley lamp from the girls' bedroom into the pantry
where she enjoyed directing proceedings, assigning veggies to the most
appropriate bins, storing things away, putting the butter and cheese with the
meat and suet in the ice box, dodging Glad and Bill as they lined up the sacks
of dry goods on the lower shelf on the right where she wanted them. The
condiments joined the remnants of Glad's daily breakfasts. Mavis's white
bread recipe she secured above the work bench with a small splinter of
firewood wedged into one of the cracks in the tongue and groove before
cutting handsome slices of the banana cake, opening up the netting umbrella
to cover it. Then she stowed the tea towels on a shelf under the work bench
beside which two separate nests grew from all the bits and pieces deposited
on the kitchen table – one containing their meagre "medicine chest" and
personal toiletries, and the other the candles, matches, batteries and so on.
The paraffin was relegated to the laundry but she left the heavy sack of lime
and the fly strips on the work bench where they'd been put, thinking to ask
their purpose. When sure they must be as good as finished, she poured the
boiling water onto the tea leaves, put the pot on the trivet next to the cake in

middle of table, and turned on the wireless just as Bill and Glad came in the front door. All she got was a crackling static so turned it off again with a shrug of her shoulders, poured the tea and took the cover off the banana cake as everyone sat down.

"So what's this then?" asked Bill, picking the cover up and inspecting it curiously.

"To keep flies off," said Glad, "It'll never get a day off, believe me."

Bill nodded and silence reigned whilst the first mouthfuls went down.

"Oh, that's good," said Bill "didn't realise how hungry I was."

"Well it's a long time since lunchtime, love. I hope you had some."

"Ummm,' he said through a mouthful of banana bread, "we had some bread and cheese and a pot of tea while Ray and the boys were working out what to do about getting rid of those bloody snakes."

"And? So what's on the agenda tomorrow, Bill?"

"Well you probably understand things a bit better than I do Glad; but basically, it's going to be business as usual until ten-thirty, eleven o'clock."

"So everyone comes over for breakfast first thing?"

"Yes, as usual. After breakfast Dulcie will take the kids down to Curly and Nancy's place and we carry on with the work over in the bails until Ray's back up crew turn up around 10.30 to check things out, if George and Bruce track them down, that is."

"His back up crew?"

"Yes, couple of stockmen he says know the lie of the land like no other, dealt with this sort of thing before, can't remember their names."

"That'll be Jacky and Bunya. Trust Dad, that's a great idea, but I didn't know they were in town."

"They're the blokes, but as I said, depends on whether George and Bruce can track them down. Who are they Glad? Ray's certainly a lot of faith in their ability."

"They're a couple of the real locals, Bill, aborigines. Spend a lot of their time in the outback, droving mainly. Absolute genius with the stock whip, both of them; it's the showiest but not necessarily the best of their talents. They'll sort things if they're around, for sure and certain. We'll know soon enough; but, don't worry, if the boys can't track them down Dad will have something else up his sleeve."

"So why would they be coming at ten thirty?"

"Good question, Dulcie. Ray thought if you put the milk down at 11 o'clock and then left, same as usual, they might just come back for more, the snakes that is. Stands to reason it'll be much easier to deal with them if we can draw them out."

"Sounds a bit unsporting really if I'm to lure them out with kindness for you lot to finish them off, like?" She shuddered. "But from what Glad's been telling me I'll be glad to be rid of them, by any means."

Dulcie reflected.

"So that means I'm to come back after dropping the girls off first thing, then?"

"Yes, sorry love, I meant to say so. We thought you should go back down for lunch after you put the milk down. I'll come down and get you when the coast is all clear."

"Well that suits me well enough. I wanted to make bread tomorrow morning and if that's the plan it'll give me plenty of time. I presume someone's told Curly and Nancy we'll be invading them again?"

"You're a cool customer, Dulcie. I'll say that for you," said Glad with an appreciative smile, "now I'd better be going, it's getting on. Tomorrow looks like being another big day. We were hoping to get the pigs installed tomorrow arvo, I'm sure Dad's lined it up, hope he hasn't forgotten," she rose to leave. "I hope the boys don't get too enthusiastic about the enlistment of Jacky and Bunya – those two only do business in the pub and the amount of lubrication required seems to vary quite considerably depending on a variety of 'things'." She sketched quotation marks about 'things' with outstretched fingers.

They laughed, walked Glad out to the ute and stood in the turnabout to wave her off into the night. Bill looked skyward but a light tissue of cloud blocked out the luminous spectacle of eternity he had witnessed on their first night here. He put his arm around Dulcie's shoulders and drew her into his body as they walked back inside, closing the door tight behind them.

"What a day," said Dulcie as they came back into the kitchen.

"I don't know whether you noticed, love, but I brought the tub up from the laundry this afternoon and put it in front room; and the bucket. Tub's only quarter full, but it's something. They're in the back corner here," he said indicating their location, "covered with the blanket; just so that you know, like."

"Oh, thank you, darling, I noticed all the pots of water on stove. I hadn't even thought of it. Ahhh, that means we don't have to go down there again until it's all been sorted." She sighed, sitting down, before continuing, "This life in the country bears no resemblance whatever to the idyllic rose covered cottages on all those calendars in the newsagents' back home, love. Remember them? Nor is it likely to, according to Glad. Snakes might be the most dangerous thing we'll come across out here, but there's a long list of undesirables, and a good few of them can cause serious grief if not death."

"I figured Glad wouldn't waste any time."

"She certainly didn't. Soon as we dropped the girls off with Mavis she was right onto it. My head is reeling from the amount I've tried to take in today, but I have managed to round them up – do you like that? It's a farming term! - into two groups. There's the group which snakes rule; members of this group can cause death, and the other group is populated by little bleeders who seem hell bent on stealing or fouling our food supply or our house, much the same as back home but with added extras – no charge," she laughed. "Did you know any of this stuff?"

"Not before we arrived, no, not especially."

"And now?"

"Try me," he said as he moved to make a fresh pot of tea.

"Well, according to Glad, the snakes' group, as I have so named it, includes some very nasty spiders, bees, wasps and, believe it or not, ants. Apparently some of the ants around here are vicious. They're big and their bite can be excruciating. I think Glad mentioned soldier ants and bull ants. Same as with the bees and wasps, their main threat is to someone who is allergic to them but from the sound of it, being bitten or stung by any of them would be no picnic. I remember learning about fatal allergic reactions when I was training. There are lots of possible symptoms; disorientation, respiratory problems, tightness in the chest, low - well very low - blood pressure, loss of consciousness, shock - anaphylactic shock it's called. It can be fatal – horrible thought especially being out here so far from help, though when I really think of it, it can happen so darn quickly it would be very difficult to know what to do wherever one was." Dulcie got up and popped into the pantry, "The spiders on the other hand are like the snakes, they're venomous – we didn't have any poisonous spiders back home, did we?"

"Not that I ever came into contact with, love. No-one ever talked about them. I don't think we could have had. Did Glad give you any idea where to keep an eye out for any of these blighters?"

"She most definitely did," Dulcie took the pannikin of tea Bill handed her and passed him one of Nance's biscuits. "From what I remember, we are most likely to get tarantula spiders in the house; there are several varieties, some quite harmless, even useful according to Glad, I think they eat flies. I seem to recall funnel-web spiders liking water, so probably the laundry or the garden might attract them, not that we're likely to be leaving water lying around unused. Favourite place for the red-backs is the dunny, which I have learned is the local equivalent of our khasi," she paused, grinning. "Bees and wasps build nests so it's a relatively simple matter of keeping a good look out for them and getting rid of nests appearing too close to, or on the house. The big ants shouldn't be a problem around the house but we'll have to teach the girls to be really careful when they're out playing, or if we go walking, or on picnics, Glad said. From what she said, they could cart off your dinner if you so much as turned your back for a minute." She smiled, "so," taking a deep breath, "how am I doing so far? It's enough to give you the heebie-jeebies, isn't it?"

"I'm impressed, love," said Bill, "bit surprised you haven't said anything about snakes yet though."

"Just saving the best 'til last," said Dulcie. The irony wasn't lost on him. "OK. There are lots of different kinds, not all poisonous. You can come across them anywhere. I think Glad mentioned carpet snakes favouring the barn because they eat mice - mice eat grain – blah blah blah. I gather they grow really big, like wrapping themselves around the rafters, and, in their favour, they are not venomous. Tree snakes come in a variety of shades. Not likely to do you any harm other than scare the living daylights out of you. So at least you get the opportunity to die of something quite harmless!" She laughed, albeit ruefully.

Her right hand rested on the table between them and Bill took it in his and gave it a reassuring squeeze. He chuckled, smiled into her eyes.

"Then there are the ones we seem to have inherited," she continued. "Some black, some brown, all venomous to differing, and many potentially lethal, degrees. One of the most venomous is the death adder which is relatively small and is, unfortunately, a well-known resident in these parts."

"The boys said pretty much the same over lunch. But I must say, the liveliest exchange was about the snakes drinking milk. I'm glad Bruce saw those snakes in the act because I think they would all have been hard pressed believing you otherwise. Bruce can hardly believe what his eyes have seen as it is. Ray Watson's never heard of the likes of it and says it goes against nature as far as he's concerned. He says snakes are cold-blooded carnivores, not mammals, and drinking milk would be unnatural to them. There was quite a debate about it. Seems you've presented them with a bit of a conundrum, love. They'll be dining out on this until a plausible reason surfaces and then some, mark my words. Oh yes, by the way, Bruce says those cats are over in the barn on other side of the cow shed, he saw them this morning."

"Oh, good, I don't think I'll feel comfortable putting saucers of milk out in a hurry."

"I have to tell you Dulcie; Ray Watson was very impressed with how you handled things, your cool headedness, like. It was potentially dangerous for you and the girls and any number of bad things could've happened if you'd done any different love. As is it, the girls haven't been the least bit spooked. I'm proud of you," he squeezed her hand again, smiling. "Hopefully we'll get rid of them tomorrow, one way or the other, and we can educate the girls calmly, without an immediate threat giving us the jitters."

He paused to reflect on things and they both finished their tea.

"So, you said there were two groups. What about the other group?"

"You're a glutton for punishment you are," she replied, scratching her head. "OK, what would you like first, the ones that eat you out of house and home, or the ones that will just eat your home?" He laughed. "No, seriously darling," she continued, "I have it on Glad's authority that there are birds here that actually tear people's houses apart. Can you believe it? We already know termites and white-ants have an appetite for houses but just so that you know, they've immigrated from wherever in solid numbers too." She paused, thinking. "Wooden houses that is. Maybe Mervyn's idea of building this place out of iron was not such a bad one."

"Cockatoos," said Bill. "They're the ones that'll tear a house apart. George mentioned it yesterday. A flock of them flew over when we were checking the motor up in the milking shed. Big birds, bold as brass; flew low over here and squawked off into the distance; loud. Tend to do their damage when a place is left empty for any length of time George said, so we should be alright, eh. Vermin, George reckons. No love lost between these people and anything that might threaten their lives or livelihoods, that's for sure."

"That's funny, Glad reckons Indian Mynahs are lice riddled vermin... and quick to take liberties if you let them. They like eaves apparently. I've seen them around – dun coloured characters with heavy kohl eye makeup, yellow lipstick and socks. Seen them?" He nodded, murmured in the affirmative; she frowned before continuing, "Glad mentioned crows too. To be honest I thought, well there's nowt wrong with them; ones back home seemed harmless enough, to my mind, but apparently I'm quite wrong, farmers don't like them. They kill things, steal things, damage crops, even attack people at nesting time; dive-bombers according to Glad. I'm beginning to realize I know Sweet Fanny Adam that's of any use to us out here."

He took her hand again, "I think 'knew' would be more like it, love. One afternoon of Glad's tuition and you've become a mine of information. I'm more and more concerned myself about how little we know, well especially how little I know, and how much there is to learn, but we've faced bigger challenges than this and come through alright." He paused and held her gaze, "At least it's nothing like warfare, Dulce. We just need to learn how to get along with nature, though they all reckon keeping the upper hand remains one of life's essentials." They held one another's gaze. "I know we can do it Dulce and the girls are just lapping it up. You notice how bonny they're looking? Besides, you know a great deal that's useful out here. I bet you still make a cracker of a steak and kidney pudding!" He'd never tried Dulcie's steak and kidney pudding, just heard about it from her brother one night in India, when the bully beef stuck in their throat and they ate it purely as a matter of survival, fortifying themselves with heady reminiscences of the good grub they'd get when they got back home.

"You've a smooth tongue, Bill Johnson, and that's a fact. I was going to attempt a steak and kidney pudding tomorrow night but I think I'll have to put it off ...."

There was a staccato tapping on the window. Startled, they looked up sharply, were relieved to recognise George, his face close to the glass, gesticulating towards the front door. Bill gave him the thumbs up as he rose to go let him in. They came into the kitchen accompanied by two men whom George introduced as Jacky and Bunya. Dulcie didn't understand their guttural greeting but smiled in welcome and suggested making a pot of tea. As they sat down she rose through a pungent, hop-laden miasma to stoke the fire and put the kettle back on.

She described the scene in a letter to her sister, Meredith, with candour: "*Honestly Merry, if I'd have bumped into them on my way home one dark night I don't know what I would have done. Two long streaks of misery if ever I saw - skinny, loose-limbed; shiny oily faces for which the word lugubrious could have been created, and black as the ace of spades. Unshod feet, broad as they were long, and they'd an invasive, musky body odour too, on top of the fumes belching forth from a goodly consumption of beer, I felt quite stifled until they went down to inspect the laundry. They were not like any visitor I've had in any home of mine I can tell you. What made matters worse, they don't talk so much as rumble into their boots so's you can't understand a word they say. I've no doubt they find us equally curious and difficult to understand – I wonder if they think we smell peculiar, and rank? To be fair, I must say Bill joined in the inspection outside and he says they were a lot more at ease outside in the open, quite animated by comparison. He thinks their mournful look is largely attributable to the way their faces are put together, but he also thought they were on their best behaviour, you know, showing respect for our home, though not altogether comfortable in it. I must say, they certainly knew what they were doing, going by the results. I feel I should get to know them better but ask myself how one would go about that. Now we must be eternally vigilant to prevent their return – the snakes I mean – and also to make sure we are not taken over by mice, rats, possums, spiders, flies, cockroaches, bees, wasps, termites, fleas.... Blah, blah, blah. This is a strange country we've come to, make no mistake. Whoever said ignorance was bliss had a very good point. If I hadn't been endowed with it in abundance even Bill may have found it difficult to get me here. Never would have dreamed I'd ever be putting snake repellent on my shopping list! I kid you not, but whatever you do, don't tell Harvey, I am trying to talk him into coming over, has he mentioned?"*

- 0 -

Cock-a-doodle, doooooo!!!!!!!!!!!

"Regular as cockwork," said Bill, making himself laugh. Dulcie giggled, "Ooo, you are a caution." They had been lying awake for a little while, sharing a precious cuddle with a baby who kicked like mad before the day's demands drew them inexorably apart.

"I slept like a log," said Dulcie "can't believe it after yesterday, what with the snakes and all that talk about creepy crawlies."

"You're made of sturdy stuff, Mrs. Johnson, and I'm going to get you a cup of tea in bed as a reward. Should I open a window before I go and get the stove going?"

"Mmm, that'd be nice. I wonder what the time is. I might get up soon myself and have a cuppa with you," she scrunched up her eyes as he caught her in the beam of the torch. "The girls were so early to bed last night they'll probably be up soon and I really want to have a good look at Mavis's bread recipe before then, make sure I get the timing right. Never used yeast before," she said, hiding a wake-up yawn behind her right hand.

"Right you are," he said, smiling as he dragged on his trousers and threw a shirt on. Before leaving he pushed out the shutter in front of Dulcie's side of the bed, secured it and leaned out to breathe in the soft pre-dawn air in which light and shade jostled for supremacy across the paddocks. Clouds sprawled on the horizon. The rooster crowed again cutting through the maniacal laughter of jackasses floating up from the direction of Curly and Nancy's.

"According to Glad those kookaburras hunt for snakes – they sound more like jokers than hunters, hardly stealthy?" She grinned as she stretched luxuriously, relishing the flow of strength back into limbs.

Smiling, he headed for the kitchen. When he got the Tilley lamp going it cast a yellow fan onto the bedroom floor. In its round golden light he cleaned out the stove, scraping the ashes into an improvised ashcan. He'd chopped plenty of wood and stacked it to the back of the alcove the previous afternoon and soon had a good blaze going to which he gradually introduced a couple of larger pieces of wood. The foresight he'd shown in filling the kettle the previous evening paid off and tea was soon brewing whilst the back door remained closed. They enjoyed their early morning ablutions together before taking pannikins of tea outside well before the day was coming atwitter.

"I like this end of the day out here," said Dulcie softly, taking in the surrounding landscape which languished in a pale grey limbo. "It is so peaceful. It has an untouched, innocent quality, unkempt, no pretensions – so extraordinarily natural and unspoiled. It's a tonic, it is."

"Deep thoughts," said Bill with mock gravity, putting his arm around her shoulders. "But I know what you mean. It is peaceful, isn't it? I'd best make the most of it before they move in the cows – if that's what they do with cows - because once they're in residence I'll be up and out before first light according to the lads. Won't be quite the same, but I think I'll enjoy it."

She tilted her head back to look him squarely in the eye. "You will, I just know it!" She kissed him on the cheek. "By the way, love, what with one thing and another I didn't get around to it, but I meant to give you all the bits of paper I collected during our shopping expedition yesterday. They all have different systems for tracking accounts, these shopkeepers, so I'll sort them out, and try to make sense of them today before I forget anything. But what am I to do with them? Best have a special place for safe-keeping, eh?"

"Did you get an exercise book?"

"I actually got two; one for your ledger, and I thought I'd use one for my own notes and lists and so on, provide a different kind of a record."

"Why not just pop it all in there for the time being, we'll come up with some sort of a system. I can't leave it too long if Ray Watson is going to inspect the books every month."

"I was thinking too, about whether we should keep a record of the animals and such like. We've already got the chooks and our new alarm clock. Glad said Ray Watson was delivering pigs this afternoon. I don't know," she broke off, "I still can't get used to the idea of pigs."

91

"They'll be right love – they'll be in the sty. Just have to be fed and I'll do that, unless Old Bronc volunteers, like Glad suggested." She gave him a sideways look but he carried on regardless, "George said something about turkeys yesterday too, before you dropped your bombshell; can't remember the details. But that's a good point, Dulcie." He gave her shoulder a squeeze, "You're right, we should keep a record of the animals; I think livestock is their collective handle. No doubt we should also keep a record of any progeny – chicks, calves, piglets, etc. They'll each have a value which will contribute to our profit."

"And for profit, read income," said Dulcie, the sound of a penny dropping, "I tend to forget we're not just doing this for amusement; and what about the eggs we collect each day?"

"Mummy, I want a wee wee and the back door is still shut," said Jess from the doorway just as a sliver of sunlight pierced the cloud on the horizon and sent long shadows rushing before it towards the house.

The day was no longer their own.

"Good morning, lovely, you just come with me," said Dulcie rising to join her, tousling her curls affectionately. "I think I'll make some porridge now you're up, would you like that?"

"Yum."

"Me too," asserted Jilly from the bedroom door, rubbing the sleep from her eyes.

Bill headed off to feed the chooks, his ears picking up the now familiar sound of Glad's ute slowing down before thrumming across the grid. She parked in front of the house and wandered over to meet him as he headed back.

"So, how're things, Bill: everything OK?"

"Right as rain, thanks Glad. George has told you what Jacky and Bunya came up with last night, I presume."

"Yeah, should work; I trust them to know what they're doing. Did George remember to tell you about Curly picking the girls up early? Should be here soon I'd reckon. He's driving over to the Pidsley's place over Ravenshoe way to pick up your turkeys this morning; wants to go early so as to be back by eleven."

92

"No, he didn't say; mind on other things, more than likely. Still, no harm done, girls are up, probably finished their breakfast by now; we'd best let Dulcie know just the same. That looks like Curly coming now," he said, nodding to indicate a vehicle approaching along the ridge, on the road from Malanda.

By six fifteen Dulcie, Bill and Glad were once again standing in the turnabout waving farewell to the slowly-departing rear end of Curly's ute, a gesture reciprocated on this occasion by the two girls through the back window and by three boisterous boys hanging out of the side window. As the ute turned the corner up near Old Bronc's patch the three of them dispersed, each privately welcoming the distraction of early occupation.

- 0 -

By eleven, when Dulcie set the two saucers of milk down in the laundry, Jacky and Bunya had made their preparations and were stationed, along with the others, ready for action. It took enormous self-control to walk calmly away, to beat the almost overwhelming desire to run willy-nilly down the hill, but she performed, performed being the right word, admirably. Once on the wide and now well-beaten path down the hill she moved quickly, anxious to be with the girls. She tried not to think of Bill's part in the ensuing action. She slowed by the rill, conscious at once of the humid weight of the louring sky and the bruised light now sullying the earlier innocence of the day. She paused to catch her breath looking back towards the house. As she did she heard a sound similar, but much magnified, to that of a wide strip of plaster being ripped with a flourish from the flesh surrounding a wound. It was followed by a loud but controlled grunt, not unlike the reaction of a victim to such treatment, a reaction with which she was poignantly familiar. As she turned to flee once more down the hill a sharp crack from above cut cleanly through the air. A gun was fired once, twice, reverberating distantly as the disjointed cries of battle floated down the hillside on a freshening breeze; then, no more. Into the following silence evidence of a distant storm rumbled.

Curly had been keeping a keen lookout for her and hurried towards the fence as she emerged through the stand of trees. Her anxiety was

93

palpable, the strained pallor of her face a marked contrast to the blooming picture of good health she had presented just a couple of nights ago. He waved and called out in reassuring greeting.

"Gobble, gobble, gobble!!! Gobble, gobble, gobble!!!" responded the turkeys.

"Sorry mate," he said as he reached the fence, "forgot about those buggers. Are you OK, you look as if you've seen a ghost," he opened the gate as the kids came running around the side of the house to join what they obviously thought was a new game.

"Gobble, gobble, gobble" they shrieked.

"Gobble, gobble, gobble!!! Gobble, gobble, gobble!!!" responded the turkeys.

"Nah, nah, nah," said Curley firmly to the kids, "that's enough. Go on, off you go and do whatever it was you were doing before. I'll call you when lunch is ready. Go on, off you go, I mean it."

"Do they always make that racket?" asked Dulcie.

"It's the only conversation they have I'm afraid, Dulce. But they're OK; they rarely start a conversation." He grinned; noticed the colour coming back into her cheeks and was grateful for the unplanned diversion. "Sounds as if everything's going to plan back there, eh," he commented.

"What makes you say that?"

"You must've heard the whips cracking?"

"I certainly heard something before those gunshots - that must have been the whips," she said, "but what's the significance?" She wiped a large spot of rain from the side of her face as she finished.

"C'mon, you get yourself inside. I'd best round up the kids. I don't think this is a paper tiger, Dulce, looks like it could be hail," but as they moved quickly toward the house the kids came galloping around the corner on stick horses yelling, "Diddle un, diddle un, diddle un dun dun!"

"Gobble, gobble, gobble!!! Gobble, gobble, gobble!!!" said the turkeys.

"OK, youse can play out on the verandah you lot, but keep it down, orright; lunch won't be long."

- 0 -

94

It wasn't long either, before they were all tucking into sausage sandwiches dripping with tomato sauce. The kids had a glass of milk with theirs, out on the verandah while Curly and Dulcie were sharing a pot of tea at the kitchen table.

"Good to see you haven't lost your appetite, Dulce," said Curly as they both tucked in. "Now," he paused to lick some sauce from the corner of his mouth, "the significance of the stock whips I believe you asked?" She nodded, mouth full. "Well apparently, after visiting your place last night Jacky and Bunya were both adamant that they couldn't do anything with the snakes in the laundry. Stands to reason if you think of it; no space to get a fair crack of the whip for one, fence is too close and those two bloody trees of Mervyn's would've been right in the way. Everyone agreed it was much too dangerous to use the guns, too many hard surfaces to send bullets spraying off in all directions, and they're none of them what you'd call crack shots, more's the worry. Belting the bastards with sticks, sorry Dulce, sounds real simple but that wasn't an option either. Cramped space for one and Bruce reckoned there were more than one or two of the mongrels."

"Oh, definitely," said Dulcie, "there were at least half a dozen though only one of 'em was what you'd call big."

"Yeah, red belly black according to Bruce, nasty customer, all the more so on account of its size. But he also said there could have been an adder or two amongst 'em. They're actually relatively small Dulcie, but they are more dangerous in lots of ways than the bigger black snake."

"So everyone keeps telling me," murmured Dulcie.

"Yeah, well, the adder's fast and very poisonous and this is their country, like it or not. Out in the open they camouflage 'emselves real good so you have to learn to have your wits about you." He paused, leaned back while Dulcie topped up their tea, "But anyway, getting back to the immediate problem. After much discussion and after everyone throwing in their tuppence worth, the boys knew they had to come up with a plan to lure the snakes further out where they could deal with 'em. That's the significance of those whip cracks, you see; they obviously had 'em out where they could deal with 'em. And I'm telling you Dulcie, what those boys can't do with a stock whip is not worth doing. You'll get the chance to see them performing at a show or rodeo or something sooner or later and you'll know just what I mean."

"Well that's a relief then," said Dulcie, "I just hope the rest of the plan has worked as well. When should we know, do you think?"

"Mummy, why's it gone dark?" asked Jess from the doorway.

"Holy Moly," said Curly looking about, "I wasn't wrong after all. Thanks Jess. We're going to have a humdinger of a storm by the look of it. I'd better go throw a tarp over the turkeys, forgot all about 'em. Haven't got long – hear it coming? You stay with the kids Dulce – probably best on the verandah, believe it or not. It'll be noisy as bug….," he swallowed the word, "one thing, but youse'll be right as rain under cover. I won't be gone long." With which he darted out the back door, slamming a battered, wide-brimmed felt hat on his head as he left.

"Right as rain, eh?" Dulcie thought quizzically; but he was certainly right about one thing, you could hear something coming – it sounded like a train off in the distance; a train with a full head of steam up, traveling swift and easy, unstoppably, in this very direction. When Dulcie reached the verandah with Jess moments later they looked over and saw that Curly had the tarpaulin secured on one side of the cage and was working feverishly to tie the other side down. The turkeys were remarkably still, silent, hunched. The rain was now splashing down in enormous individual droplets, rapidly growing in number, the noise growing in intensity, ever closer, more urgent. The atmosphere felt bruised, the oxygen crushed out of it, its turbulent remains careless of any obligation to human life. Dulcie looked out through the blue light towards home but could see no further than the copse of trees, the hill beyond now shrouded in sheets of slick billowing rain which soon beat a ragged tattoo on the tin roof. Jess went inside to tell the other kids to come and watch because there was a dirty big storm coming. Where had she learnt that? A clattering scattering, as of a casually thrown handful of rocks skittering across the roof was followed rapidly by another, and another, heralding the arrival of hail. Curly ran hard for the front steps, head down, arms crooked up around his ears, hands covering the back of his head, holding his hat in place. He arrived on the verandah with obvious relief, blood flowing freely from a wound on the back of one hand. "No bloody fun being out in that, they're big bastards," he said superfluously as the breathless welcoming committee gathered him in, no one hearing a word he said as the full fury of the storm pounded deafeningly on the roof. Dulcie had never seen anything like it, hailstones the size of eggs bouncing down from the roof, bouncing from the stairs up onto the verandah, wreaking a furious icy havoc in its wake. The omnipotence of the storm was at once exhilarating and frightening; the kids dealt with it by going berserk in the front room, soundlessly shouting their heads off, screeching with laughter, showing off flagrantly to hide their scared bits. It lasted an interminable 10 minutes. Afterwards, as they all looked around in amazement at the surreal white landscape oozing lazy drifts of mist into the languid almost post coital atmosphere each felt the peculiar isolation of imprisonment inside a vertiginous bubble of distant, distorted sounds, lingering remnants of the storm's vehemence etched indelibly into their eardrums.

The kids blew a clamouring bubble, a plea to go out and explore this strange new world of white ice, to which Dulcie agreed with a concomitant nodding of the head; but she felt as if she was talking under water when she suggested to Jilly that she might like to have a nice rest first. Gratifyingly, Jilly not only understood, but acquiesced without a murmur, taking herself promptly off to curl up on the couch with her head on one of Nancy's crocheted cushions. Curly headed off down the front stairs. When he came back he reported, as if from a great distance, his voice pinging off a wobble board, "turkeys are OK, just sulking," and then left again, mumbling to himself and shaking his head ruefully, to see how his garden had fared.

Dulcie sat on the verandah, elbows on the table, forearms crossed, hands clutching her upper arms. Her bubble now held her suspended in an eerie, unnatural quiet. She knew it was unnatural because she could see noise happening; the kids playing vociferously over by the fence, water dripping from the edges of the guttering, a fly which had to be buzzing as it flew reconnaissance back and forth above a small piece of sausage stuck to the table. She instinctively exercised her lower jaw, moving it from side to side, up and down. She generated a couple of exaggerated mock yawns; pinched her nostrils together, closed her mouth and gently tried to blow through her nose; swallowed several times. She hummed, meanwhile racking her buzzing brain for other possible remedies and then, just as her 'bubble' seemed to burst she heard – "Dulcie, hoy Dulcie," – knew it was Bill before looking up to see him coming through the mist, out of the trees, waving, a big smile on his face. The concern for him she had denied lurched to the surface and her bottom lip trembled as she stood, waving back as she set out to meet him.

- 0 -

They walked slowly back up the hill through the detritus of the storm; trees stripped of leaves, branches strewn, grass pummeled, mist issuing from crevices plugged with ice, the atmosphere a milky wash shrouding the hillside and magnifying the sound of the now feisty rill on its headlong rush to the already swollen river. At home a faint whiff of Dettol met them at the front door but it was all that was left here of their crude 'facilities' which had been returned to their rightful place in the laundry. Their footsteps echoed hollowly on the bare wooden floor. Hers took her automatically to the kitchen where she stoked the fire in the stove, added wood, weighed the kettle automatically in her right hand before putting it back on the hotplate. The soothing ritual of preparing tea dispelled the spectral fear of loss which shimmered like a mirage at the edges of her life. As she laid out the tea things, the mirage receded back into a peripheral consciousness, her thoughts regained order, her resolve regained strength. *"The snakes are gone. We survived the storm."* She called to Bill that tea was ready and he came to join her in this pastime which so punctuated their lives.

Before he sat down he turned on the wireless, grinning at Dulcie as the rich tones of Alan McGilvray filled the kitchen, "Ring turns, runs in bowling to Mansell; it's a ball well-pitched. Mansell moves forward, drives, Hole at cover tries to cut it off. He's beaten by the pace of the ball and it races away for four. APPLAUSE! A rare boundary to excite the crowd and Mansell takes the score to 169 for the loss of six wickets as South Africa moves stoically towards Australia's first innings score of 280, with the loss of two quick wickets in the morning session after reaching 273 for eight on the first day's play."

"It's all double Dutch to me, darling, but he's a nice voice, that announcer," said Dulcie.

"Alan McGilvray, Sydney man, played a bit of cricket in his time. We've heard him commentating with John Arlott's crew on BBC radio back home. Can't say as I'm much of an aficionado of the game either Dulce, but I would have sworn there were only six balls an over; but not in this match. I've paid enough attention to know they're bowling eight; beats me," a revelation which left Dulcie incuriously unmoved.

As she sat sipping her tea, Dulcie noticed with pleasure that the kitchen had taken on a new character. The stocking up of the larder, stockpiling of the wood and so on had not only made it look homelier, but it had also lent a roundness to the quality of sound in there – it was cosy, it felt like home, it had taken on an infinitely improved timbre. The rhythmic description of the game held them under its companionable spell and Bill was gratified to see the colour flowing back into Dulcie's cheeks, the dissipation of worry lines from around her eyes. She took the program guide from where it was wedged behind the knife block and started to study the daily offerings, making a mental note of a breakfast program called Russ Tyson's Hospital Half Hour, during which Mr. Tyson apparently played the favourite tunes of family members unlucky enough to find themselves in hospital requested by family members lucky enough not to be. A regular afternoon show called Blue Hills, described as being a radio drama written by Gwen Meredith [of whom she'd never heard], caught her eye simply because she liked a good serial, which it may well be. She was pleased too to see that a children's program was broadcast at 4 o'clock every afternoon during the week. Jason and the Argonauts, which sounded a bit boyish but would, hopefully, entertain the girls.

Bill turned the volume up a bit asking, "That all right, love?" to which she absentmindedly nodded, as he went out to the laundry to fill the copper and set the fire under it, thinking a good scrub in a nice warm tub would restore more than their cleanliness this evening.

The Australian team's twelfth man, Richie Benaud, had just brought drinks onto the field when a thrumming on the cattle grid signified Curly's imminent arrival. They went out the front and watched the slow approach of the ute, taking the high ground to straddle the twin rain-filled ruts, but throwing up plenty of mud nevertheless. He pulled up in the middle of the turnabout and the two men eased the cage and its still sulky cargo down onto the ground. When they opened the door the turkeys, following the big tom's lead, strutted forth, their ebullience restored by freedom, with much gobbling and posturing to the huge amusement of the kids. Jess and Jilly couldn't believe they were not only coming to live here, but that they could also run free, wherever they liked.

Bill scattered a couple of handfuls of feed for them over near the feed bins, a popular move which attracted their immediate attention. Then the men returned the empty cage to the back of the ute as the kids went off, with Dulcie's blessing, to explore in the cow shed. Curly grabbed a cardboard box from the floor in the cabin and unpacked the contents onto the kitchen table as Dulcie washed the pannikins and spoons and emptied the teapot. She came back to a pyramid of canned baked beans on the table, "something nice and simple for our tea."

It was early when they fell into bed that night, full of baked beans, sausages and toast, freshly scrubbed, replete; depleted. The day had passed with uncanny silence into night, a result of the storm according to Curly. As they lay on the edge of the valley of sleep, the solitary cry of a mourning curlew haunted the thronging silence of the night, accompanying them down into the transient death of sleep.

Chapter Four

Milestones......

*T*hey looked back on that day many times during their lives, as a family and individually. Then it was called, depending on what had occasioned the reminiscence, "the day we got rid of the snakes,", or "the day we got the turkeys" or "the day of that dirty big hail storm!" But there was one aspect of the day on which Dulcie and Bill agreed without hesitation. It was the day after which they woke up feeling at home.

Their sheer survival of it, the fact that they had prevailed over its challenges engendered a sense of belonging, and cemented them somehow to this next bucolic phase of their lives together; a bond strengthened by the existence of a freshly and generously stocked larder for their exclusive personal wellbeing. Optimism in the future poked its nose through the long, cold reality of their post war lives together, like the first intrepid snowdrop of spring.

The farm was stocked as Ray Watson had finally decided, with 60 Jersey cows and a bull, ducks, the turkeys of course, and pigs – three sows and a cantankerous boar. Apart from the cats who largely inhabited the happy hunting ground of the corn shed, other working animals were brought in; first off, a couple of stock horses, which Bill and even Jess took to immediately though, not surprisingly, Dulcie and Jilly didn't. Old Bronc was quick to visit after spotting Ray Watson and Bruce unload them off the horse float in the turnabout. On horseback, he'd maintained an orbit of the farmhouse of ever diminishing circumference, making the occasional incursion only when he spotted Bill out and about on his own. As far as Dulcie went he was keeping his distance, testing the waters, trying to work out his standing with the lady of the house, whether his persona was "grata" or "non grata".

Then there were the dogs, a couple of kelpies, sharp as tacks and always raring to go. Without their skills and practical intelligence the milking would have probably taken place every two days instead of twice daily. For a while, albeit a short one, Bill thought of them as Hup and Hup Hup, just from listening to George or Bruce putting them through their paces out in the paddocks. It was only when he was out with Curly, who used a spectacularly piercing whistling technique to direct the dogs at their task, that he learnt their names were actually Reggie and Fred. Bill enjoyed this induction into dairy farming and, being intelligent, observant and keen as mustard to make a go of things, he learnt quickly. According to Dulcie who was frequently surprised by things he knew or could do, "he can turn his hand to anything, can Bill." During the first week after the herd was moved in Ray Watson made sure Bill had help, but it wasn't long before he and Old Bronc managed the herd comfortably and effectively with no other assistance than that of Reggie and Fred to whom, in the main, they both confidently deferred. As Bill told Dulcie more than once, dogs seemed to obey him if he got things right and to do their own thing if he got them wrong, which he suspected was most of the time, though definitely not always and increasingly less so.

- 0 -

During the weeks leading up to Christmas the boys managed to put a line through most of the major jobs on Glad's To Do List and the farm started to hum. The only big thing they didn't get around to was reinforcing the pigsty and checking the fencing around their patch, which degenerated into a quagmire within days of their arrival. The boar was a big, obstreperous animal whose occupancy dampened any enthusiasm any of them might have had for the task. Once the pigs were installed the chore was somehow constantly relegated to the bottom of a seemingly self-perpetuating list, the accomplishment of any other item somehow revealing an additional need of greater urgency. It was also fair to say they'd settled in like pigs in the proverbial, and it was with a clear conscience that other restorations gained the ascendancy. Restorations which, to Dulcie's womanly satisfaction, greatly improved the 'homestead' as they jokingly called it. Initially they were mainly improvements Bill had promised himself he would carry out the day he had crept down the side of the house with Ray Watson, Bruce and George half

106

expecting to see the laundry seething with snakes, only to be confronted with the pathetic sight of the crude makeshift facilities he and Dulce had rigged up for themselves as best they could.

Their first project around the house was to re-establish a veggie garden in preparation for which they cleared a lot of rampant growth from out back, weeds, old inhabitants of Mervyn's veggie patch gone feral. Bill cut the grass around the house with a scythe, thinking to encourage a lawn, but aware too of the practical safety of the clear view it provided. It was equally, if not primarily, important to clear a way to the outhouse, a flimsy structure which seemed to lean slightly to one side. The pit itself had been checked out and found to require no further preparation for use other than to make it comfortably accessible. It was deemed ready when a path to it from the laundry was laid using smooth, sunken rounds of wood, Penda most likely, set out like stepping stones which stood out clearly in the red, red dirt, and when the rampant vegetation had been cleared from its walls and surrounds. The big bag of lime and the ashes Bill saved fastidiously from under the stove and copper each morning were transferred to separate, covered containers and moved into the outhouse, each with its own scoop. Jess and Dulcie's introduction to the use and maintenance of a pit toilet was completed; the routine starting with a thorough inspection of the interior of the outhouse itself, especially behind the door and under the seat to ensure one wasn't in unwelcome company. Which was all very well, but neither of them ever got over their constipating fear of going into that perennially dark, isolated place, expecting to be bitten fatally on the bum at any moment by a snake or a spider. Bill wouldn't let them take a lamp in with them - in case they blew themselves up. So, without exception – that is, everyone including Bill - they all left it 'til the last minute and then sat, door open, allowing the view of the garden to distract them from their fear of the Grim Reaper's servants whilst their daily evacuation took place; it was an exclusively daytime occupation - after dark anywhere else provided a preferable receptacle. Dulcie allowed Jess to use the commode if she just wanted a pee, citing the efficacious effects of urea on her hydrangeas around which she regularly emptied the diluted contents of the pot.

As far as the regeneration of the veggie garden was concerned, Mavis Johnston became their chief adviser and willing assistant. It happened over afternoon tea on her second shopping day when Dulcie gave an account of their horticultural activities, "We've cleared the space like, and managed to save a few of the plants as were already there, some herbs and a pumpkin vine which Bill has cut right back; and there's a lovely passion fruit vine growing over the shed, but we've no idea really what we should do next; what with things being so topsy turvy here as far as seasons go. I mean, it's December and not a sign of snow in sight; but to be honest with you, Mavis, we're neither of us gardeners really, we've such a lot to learn." Mavis responded with enthusiastic advice and the benefit of her personal, physical assistance, a spontaneous gesture from which an enduring friendship flourished to their mutual benefit.

After much mumbling, reckoning, toing and froing, and enigmatic tinkering in the back shed, all of which Dulcie observed without remark, Bill called her out into the back garden one day to see what he'd been up to. He'd converted the otherwise useless pole out the back near the tank into a flag pole.

"So's you can send me messages when I'm out in the paddocks, love. I've checked, and the only place I can't see the top of this pole from is beyond the rill in the low paddock over near the Coughlin's – you know where I mean? And I'm rarely down there, unless I'm with you. I can see it plain as day from everywhere else. Real easy to run up a flag, change one, see," he said, showing her the way the ropes ran through the loops he'd manufactured, and where on the rope he'd attached the loops for tying a flag.

"Well I never!"

"It's really simple see, just straight up and straight down. You tie off the rope on this bracket here like this, and coil the tail end loosely over this hook here when you're done," demonstrating as he spoke. "We just need to develop a code. Have a think about it. Nothing complicated, mind." He paused, "First and foremost though we need some coloured rags, especially one for when the baby comes. What do you think?"

"You're a clever devil, Bill Johnson – I'll give you that. You weren't in the Kings Signals for nothing, were you love?" she gave him a broad smile, a peck on the cheek. "It's a grand idea. I'll have to put my thinking cap on about what sort of messages I might need to send."

"What about yellow for GRUB'S UP? It'd be a good start," he laughed.

"Give over," she said, giving him a nudge with her elbow. "Belting the old fry pan with a metal spoon seems to be doing that job quite nicely, to my way of thinking."

"Yellow flag wouldn't set the turkeys off though, would it?" he persisted, grinning.

She looked to the top of the pole and reflected a moment, "It's a good idea, it really is. There's no knowing what could happen if we had any sort of emergency. It's not as though we've next-door-neighbours near at hand, is it, or a telephone to summon help? In a way it's quite liberating having all this space to our selves, but it has its drawbacks too," she was just thinking out loud. "I agree with your number one priority. It's crossed my mind more than once. If my waters break and you happen to be out there I know I'll feel a lot better being able to let you know. I'll have to have a good look for something to use; not too long to go now. It'll soon be Christmas," she paused, massaging her lower back as she gazed up at the top of the pole, "Doesn't feel like it though, does it, this heat 'n all? I wonder how the locals celebrate Christmas," she finished with the afterthought.

- 0 -

Ray Watson turned up one day, still well before Christmas, with a bloke from Piper's Plumbing Service, as testified by the sign on the back of his van which included, to Dulcie's private amusement, the slogan "Don't sleep with that drip tonight". He introduced the fellow as Jack Piper. That she was tickled pink was obvious when they explained the purpose of their visit and proceeded without delay to prepare for the installation of pipes to provide a water supply to the kitchen via a tap over the workbench. It ended up taking nearly a week of intermittent labour to get the job done, but, ahhhhh, the difference it made, even though they still had to carry the basin out to empty it.

Mindful of the imminent arrival of the baby, they decided their priority indoors would be covering the floor in the kitchen first and then the living room. They didn't have any real money to spend so Bill put out feelers through Curly and the boys for some second hand lino, if anyone was doing some home improvements and needed to get rid of their existing floor covering. They put it about that they couldn't pay much but would be happy to come and pick it up from anywhere within reason. Curly had promised them the use of his ute if the one Ray Watson was having fixed up for the farm wasn't ready before something turned up.

Dulcie joined Glad on a trip into Atherton before Christmas too. To her amusement she discovered artificial holly complete with red berries in the newsagent's and she purchased a few sprigs, deciding on the spur of the moment to make a nice plum pudding for Christmas Day even though it was too late to really do it justice, the way her Mam did. It would be nice touch of home though, decorated with holly and served replete with thrupenny bits and a nice bit of custard. She bought a few small things to put in stockings for the girls too, comics, colouring books and pencils and a couple of miniature animals, carved in segments, hand painted and strung together with elasticised string which was threaded through a pedestal. When you pushed in the base of the pedestal which was like a plunger, it caused the animals, a cow and a giraffe in this case, to collapse over the side of the pedestal in a bedraggled heap, only to leap back to attention when you took your thumb off the plunger at the bottom; by wiggling the plunger about at different angles you could have the animals adopting all sorts of bizarre postures. She and Glad had a good giggle about these antics before she made her mind up about the purchase.

On that same trip she found, at a very reasonable price, a good, long piece of cotton gingham in red and white checks which she purchased to make curtains for the kitchen window and to hang from edges of the work bench, covering the shelves. It would make a good project for after the girls' bedtime, when she and Bill sat in the kitchen and talked, usually with a music program on the wireless quietly in the background. This was when he did the books too, and sometimes they read by the light of one of the big mantle lamps, but whatever their occupation they never lasted long, early nights

110

being essential to mornings equally so, and strenuous days between. It was a blessing in disguise really. The relentless work provided a permanent distraction from the fact that cultural pursuits in these parts were thin on the ground and there was little to do by way of entertainment or amusement. They had themselves and the radio, and if things continued as they'd started they could look forward to a few games of cards every couple of weeks with Nancy and Curly. One would be wise to keep one's sense of humour.

- 0 -

They woke well before dawn, rose before the cock crowed and performed their early morning ablutions together, enjoying the intimacy of the chiaroscuro lamplight in the kitchen while the stove heated up and the kettle came to the boil. The dipping, swooping light of the freshly lit Tilley lamp cast a golden glow on skin like silk, and wrapped their private treasures in folds of darkness. It was a precious time together.

By the time tea was brewed they were dressed and ready for their day's work but always had their first cuppa together sitting at the kitchen table, or preferably, on the log out front, weather permitting, before Bill and his offsider for the day set off with the dogs and horses, heading out in the dim predawn light to bring the cows in for milking. By five, five thirty the diesel motor was humming and the first batch of cows was bailed up, ruminating over a feed trough sparingly laced with molasses as the suction cups of the mechanical milking machine drained away their cream rich milk dispatching it via the separator to churns headed for the cream house or buckets headed for the pigs' troughs. The cows came in one end of the shed and were driven out the other, in the direction of a small reservoir replenished from a subterranean spring by the windmill in between the corn shed and the shed which housed the tractor and the farrowing accommodation, should one of the sows bear a litter.

After the morning session, the cows were herded back out to pasture by seven, by which time the girls were up and dressed and a big pot of porridge was ready to tuck into with an enormous dollop of cream each and honey trickled in a crisscross pattern over it. The family ate together, engulfed by the aroma of baking bread which would be ready for lunch, light and crusty. The girls liked nothing better than a nice big slice smothered in butter and vegemite. Jess and Jilly had been protected in the main from the food shortages in England and were quick to take these things entirely for granted, but not so Bill and Dulcie – years of deprivation occasioned by scarcity and food rationing would be hard to forget.

As soon as he'd finished breakfast Bill bade his family a good morning, kissed Dulcie on cheek and returned to the milking shed to clean and sterilize the equipment, ensure the morning's produce was chilling nicely in the cream house ready for collection, and shovel up any drier, collectable droppings before hosing down the concrete to clear it of the looser, grass green offerings. The girls went off to feed and water the chooks and collect the eggs which they brought down to the kitchen in the tin bowl they measured the feed with; eggs often still warm with the body heat of the hens who had so recently produced them. They scattered a smattering of feed for the ducks and the turkeys too, and amused themselves goading the turkeys into strutting "Gobble, gobble, gobbling" until Bill called them to order from the milking shed or Dulcie came to the front gate to yell at them all to "pack it in!" The plain fact was, the turkeys were easily roused and the day resounded richly with their gobbling; if the girls were around they never could help echoing their call, a recipe for perpetual commotion if ever there was one.

One day after the other, after the other called their attention to new responsibilities as Ray Watson slowly broke them in to the rhythm of farming life. For a time Dulcie struggled just to keep clean clothes on their backs and food on the table being, as she was, both heavy with child and new to the rigours of such unsophisticated living. Although there was no repeat performance of the hail storm, a rare occurrence by all accounts, since then it had rained almost every day bringing with it an abundance of red mud and a dearth of suitable places to dry things.

Washing, which was an arduous chore anyway, became even more difficult to keep up with. Her equipment consisted of the copper, a copper stick, three soapstone laundry tubs, a tap with a length of hose attached to it supplying gravity fed water from one of the tanks, a washing board – her skiffle board! - and a hand-turned mangle. She was well aware that having

112

three laundry sinks and a water supply was still considered a luxury in these parts but simply couldn't imagine how anyone would manage if they had to cart water from a creek in old kerosene cans, the lot of some, she heard, even now. After a period of trial and error she found the only way she could manage was to bring a batch of washing to the boil and soak it in soapy water in the copper every night except Saturday. Immediately after breakfast in the morning, when the fire Bill had lit first thing was getting low, she gave the washing a good drubbing, prodding it with the copper stick, occasionally using it like a pitchfork to lift a batch high above the water before letting it fall back. Even in the relative cool of the morning the salt from freely flowing perspiration stung her eyes and her light shift clung to her body. The concrete floor was hard on her feet and legs, her back ached. She soon learned how much wood she needed to just bring the water to the boil and once she had given the load a good pummelling with the copper stick she left it and attended to other chores until it cooled down, taking a pan of the hot water from the copper to the kitchen to wash up the breakfast things.

When she came back she wielded the copper stick once more to transfer the contents of the copper to the first sink, leaving the plug out. Copper emptied, she pressed down on the clothes in the sink to squeeze as much soapy water from them as she could, put in the plug and ran clean water to cover them. Agitating them soundly to release all the soap, she wrung them out individually and dropped them into the blue rinse in the second tub. The final step, she never bothered with starching anything, was to put each item individually through the rollers of the mangle which was attached across the third sink with a tray behind the rollers to catch the finished articles. Then she hung the clothes out to dry using wooden pegs. On a rare fine day they'd go on the long lines running down the side of the house and garden but more often than not she had to hang them on the lines Bill had strung up across the end of the kitchen in front of the stove. Until about April the following year the kitchen rarely without washing hanging in it to dry.

After finishing the washing one day she was sitting at the kitchen table sipping a nice fresh cuppa, recuperating her strength for the task of preparing lunch, when she saw that she had left the copper stick on the table.

She gripped it in the middle between her thumb and a couple of fingers and gave it an idle twist, setting it spinning in slow, lazy circles. When it stopped she noticed something engraved down one side, below the knob which formed the handle. She picked it up, inspecting it closely. Slowly she read out loud, "Isa pot stick is my name, poking clothes is my game." She laughed, wondering who had gone to such trouble to embellish a humble copper stick so. "*If life could be so simple*," she thought, the relentless treadmill to which they seemed anchored in mind. With so much to do, they were hard pressed to find time for even a little recreation, but even so, after the baby was born they would have to take a bit of time and trouble to find out what went on around here for entertainment, or just to let their hair down and have a bit of fun.

- 0 -

During the day the girls spent a lot of their time exploring the rill which Bill had declared safe after a thorough inspection from its entry onto the farm to where it disgorged itself into the creek which ran along the down side of the southern paddock before crossing under the Skennar Bridge on the road to Malanda, on its way to the Johnstone River. During Jilly's afternoon rest time Jess explored further afield, finding, amongst other things, her own secret hideaway up on the hillside beyond the windmill. Her explorations took her further afield too, but she kept all her findings to herself, partly because she liked having her own special places but also because she didn't want to get herself into trouble for travelling too far afield, even though, to her mind, she was always very careful like Mummy and Daddy said.

Even after Jess started school, one of their favourite pastimes was being allowed to help with the milking. Helping mainly involved keeping well out of the way of both the activity and the cows, by staying in the equipment room where they were inveigled by the whirring noise of the separator which cut through the clanking, lowing, scuffling sounds of milking time like an exotic musical instrument; they loved dipping into the molasses bucket too and licking its rich, sweet, stickiness from their fingers. Nor did they tire of watching Bill filling up the family milk churn with fresh milk, hand milking

114

the 'same' cow each day because her milk was "the best of the lot". Although a complete novice to start with it wasn't long before he was boastful of the strong jet of milk he could send in a continuous whooshing spurt to fill the pail quickly with frothy sweet smelling milk and sometimes even sent the odd squirt in search of a wide open mouth. He rarely scored a direct hit even though the girls leapt and bobbed in an effort to abet his success; the pastime was a source of much hilarity and skylarking. Their interest waned however, when it came time to feed the pigs with the watery looking skim milk drained out of the separator and they were quite content to watch Bill stagger off with sloshing buckets, one in each hand for balance, the sinews and veins in his neck standing out with the effort.

- 0 -

As if in testament to a continuing connection with all they'd left behind, Dulcie quickly re-established their old family traditions of a later, and more leisurely breakfast on Saturday mornings and a cooked lunch on Sundays, though at first they were hard pressed remembering what day of the week it was. If it hadn't been for Russ Tyson wishing them a good weekend on the ABC every Friday after the Hospital Half Hour with the promise of joining them again bright and early on Monday morning, they would have simply soldiered on regardless.

In no time, it seemed, Christmas was upon them. Glad had invited them to attend the midnight mass at St. Matthew's Church of England in Malanda and the celebratory breakfast afterwards, but they weren't ready yet to make their social debut, and cited Dulcie's advanced condition to decline with good grace. Fact of the matter was, they had not been church goers for some time and it wasn't a pastime either of them felt a need for. They decided to have their own quiet celebration, and Nancy and Curly accepted their invitation to visit in the afternoon with the boys for a few games of Canasta and a nice bit of tea. If it rained the kids could play in the front room which was still devoid of furniture, and they could all sleep in the girl's room if Nancy and Curly ended up staying late. As far as chores went, they all intended to do the bare minimum.

Bill's chores on Christmas Eve gave him several opportunities to listen to bits of the broadcast of the first day of the second test match between Australia and South Africa. Early that morning, before going out to round up the cows, he killed one of the chooks to have for Christmas dinner, as suggested by Ray Watson. Following the farmer's good advice he removed the bird from the roost with relative ease and took its head off with an axe on the big stump in the turnabout in virtual darkness. What nearly did unnerve him was the frantic flapping of the headless bird which seemed to go on for an age but could only have been a minute or so at most. When it eventually stilled he hung it up by the feet in the separator room to drain. He sloshed plenty of water on and around the stump which got rid of the bloody mess, but the almost metallic smell of the first spurt of blood remained in his nostrils, staying with him throughout the morning. He planned to pluck and dress the bird later in the day when the girls were playing away from the house, probably down by the rill if they ran true to form. He didn't want to spoil a special Christmas treat with intimate knowledge of its means of procurement.

It was a beautiful fine day, rare for this time of the year and at around eleven o'clock, having seen the washing on the line and the girls walking up the rill towards Foresters' Track, he took the dead bird down to the laundry where Dulcie had the copper quarter full with fresh water coming nicely to the boil just as he'd asked her to do when she finished the washing. He threw the chook into the water and its severed head into the fire. After a minute or two he rolled the now bedraggled looking carcass around with the copper stick until the feet were sticking up out of the water and, clutching one of them with a wad of cloth over his hand, hoicked it gingerly out of the water and into the first tub, letting it go as he stood as far away as possible to avoid the hot splashes it sprayed in transit. They both let out a big sigh of relief as the chook hit the bottom of the sink. After a minute he ran cold water over it to cool it down to a comfortable handling temperature, then gave it a good squeezing in a downward motion from the neck before patting it all over with the cloth getting rid of as much excess water as he could. To pluck it he transferred it to the second tub which Dulcie had lined with several layers of newspaper. Still following Ray Watson's advice, he started with the big wing

116

feathers. He was surprised at how easy the task was made by the dunking in hot water. What it had done was to melt the fat around the pen of the feathers so that they slipped out readily. Even so, it took him about twenty minutes to pluck the fowl to his satisfaction, a fact he thought best kept to himself. He removed the drip tray from the mangle and placed it over the first tub, providing a clean base on which to gut the bird, which he did with trembling fingers, taking care not to rupture the intestine. He was looking forward to this roast, was determined not to stuff the bird before Dulcie got to it with the sage and breadcrumbs; finally he cut off the feet which he saved along with the edible viscera for Dulcie to enrich the gravy. The rest he wrapped in small newspaper parcels and stuffed them patiently into the fire under copper one at a time.

Dulcie had gone in to prepare lunch, closing the back door quickly as the pungent smell of the burning head rose from the fire. When she'd finished making their sandwiches she put a fresh kettle of water on to boil and went out the front. On the spur of the moment she decided, instead of summoning the girls by banging on the fry pan, to go up to fetch them, find out what their day's new or continued fascination was. It was uplifting to walk under a clear blue sky albeit through the rust red dirt which clogged moistly around the paspalum tufts and created a squelching, sponge-like mat which 'blew raspberries' and bubbled underfoot. Tomorrow might be nice too she thought, forgetting her red-speckled legs and looking skyward seeking affirmation.

- 0 -

Before the girls went to bed that night they all joined in to decorate the kitchen, festooning it with brightly coloured strips of crepe paper, stretching them in twisted strands from both sides of the room to meet in the middle of the ceiling where their higgledy-piggledy confluence was hidden by a big green paper bell which Bill nailed to the spot. It had sat on the table looking like a slim, half-bell-shaped book, but when the covers were drawn back and clipped together with its soft metal catches a bell of skillfully interlaced leaves of bright forest green was created. Red berries hung from the gold tassel Bill used to secure it to the ceiling, drawing a chorus of appreciative "ahhhs!!" from his avid audience. Under Dulcie's guidance they then arranged on the table a bottle of sherry, two glasses and two slices of cake on a plate, refreshments for Santa Claus and his helper when they called in under the cover of darkness, when everyone would be asleep. Jilly was concerned that Santa wouldn't know where they'd moved to and Jess was sure he wouldn't fit down the chimney which was nothing like the one they'd had at home. After copious reassurances that everything would turn out alright, they went to bed and slept almost immediately.

Bill and Dulcie listened to a summary of the days play in the Test Match as they made preparations for the morning. They learned from a familiarly English-sounding commentator that South Africa had won the toss and opted to bat. After a shaky start they'd been rescued by sound batting performances from three of their bowlers, top scoring Murray, who was last man out, bowled for 51 by Benaud in his first outing for Australia, Mansell who was bowled out by Lindwall for 24 and Tayfield who was caught by Langley off the bowling of Miller. By close of play, Australia was 0 for 26 in response to South Africa's first innings score of 227 in an entertaining though unremarkable day's cricket. Bill said he reckoned he'd get a bit more excited about a test match between England and Australia, but it wasn't bad entertainment all the same, given the chance to listen. Preparations finished they drank a glass of sherry and shared the cake and then, with rusty but gay abandon, they had another sherry, left everything where it was and went to bed where, after a gentle, loving spoon-shaped union, they too, slept soundly.

The following day, their first Australian Christmas dawned clear.

"Two fine days in a row," said Dulcie, as she and Bill sat out the front enjoying their first cuppa. "Couldn't have asked for a better Christmas present if we'd tried, eh? It's a pity to waste such a good drying day - I think I should do a load of washing after all, love. I'll regret it if I don't."

"How about you get it going early, Dulce, and I'll finish it off when the milking's done? You've got enough on your plate in the kitchen today, love, no pun intended, and I'm looking forward to the results." He gave her a kiss on the neck and rose to go and meet Bronco who was lurching towards them on his docile white mare, a lighted lantern held aloft in his right hand. "Looks like Old Bronc's full of the Christmas spirit already," he grinned at her as he opened the front gate, "I'd best head him off at the pass, love, out of harm's way."

Dulcie slipped quietly back indoors amazed as always at the girls' ability to sleep through the early morning chorus, especially the rooster's persistent crowing. She took the Tilley lamp down to the laundry and sorted a load of washing into the copper, added soap powder, filled it with water and set the fire beneath it. Having space to keep the chopped wood dry under cover in the laundry and the kitchen was an absolute godsend, and before long the fire was burning strongly. She added another small log before going indoors to do as much as possible before the girls woke.

By the time the girls bowled into the kitchen, chirping like crickets about the treasures they had found at the end of their bed, she was preparing the stuffing for the chicken and the natural, slightly medicinal smells of fresh sage and mixed dried herbs mingled with the more earthy aroma of frying onions and chicken liver.

"Mmmm, heaven," she thought.

"Yuk, what's that smell," asked Jess, wrinkling her nose as she came down the stairs. Jilly held her ground on the top step.

"Happy Christmas," Dulcie said gaily, pushing the fry pan to the side of the hob and moving quickly around the table to gather them into her arms. "That's just a special treat for Mummy and Daddy," she said, "You don't have to have any if you don't want. There will be lots of yummy things for you to have. But what do we have here?" ... feigning great surprise at the sight of the red and white checked Christmas stockings each of them was clutching. "Come and show me," taking them by their spare hand and leading them back into their bedroom where they quickly hopped up onto the bed, intent on their Christmas booty. Dulcie pushed out the shutters, letting in the crisp morning light and the sounds of milking time; the lowing of cows, the clattering of their hooves on the concrete, the rattling of the chain on the metal gate to the holding pen, the excited yapping of the dogs further afield, the drone of the diesel motor and whine of the separator. Then, coming to them from the high side of the eastern paddock Dulcie suddenly heard snatches of *I'm dreaming of a white Christmas*. Hot tears suddenly filled her eyes and she almost gagged on the lump in her throat. She gripped the window frame fiercely in an effort to control her emotions, her knuckles white. Then, to her astonishment, she heard, stronger and a bit closer now in Bronco's distinctive tones, *Roll her over, in the clover, roll her over, lay her down, and do her again.* These bawdy words were more effective than a dose of smelling salts and she came to, feeling contrition at her momentary lapse. "He's well in his cups," she thought, pulling herself together, "So he's an excuse." She turned her full attention to the girls who were utterly absorbed in, and thrilled to bits with all their little presents, and soon tucking into the breakfast of bananas and shortbread biscuits they found in their stocking; as Dulcie had said to Bill when they'd been filling the stockings the night before, "Down there for dancing love, up here for thinking."

When Bill came in from the milking he breathed in the aroma of baking bread and rich sage stuffing appreciatively as the girls demanded clamourously to share with him their good Christmas fortune. Afterwards, he and Dulcie sat down to tea and toast for breakfast and exchanged the gifts they had each taken pleasure in smuggling in and keeping hidden. The first package Dulcie handed him contained a single breasted, pin-striped vest which looked as if it had once belonged to a suit.

"Very dapper," she said, as he tried it on, "fits you perfectly, darling."

"I rather fancy that," he said, "Thank you, love, I think I'll keep it on."

It was a sartorial style his family would remember. That afternoon Dulcie crept up by the side of the house and managed to get a photograph of him and Bronco standing in the turnabout next to Bronco's white mare, the two men completely engrossed in conversation. It was a marvelous photograph as they eventually discovered many months later, when Harvey turned up and developed all the pictures they had taken since leaving home in England. Only then could they carefully choose the ones they would have printed, a project which, as it happened, took yet another several months.

Bill was surprised when Dulcie handed him a second package and apologised for having but the one small offering. Though small however, it seemed to carry significant weight, beautifully wrapped and tied with ribbon as it was. He handed it to her with obvious pleasure. "Happy Christmas, love," he said, looking into her eyes as he placed it in her hand. She unwrapped it with trembling fingers.

"Oh, Bill, you shouldn't have, darling," she said opening the small, black, hinged box to reveal a gold ring inset with an opal. It was almost the twin of the one she had lost down the plug hole during the voyage, their betrothal ring. She hugged and kissed him, "but I'm so glad you did," she finished with tears shining in her eyes, "it's beautiful. Oh, thank you darling. It means such a lot. Oh dear, my nose is weeping," she said, holding the back of her hand to the offending appendage.

He handed her his handkerchief and tore the wrapping off his second present. "That's a cracker, Dulcie," he said, inspecting the cover of a paperback of Zane Grey's novel, *The Mysterious Rider*. "Must be one of the few of his I haven't read yet. You're a canny shopper Dulcie, make no mistake - I'll look forward to that, love."

"That's good. I didn't think you'd read it, but the shopkeeper said you could exchange it if you had anyway," said Dulcie, "I couldn't believe it when I saw it. I got it at Andy Maule's Newsagency in Mareeba, when I went up there with Glad that time. He's a good selection there, darling, and he's a tobacconist too. Worth a visit when you get the chance to get over there. It's in Byrnes Street from memory. Gave me thru' pence off, he did!"

"I meant to ask you at the time, what was Glad doing in Mareeba, do you know?"

"She went to see someone at the Mareeba Bacon Factory I think. As I recall she said that's where most of our pigs will go – any exception going to Bronco as part of some sort of special arrangement which is good for all of us apparently. It didn't take her long because she joined me at the newsagents and I hadn't been there long."

"Ah, so that's where they'll go," another piece falling into place.

They were in good spirits and working together they had the washing on the line in double quick time. Then Dulcie put the potatoes on to par boil in readiness for roasting. They were going to have the chicken stuffed and slow roasted which would give off lovely pan juices for a good rich gravy, roast potatoes, pumpkin and onions and boiled cabbage tossed in butter with crispy bacon pieces and lightly peppered. After that there was plum pudding

121

and custard. The pudding had been soaking up the sherry these past couple of weeks and might be a bit rich for the girls but they would be happy just with the custard, one of their favourites. She couldn't remember the last time they'd had such a meal and hummed as she worked, trimming the table setting with pieces of holly and polishing the cutlery and cruet, for what it was worth. She didn't have a fancy sauce boat for the gravy but knew it would taste just as good out of a pannikin. To her way of thinking, she would rather have good tasty gravy from a pannikin than gruel from a silver sauce boat any day.

They would have their Christmas dinner at 12.30 giving them plenty of time to enjoy the meal and clear up before Curly and Nancy came.

All in all it was a good day, full of good will and small but special treats for everyone but although Bill and Dulcie went through the motions cheerfully, each suffered sharp pangs of homesickness, during which they longed for the void in which they found themselves to be filled with family, friends, the institutions of their previous life, so recently abandoned, so patently and thoroughly gone.

Bill thought especially of his father whose health was failing though he was not much past 50, his lungs eaten away by the foul air of industrial England and the rigours of the first war. Bill was the eldest of eleven children, ten of whom had survived the second war. He and Dulcie had spent their first four years of married life living in the attic of his family home, waiting for housing. Ironically they had moved into a brand new home just three months before news came through of their sponsorship and assisted passage. His youngest sister was only eighteen months older than Jess and the two of them had been great mates. It saddened him to acknowledge that she'd be a virtual stranger to him if they were lucky enough to meet again, but when he looked about him now, the sight of his family sitting down to a hearty Christmas dinner, and the rude good health and happiness which radiated from their glowing faces, brought him back down to earth where he felt pleasure in having made a good choice.

Dulcie, also the eldest though only of five, missed her siblings and her mother's comfort even more so than usual, Christmas being, traditionally, a time of family reunion. She deliberately shunned, however, any thought of her father whom she had not forgiven, not on any account. Dulcie had been his favourite, for which she'd been teased relentlessly for years by her three brothers and her sister, Merry, and she had grown up believing that all he wanted for her was her happiness. He had, however, demonstrated otherwise in such indelibly hurtful ways that she still felt betrayed and belittled even now, some seven years later. Although her marriage to Bill had been, of necessity, a hasty one, she had been, and still was, head over heels in love. She had been cut to the quick when her father's highhanded displeasure had made her and her love for Bill fugitive from the family on her wedding day. He had disallowed their attendance at the celebration of the marriage and not one of them had been present, each anxious not to make life more difficult at home for Ma.

Subsequently she'd come to believe that all he'd really ever wanted was the personal gratification of vicarious pride in her professional achievements and successes. He'd no understanding at all of the enormous emotional costs of those achievements; the difficulties she'd had to overcome during those hideous years of dealing day after day with the tatters of humanity, shredded bodies and minds rained relentlessly down on them by the conflagration of war; her earlier love for a man capable of hiding the extent of his wounds until an incident in the ward with another patient propelled him over the edge into a state so demented the doctors gave him little chance of ever completely recovering – his affliction the extreme psychoneurosis of shellshock. In reality, this trauma to someone to whom she had become so attached had left her reeling, close to an abyss of unmitigated despair. At that time the daily rigors of coping with the gruesome demands placed on her profession by this unholy war actually helped her through to some extent, leaving her physically and mentally devoid of any real energy for self-pity; but at the same time the situation had also denied any opportunity for grieving and, though invisible, the wounds existed to this day.

Now, when she thought of her father, his meanness of spirit, it riled her. It also made her sad; she missed something she'd come to believe she hadn't had in the first place. She worried about her Mam too, being under the thumb of 'the old bastard' as she and Merry now quasi-jokingly called him.

123

Since they'd left, recent though that was, she'd thought a lot about her need for family, had convinced herself that Harvey, the next born and just two years younger than her, was the only one with the experience, imagination and maturity to pack up and come to settle out here. He'd been in the RAF during the war and spent a lot of time in Egypt, ground staff, maintaining the fleet based in Cairo. He'd grown accustomed to the warm weather there, thrived on it. Back home in that foul winter of 1947 he'd suffered grimly with a terrible bout of bronchitis and in Merry's latest letter, which she would read again tonight as a Christmas treat, she said it had come back again, as it had every year since. Even at this early stage of their settlement here she was working on him, and she had no intention of letting up, knowing instinctively that her success would be very much easier whilst he remained a single man.

- 0 -

The week between Christmas and New Year had a highlight. Mavis and Reg Johnston paid a visit the day after Boxing Day, something Bill had known about but somehow forgotten to tell Dulcie. It was early afternoon and Bill was chopping wood out the back when the familiar thrumming of the cattle grid caught his ear and he looked up to spot the Model T laboriously negotiating the track towards the turnabout. He called to alert Dulcie, apologising for not having let her know sooner, and they went out the front together to welcome their visitors.

"Hello, Mavis love – Merry Christmas! It's so good to see you. Silly so and so forgot to mention you were coming," Dulcie nodded her head in Bill's direction, "otherwise Jess and Jilly would be here – would have insisted on it in fact," she laughed gently. "As it is they're down playing at the Coughlin's place, making the most of the dry weather. They'd be ever so sorry to miss you – let's hope they'll be home soon."

True to form Mavis had arrived laden with goodies from her kitchen and produce from the garden. Reg brought a couple of bottles of beer which he and Bill shared, sitting on the log out the front listening to the cricket. Earlier in the day the commentators had been rhapsodic about the South African performance in the field the previous day. The visitors had dismissed the home side for 243 in, according to the commentators, "as fine a display

124

of out-cricket as either side has produced in the series to date," before eventually retiring themselves without loss of wicket for six runs, just 10 runs behind the Australian side.

"Did you manage to catch any of it, Bill?" Reg asked conversationally at the end of an over.

"No, I didn't. To be honest I forgot all about it. There were a few things needed seeing to around here."

"Well Tayfield made their day for mine," said Reg. "Apart from Miller, the middle order batsmen just couldn't handle his offbreaks. Their bowlers Murray and Watkins were both nursing injuries of some sort, but after Tayfield saw Morris off with a spectacular caught and bowled," he thumped a knee with one hand, "Cheetham just seemed perfectly happy to let him take up the slack. Not bad tactics as it turned out, eh?"

"Six wickets, wasn't it?" said Bill.

"Yeah, that's right," said Reg, "but the killer was he got three of them for just one run – Ring, Miller and Johnston. This bloke Endean, who's batting now, took a smashing catch on the boundary to dismiss Miller and that really seemed to knock the stuffing right out of our lot, to be honest."

They turned their attention once more to the broadcast, not saying much, neither needing to, as the commentary of Alan McGilvray and his cohorts spun a web which drew them right into the Melbourne Cricket Ground where the South Africans, after a solid display during the morning session, were continuing in much the same vein after lunch. Even Bill could tell that something out of the ordinary was taking place.

The statistics at the end of the day's play were a testament to that fact, and indeed, when umpires Elphinstone and McInnes pulled up stumps on Day 5, a couple of days later, in their second innings Australia were all out for 290 and South Africa the victors by 82 runs.

- 0 -

While the boys listened to the cricket out front Dulcie made tea for Mavis and herself and was pleased to have fresh scones to offer with clotted cream from the top of the milk, and the strawberry jam Mavis had brought with her. They settled themselves at the end of the kitchen table further from the stove. The clothes lines strung up in front of the stove were empty for which Dulcie was grateful, today being their fifth fine day in a row, barring one fairly light shower in the afternoon on Boxing Day. Mavis produced a gaily wrapped package for Dulcie which turned out to be a bottle of lavender water, "Just a little something to help you cope with this stinking weather," and a tin of Mackintoshes Quality Street for the girls, "I hope you don't mind them having sweets," she said, "but I just couldn't resist the tin. I've not seen this one before and I thought they might like it too, that lovely English street all covered in snow. It could probably be around the corner from where you lived."

Dulcie laughed, "So long as they don't mind sharing, I don't mind at all – these're my favourites," she said, holding the tin in her hands, inspecting the scene depicted on the lid and around the sides. "I must confess that by Australian standards everywhere in England is not that far away from anywhere else, something I didn't properly appreciate until I left I must say. But you're right, this street is so familiar to me I feel I know it. The Macintosh factory was in Halifax, in Yorkshire – just a short trip by bus or train from where I grew up in Oldham. Used to go there on school outings, went to one of the woolen mills on one occasion." She poured the tea.

"Did you ever see the movie they made before the war called Quality Street, with Katherine Hepburn as Miss Sweetly – and, oh, who was the fellow who played Major Quality? Married to Joan Crawford he was, and chocolate-box handsome you might say? Made lots of films; funny name, French I think."

"I can't help you there Dulcie. I didn't see a movie at all until after the war. I'll never forget my first one – it was Duel in the Sun, with Jennifer Jones and Gregory Peck. Ohh, she was gorgeous. It was on in town and I managed to talk Reg into taking me. I did enjoy it, and so, fortunately, did he," she tilted her head in the direction of the log where the men were sitting out front.

"Bill and I went to see that not long after we were married. One of Bill's favourites she was," said Dulcie.

She sipped her tea before topping up both their cups Mavis having pushed hers forward as she picked up the pot. "Quality Street was well before that though, prewar as I said. I think it came out at around the same time as these did," she patted the tin. "I would have been about 13 or 14 and by then Dad would let me go to the cinema with a girlfriend on a Saturday afternoon. I hero worshipped Katherine Hepburn I did, she was ever so modern – 'tray' sophisticated. She had a lot of nerve to wear trousers, she did, but jeepers, could she wear 'em, eh?"

"Yes, and she always looked so chic I thought. I still couldn't dream of it."

They smiled at one another, happy to launch into reminiscences of past pleasures shared. They helped themselves to another scone and accompaniments,

"Franchot Tone!" blurted Dulcie.

Mavis laughed, "Oh, I know him. He was in *Every Girl Should be Married*."

"You're right you know," Dulcie mumbled through a mouthful of scone.

"I went to see that with my Mum, Reg wouldn't hear of it. Now, Franchot.... Is that how you say it? Anyway, he was the playboy wasn't he? The one who fell in love with whatshername, the one who wanted to marry Cary Grant? He was a confirmed bachelor so she had a lot of scheming to do and used the playboy unmercifully."

"That's him," said Dulcie, patting the table top for emphasis, "one and the same, and he played Major Quality in *Quality Street*." They both laughed, pleased to have found a mutual memory, another point of connection.

"And I think it's 'fran- show'," said Dulcie, "not 'fran-tchot'.... But with a French accent instead of a Manchurian one."

They giggled. They attended to the scones. Their eyes met conspiratorially and they were drawn closer by these shared memories.

"So where is your Mum now, Mavis? Is she in Malanda?"

"No. Mum and Dad are on Watson Road at Minbun, out along the Millaa Millaa road, past Tarzali. It's not that far away but it's a dirt road and it's shocking during the wet season. Reg and I try to ride over to see them at least every couple of weeks."

"So, they're farmers then?" asked Dulcie.

"Yes, dairy farmers, their cream goes to Millaa Millaa. Dad is a local boy. He grew up on the family farm on Brooks Road, closer to Millaa Millaa. Grandma and Grandpa Woods are still there but they rented out the farm and retired a good few years ago now. I was quite small when Mum and Dad bought their place. I know you think this place is primitive but it's positively sophisticated compared to what Mum had to make do with, and she wasn't born to the land either."

"So she's not a local girl then?"

"No she was born in Dapto, down in New South Wales near Sydney. Her dad worked on the Bulli Pass Road, not that I expect that means much to you, eh? Ah, the stories she tells. She went to two schools when she was a kid, both at the same time," Mavis laughed. "The teacher used to teach three days at one school down river and two days at another school up river. She was one of ten kids and Grandma insisted that those that were old enough went to school every day so they had no choice but to follow the teacher about. Even so, Mum was only 11 when she went out to service to earn the princely sum of twelve shillings and sixpence a week. Hard to imagine, isn't it? She was still very young when she went up to Sydney, 13 or 14 I think. She used to live in and provide care for elderly people or invalids. She met Dad in Sydney when he was there on holiday one time though I am not sure of the circumstances."

"Oh dear, I know all about where following your heart can get you," said Dulcie, smiling ruefully as she looked about her.

"Yes indeed," Mavis agreed, "though I don't think the change for Mum would have been quite as drastic as the changes you've encountered somehow. All the same, one of Dad's favourite stories is about how she appeared in high heels and white stockings the first time she helped with the milking. Can you imagine? The dirt's just as red over there as it is here, believe me."

They were still laughing when Bill came in to get the second bottle of beer.

"You sure that's tea you two are drinking?" he teased. "You've been giggling your heads off for the last six overs," he smiled as he headed back out the front.

Dulcie rose to rinse the cups and make another pot of tea.

"It's interesting that you mentioned Katherine Hepburn wearing trousers in those movies in the thirties," continued Mavis, "because Mum still talks about how dirty her skirts would get around the edges and how much easier it might have been to wear pants like the men. She didn't though, because it would have been considered vulgar. It just wasn't done. She would never go without a corset either, even when she was milking, regardless how hot it was. It's hard to credit that a thoroughly sensible woman, which she undoubtedly is regardless of the high heels and white stockings episode, could be such a slave to social mores. I mean she was stuck in the middle of nowhere; there was little chance of meeting anyone from one day to the next, and I'm afraid it took all one's energy and time just to sustain life. I don't know how they did it, maintaining those dress standards while putting up with such hardship on a daily basis, but the women were all the same apparently. It's just the way things were. Things really have changed a lot, haven't they, even though, like you, I still can't imagine wearing trousers?"

"I don't know about here, Mavis, but the war changed a lot of things in England. The contribution of women to the war effort simply couldn't be denied, not by the government, not by the men folk, but even more importantly to my mind, not by women themselves. I imagine women had to keep a lot of things going here too, while their men were at war. It's changed certain perspectives forever, to my mind."

"Yes, well, the war certainly changed the course my life might otherwise have taken," said Mavis lightly. "I met Reg at a dance in Tolga in 1943, I was 18. There were thousands of Australian soldiers camped in the Tolga district back then and the local people did their best to provide entertainment for the troops. I think the men enjoyed the break from camp life which by all accounts was pretty tedious, and their spending money provided quite a boost to some local coffers too. Reg's from Townsville. He's adamant that he would never have traveled to Tolga off his own bat, not in his wildest dreams, never having heard of the place, so the war did him a favour he reckons," she smiled coyly. "We were married in Cairns in 1948, in the same church Mum and Dad were married in. We moved about a bit at first but ended up here in Malanda when Reg landed the job at the butter factory just over three years ago. We both really love it here and it's good to be close to Mum and Dad."

She paused wistfully and Dulcie waited, sensing that Mavis hadn't finished.

"If only I would fall pregnant," Mavis finished wistfully.

"Aahh," said Dulcie, and patted Mavis's hand as the excited trilling of the girls could be heard through the open back door from the direction of the rill. They had obviously spotted the familiar form of the Model T sitting in the turnabout. To their uncomplicated minds that car meant Mavis, and Mavis meant treats.

"We should talk about it, Mavis, if you want. Next time I come into town, eh, or you're always welcome here? Now's not the time unfortunately, the girls will be here any minute so you'll be inundated."

"Thank you Dulcie, I'd like that. It would be good to talk to someone."

- 0 -

With the arrival of the New Year the days grew hotter and there was a tendency to high activity at each end of the day, starting with the milking on both counts. Close as she was to confinement, and being totally unaccustomed to such long periods of unrelenting heat, Dulcie found conditions enervating. She felt guilty about the extra work that fell to Bill but knew she needed to remain strong for the birth. For his part he was adamant that she conserve her strength and was relieved that his current work routine provided ample time for some of the domestic chores which usually fell to her. The main priorities on the farm during the heavy wet weather were the milking and generally managing the herd, maintaining the equipment, careful storage of the cream in the cream house, transporting the milk churns up to the road on the back of Bronco's old dray, as it so happened, on Mondays, Wednesdays and Fridays for pick up by the butter factory truck, and making sure the rest of the farm animals were fed and watered.

130

He chopped the wood, did the bulk of the washing and prepared the bathtub in the evening. The times they enjoyed most together during these hot, wet, steamy months were their predawn ritual which they followed religiously and the time they spent pottering in the garden on the occasional clear moonlit night.

On the 13th January 1953 at about 10am Bill and Old Bronc were high up in the top paddock with the stock horses, trying to improvise a way to bring a couple of large logs down to the house where they could be cross sawn and chopped when Bill suddenly noticed the yellow flag flying. He almost choked on the heart now stuck in his throat as he turned to Old Bronc, saying with uncharacteristic intensity, "Sorry mate, have to go, it's the missus, it's the baby, some things just don't wait for anything!"

Old Bronc could feel the heat of urgency emanating from him, told him to be off and look after his "lady love", saying he'd take care of the horses. Together they quickly unhitched the special harness they had rigged up for the task in hand and Bill took off on Big Red, a small, black, but very dependable horse.

Chapter Five

"God must be sleeping............"

*D*espite the cool exterior he had shown all day, to Dulcie and the world at large, he could not deny his inner turmoil. He was on the road from Atherton to Malanda. It was late on Tuesday 13 January 1953. As he began the drive back home from the hospital he reasoned with himself that the queasiness roiling in his gut was probably the culmination of months of uncertainty about his family's future. Since their arrival here he'd seriously questioned the wisdom of his decision to come and only recently, as he had begun to find his stride and to winkle out the opportunities of their new situation, had he cautiously breathed that first shaky sigh of relief that his decision to emigrate had been a step in the right direction, towards a safe and happy future for them all, including, he hoped, those to come. His concern for Dulcie during the delivery of his boy exacerbated the raw emotions surging through him – oh, yes! A piercing shard of sheer elation ran through him at the thought of it, he had a boy; he'd managed to put 'the tassel' on this little whippersnapper. All the same, he was hard pressed now, as he set off in Curly's ute back in the direction of Malanda, to know what had swamped him most when he had been told that mother and son were doing well. Was it relief, pride, elation, love or fear? He felt disquieted at being ambushed by fear. He'd not suspected its latent presence, but recognised it now as a sense of potential inadequacy, the fear of failure. He met it head on, characteristically refusing to let it get the better of him, but he was at a genuine loss to know what he had learnt of life beyond familial love and respect that he could teach a son with pride and pleasure. He had never had any such misgivings with his daughters. He found it sufficient in their case simply to love and to provide for them, to give them affection and lead them by example, and to allow Dulcie to take care of their lives' mysteries. A son was a different matter.

The night was fine but the moon, in its third quarter, was only dimly visible through a fine tissue of cloud when he left the hospital. Out on the road, for much of the time, the beams from his headlamps were cowed by the pitch dark into mere puddles of light sucked into the sodden floor of a narrow, leafy, dripping, muddy tunnel, contained above by the murky reflection off the canopy of the rainforest. It was reminiscent of driving during the wartime blackout and he was on edge, never knowing what might be around the corner. His old distaste for night driving stuck in his craw forcing his body upright, tense over the steering wheel, knuckles white with the effort of holding his course in the slick, red earth. He sighed in gratitude when he got through a treacherous stretch of dirt and back onto the bitumen again, but almost immediately another vehicle came around a blind corner, hogging the middle of the road and his spontaneous evasive action sent him skittering along the soft edge of the road, cursing and battling yet again to keep the ute under control. The interior of the cabin was filled with the staccato percussion of gritty earth battering the inner mudguards and undercarriage, thrown up sharply by the slewing motion he battled to control. He blinked rapidly as he brought the ute to a skew-whiff rest, half on the hard surface, half off, and behind his fluttering eyelids a rapid sequence of black and white images from the carousel of an earlier memory fleetingly passed. A quiet curse, part frustration, part fear, escaped his lips, self-acknowledgement of the personal physical vulnerability he was acutely aware of. He tore himself back from this intrusive past, brought the ute to rights, and proceeded determinedly on his way, thankful that home was now close and soon the road would be not only sealed but also open, with cleared, farmed land on either side.   Hallelujah! The conditioned desire to praise god for life's mercies registered in his consciousness… "this 'Jah' has a lot to answer for," he sighed as he settled to enjoy the short run in to home.

He slowed as he passed Ray Watson's homestead, noticing the lights on the verandah and in one of the front rooms of the house. Realizing how hungry he was, and thirsty, he decided to pull in at home instead of driving straight through to the Coughlin's and as he slowed to take the turn he saw the spectral vision of Old Bronco striding down from his humpy, eerily lit by a hurricane lantern swinging rhythmically on the end of a pole. He pulled up

136

a few yards inside the cattle grid, put the handbrake on and jumped down from the cabin as his eccentric neighbour lurched to a halt on the track just ahead.

"So, everything's all right then, is it?" Old Bronco cut straight to the chase.

"It is that," Bill gripped the hand being proffered, "she's given me a fine strapping lad," smiling broadly as they shook hands.

"Aye, but that's fine news, fine news; congratulations my friend - heartiest congratulations; a relief to have the babe safely in your arms, no doubt?"

"No less on this occasion than ever before, and that's a fact," Bill said. "They're both doing well as they say in hospital parlance, everything went well, and there were no problems, though Dulcie's a bit tired, naturally enough. They've suggested keeping her in for a few days to get her strength back and I'm grateful that's possible. A few days' rest and being waited on will do her the world of good. She's done well, Athol, she's done very well."

"Aye, well this is all fine news indeed. Do me the honour, Bill, if you would, and accompany me to my place to drink a toast to your dear lady and your new son," in that formal style of speech Old Bronco was wont to adopt.

Bill was surprised and, in fact, touched by this unexpected invitation. "Thank you, Athol, but I'm famished. I was just going to get myself something to eat and have a cuppa before going down to Curly's to pick up the girls. It's been a long day."

"I've a billy of tea mashing, a good ham. I made fresh damper this evening, it being fine and there's bananas, pineapple…. allow me to look after you, and when you've eaten, then we'll enjoy a small libation to wet the baby's head! The young ladies will be well asleep by now. What do you say?"

Bill had often wondered how Old Bronco lived, his gaze frequently drawn to the humpy which dominated the clearing on the crest of the rise above where they now stood, on the northern extremity of the farm, but he'd not yet been up there. Apart from a serendipitous opportunity to satisfy his curiosity, the victuals being offered sounded good too, but his real reasons for accepting the invitation were the genuine warmth of it and his spontaneous realisation that he would enjoy the light relief of company after what had been an anxious, lonely wait during Dulcie's travails, and the ordeal of the drive back from Atherton.

"Since you put it like that, Athol, you've talked me into it," he said, "and the honour will be mine. I'll just turn off the motor," he finished, walking back to the ute where he leaned in to douse the lights and turn the engine off. Slipping the key into his trouser pocket, he joined Old Bronco and they clambered through the fence to walk up the hill. On the way Godiva appeared softly out of the darkness to nuzzle Old Bronco's shoulder. Without breaking stride he absentmindedly scratched her under the chin and patted her neck before gently slapping her on the rump to dispatch her back to graze, and the stillness of the night was briefly broken by the voluptuous clopping of hooves sucking up a soft, damp redness of earth as she startled away.

As they reached the clearing Bill expressed surprise at seeing a second humpy of sorts set further back. He reconnoitered the new territory instinctively and observed that this second structure was shielded from view from the south and the west though probably visible from Foresters Road, a road he'd not yet had cause to travel.

"Aye, that's my smoke house, amongst other things. Sleep there during winter – warm as toast. Tight as a drum in a storm it is, too," Old Bronc furnished this information as they walked up to the campfire set under a tin roof in front of the main structure, "and makes as much din," he finished with a wry grin. Bill was amused by the analogy. In the dim light the smokehouse looked like half a corrugated iron rainwater tank that had been cut in two from top to bottom and the two halves laid end to end to form a hangar like roof supported by low slab walls. Looking at it, Bill thought that even in the middle a man would be hard pressed to stand up. It appeared open at the featureless end facing them though its interior was not visible and this may have just been a trick of the light. There was a bent stove pipe chimney protruding at a rakish angle from the back of the structure. Old Bronc pointed Bill towards a log by the fire, and bent to pour a pannikin of tea from the billy. "Tin of condensed milk in that box just behind you," he said as he handed it over. He put the billy down on a flat rock in the wall containing the smouldering fire and plodded off with his deliberate, old man's gait in the direction of "the smokehouse" whose gloomy interior soon swallowed up his stooping figure and the light from the hurricane lamp giving lie to the notion that it was open ended.

In his absence Bill satisfied his thirst and his curiosity with equal enthusiasm. The tea was a new experience, laced with smoke and thoroughly mashed as it was, but it was hot, and it was wet and it was sweet, and such was his need it hit the spot as well as a fine Orange Pekoe freshly drawn. He drank thirstily as he inspected the main humpy, outside of which he sat. It wasn't large and could only, he surmised, provide very basic accommodation; somewhere to sleep, and somewhere to keep limited personal effects, certainly no kitchen, apart from where he sat, and a bathroom was out of the question; he ruefully remembered his own present lack of a bathroom, but in truth it was a condition with which he was well accustomed even back home. Through the open door, the inner walls appeared to be covered with something but the light was so dim he couldn't make out the substance of it. He observed a number of books propped up on a bookshelf which looked to be improvised out of a kerosene case turned on its side. He and Dulcie knew something of the kerosene case culture themselves and appreciated, like most of the local denizens, the advantages of versatility at the right price. He wondered what constituted this particular library, thought to ask some time. The sparseness of the living quarters before him reminded him of his time in India serving in the Royal Signals, the treasures he could see now a reminder of what he had chosen to surround himself with at that time – books, letters, photographs, the sketches he loved to do of scenes graced by Indian women elegant in traditional dress, captured during his rare, therefore precious, free time. The construction of the humpy intrigued him, and when Old Bronco returned with provisions, he expressed his interest as he fell gratefully upon the repast.

"Interesting place, Athol, built it yourself, did you?"

"Aye, I did. Mervyn helped out at the start, he was a mere sapling then, aye, and then when George arrived he took an active interest. But I've added to it over the years." He paused in reminiscence, and glanced up at his home, "She's a bit of a hybrid, you might say; grew out of what was available at little or no monetary cost. Not exactly begged, borrowed or stolen but not

139

far off; same now, always been the same. Always need the money I come by for other things."

"Hard work by sound of it and patience a virtue," Bill empathized.

"Hard work orright. And it were a slow process. I lived in a tent for nigh on two year, which in itself was a big improvement on dossing down under Skennar's Bridge I can tell you," he paused, reflecting.

"Aye, we hadn't much to work with but we were discerning all same. Her walls were split from maple off the land, and the rafters crow's foot elm, all done right here with a maul, wedge and froe. Right lucky we were, to get sheets of corrugated iron for the roof. It was dead hard to make shingles with our primitive set up and it were a great relief when the roofing fell into our lap, as it did, so to speak," he nodded towards his roof.

"A real boon, that were, wet season being as is. Yon house of Mervyn's, your place, grew out of that same circumstance, another man's cloud providing our silver lining, though she's a bit rusty looking now." He chuckled as he looked towards his home, nodding his head for emphasis as he continued, "many an hour I've spent plugging cracks in wall with soggy newspaper and old corn husks to keep out draughts, or rain, or serpents; still have to do it from time to time, but the iron roof has kept me sheltered from the outset."

Bill drained his tea and Old Bronc paused to replenish the pannikin and throw another small log on the fire.

"You're welcome to visit any time, Bill, for a good look around; daytime's best, when it's dry. I've an earthen floor, same as in yon kitchen," tilting his head in the direction of 'Mervyn's' place, "and I've found many a use for a kerosene case as you've no doubt noticed, but the beds are a treat, here and in smokehouse. Fashioned from saplings and corn sacks, they are, same as early settlers made 'em, and they couldn't be more comfortable; made 'em under Mervyn's instruction and guidance. He's a canny lad, is Mervyn," he paused, "So here I am, Bill, living in the lap of luxury and nary a bill to worry about. Never been very good with bills," he concluded with a self-deprecating snort.

"A big advantage having no bills," Bill agreed, "never more so than when there's no money to pay them; a condition I'm not entirely unfamiliar with." He brushed the crumbs from his hands and wiped the corners of his mouth with his fingers, finally smoothing down his top lip, where his moustache used to be, habitual post prandial grooming no longer necessary.

"Thank you Athol, that was good ham, very good ham, lives up to your reputation," a long, satisfied sigh escaped him, "it was just what I needed, it was, all of it; very satisfying, I feel almost human again."

"The goodness of my ham owes another debt to patience, make no mistake, learning right wood to burn in the smoking of it. Wasn't always that good," Old Bronc rose, removing Bill's empty plate and pannikin, "but now that you are replete, an important toast is to be drunk."

He went indoors eagerly, returning with a bottle of Old Digger Bundaberg Rum and two pannikins. He unscrewed the metal cap and poured two generous measures ceremoniously into the pannikins, "This bottle has been awaiting just such an occasion," he said as he passed Bill one of the pannikins and sat himself back down on his log. "A drop of this to wet your wee son's head, Bill, and your restoration will be complete. To the boy," he finished and they clanked their pannikins together.

"To young John," said Bill, whereupon Old Bronco took a robust draught from his pannikin with relish whilst Bill, who followed suit, found the emphatic presence of the uncut spirits on the back of his tongue a challenge. He exercised great self-control to stifle a cough which he knew, if he let it take shape, would lead to others. His eyes watered. He put the pannikin down, gulping to drown the fire at the back of his throat, took his makings out of his top pocket and set about building a rollie, feigning an insouciance he wished he felt.

"Ah, so it's John then," said Old Bronco after a time, "after his Grandfather maybe?"

"No, Athol, no," replied Bill, breathing freely again, "after a brother I lost during the war. Only eight he was, poor little blighter," said Bill, lighting his cigarette. He dragged himself back once again from the brink, "but Dulcie insists that his full name be William John Johnson, though we'll call him John," he took another, more circumspect sip of rum as he finished. He was getting its measure.

Old Bronco paused, nodding in tacit understanding of this commemorative gesture and the depths from which it originated. He allowed a respectable time to pass in companionable silence before he went on to ask, "So you met your lovely lady during the war, Bill?"

The question was all it took. Just as he had reacted spontaneously out of a personal, emotional need, to his neighbour's invitation to take food and drink, Bill now ceased fighting with the past, and embraced it in an instant, ready to revisit memories he knew Eternity itself wouldn't erase. Taking another, fuller taste of the rum he prepared to tell the story as its fire reached his belly and he allowed himself to be sucked down into the past.

- 0 -

William Johnson was born on 16 December 1921, the first child of Clara and William (Bill) Johnson who had married on Christmas Day in 1920. They had lived for a time with Bill's parents in Birmingham in the West Midlands of England, their home town, before moving to a council house which became available in Brearley Road, close to the city centre and handy to the tramways where Bill worked. Clara had met William when he was swimming in the canal near her place one day. Conditions were tough in post war England, and in time, she learnt from him, under an oath of the strictest secrecy, that he didn't swim in the canal for pleasure.

"Sometimes," he'd said, "when a barge comes through, it touches bottom in these shallow sections so bargee throws some of his cargo overboard to lighten load and be on his way."

"Ah," she said, the penny dropping, "and most of the barges along here are carrying coal."

"Aye, and since you've cottoned on so quick, you can understand why I've sworn ye to secrecy. It's taken me a while but I know the spots where they run into bother so I've a steady supply of coal, mine for the taking. It keeps me going and I sell some to neighbours from time to time, make a bit on the side like. Strange place for a coal cellar, eh, bottom of canal."

Having been one of the "lucky" ones to have returned intact from the horrors of trench warfare at the end of the First World War, albeit with

142

memories of an inhuman experience no amount of time would expunge, he now succumbed to the insidious effects of the coal dust in the water, a danger of which he had been ignorant. It was just around the time Clara, whom he called Mick, married him that he went totally deaf and nearly blind. It was a huge relief to them both when Bill's eyesight returned after a short while, brought about by a total ban on his canal activities and liberal doses of Mick's tender, loving care administered under the guidance of their local doctor. A small operation a little while later also restored his hearing, and he made a somewhat jittery journey out of the silence to which he had become accustomed.

Whilst he recovered quickly and fully from these physical impairments his memories dogged him; those he managed with large doses of denial aided at times by liquor and even larger doses of humour which cocooned him and, more importantly to him, shielded his much loved and ever growing family from any intimate knowledge of what his war experience had actually been.

As the eldest, Bill's early memories of his father were of the hilarious buffoonery with which he parodied many aspects of a soldier's life and lot. His Dad's Chinese Whispers story amused him for years: *After several hours hunkered down in their trench, the CO decides, in response to a prolonged lull in enemy fire, that it is time for retaliatory action. He turns to the man next to him and asks him to pass an order down the line to the other twelve men in the trench, but to keep their voices down as he wants to retain the element of surprise in his planned attack. The order - "Fix bayonets, we're going to advance!" - is received by the last soldier in the trench as "Give me two and six we're going to a dance!"*

There were many stories, all taking the mickey out of a grim reality, and they became part of young Bill's folkloric memory. As a little un he'd clapped his hands and laughed at his Dad's antics – presenting ahhhhms with exaggerated precision, clunking his heels together and saluting with a rigidly vibrating arm and hand whilst shouting something sounding vaguely like "Yassah, sahnmajor, sah!! Sah!", or performing in his heavy work boots an extraordinary, very loud high stepping manoeuvre choreographed to assist a soldier in the execution of a right-hand turn before continuing on his way. In time these antics of his father's ceased, but his memory of them remained vivid.

His first big personal memory was of buying his own bicycle, albeit a second hand one, with money he'd earned selling newspapers and doing odd jobs for the neighbours. He was twelve at the time and by then he'd already learned to ride on his Mom's bicycle which he could strip down and rebuild virtually blindfolded. He was a quick learner and grasped mechanical concepts almost intuitively, but the acquisition of his own bike was a milestone which taught him something more of his potential and capabilities. He'd learned that if he wanted something badly enough he could have it, provided he was prepared to work hard and give up things of lesser importance in favour of his goal. He also learnt, through his Dad's frequent reminders that he was lucky to have such talents and that good luck is not to be sneezed at; he was charged with the responsibility to make the most of them.

At fourteen, by which time he had a sister and four brothers, he left school to take up an apprenticeship in a nickel plating factory. In the months leading up to this, he'd become aware that things weren't quite the same at home as they used to be, nor were they on the street. They never actually went hungry but it dawned on him one day how long it had been since they'd had a spotted dick, or a treacle pudding and custard, his Dad's favourite. In fact it dawned on him that his younger siblings probably didn't know what a spotted dick was, let alone whether they liked it or not. He'd noticed other things too. His Dad still worked on the tramways but he was home a lot more often; the news on the wireless and pictures in the papers were full of strikes and hunger marches, and the anger and fear in the faces of the men queued outside the Labour Exchange in town were unmistakable, even at his tender age, as was the worry which etched itself into his Mom's usually cheerful face; the confrontation of these things scared him so he privately denied their existence, deliberately shunning reflection upon them.

When the opportunity of an apprenticeship came up and the idea was put to him by his Dad that if you put something in instead of taking something out, the value of your action was twofold, he'd understood. He'd a sense of his good fortune arising out of the cheapness of his young labour

144

but it was clear his earnings, however modest, would help ease things at home so he took the opportunity enthusiastically, determined to make the most of it. His education had been rudderless anyway, an education was just something you were supposed to "get", and he looked forward to having a paid job, being a man, helping out, laying down a good foundation for the family he already entertained hopes of having himself one day. When he made his first contribution to the household, an agreed sum which he paid to his Mom, he was proud to do so. They had a treacle pudding with custard that weekend to honour the occasion, but they didn't talk about it outside the four walls that contained them, nor did it become the regular treat of distant memory. He learnt early to keep his cards close to his chest. It was 1936.

But still, to him, his future looked rosy.

He enjoyed working in the factory and got on well with the other men, including those foremen, and there were a few, who took the trouble to make themselves known to him. He learnt a lot through the smoko grapevine about the European goings on at the time, all from an acutely different angle to that gleaned from around the family table or the wireless. Another war involving Britain was becoming a serious possibility and all around him people suddenly had the wind up them. When civil war erupted in Spain that July it was much talked about by his workmates, especially when the fascist governments of Germany and Italy supplied aircraft manned by 'volunteers', and set about using the war 'as an opportunity to test bombing tactics,' according to many, including attacks on both Madrid and Guernica. At the cinema, newsreel footage of the aftermath of those raids contained horrific images of the mangled bodies of women and children killed in their homes whilst innocently pursuing their everyday lives. After the raid on Guernica there was a large, picture on the front-page of a newspaper showing a mother, disheveled and blood-spattered, sitting in the street with shattered buildings just behind her head, holding up her tear-stained face towards the cameraman. She has her mouth open, crying; her hand is raised as though for help; across her soiled lap lies the tiny body of her young child, clothes tattered and disarrayed, some wounds evident. It shook Bill to the core. When he saw it the realisation that '*this could be Brearley Street and Mom with young Dave*' overwhelmed him.

He was not alone in this realisation. ARP preparations were taken more seriously as the prevailing winds of imminent war fanned a widespread fear that new technologies, including larger aircraft that could fly further, faster and with larger payloads, had empowered the enemy to bring the next war home to them, and you wouldn't necessarily have to 'join up' to see action. The involvement of family and friends in a range of ARP activities became a regular topic at smoko. His own brother Doug, who was a Boy Scout was already rattling on at home about the messenger training he was doing, which included basic First Aid. He came upon a handbook entitled "Anti-gas precautions and first aid for air raid casualties" at home in the living room, which Doug knew nowt about when he quizzed him so he presumed it was his Dads. He read it and was disturbed by the contents, the enormity of the task which might lie ahead. In January 1937, the first official radio broadcast on ARP matters described some of the government's plans and appealed for volunteers for the ARP services.

In fact, ARP – or more precisely, air raid precautions – had been introduced as early as 1 April 1935, an inauspicious date which no doubt contributed to the popular view that they were a 'bleeding joke'. Nobody had got all that fired up about it. But by 1937 the perceived need for ARP was gathering momentum and the measures prescribed became recognised as a potentially new way of life. By association, it now also seemed self-evident that war was on the way. It was simply a matter of when.

Smoko conversations at the factory covered the lot, oft times drenched in the dour cynicism of dyed-in-the wool skeptics. The views they aired were disparate; according to some there was a load of politicking codswallop going on and there was no real threat as "we're simply too far away", whilst others maintained phlegmatically that the government couldn't organise a bun fight in a bakery and if the heavens were to rain bombs they would all be dead ducks so what was the point? There were even those who were of the mind that Hitler could probably run the country a bloody sight more effectively than the idiots in Whitehall and that resistance to any advances he might make would simply be counterproductive to the country's best interests.

146

There were those, however, who viewed the outlined requirements for self-preservation with greater gravity and discussed the whys and wherefores of proposed civil defence activities, and the hows for success. Bill gravitated towards these men, and learned substantially from them, many of whom were World War I veterans like his Dad and not ignorant of warfare's destructive potential and how simple precautions could be the difference between annihilation and survival. What he learned didn't ease his qualms.

For a time they'd all muddled along, simply doing the best they could, but on January 1st 1938, with the promulgation of the ARP Act local authorities were charged with the responsibility to set up wardens, first aid, emergency ambulance, gas decontamination, and rescue, repair and demolition services as well as setting up first aid posts, gas cleansing stations and casualty clearing stations. They also had to virtually triple local fire services via an Auxiliary Fire Service. The reception to all this was still mixed, by the population at large and local authorities alike but the upside was that government grants were available to local authorities to cover a very large percentage of the costs of introducing ARP schemes. The great majority of ARP workers at that time were part-time, unpaid volunteers with paid employment, like his Dad, who were expected to work for a maximum of 48 hours a month. Many of them, however, were otherwise unemployed, and a job, at the time, was after all a job; for some occupation helped restore dignity. It was announced in parliament, in February 1939, that full-time ARP personnel were to be paid three pounds a week for men and two pounds a week for women. The fortunes, and the attitudes, of many improved, a corollary to which was improved competency in the essential 'neighbourhood' services to look after themselves in a domestic war zone. Others however, though vehemently castigated by the country's more solid citizenry for doing so, just took the money and devoted their efforts to the avoidance of any real work or potential endangerment. To date the country had only been involved in civilian war games, no big deal. In Birmingham the unemployment rate, already low compared to that of other cities, plummeted. ARP pushed ahead, fuelled by a collective understanding that the city's industry, being vital to the war effort, would likely be a strategic target for the enemy. It wasn't hard to work out.

Bill's Dad had believed that as far as the draft went he was 'scrapings' – well and truly on the bottom of the barrel - so he had put his hand up early for civil duty and became a local warden, opting to undertake his duties close to home rather than near his place of work. Things didn't always go smoothly. One evening, after they'd all finished their tea and the youngsters had left the table to do their evening chores, he surprised Bill and Mom by mentioning 'a bit of bother' he'd had that afternoon with old Mrs. Noakes down the road.

"A bit of bother? Whatever do you mean?" Mom had asked incredulously. She knew full well that as a rule he was anything but confrontational, having only convivial words for a person, an approach that came naturally to him and usually got him his own way without any attendant ill feeling. It was a simple story. Clad in his official warden's uniform - comprising embroidered armband, helmet and clipboard - he'd gone to interview Mrs. Noakes to complete the standard household questionnaire. All the wardens had to conduct these interviews to create a Household Register of everyone in his sector: his being both sides of Brearley Street, east side of Hospital Street between Brearley and Tower Streets, and both sides of Tower and Lower Tower Streets about 120 households all up, two pubs and several shops. Up until now, he'd found his neighbours, many of whom he knew, cooperative if sometimes grudgingly so, but Mrs. Noakes had taken grave exception to his "snooping and prying" into her affairs and refused point blank either to answer any questions or to allow him inside to carry out any sort of inspection and ended up slamming the front door in his face. *"Too old for hanky-panky, surely,"* young Bill had thought, though keeping a straight face and his lips sealed. Mom, however, admitted right away familiarity with the old biddy's difficult nature and offered to have a word with her the next day.

When Mom left to tend to young Margaret, our Maggie as she was called, his Dad had elaborated, at Bill's request, on the responsibilities he had as local warden. In the event of an air raid it was crucial that he know his sector intimately so that he could report efficiently to Incident Control Point about the nature of any damage, and any specialist rescue services required to deal with the situation. When those services arrived, he should further be able to provide detailed information which would help mount the most effective

148

rescue operation. This was all in theory of course, and fact of the matter was that he may have to marshal whatever manpower was readily available and simply do the best they could if said services didn't arrive. This was all news to Bill; '*none of the men at work know owt about this*'; well they certainly hadn't spoken about it at any rate.

"What sort of information?" he'd asked.

"The lot, lad," said his Dad. "The building; who lives in it, and of them, who would likely be there at said time; where they would normally take shelter; where they would likely have been at the time of the explosion; their personal mobility; where the stopcocks and switches are located; as if you lived there yourself," he'd said emphatically.

"That's why we're to use the questionnaire," he'd continued, "to make sure we don't miss anything. And I have to commit this lot to memory, you understand, as well as keeping the Household Register. To my mind, it makes good sense – and if you ask me, anyone with any sense would be willing to cooperate."

"Do you think it will happen, Dad? Bombing? Here?"

"Aye, lad, I'm sorry to say that I do. War is inevitable. They have the means and in my opinion they won't hesitate to use 'em. It'll be no picnic when they do; for both sides," the sombre response chilled the pit of Bill's stomach quenching the myriad questions fluttering in his mind like moths against a light. "They'll be delivering our Anderson Shelter soon, lad," his Dad had continued, "so I'll need your help to get it installed."

"*This is serious*," Bill thought.

- 0 -

The house was two rooms at ground floor, two bedrooms and two attics. It was all gas lighted and the gas stove was at the top of the steps leading to the cellar where there was just about enough room for the stove and someone to stand in front of it to cook. Behind the house were a couple of laundries, both unlit, which Mom called the brewus, and a brick paved yard with a rainwater drain, or sough, in the middle. The dustbins were kept in this area. The brick paving led past the little japanning factory which had been there since before the Johnson's arrival, past the two boarded up

149

lavatories, one for them and one for the factory, to the garden. From the end of the factory to the top of the garden was about 27 yards so the kids had plenty of room to run around.

Bill and his Dad erected the Anderson Shelter in the back yard a few weeks later. It was about seven foot long by five foot wide. They dug a hole about three and half feet deep and dropped the shelter in. The floor of the shelter was packed earth covered with a tarp and around the front entry they placed three wooden chests filled with soil. Finally, over the top went a big wooden door also covered with soil to form a tunnel to the entrance. The whole thing looked like a mound of earth in the garden. Little did they know what was in store for them, but they were as prepared as they could be and his Dad was pleased to set the example.

- 0 -

Throughout his apprenticeship he'd never failed to pay his Mom for his board and lodging on pay day. Neither had he failed to save a bit. It was his first self-imposed rule in life, the perspicacity and effectiveness of which he had learned empirically, and enjoyed the results. After starting work he quickly took up the habit of smoking, putting himself on a more equal grown-up footing at smoko, though not at home at first, having an intuitive understanding that Mom would not be best pleased. He indulged himself in other ways too; books, the cinema, and dancing, with its attendant society of young ladies, were particular weaknesses, but his growing nest egg, modest though it was, not only brought him satisfaction but opened his mind to hitherto unimagined possibilities.

Then, on the 3rd of September 1939, just a few months before his 18th birthday, the Prime Minister, Mr. Neville Chamberlain of whom his Dad couldn't stand a bar, made an announcement on the wireless. It was a Sunday afternoon and he'd been sitting at the kitchen table with his Mom having a cup of tea. They'd been enjoying a bit of an Indian summer and all the others were off out doing something except for young Maggie who staggered between items of support, chair legs, table legs and such like, practising her new found ability to walk. He'd had a rare attack of somnolence and stayed in, ostensibly to finish the book he'd been reading.

I am speaking to you from the Cabinet Room at Number Ten Downing Street. This morning the British Ambassador in Berlin handed the German Government a final note, stating that, unless the British Government heard from them by 11 o'clock that they were prepared to withdraw their troops from Poland, a state of war would exist between us. I have to tell you now that no such undertaking has been received and that consequently this country is at war with Germany......

Though expecting war, its advent came, nevertheless, as a serious jolt. "*Bloody hell, this is it. We're at war,*" he'd thought, which was something of a reaction from him who didn't use swear words much, and much less thought them. His Mom's stricken face seemed to reflect the exact same thought with all its attendant fear and despair. With this pedestrian announcement, concocted in almost peevish diplomatic bureaucratese, Britain had indeed declared herself to be at war with Germany, and, unbeknownst to him, the previously unimagined future possibilities and potentialities he had so recently courted were to be buried six years deep in a war which eventually shook the whole world, a war of which there were no real victors, and from which no one anywhere could simply go back to take up where they had left off. Any who thought the war a simple detour on the path to their future, discovered as Bill did, that unlike most detours which only bypassed a temporary problem this one lead inexorably to a destination quite different to the one they had been setting a course for; the future they had previously looked towards was irretrievably lost, and although undefeated, his motherland was to be sorely wounded and severely diminished.

It was a given that he would follow in his father's footsteps and enlist to serve the King in the defence of his mother country. There was no discussion about it. He volunteered, lodging his application just before his 18th birthday, in December 1939. Eager though he was he had learnt early on that 21 year olds were being enlisted first and figured he might have a wait before he heard from the authorities. He was right, it took nigh on two years.

- 0 -

Their first indication of bother had been the initial reaction of Whitehall to Germany's invasion of Poland on the 1st. September which had been the immediate enforcement of the blackout even before Chamberlain's declaration of war two days later. The heart wrenching evacuation of all the kids of school age from major cities to billets in the West Country also began on that day. Doug who was nine and a half and young John who was six were issued with gas masks one day and a day or two later were shunted onto a train at New St Station in Birmingham bound for Abergavenny, close to the border of Wales and England. It was their very first train trip so their evacuation felt more like an exciting adventure at first, until the reality of not going home hit them.

Meanwhile, at home, the benefit of long term preparations for ARP was immediately reaped by some whilst others, who had been less than diligent in following prescribed procedures, now found themselves unprepared and suffered the frequent inconvenience of having to "Put that light out!" until they installed curtains which met the total blackout standards. Whilst domestic compliance remained patchy for a time, a seriously enforced requirement of the total blackout conditions was that night driving be completely unaided by headlights. Learning to drive in the complete dark was a challenge many had to meet and Bill, who had progressed to a motorcycle soon after his 17th birthday, was not shy of taking it on when his opportunity came. It was a scary business but he remained unscathed. There were plenty of dingles under cover of dark, no question, though very few reported, to the relief of the constabulary. His bike was the apple of his eye. It was a second hand 1932 BSA Blue Star 350cc, produced by the Birmingham Small Arms Company in their factory in Armoury Road in Small Heath, an area centred around Coventry Road, that formed part of the main route from Birmingham to Coventry. He was inordinately proud of it.

Whilst awaiting call up he continued working at the factory which was systematically adapted for munitions production to help meet war time demand. The work practices of all the men changed radically in response to the new production line, and to the now strictly enforced ARP. At night he also did, voluntarily, but according to a roster laid down by factory management at the behest of the local warden, his share of fire-watching shifts, stationed on the flat section of the factory roof, protected solely by a tin helmet and equipped with a simple stirrup pump and a bucket of water, buckets of sand and a whistle; and, of course, his sodding gas mask which everyone, man, woman and child, was now required to carry at all times, which of course they didn't because they forgot, or they thought it was a load of old cobblers, or they just couldn't be bothered. The fire-watcher's aim was simple, use sand to put out any incendiary bombs which fell, douse any spot fires caused with water to hand, or at the very least get word to the local fire service before any real fire took hold. The job lost its attraction, if indeed it ever had any, when, from the end of 1940 the Germans started to use an explosive incendiary which was aimed precisely at those engaged in putting them out. Soon after they began to burn these devices would explode, showering anyone trying to put them out at close quarters with burning magnesium. Bill had known more than one of the local men killed in such circumstances, and others seriously burned. He counted himself lucky to be spared. He became grimly conscious of his youth and optimism ebbing away amidst these wartime rigours.

- 0 -

From the onset of Hitler's expansionist activity, everyone had been hungry for news, and for a time they'd been afforded some information, but after the declaration of war, and during the immediate lead up, all they got from the home news service was a starvation diet, not even a slow drip. Television broadcasting ceased. They were not to be defeated by this propaganda of silence. It didn't take long for those not yet engaged in the activity to work out that with a bit of twiddling the old crystal set could pick up broadcasts from abroad loud and clear, Berlin in particular. The Hun was obviously boosting transmission strength to engage in a different kind of war, and the Italians likewise. Their broadcasts were entertaining and informative. They enjoyed a wide audience in Britain, relating sympathetically, as they did, to many of their listeners.

The Johnson family, like many others, kept their wireless tuned to the BBC in case something of genuine interest or importance came on, but became regular listeners to Lord Haw-Haw, for one, broadcasting from

Berlin. It was a popular national pastime. The man pitched perfectly to the disenchanted ordinary man and woman in Britain whose plight he uncannily understood – treated like mushrooms they were, kept in the dark, fed on shite. He seemed genuinely to speak to them, to know about their difficulties and frustrations and the ignorance in which they felt they were being kept. Haw-Haw impersonators burgeoned. Arthur Askey joined the spate and his already robust, everyman's-comedian popularity waxed. After a Haw-Haw broadcast one night, Mom bowed and said, "Ay-Thang-Yew" and they all laughed their heads off.

Early on, in 1939, when Haw-Haw had appealed especially to soldiers' wives because, according to them 'he seemed to be the only person interested in them', they'd all wondered who he really was, with that strange pretentiously superior drawl; definitely a bit of Irish in there said some, who turned out to be right. Bill first learnt from the lads at the factory that Haw-Haw had been identified as William Joyce; born of Irish parents in America, with a First Class degree from the Birbeck College, of the University of London, and at one time not only a member of Mosley's British Union of Fascists but propagandist to the man himself. Bloody hell!

Haw-Haw had wooed them with his wit and understanding, but once the so-called Phoney War was over he changed tack. Now he started his broadcasts with: "Chairmany Calling! Chairmany Calling!" – following up oft times with predictions of where the next bombs would be dropped, and those who were the recipients learned that he was punctiliously accurate. News of his prescience traveled and he went rapidly from joke-object to a figure whose vituperative, corrosive revelations were feared; feared because believed.

Mom's indignant reaction changed to "It just makes you want to spit! The man's playing with us!" Maybe ignorance really was the preferred option, if not bliss exactly.

- 0 -

Some events on the home front simply couldn't be kept under wraps, wartime reporting restrictions or not; the Luftwaffe strikes on London on Saturday 7 September 1940 were one such occasion. The peoples' grapevine

154

reached far and wide. Black Saturday, as it soon became known, marked the start of the big blitz on London, and reports of the devastating impact of the repeated waves of bombing sent many flocking to the pubs and gin palaces up and down the country to imbibe in inebriating, anaesthetising quantities their favoured drop of black market alcohol.

In one of his infrequent broadcasts in July that same year Churchill, in his unmistakable, half-slurred but defiant, aristocratic tones, had warned them: '*Here in this City a refuge which enshrines the title deeds of human progress and is of deep consequence to Christian civilization; here, girt about by the seas and oceans where the Navy reigns; shielded from above by the prowess and devotion of our airmen – we await undismayed the impending assault... We shall seek no terms, we shall tolerate no parley, we may show mercy – we shall ask for none.*' They hung on to every word and grew in collective stature through him. Believed in themselves then, they did.

At the commencement of the big blitz in London, the Midlands braced themselves for similar attention. Birmingham was under repeated, heavy attack and young Doug and John who had returned home during the so-called 'Phoney' war were packed off once more to the West Country, this time to a place called Aberaman. They were accompanied on this occasion by Dave who'd turned five in January. Being the oldest of the three, Doug had made his Mom a promise that he wouldn't let them be split up, so she might be able to come and visit them one day but even so, she cried for days after her young boys were taken, though she'd put on a brave face to see them off on their 'adventure'.

In the snatches of time available, the Johnson household quietly discussed around the family table, a plan of action for any number of potential scenarios in which the destruction of the family home, or other significant losses, might occur. They epitomised the indomitable character of their countrymen, with their ability to bend with, and their refusal to bow to, whatever was thrown at them. They were kept busy for the most part working for the war effort; in their spare time they maintained their ground, limiting death and damage to the best of their ability during air raids, and training, or training others, in vital survival skills when the Hun let them be.

Life was no bowl of cherries.

- 0 -

The factory where Bill worked was located on a ridge overlooking neighbouring streets on the eastern outskirts of the city and from the roof there was a good open view east, sou' east, towards Coventry, just 18 miles down the road. A couple of months after that massive blitz on London commenced, it was actually on Thursday 14th November, he was rostered on for fire-watching. Suddenly, just after 7 pm, one explosion after another bloomed in the distance in a precisely orchestrated formation. By his estimation, they were pretty close to, if not in, Coventry. More explosions followed rapidly in a continuation of the structured sequence and his gut told him that it was Coventry and Coventry was under a sustained and serious attack. Nothing like this had ever happened on his shift before. He dithered. What should he do? Stay to honour his obligation to the fire watch or go to tell his Dad what was happening out there. There was almost certainly something they could do to help; as one of the wardens, Dad might even have been called in by now. By 8 o'clock a fiery glow, not unlike the setting of a tropical sun, filled the sky and, as he learned later, that was also around the time the first of the incendiaries struck the cathedral; the Coventry and Warwickshire Hospital being already aglow by then with incendiary bombs. He could hold his post no longer. He leapt on his motorcycle to hurtle through the blackout like a bat out of hell - a bat into hell more like! - straining to see fellow travelers on eerie streets glowing dully in the red light of Coventry burning.

By morning, with drizzle in the air, it looked, and felt, as if that whole city had been destroyed. He'd gone with his Dad, his Dad to help organise, and he to assist as directed, the rescue effort. Amid the destruction of the houses and factories, the cathedral, the gardens, the streets and hundreds of the city's inhabitants, he sensed most strongly an undeniable loss of the past. The collective achievement and memory of centuries had been wiped from the face of the earth. Death was everywhere. He was changed forever by the experience.

Just five days later, on the Tuesday night, the BSA factory in Small Heath, back home in Birmingham was hit directly by two German bombs in a devastating air raid. The hit was not mere happenchance, the factory being an obvious target for the Luftwaffe and more than likely marked on every German navigator's map of the area. The city had had more than its 'fair' share of the Hun's attention, but on that particular night the air raid was a big one. At 9.25 pm a low flying aircraft dropped two bombs on the BSA works catastrophically damaging the southern end of the New Building in Armoury Road.

Word came through quickly. Bill was not on fire watch at the factory that night and, Brearley Street having survived the raid intact, he left Mom with Dick and the girls in the shelter and went with his Dad to assist as best they could at the scene. They were quickly marshaled into appropriate occupations by the local wardens. Rescuers rushed to the scene from all points of the city and beyond, including the BSA's own fire brigade who pumped the Birmingham and Warwick canal dry that evening in their attempts to control the fire, assisted by upwards of 60 fire crews also in attendance.

As was their habit, the night shift in the factory, had remained at their machines till the last moment that night and the casualties were high; brave men, many now dead. The explosion had caused the concrete floors to collapse trapping both dead and survivors. A roll call after the event revealed 53 dead and 89 injured. One of the last survivors to be pulled out had been entombed for 9 hours and as they brought him forth into the grey dawn it reflected in the grim, grey tear-streaked faces of rescue workers, faces grown older overnight, full of despair at where it would all end. The effort of the rescue workers was superhuman, fuelled by adrenalin, by fear and by their determinedly optimistic belief in the possibility that they could save yet another from the wreckage. But it was not to be. It was six weeks before the last of the bodies could be removed.

Bill fell into bed that Wednesday afternoon, smeared with the grime of blood, sweat and tears and cried afresh, albeit briefly, rescued from misery by the blissful unconsciousness of sleep. He was still only 18 years old; he felt a hundred.

True to form, in accordance with wartime reporting restrictions, there was not a single mention of the event in the newspapers or on the wireless.

Brearley Street itself remained relatively unscathed during the bombing raids over Birmingham until one day, early in 1941 when their luck ran out. Bill was at work when it happened, but word reached the factory quickly that Brearley Street had suffered two direct hits in a rare, daytime wild cat raid. The foreman on duty sent Bill off to assist, with a parting wish for his family's wellbeing.

He jittered from the factory to home through a buildup of wartime detritus, making the journey in double quick time. Turning into Brearley Street from the chaos of rescue vehicles and salvage activity on New Town Row he propped sharply, almost toppling from the bike. A wave of shock ran through him at the sight of a nearby neighbour's home razed to the ground, and a sibilant buzz electrified his very being, raising the hair on his arms and the back of his neck. Relief akin to elation ran through him as he took in, up the road, the sight of his own home, intact. Further on he could see that their local, the Rose and Crown up on corner of Brearley and Hospital Streets was gone. Amidst the tumult in his mind, he saw that it was number 64 that had been laid waste, reduced to little more than rubble. He was not conscious of leaping off his bike and propping it before rapidly approaching a couple of people in the middle of the road nearby; a man sitting, utterly distraught, clutching his chest as he rocked back and forth, the other, a young woman he recognised from the alterations shop up in the High Street, crouched beside the keening figure, offering comfort. Before them a team of rescue workers was strung out over the mound of rubble, ears to the ground, listening for signs of life. Before he reached them, the young woman rose to meet him and Bill recoiled with shock as he saw, when she moved, that his neighbour clutched to his chest a severed hand. Bill saw it, suddenly and with absolute clarity. The highly polished nails, shining pristinely amidst the grime, were a vivid embodiment of her vibrant personality, as were the rings by which Jack Tynan had identified this remnant of his wife. Bill gagged on the liquid rushing into his mouth, turned aside and spat, concentrating at the same time on controlling other bodily functions. After a timeless moment, his self-control partly restored, he succumbed to being drawn aside.

"You're the local warden's boy aren't you?" she asked, as he forced himself upright, wiping his mouth with the back of his hand.

"Aye, Bill Johnson," he gargled raggedly.

"Your family's all fine," she said. "Your Mom's manning a tea wagon. They're set up in Summer Lane, and your Dad's further up dealing with operations at the Rose and Crown. Direct hit by a flying torpedo – not sure how the patrons fared." She drew a sharp breath before continuing. "You'd best go see your Dad, find out how best you can help. Check in with your Mom on the way though, mmm? She'll be pleased to see you."

She grimaced, "All the indications here are that Mrs. Tynan took a direct hit; blown to bits more'n likely. No trace ..... save what yon poor soul ......" she paused, "I've been given the nod there's no sign of life in that heap. We've turned off gas and water to area naturally, but all services seem to be intact here- sappers'll be moving on shortly. You could let your Dad know if you get there before us." They'd moved away from the umbra of Jack Tynan's grief to talk and looked back now towards the cone of solitary existence in which the poor man rocked, inconsolably bereft, holding tightly to his breast the hand of the only woman he'd ever loved, she with whom he had spent the best 25 years of his life.

Bill thanked this Good Samaritan seamstress and focused his mind on Summer Lane and his Mom; he would go from there to home if need be, otherwise he would go and see if he could help his Dad. He turned, numbly, disoriented. Locating his motorbike, he walked towards it in an almost hallucinatory lightness of head, though firmly anchored to grim reality by the stone that was his heart.

They had a makeshift tea down in the shelter that evening, eating their bread and jam in silence, each lost in their own thoughts. Suddenly young Eileen turned to Mom and said very quietly, "I think God must be sleeping Mommy, don't you?" The silence in the room deepened as Mom stroked the little one's hair.

"Gaffer at pub says anyone's welcome to help themselves to the coal in pub's coalhouse. Bloody miracle it's still standing, but it is. Maybe you and Dick should go down first thing tomorrow with a couple of buckets, Bill. It won't last long."

159

The boys agreed and silence fell once more. The Anderson Shelter had seen it all; the laughter and the tears, the fun and games and the fear, the uneasy sleep that finally claimed them; but never before had it witnessed the silent despair which seemed to grip them all that night.

- 0 -

"Egad Athol, during that time the fear that stewed in the gut signaled its bilious presence to your every companion, chosen or circumstantial, wherever the meeting place; be it during preparation for action, or down in the bomb shelter according to ARP. We all reeked of it. It was a national condition, and not peculiar to our precious kingdom, no doubt," Bill paused, completely lost in his reflections, "I thought a lot about it, the fear, and I still don't know whether having the time to do so was a blessing or a curse. Though I did come to a personal belief that what I, personally, feared was not death, but pain, and physical pain was but a small part of it. What I truly feared was the loss of my family or the loss of life as I knew it. Either would be very bad, both – unimaginable! Though many had just such experiences, poor sods."

-0-

He was finally called up in October 1941. Ironically the immediate effect of his call to arms was to take him away from the living hell being perpetrated on civilian society. He attended three weeks of army training just outside of York. The activity was intense; route marches, 10 miles in two hours with full pack, and rifle. Egad, but he learned to hate new boots and brass monkeys! Yorkshire was beautiful, to be sure, with its hills and dales, rivers and lakes, but it was most outstanding in his memory for the freezing cold into which he stepped each morning to find out how they were going to wear him out today, and to discover that the hills and dales did for them all – wasn't there any flat land in these parts. There were some nice ATS girls in the training camp but by the end of the day the men, himself included, were too knackered to bother them.

Immediately after training he was put in the Rifle Brigade of which his prevailing memory was the square bashing – being marched on the parade ground at 180 steps a minute, fully 'got up' and armed, to what purpose he failed to deduce, but Geez it was fast and one's weaponry heavy. If the purpose was simply to wear a man out, it worked like a charm. When he finally finished up as a dispatch rider he thought, "Wonders will never cease; someone in personnel must have read my file!" The job came with a 500cc BSA - he was chuffed to bits. He revelled in his good fortune and actively enjoyed running about all over the Yorkshire moors, doing what they called "Schemes" battles – live ammo 'n all - the aim being getting to where he was going in one piece as quickly as possible, whether on a road or off, and keeping safe whatever 'orders' he carried . He was surprised at how much steam he had to let off, but relished the opportunity to do so, the activity serving to vanquish his perennial concern for his family to a more manageable subconscious level.

Once fully operational, he found his days blurred into one another. He enjoyed the challenge, the relative freedom and variety of a dispatch rider's life, oft times sleeping where he could, when he could, never really knowing what each day would bring. There was little chance to form friendships, he found himself alone, and a loner to a large degree, but the job had its benefits. He remembered vividly some of his chance meetings and nocturnal adventures, one of them during the period when the whole country was preparing for the Allied invasion. Americans had been arriving by the boatload – packed in like sardines. Having absorbed *undismayed the impending assault,* the nation and its Allies were, at that time, preparing to offer their collective *blood, toil, tears and sweat* to *fight them on the beaches* - the beaches of France, that is. On the occasion in mind he'd spent a memorable night in a pub in Newton Abbot – The Commercial Hotel - one of 39 in the town according to the local gent he'd bumped into, literally, in the pitch dark of a moonless blackout.

Having been given directions, he'd stumbled into the entrance, pushed open the door and walked in past a light-shielding curtain to find himself in a tiny lobby into which trod the proprietor, clad in plus fours and hunting shirt and glowing with rude health – "*or,*" Bill surmised, "*an alcoholic flush more like?*" This vision augured well for the quality, and availability, of the ale in the establishment and he decided on impulse to stay to enjoy a pint before asking the whereabouts of the nearest billet, and the CP he was to report to first thing tomorrow to receive orders. He happily received the news that although the Guinness was 'used up', rations of ale and stout were still available, and there were sweet or rough cider, ginger beer, or a swig of peppermint, "if any of these takes your fancy!"

The bar room contained all the usual suspects, a smattering of civilians and military personnel, locals and transients. The babble had a twang to it that night, emanating from a group of American soldiers playing cards at one of the tables. He bought a pint and sat at a table near the action, listening idly to their chatter as he rolled a cigarette. They were playing poker but a quick game it wasn't.

"Now you owe me five sixpences."

"Yes, that's 'two and six'; here you are."

"What do you mean, two and six – two what and six what?"

"Oh, that's a florin and sixpence, or to make it simpler, two shillings and sixpence, or a half-crown, or –"

"Wait a minute – how much is that in English, I mean American?"

"Fifty cents."

"Why the hell didn't you say so; on with the game!"

He'd taken a draught of ale to hide his amusement, not wishing to cause offence, but one of their compatriots, an onlooker of the game, had noticed the glint in his eye and came over to join him, extending his hand as he arrived at the table.

"Pfc. Harry Golinos," he said, "I couldn't help but notice your interest and amusement."

Bill had risen from his seat, "Bill Johnson," he said, shaking the proffered hand before indicating the vacant chair opposite him at the table.

Harry Golinos settled himself cheerfully as he launched into conversation, "In the few weeks we've been here," he said, "most of the men have come to grips with the local situation as regards whisky and women but, as you've just witnessed, they don't yet have the measure of English currency; not its value in relation to American money nor the notes and coins themselves; can't say as I'm any different in that respect."

162

Bill considered the problem, one he'd not encountered himself, never having travelled to foreign shores. He took another sip of ale, "Why not gamble with American money," he asked, "for simplicity's sake?"

"Nice try Bill, but not possible," Harry responded, "Regulations don't permit us to carry American money. We could use it on the ship, coming over, but it all had to be cashed in at the end of the voyage," he reflected briefly before adding, "and honestly, some of these guys only have money for a day or so after they're paid anyway, wherever they are, whatever the currency."

"I didn't think of that," Bill said, nodding his head as the penny dropped, so to speak, "Stands to reason I suppose - something to do with legal tender." He paused reflectively, "Well, they could always use match sticks with a set value in American money and work out the sums after the game?"

"Yeah, that might work if you take the alcohol out of the mix – would definitely save the army money too," Harry laughed. "That way they wouldn't need to carry around a bunch of this strange, and weighty, variety of coins you English seem to need. We've only been here a few weeks and everyone's wearing holes in their pocket linings – no joke, no joke, really, it's true. And as for your bank notes!" warming to the subject now, he shook his head in disbelief, "a man could wrap a gift with one of your five pound notes."

"You'd be lucky to have one of those in your kick," interjected Bill, for whom a fiver represented best part of a fortnight's pay at that time.

"Right enough," agreed Harry, though better paid than he knew Bill to be, "but we saw a full set of British currency when the finance department changed our money over before we disembarked in Liverpool and that white five pound note was much remarked upon. Even the pound and ten shilling notes are large - if lacking in substance. Some of the lads reckoned them for being soap-advertising coupons; like the ones distributed back home." He smiled to soften his critical observation, "But we learned an interesting thing from one of the MPs who came aboard to guard the gangplanks during our disembarkation - mine of information those guys. He reckoned not too many English even know it."

"What's that?"

"Let me show you," said Harry, removing a new-looking wallet from the left-hand breast pocket inside his jacket. "This was one of my first purchases here," he said, waving the wallet in the space between them, "to accommodate the size of these durn notes!" He paused, unclipped the wallet to extract a pound note. "You'd think a flimsy thing like that," he said, smoothing the limp and somewhat crinkled note on the table, "would be dead easy to counterfeit, wouldn't you?"

Bill concurred, though never really having considered the question.

Harry took the pound note and tore it a quarter of an inch, revealing a thin strand of silver. "That silver strand runs all the way around at the edge," he said. "You can always tell by that whether a note's genuine or not – and you see that water mark when you hold it up to the light?" he demonstrated, and passed the note to Bill for like examination. "Well I have it on authority that it can't be duplicated. So, how about that?"

"Well I'll be," said Bill, "you learn something every day," the information being, indeed, news to him. They paused, looking around, having become quickly comfortable in one another's company, and taking a particular interest in the activity around the game being played under a gathering fug of cigar and cigarette smoke. Bill set about rolling another cigarette as Harry put his pound note away.

"So, if you're all headed for Omaha Beach, Harry, you'll no doubt have to come to terms with French currency too in the not too distant future, eh?" Bill asked quietly, so as not to be overheard by others, as Harry brought his attention back to their conversation. The question was skirted warily at first - "TALK COSTS LIVES" screamed a poster on the wall near the bar, a fact drummed into all servicemen from day one - but it embarked them on a night long conversation fuelled in part by the conversion to their host's fine ale of a noticeable chunk of Harry's tatty pound, and all the loose change Bill could muster. Contemplation of the potential transience of a man's life at the meat grinder which was the front line created a thirst in a man; equally so the oft imagined opportunity to "Chercher la femme" in gay Pareee – which they agreed as good a carrot as any for getting themselves through this war both unscathed and victorious. The following morning, each woke in his respective camp to pay yet again, albeit in currency of a different kind, for the conviviality of their chance encounter. Although the only occasion on which they met, it was an occasion committed, nevertheless, by Harry to his diary – strictly against regulations of course! - and by Bill to that place where the memory keeps its treasures; items worthy of revisiting from time to time, to savour the uplifting splashes of colour they cast randomly in the weft of life, and in doing so, render the drab and oft tortuous warp tolerable.

- 0 -

Soon after that chance meeting, on a similarly pitch, moonless night, whilst hurtling between the origin of the orders he carried in his satchel and their intended recipient, his lights went out – literally, physically, personally. He'd been hugging the left edge of the narrow road from which a cliff-like embankment rose abruptly. As obliged to do, to fulfill the instructions he had been given, he blindly and trustingly negotiated at full speed the sharp turns and rolling hills of a 'pinball' highway, shielded from any view of the surrounding landscape by high, thick, ivy-covered walls of rocks mortared with clay. No doubt, as was much discussed, this terrain would prove disadvantageous to the Germans were they to attempt an invasion of England, but it was equally true, especially at night during black out conditions, that it also seriously hampered the operations of the allied forces mobilizing for the European invasion; accidents were many.

He had collided with an armoured vehicle attached to the Middlesex Regiment, part of a convoy heading for Southampton. He hadn't seen it, didn't feel a thing when the Bren gun rode over the entire right side of his body. 'Didn't know what hit him!' as the saying went. When his lights came back on several days later in hospital, he felt plenty. His first conscious realisation after this fortunate resurrection was that the major threat to his existence for some time to come probably lay in the possibility of Jerry dropping a bomb on the hospital; that, or falling prey to a malignancy spawned by this singular breeding ground. Neither of these potential fates befell him, but his recovery and rehabilitation took several months, a period of which he had little recollection.

165

The most memorable event during his convalescence was a visit from his father, a visit he keenly anticipated for the two weeks between learning of it and the date for which it had been set. When the time came and he first clapped eyes on his dad, the inherent joy of the occasion dissipated, the energy regrouping in a dark gruel of apprehension and concern. The weight his dad so clearly carried was quickly shared after their initial reunion and greetings - the news of young John's death, from meningitis, whilst billeted in the West Country, safe from the bombing assault on Birmingham. "Your Mom's taken it very hard, lad, very hard. But she's kept busy with the young uns which is a blessing," he paused, "and there's another on the way," his Dad had said with a sigh. Their grief was palpable, a dark mantle enshrouding them, but they rallied and his Dad related, among the more positive aspects of their present circumstances, "We've been moved to another house you know lad. Bomb came alarmingly close to Brearley Street house, split it from top to bottom; we've a lot to be thankful for, I can tell you. They've moved us to the eastern outskirts of Birmingham, 88 Kelynmead Road, in Kitts Green. Here, I've written it down for you," a scrap of paper changed hands, "I've been relieved as Warden at Brearley Street and just do as I'm bidden now, but we're not getting nearly the attention we were from Jerry, lad. Well, not those unmerciful, bombing raids anyway, though we've all got a constant ear out for them bloody [rhymes with woody] doodle bugs."

During his rehab, Bill also had a visit from Personnel; a couple of officers who mentioned, amongst other options, the possibility of training for the Royal Signals Corps. The dissemination of intelligence from behind a desk instead of astride a motorbike didn't strike quite the same chord, but he was glad to put his hand up nonetheless. Although no coward, and never likely to shoot himself in the foot just to escape front line duty, he couldn't help the considerable relief he felt at the unlikelihood, in the Royal Signals, of ever having to contend with the front line. Little did he know! He ended up in Holmfirth in Yorkshire to do the training which was intensive. He welcomed the new mental activity but what he appreciated even more was the social opportunity he'd not enjoyed as a dispatch rider. One chap he really hit it off with, being of like interests, was from Oldham, not far off, on the outskirts of Manchester. Frank Howard, a good few years younger than

166

he was, had been put here from the very start of his stint in the army by poor eyesight. They shared much of their free time, and as luck would have it, both ended up getting their ticket at the same time with a New Delhi posting attached.

The circumstances leading up to their embarkation to undertake their new posts opened a course of events neither of them would even have tried to predict. As was routine army practice, a few days before their scheduled departure they were granted embarkation leave. Frank took the short trip west to Oldham to see his Mum and Dad, younger brother Eric and his sister Meredith, the ten year old baby of the family. His older brother, Harvey, was stationed in Egypt, serving with the RAF, and Dulcie, the eldest, had spent the last few years living in the nurses quarters of whatever hospital she was attached to, firstly in training and then in service. He didn't hold much hope for bidding either of them farewell.

Bill had considerably further to go, and considerably more, by sheer weight of numbers, to contend with when he got there. He headed south on the train, pleased to be walking freely, limp only slightly discernible. He knew the boys were back home and looked forward to seeing his family but knew parting would not be easy. They were a passing parade in his mind's eye - Mom and Dad, his beautiful sister Clara with whom he felt a special bond, and who, though younger than him, had somehow assumed the role and responsibilities of the eldest with the birth of Dick, the next in the line; then there were Doug, Dave, Eileen, Maggie, Helen, and Joyce, the baby, whom he hadn't even met yet. Well, he'd see most of them. He especially hoped, though against the odds, to see Clara. He'd heard from Mom that Clara had joined up, recruited into the NAAFI. After training – on how to serve tea and buns, according to Doug, who deliberately made light of this terrible loss of Clara to the outside world – she was stationed in Manchester. His throat constricted as the certainty of not seeing Johnny struck him, not on this visit, nor any other. Dick had signed up with the RN, was at sea as far as he knew, but he should see all the others. He'd just have to take it *"as it comes"*.

He was pleased to be travelling by day, afforded the distraction of a mesmeric ribbon of countryside slipping by, rather than scuttling mole-like through the night in a blacked out burrow of morbid introspection. In

167

hindsight, it was a good visit, but by the time he returned to holding camp he was emotionally drained. He was eager to get cracking, to be mobilized, taking up his new post in India, setting off on what might turn out to be a bit of a lark.

Frank was already back in camp when he arrived and greeted him with, "You wouldn't Adam and Eve it, Bill, but embarkation has been delayed. We've been given three more days leave."

"Hells, bells ....!" the curtailed expostulation said less than Bill's body language as his determined optimism fled with the wind knocked from his sails. He couldn't bear a second parting, once had been hard enough; a second wouldn't be fair to any of them. All this flashed through his mind in a trice. It happens. Guards drop. Friends intuit.......

Frank twigged, "Yeah, I know what you mean: couldn't organise a piss up in a brewery this lot." He continued quickly, without pause, "Why don't you come to my place with me, Bill? It's Saturday tomorrow – we could go to the Trocadero, up in Chadderton, kick our heels up. Never know your luck in a big city, eh? What do you say?"

So off they went for a bit of R and R in Oldham, accompanied, unbeknownst to them, by one of the Moirae, or was it Shai?

- 0 -

"We went to the dance that Saturday night, Athol," recalled Bill, "and made quite a night of it. Sunday morning, latish, we were lounging about in the sitting room at Frank's place with Merry, his young sister Meredith, being a lot livelier than either of us was up to accommodating. She was a bubbly girl, irrepressible."

He smiled and shook his head as the wake of the memory rippled through him.

"I remember standing up to stretch, twisting to the left, and suddenly I was held in the direct gaze of the gentlest, kindest eyes I'd ever seen. It was a framed photograph of Dulcie, Frank's older sister, in her nurse's uniform. There was nothing glamorous about it, but I found it strangely and deeply affecting. Before I left I asked Merry for the address of the hospital where

168

she worked and I wrote to her soon after arriving in India. She wrote me back and they were the first of many letters to and from."

He wet his lips with the surface of the rum in his pannikin, licked at it, and breathed deeply.

"We didn't meet 'til I was de-mobbed after the war, Athol, though I always felt as if I'd met her on that Sunday, on embarkation leave with Frank at her place."

My beloved Divine Mother
Dance with me
under the soft moon shining
in the wide open fields
far beyond the toil and trouble
of my busy mind

Chapter Six

The rhythm of life..........
Sus scrofa domesticus ....

*T*he sights, sounds and smells of the hospital ward wrapped their familiar cloak about Dulcie as she sat stroking her son's head whilst he hungrily sustained himself, enthusiastically breaking a fast of all of four hours. She absorbed his contentment, and the warm, milky smell of her newborn whom she had changed and sponged down before putting him to her breast. She would never cease to marvel at the extraordinarily soft, velvety pliability of extreme youth. Young man though he was, his vulnerability and utter dependency on her was no different to that of his sisters before him, and she was now quite naturally given up to his every need for as long as he needed her.

The radio on the ledge below the only fixed window in the ward was tuned in to Russ Tyson's Hospital Half Hour, a half hour during which Mr. Tyson regaled the inmates of hospital wards up and down the country with music and special messages of love and encouragement from those of their well-wishing families who had managed to get a request through. It was cool, if clammy, in the ward and the early light of day augured rain, bore its memory. Johnny fed well and was soon replete, burped and ready for a recovery kip. Just as Dulcie was tucking him back into his hospital crib Russ Tyson announced, "And now, for Mrs. Dulcie Johnson a special cheerio call with lots of love from your loving husband Bill and daughters Jess and Jilly. Mrs. Johnson is enjoying a nice rest at the Atherton Hospital after the birth of Johnny, the Johnson's first little Australian and indeed their first son. This song comes to you especially from hubby Bill, Mrs. Johnson: here's Al Jolson, and *You Made Me Love You.*"

"Hey, Dulcie, this's for you, love," said Betty, a neighbouring patient.

173

"Well I never," said Dulcie, her face glowing with emotion, "Whoever would have thought it?"

She sat on the edge of her bed as the ward filled with the inimitable sound of Al Jolson over whose death she had wept bitter tears not two years since.   Visions of her early days with Bill filled her mind, bobby socks, dancing, sitting in the back row at the movies, yearning for him every moment he wasn't there.......

> You made me love you
> I didn't wanna do it
> I didn't wanna do it
> You made me want you
> And all the time you knew it
> I guess you always knew it
>
> You made me happy sometimes
> You made me glad
> But there were times
> You made me feel so bad
>
> You made me cry for
> I didn't wanna tell you
> I didn't wanna tell you
> I want some love that's true
> Yes I do, 'deed I do
> You know I do
>
> Gimme gimme gimme gimme what I cry for
> You know you've got the brand of kisses
> That I'd die for
> You know you made me love you
>
> You made me cry for
> I didn't wanna tell you
> I didn't wanna tell you

I want some love that's true
Yes I do, 'deed I do
You know I do

Gimme gimme gimme gimme what I cry for
You know you've got the brand of kisses
That I'd die for
You know you made me love you

Betty laughed as the song came to an end, "And look where that's gone and got you darling!" she said.

"And this is only number three, Betty," grinned Dulcie, "there'll be more, you mark my words," and they both laughed.

Bill was grinning from ear to ear when he turned up at about two o'clock to pick her and Johnny up to take them home.

"I can see from your face that you heard it, love. I was right chuffed they could oblige me, to tell truth."

"Thank you, darling. It were a surprise to me and all, no mistake; and a real treat." She sighed and kissed him lightly on the cheek before turning to Betty to say 'Ta Ta For Now', TTFN as they said back home. The usual hospital bedside exchange between inmate and escapee took place after which she took Bill's arm.

"Come on, love. Everything's in here," patting the small case on her bed, "except for his nibs," she said, stooping over the hospital crib to pick up the sleeping Johnny.

Although the road was slick as ever and the ute skittish, the drive back to Malanda in daylight and in company was immeasurably better for Bill than the trip of just a couple of nights ago. The girls were at Mavis's place so they were heading there first before going home to a 'little surprise'. Dulcie stopped guessing at what that might be when it became patently clear that he had no intention of letting on.

Much as Bill knew Dulcie would like to spend some time with Mavis, and Mavis with them, he stressed the need to get back home to milk the cows…... "and I've got to get the ute back to Curly tonight. He needs it first thing tomorrow."

"No further word on the ute for the farm, then?" Dulcie enquired mildly.

"No love, but Ray Wilson's been hard to nail down. His missus is in some sort of crisis and I think it's taking all his attention and energy at the moment."

"She's in Atherton Hospital," Dulcie rejoined. "Nancy told me when she popped in to see me yesterday."

"Yes, I think it must have been Ray who nearly drove me off the road when I was coming home on Tuesday night. Porch light was on at their place as I drove past and George reckoned it was still on in the morning. Not like Ray that."

"From what Nancy said, she's right poorly. It doesn't sound very hopeful to my way of thinking; terrible shame. We'll just have to bide our time, love, can't pester him now, I agree. Not sure that we have a right to, any road."

"I'm not worried, love. I'd be more concerned about things if you could drive and not having a vehicle was keeping you housebound, but as things are it doesn't make a blind bit of difference to you. We've already a lot to thank Curly for, and I've the feeling he'll see us right til something turns up. I think he and Nancy are just dead pleased to have neighbours again."

"Glad'll look after me. Though she's her Mum on her mind too, poor love."

"I had a long chat with Old Bronc the other day. He offered the use of the dray to go to town if we got stuck. And, as you well know, what a difference a dray makes…" he ended up singing the last bit to the tune of Stanley Adam's popular song. They'd danced to "*What a difference a day makes*" at the Café Anglais on a rare trip to London when Jess was a couple of years, and considered old enough to be left with his Mam. He remembered it now, having gone down especially when they'd heard Harry Roy had formed a new dance band especially for the gig. Egad, but it seemed his mind's eye beheld another world.

176

"You're a daft aputh, Bill Johnson," they looked at one another and laughed out loud, disturbing young Johnny, but not for long; he was soon lulled by the clucking of his Mum and the rhythm of the journey.

- 0 -

"What a difference, eh?" asked Dulcie, inclining her head towards the floor as she blew on her tea, last cuppa of the day before retiring.

The girls had gone to bed at their usual, early hour, worn out by the excitement of the day's visit but both vaguely aware that things had changed around the place. Jess was happy to meet her little brother, no initiate to the concept of having a new, much smaller member of the family who seemed to demand a proportionately larger share of her Mum's attention. On the other hand, Jilly wasn't quite sure about the turn of events, trailed Dulcie's every move, and snuggled up at feeding time.

"And it'll make an even bigger difference when I get the other lot down in the front room, love,' he was referring to the roll of lino he'd not yet laid.

"Is it same colour as this?" Dulcie looked down at the dull, brick red lino on the kitchen floor.

"No love, it's floral. Different coloured roses I think, on a grayish background with green leaves." …..

She'd always liked the way he noticed such things.

….. "And it's a different quality, thinner, shinier surface. Not what we'd have chosen but beggars can't be choosers and it'll certainly liven the place up. I thought I might give the room a lick of whitewash before laying the lino, I found half a tin out in shed which should be ample."

"We won't know ourselves, darling," she sipped her tea. "So, where do these Starrenburgs live, and how did they hear about us? Not heard them mentioned before."

Bill chuckled as he recalled Reg Johnston's story.

"Well, I think we've you to thank for the lino, darling."

She looked baffled, "Whatever do you mean?"

"Well, the Starrenburgs have a fish and chip shop come café in Gordonvale; it's south from Cairns, out past Edmonton where Joe at the

177

hotel lives, remember?" She nodded as he continued, "Apparently Reg Johnston's on good terms with the old man. He's been dropping in there for a good few years, for a cuppa or a feed before driving back home up the Gillies."

"But this can't have come all the way from Gordonvale, surely!" exclaimed Dulcie.

"No love, no, you're right; and the Gillies is closed at the moment anyway, on account of the wet. No, what happened was Reg and Mavis went down to Cairns a week or so back to spend a few days. Well, you know how they both like touring about. One day he decided to take Mavis out to Gordonvale for a spin and a bite to eat, and they got chatting with old man Starrenburg, as Reg calls him, and for some reason the old man brought up that business about you feeding the snakes," he laughed quietly. "No doubt about it, darling, you've made a bit of a name for yourself. Anyway, one thing led to another and Mavis mentioned we were on the lookout for something to cover floors." He paused, looking at her still bemused expression. "Well, as luck would have it, the Starrenburgs have just bought a place over at Peeramon which needs a bit of TLC before it's reopened; an old public house I think it is, and that's where the lino's come from. Peeramon's just a few miles over the way and the road's not too bad. Reg and Curly and I went over on Wednesday to pick it up. I had a bit of a head on me that day, I can tell you."

"A bit of a head on you?"

"Bit too enthusiastic wetting young Johnny's head with Athol when I got back on Tuesday night; he ambushed me I'm afraid love."

"Ah well, it's not every day a man gains a son," she stroked his hand, "speaking of which, I should go and get some rest before he wakes up demanding his next feed, darling."

- 0 -

It was about 3.15 in the afternoon a week or so later and Dulcie had just tucked Johnny back into his basket to sleep. She'd sat in the rocking chair in the living room to feed him, enjoying the lingering smell of the whitewash and the bright new air the lino lent to the room. The heavy

178

morning rain had abated and she was sitting in the kitchen enjoying a nice cup of tea, listening to Blue Hills on the wireless. She had very quickly become a devotee of the radio serial and tuned in every weekday afternoon at 3 o'clock. In this episode, Dr. and Mrs. Gordon were expecting a visit from Peter Frobisher, and Mrs. Gordon was just discussing afternoon tea arrangements with Hilda when Dulcie was dragged back to earth by an almighty commotion outside; dogs barking, the high pitched shrieks of Jess and Jilly, the turkeys suddenly going absolutely berserk and a guttural squealing the likes of which she hadn't heard, not in all her born days. The hairs on her arms stood on end as she heard Bill urgently shouting Jess's name from up in the top paddock where he and George were clearing the land of Penda roots, preparing it for ploughing in readiness for planting a winter crop. She dropped her pannikin on the table and raced to the front door just in time to see Jilly scale the front gate, and leap over barely touching it in transit. She ran down the steps and gathered Jilly up as she rushed to the gate to see what in the blazes was going on.

What a performance. George was riding Big Red at full tilt around the corner of the grain shed, heading for the turnabout with the dogs streaking ahead of him. Bill was running down past the windmill through a fluster of turkeys which were almost in flight as they headed upwards and outwards, into the top paddock; a cacophony of gobbling strident above the fearsome squealing and clattering coming from the cow shed. Her relief was profound when she caught sight of Jess, standing on top of the cabin of George's ute at the far end of the turnabout, yelling to Bill, waving her arms in the direction of the cow shed. George whistled sharply and Reggie and Fred ran round each side of the cow shed. Pulling up over by the cream house, George turned Big Red sharply, his attention keenly focused on the open doorway to the cow shed. The clamorous barking and squealing now coming from inside was punctuated by loud bangs and crashes as the boar bounced off the corrugated iron walls of the shed in its frantic attempts to escape the dogs.

By this time, Bill had reached the ute, clambered up onto the back tray and gone to comfort and protect Jess. All of a sudden, the pig shot out of the shed like a torpedo with ears, covered in mud and propelled by the impetus of its speedy escape straight for the front gate of the house.

179

"Bloody hell!"

Dulcie clutched Jilly to her and ran instinctively for the safety of the house. "Get inside and shut door!" Bill yelled at her from the back of the ute and she was only too happy to oblige.

The dogs held back and the pig slowed to a trot, lifting its head to size up its situation. George rode Big Red round on the near side of the hesitant boar, heading it off from the house. The horse snorted, the pig snorted, and George grunted as he pulled sharply on the lasso he had launched towards the animal. Dulcie, not knowing what to expect, was amazed to see the pig go down. George was off the horse in an instant, pulling hard on the rope to keep his squirming, squealing captive down. He yelled to Bill who had leapt down from the ute to sit on the animal's head.

Dulcie couldn't see much of how they dealt with the beast, but it was well and truly trussed when George and Bill between them half hauled, half carried it back to the pig pen to release it. Then Bill went to rescue Jess, carried her back to the house on his shoulders, taking her around to the laundry where she could be given a good cleaning up before going inside. He left the three of them sitting on the back steps, all mud spattered, tear streaked red mud on the faces of his young daughters, but all clearly quickly regaining their equilibrium now that danger had been averted.

"I do wish this weather would heal," said Dulcie as he departed into the gloom.

While Bill and George made the long overdue repairs to the front of the pig enclosure Dulcie lit a fire under the copper and prepared an impromptu bath for the girls, partly to restore them to cleanliness and partly to sooth their bruised spirits. She quickly cleaned herself up as best she could at the kitchen sink; laid their night clothes out for them in the kitchen and got their towels ready. Whilst they shared the bath she opened a tin of baked beans for them to have on toast for their tea, put the kettle on the hob to make a fresh brew, and went and closed the front windows in the girls' bedroom. In her and Bill's bedroom, to her great satisfaction, her wee son continued to sleep in blissful ignorance of the afternoon's escapade.

When Bill and George eventually came in for a smoko, they found the girls giggling about how Jilly had managed to get over the front gate in one huge jump, and how Jess had managed to climb right on top of George's truck without even thinking, which the girls agreed was pretty clever even though Jess couldn't find a way down afterwards. Dulcie exercised restraint, keeping things as low key as possible, and packing them off to bed quick smart, before they got overexcited, though she did allow them a Tilley lamp so that Jess could read a bed time story, *The Tale of Mr. Tod*, their current favourite of *The Original Tales of Peter Rabbit.*. Old Bronc was rounding up the cows and George had offered to stay and help out until milking was well under way.

The days were already noticeably shorter since the summer solstice, only a month or so ago and still it rained.

- 0 -

"Ahhh, that feels better," Bill said as he came up the back stairs briskly toweling off his back, "thanks for that, darling; makes all the difference."

Dulcie had heated more water in the copper after the girls had gone to bed, sensing his need after a day like today. He'd finished the milking with Athol who'd seen cows back out to pasture whilst he'd hosed down the stalls, cleaned the lines and equipment, stowed the cream in the cream house, replenishing the water in the channels in the concrete floor at the same time, and finally carted the skim down to the newly secured pig sty. It was late, a lot later than usual to be eating.

"Come on, love, sit down and eat. It's been a long day."

"Young Johnny alright is he?"

"Good as gold, darling, regular as clockwork. Slept during the commotion and had his last feed about an hour and a half ago. Come on, eat up darling."

And so they ate, in silence, until the edge had gone off their robust hunger.

"What a day, eh?"

"It was 'n all, but at least no one was hurt, love. As you saw, Jess and Jilly are fine, absolutely fine. They'll probably be talking about it for weeks."

She laughed.

181

"I'm glad to be able to laugh about it. I must say I wouldn't have believed George could move so fast as he did when he brought that pig down. Jilly and I were watching from the girls' bedroom and we could see him whirling that rope around," said Dulcie. "Well, I thought he was just going for its head, you know, the way they did with the steer in that Western we went to see that time. We could neither of us believe our eyes when the pig dropped to the ground. You should have seen the look on Jilly's face. Eyes like saucers she had! How on earth did he do that?"

Bill chuckled in amusement. "Funny thing is Dulcie, he doesn't rightly know, reckons it was a complete fluke snaring the boar's front trotters like that," he paused, as the activity came back to mind. "It's actually called hogtying, what George did afterwards, but he's never actually tried it on a hog before, usually on calves and things. Apparently they usually wrestle an animal to the ground before tying it up. Essential skill for a cowboy, that is. They have competitions at the rodeos, camp drafting I think George said it was. According to him, they sometimes do it to load a cantankerous animal for market or to restrain a beast so as to carry out procedures it doesn't much fancy, like branding or shoeing."

Bill laughed at the memory of George's amazed reaction to his own feat earlier on. "I must say I was impressed. He had the pig on its side when I got there and after I sat on its head, which was not the most comfortable position I've been in, I can tell you even though its tusks had been cut, George slipped the loop off one front hoof and pulled the other leg back across one of the hind ones and secured 'em both with a quick hitch," he enthusiastically demonstrated said moves, "Then, he wound the lasso and looped it around front and back hoofs together. When he'd done that we rolled the pig over on its other side, and George secured remaining legs, fore and aft, same as before. As you can imagine, by then that pig was a dead duck."

"You just can't help yourself, can you darling?" Dulcie rejoined, laughing quietly as she added, "But you make it sound easy."

"There's a bit lost in the telling then, Dulcie. Pig weren't exactly lying there being cooperative, as you would have noticed." He shook his head, "I couldn't do it in a month of Sundays, and that's a fact. He's a skillful animal handler, is George. I'll never match him in that regard."

"Well, you've not had the country life, love, the experience. I, for one, think you're doing alright."

"Well, George reckons we're doing alright, and having seen him in action, his word carries some weight. It's a start, Dulcie. It's a start."

"It is and all, Bill Johnson. It is and all. Only a week now love, 'til Jess starts school; Tuesday 27th to be exact. Things will feel a bit more normal then, won't they?"

- 0 -

"Plurry hell, that Constantinus knew what he was talking about when he gave everyone Sunday off except the farmers!" It was a Saturday morning and Bill had just had a visit from Ray Watson to check on preparation of the top paddock, see how things were going generally. He'd seemed pleased with progress though Bill could see that even after a concerted effort for nigh on three weeks they had a ways to go yet. It was hard work. They were clearing the penda roots which formed a tenacious subterranean network across the entire top paddock which had been earmarked for planting corn this winter. Impossible to till the soil until the roots were eradicated. Apparently this land had once been virtually covered with *Xanthostemon whitei*, commonly known as red penda, a very large tree which grew up to 50 foot tall. There were several down by the creek which flowed under Skennar Bridge. He found the clusters of yellow flowers on the ends of their branches attractive, but their new leaves were hairy, irritating, and he'd warned the girls not to play around them.

It was about quarter to ten and Dulcie was making a batch of scones, just in case Mavis and Reg dropped in which they might do as it was Saturday. Bill walked into the kitchen to be greeted by a very floury wife and the lively sound of *It don't mean a thing (if it ain't got that swing)*.

"Ee up, what's this then?" he said with a grin as he clasped Dulcie firmly to him and quick stepped her into the clear space in front of the larder door.

183

"Give over, you daft aputh," laughed Dulcie, "or we'll have flour all over the place!"

"But this is wonderful, Dulcie. If it isn't Lester Young I'll eat my hat," he manoeuvred her back to her place at the table, his enthusiasm undampened.

"Yes, this chap fancies Lester Young, plays him quite a bit."

"So it's a regular programme then?"

"Aye, love; Rhythm Unlimited, the announcer's Eric Child; remember him from the BBC? It's on every Saturday morning at half nine. It's only on for half an hour but he plays some wonderful music."

Lester Young came to an end and Eric Childs briefly introduced a 1952 remake of *April in Paris* by the Sauter-Finigan Orchestra.

"Right, then, it's a date; next Saturday morning 9.30 in the front room, we'll dance; gives us a week to polish up our dancing pumps, Dulcie."

"Do you really mean it?"

"My very word I do."

"What a right nice idea, darling, I might even get all dolled up for the occasion!"

Bill went through to the laundry to clean himself up as Dulcie popped the scones in the oven. They were just sitting down to a nice cuppa when Rhythm Unlimited came to an end with Count Basie and his Orchestra and *Lullaby of Birdland.* According to Eric Child's intro it had been recorded live at Birdland earlier in the year.

"He's certainly up to date with his music, I'll give him that," Dulcie commented as she poured.

When Bill went out the front door, heading back up to the top paddock, a quick snatch of the song floated back to her................

> And there's a weepy old willow
> He really knows how to cry,
> That's how I'd cry in my pillow
> If you should tell me farewell and goodbye.

- 0 -

It was on Tuesday night, after Jilly had gone off to bed, uncomplainingly alone for once, that Dulcie decided she would set to and iron her favourite dancing skirt, well her only dancing skirt really, to wear on her big date on Saturday. Bill had pumped up the mantel lamp so that it gave a nice bright light and Jess was sitting at the end of the kitchen table doing her homework. He'd also filled the fount of the old Coleman iron with kero, fired her up and fiddled with the key wrench until the fuel seemed to be flowing at about the right rate. This particular model, which, he reckoned conversationally as he fiddled around with it, was made around about same time as he was, wasn't pressurised by a separate pump but instead was gravity fed from the fount which created sufficient pressure to fuel the burner. Once Dulcie had got used to the noise the jets of flame made, which was not unlike the sound of an oxy acetylene torch, she said it weren't bad to use if a bit on the heavy side. Wielded the right way it certainly did the job. Her dancing skirt looked lovely when she'd finished. She'd felt dead guilty about the amount of fabric in it when she'd bought it, but it were ready made from Marks and Spencer who'd managed to make nice things affordable, coupons or no coupons, even this take on Dior's New Look evening ensemble. She remembered her excitement when she'd bought it in 1947, not long after Jess's birth. She'd dig out the strapless boned top that went with it before Saturday, a suddenly necessary prop in the poignant need for glamour that accompanied her girlish anticipation of their dancing assignation.

She clipped the skirt on a hanger and hung it on the nail on the back of the bedroom door. Expecting young Johnny would be waking up and seeking attention any minute, she decided to pack it in. She put the ironing paraphernalia away and pulled the kettle back onto the hob, put tea leaves in the pot.

"So how's the homework going Jess? Sums eh?" Dulcie had spotted Jess's little fingers working away under the table as she stared in concentration at the exercise book on the table.

"They're just adding and taking away sums, Mummy, but they're bigger than I used to do. The teacher showed us how to carry one with the adding up and how to borrow one with the taking away. I've nearly finished. I think I've got them right."

185

"Daddy'll check them for you when you've finished, lovey," Dulcie said as she poured the boiling water over the leaves, "but don't be long now, it's nearly time for bed."

Making the most out of the bright lamplight, Bill was engrossed in The Mysterious Rider, but he was quick to respond, "Come on then, give us a look."

"In a minute, Daddy; I haven't finished the last one yet."

"Alright, alright, whenever you're ready kiddiewinks, no rush," he said affectionately, and went back to his book. Dulcie departed quickly for the bedroom to pick up young Johnny who had woken right on cue and was giving his lungs a right royal workout in the quest for attention.

- 0 -

Early rain cleared quickly on Saturday morning and the girls ran out to do their chores straight after breakfast, both in high spirits because Jess had the day off school and Dulcie had agreed that she could finish her homework tomorrow. Over breakfast they'd said something about checking their favourite place for tadpoles and going to explore up the rill but Dulcie had only half an ear on their chatter. Her thoughts were occupied with the timing of preparations for her big date. Bill was similarly distracted, under pressure to get back out and finish the morning detail early so as to have time to get back and dress for the occasion he himself had suggested.

Dulcie hummed lightheartedly as she cleared the kitchen table, dispatching leftovers to the appropriate feed cans out by laundry steps, most going into the pigs' slop bucket. She was early tending the washing and managed to get most things done before young Johnny woke, demanding attention. As was the case with all of her children, once she gave herself over to their nurture she became completely lost in a cocoon of mothering, totally absorbed in their needs and wellbeing. After settling him back down, clean and contented, she checked the time and decided on a cup of tea before decking herself out in all her finery. She automatically lifted the kettle to check the contents, pulled it back onto the hob and put the leaves into the pot. The wireless was already on the little table to the right of the door, under the .303 and Dulcie had earlier added a jam jar containing a couple of their first hydrangeas, of nondescript colour but with a lush abundance of tiny flowers in their large, pompom-like display and a light, sweet scent. She'd removed most of the leaves as Mavis had recommended, so that the blooms would last longer.

She made the tea and took her cup to the bedroom. Young Johnny was clucking, and sucking at his fist lackadaisically, on the verge of sleep. She changed quietly and carefully, silently cursing only once as she strained to get the waistband of the skirt done up. Then she sat on the side of the bed before the small mirror hanging from a nail in the 4 x 2 structure of the wall on her side of the bed, and carefully applied a light dusting of face powder and the special lipstick she had bought because it exactly matched the colour of the necklace she favoured with this outfit. She gave her hair a final grooming and found, as she stood up, that she felt strangely excited and slightly shy of seeing Bill, done up to the nines as she was. It had been such a long time. Taking a deep, calming breath she left the bedroom and pulled the door quietly closed behind her.

"Perfect timing," said Bill, as he turned from the wireless at the sound of her entry. "And looking a real Bobby Dazzler, darling," he said.

Dulcie was taken aback as she turned towards him. He looked so handsome, strong, restored to the sartorial standard he had always so fastidiously maintained. His suit fitted him well, just a bit tight in the shoulders maybe. He took her breath away just as he had when they'd first met, after corresponding for all that time.

"Come on, love," he extended his hand, "we'll be off any minute."

He turned up the volume and the room was filled with the fading sound of Rhythm Unlimited's signature tune. Eric Child was quick to introduce the opening song of today's programme; *I don't stand a ghost of a chance with you,* from one of his previously confirmed favourites, Lester Young, band leader / tenor saxophonist, the band being joined for this song by Billie Holiday, his Lady Day.

They smiled broadly with pleasure as Bill met Dulcie half way, which wasn't far for either of them, and slid her smoothly into a slow foxtrot. You really could almost hear the words to the song through Lester Young's beautiful sax.

I don't stand a ghost of a chance with you.
I need your love so badly
I love you oh so madly
But I don't stand a ghost of a chance with you
I thought at last I found you
But other loves surround you
And I don't stand a ghost of a chance with you
If you'd surrender
Just for a tender
Kiss or two
You might discover
That I'm the lover
Meant for you
And I'd be true
But what's the good of scheming
I'm dreaming
For I don't stand a ghost of a chance with you
Cuz I don't stand
A ghost of a chance
With you

They were suddenly as one, joined in a harmonious celebration of the music, sharing a magnetic physical unity, Dulcie instinctively assisted by the guidance of his left hand which rested gently but firmly between her shoulder blades, their bodies not touching. She drifted in his arms, couldn't believe it when the music finished and Eric Child introduced the next musical item in his programme.

A change of tempo now, and who better to provide it than Thelonious Monk with his take on Carolina Moon. Recorded only last year, it's what we've come to expect of Monk, quirky, idiosyncratic, stripped of corn and syrup. It's what you might call a jazz waltz, which in jazz speak is any piece in triple meter, commonly written in 3/4 time but you'll note as you listen to this, that he's got 2 different rhythms going. He's got the rhythm of the melody on top, and this real double-time 8 beat piece going up underneath it with Art Baker's drums. Enjoy.

They faced one another, engaged for action. When the music began it filled them both with its rhythmic energy; they were off, slip sliding away in a swirling embrace which Bill controlled carefully to keep within the narrow boundaries of their unfamiliar dance floor. It was a short but exhilarating dance after which they spontaneously applauded warmly as they stood apart to catch their breath. When Mr. Child introduced the next piece, he first promoted the final offering of the day's programme, a classic Eddie Condon band with a version of Fidgety Feet which was over 12 minutes long.

"Come on, love," Bill took Dulcie by the waist and propelled her towards the rocking chair, the only seat in the room. "Let's take a break so we can let it rip with Fidgety Feet, eh?"

"Good idea," said Dulcie, "I'll just go and get us a jug of water, should have thought of it earlier."

As she left *Is you is or is you ain't? (My baby)* by B.B. King filled the room and she cast her eyes back towards Bill, hating to miss a moment of it, but appreciating the break all the same. Bill had turned the volume down a bit when she came back.

"Refreshments," she said, handing him a pannikin of water.

"Just poked my nose in the bedroom, darling. Lad's still sound asleep," he said, "wouldn't surprise me if Eddie Condon's band brought him back to join us."

"I'm not worried, love. Even if he does wake up he'll soon be off to sleep again, bless him."

They stood leaning on one of the window ledges sipping their water and looking out under the corrugated awning towards Old Bronc's place where a thin streamer of wood smoke fluttered upwards and outwards from his smokehouse. BB King kept their feet tapping to the end.........

> Is you is or is you ain't my baby
> Maybe baby's found somebody new
> Or is my baby still my baby true?

They left their pannikins on the ledge and took up their position in the middle of the room as Eric Child did his stuff.

Thank you Mr. B B King.

And now, as promised, one of the regular features of my programme for no better reason than his amazing ability to gather together wonderful groups of all-stars and produce exciting, spontaneous and very coherent music, a classic Condon band that really wails on this marathon rendition of Fidgety Feet broadcast last year on a return visit to Chicago, with Edmond Hall on clarinet, Wild Bill Davidson on cornet, Cliff Leeman, drummer, trombonist Robert Dewees "Cutty" Cutshall, Gene Schroeder on piano, Bob Casey on bass and who else but bandleader Eddie Condon on guitar.

Bill turned the sound up and after a droll quip from Eddie Condon to his live audience, the band was into it; and so were they, launching into a quickstep, their old improvisations flowing naturally back as they gave themselves up entirely to the music. Their feet flew and they moved together fluidly, energetically, held together as if by a force field. It was indeed a marathon but the music sustained them, held them captive, refused to free them. They knew the song well and celebrated the refrain by singing out loud the last couple of words of each line.

> I've got fidgety feet, fidgety feet, " fidgety feet!"
> Oh, what fidgety feet, fidgety feet, " fidgety feet!"
> Say, mate, come and be my "sway mate";
> How can anyone resist that "rhythmical beat"?
> You will never go wrong, never go wrong, never "go wrong"
> If you toddle along, toddle along, "toddle along".
> All I need's a partner to make "my life complete" -
> Two more fidgety, "fidgety feet".

The end was dramatic after the frantic activity; their laughter and applause rang out as Eric Child bid his listeners farewell until next week and the programme theme took over the airwaves. They were both breathing heavily but Bill drew her to him and held her close. Any chance of a bit of canoodling was, however, confounded by the sound of two small pairs of hands clapping.

They turned towards the front door where Jess and Jilly stood on the middle step, looking in, wide-eyed, and grinning shyly.

"Oh Mummy, you look like a princess," said Jilly.

"Thank you, darling," said Dulcie, turning the wireless down, "but what are you doing back so soon? I thought you two had lots of exploring to do."

"We found this new place with tadpoles," said Jess, "So we came to get a jam jar so we can collect some. They haven't started growing legs or anything yet and we want to watch them. Can we, Mummy, pleeeeeeze?" Their room already had more than its fair share of specimens, alive and dead, animal, mineral and vegetable, but it was hard to complain about their insatiable curiosity.

Dulcie noticed the state of their wellies, "You wait there," she said, "and I'll see what I can find."

"Don't worry darling, I'll get him," said Bill as a lusty yell issued forth from the bedroom, "I didn't think there was much chance he'd sleep through that."

- 0 -

"Daddy, how do you spell 'pineapples'?"

Bill had just come back into the kitchen after going out to check up on why the dogs were making such a racket. He hadn't actually seen anything but could only imagine that he'd scared it off, whatever it was, as the dogs soon settled back down. He lowered the wick in the Tilley lamp as he came in and hung it back on its hook on the wall.

"Pineapples, darling, is P-I-N-E-A-P-P-L-E-S," he spelt it out slowly while Jess took it down, head bent over her exercise book. He looked down at her work, noting how different the small, neat printing was to the printing he'd learnt at school. "You writing a story then?" he asked.

"No, it's a composition. It's got to have a beginning, a middle and an ending and it has to be about a person; and we have to give it a name," she said, parroting off the teacher's instructions. "I'm writing it about Old Bronc and calling it Our Neighbour."

191

"That should be interesting," he said, "but it's past your bedtime kiddiewinks, so you'd better pack it in for tonight. You don't want to get me into trouble with your Mam now, do you?"

"No, Daddy," she said, slowly packing up her homework; ever reluctant to go to bed, convinced like most children that she was going to miss out on something by succumbing to sleep. She knew not to argue with her dad though, and planted a goodnight kiss on his cheek.

"Can you see your way alright, love?"

"Yes thank you Daddy. Goodnight."

He pumped up the lamp until the mantle shone brightly, filled the kettle and put it on the stove before settling down to do his own homework. They'd developed a pretty good system for keeping farm records but so far the story told by his meticulous columns of figures held no promise of a financially prosperous future, blind Freddy could see it. A steady but modest income from the sale of cream provided for running costs and their general upkeep but barely met the seemingly never-ending maintenance expenses. He couldn't complain about Dulcie's frugality. They ate well, nothing wasted. Cutting down on meat and making a few other economies helped a little, but it was maintenance and cost of farming essentials, fuel and feed, that really bled the coffers dry. But still, he thought, there'd soon be more produce from the garden, potatoes and winter greens would be first, and there were a few pigs ready for market. He was dead keen to see what they might fetch. He'd just set about recording the last week's outgoings when Dulcie came into the kitchen.

"Have you taken a good look at your son lately, darling? He hasn't half got some size on him, and it's no wonder, the way he takes his feed."

Bill hoped the pigs had grown with such efficiency as he murmured his agreement. She busied herself making tea.

"I heard you talking with Jess earlier. She wasn't going on about going to church was she, darling?"

He looked up, surprised, "Going to church? No, love, she wasn't. She just wanted some help with her homework," he paused, "with spelling, that's all."

"It's a cracked record she's becoming on the subject of church. Comes home from school full of it, she does. Says everyone goes to Evensong on Sunday night and the kids are all allowed to play together afterwards while the parents have cups of tea in the church hall. Beginning to think she's deprived, she is."

"Well you'd better knock that on the head quick smart, love. It'd be hard enough to manage in the daytime, but it's out of the question at night. Besides, I'm not sure I'm that keen myself. What about you, love? You interested?"

"Not really darling, I'm not fussed either way," she poured their tea. To her mind the futility of 'worship' was a recent personal lesson shared by millions. "I didn't think we'd any option what with not having transport, but it's nice to know there is some sort of social life in the town."

She passed him the biscuit jar and pulled her Quality Street sewing tin towards her. There was always something needed mending, "*Still a right Sew and Sew I am*," she thought.

-    0 –

Our Nayber

Our nayber's proper name is Athol Wadkins. I asked him how to spell it and he rote it down for me. My Dad calls him Athol when he talks to my Mum about him, but most of the time evryone just calls him Old Bronc becorz he rides his horse evryware.

Dad says Old Bronc's house is a humpy but Old Bronc says it is Buckingham Palace. He has two houses. He hangs pig up in one to make it into ham. In the other one he has lots of pichers of pritty girls on the walls to keep him warm. He grows pineapples and bananas and he helps my Dad to milk the cows.

He choos terbacko and his horse is called Godiva.

The End

- 0 -

Dulcie was agitated. She could see the men up in the top paddock, spread out along the skyline, planting corn. When she thought about it, she didn't really know exactly where Jess and Jilly were. Exploring was a word they used to cover any number of actual occupations or locations few of which she was in the least familiar with. *"There'll have to be a few changes around here,"* she thought grimly as she paced the floor – their dance floor as it happened, but dancing was the furthest thing from her mind. Feeling guilty and responsible, she thought, *"I am so stupid,"* with which, her mind made up, she found the yellow flag in the kitchen tidy and was soon running it up the flag pole out back. She came straight back inside and as she strode through the kitchen towards the front door Jess's exercise book, which sat, open, on the kitchen table, drew her attention with the morbid fascination such as attracts people to witness the desperation or demise of strangers involved in accidents.

- 0 -

At that very moment Jess and Jilly were, indeed, absorbed in high adventure. Earlier they'd spent quite a lot of time trying to catch a lizard; any lizard would have done of the many coming out now to bask in the sunshine. They'd been trying for the last few weeks, since the big rains had stopped, but no matter how hard they tried they simply didn't have the speed or dexterity or prescience to bag one, which was probably why they kept on trying. Now, their lizard catching muse having deserted them, they were up on the rocks near where the rill entered the property in the top south paddock, close to Forester's Track, looking down on the Coughlin's house, and they'd found the strangest creature they'd ever seen. They rushed away on their first encounter, full of terror, shrieking to relieve their anxiety. Having put enough ground between themselves and it, they flopped down by the rill to recover from the shock but soon decided to go back, armed with sticks, to see if it was still there. Jess was the one to find it and poked tentatively at the strange, snakelike head with her stick, closely attended by Jilly who was caught between being scared out of her wits and utterly enthralled. To their astonishment the creature vanished.

194

"Where's it gone," cried Jilly with a quick intake of breath, eyes wide in amazement.

"I don't know; but it's gone."

Gone it most certainly was. They stooped down and stared at the empty space before them. Empty that is, except for the abundant paspalum and a myriad rocks worn smooth by the rub of nature. One of the rocks had pretty markings, quite different to the rest.

"I think it went in that rock," said Jilly, pointing her stick at it.

"Probly. That's what it looked like, but how could it?"

Jilly was sitting on her haunches peering intently at the rock. She shrugged her shoulders almost up to her ears as if to say, "How would I know, stupid?"

"I think we should wait, watch to see if it comes back," said Jess, "and I think we should be really quiet or we might scare it off, so shhhhh....." and they nestled in the grass, lying flat on their tummies, elbows on the ground, chins cupped in their hands, emboldened by the apparent timidity of the creature.

- 0 -

It was at about this time that Bill stood tall for relief, stretching his body out of the slight stoop of corn planting, the small of his back giving him curry, tying other things up in knots. He could see the girls over in the top south paddock where they had been, flitting here and flitting there, for much of the morning. He smiled with pleasure, and then the yellow flag caught his eye, caught in his throat. Calling an urgent message to Curly, the nearest to him, he dumped his seed bag at his feet, and took off quickly on foot down the slope towards the house, a chaos of potential disasters churning in his mind. Dulcie, who was watching from the living room, came out to the gate to meet him, her agitation evident.

"What's wrong, Dulcie? What is it, love?"

"Where are the girls?"

"They're up by the rill in the top south paddock."

"You've seen them then?"

"Aye, love, I have, they've been playing around in the same spot for ages," he said, exasperated by her questioning. "Tell me, what's wrong? If something's happened I need to know - what is it?"

"I came across this when I was cleaning the girls room," she brandished Jess's exercise book, "and I had a look at her work; for interest's sake." She drew a deep breath, "well, I'm glad I did because it seems to me there's a few things need dealing with around here, and I'm worried about what's been going on," it came out in a quavering rush, through trembling lips, "and I feel responsible. I haven't protected them as I should," she wailed, wiping her weeping nose on the back of her hand, sniffing to stem the flow.

Bill was completely taken aback by both her words and her tears.

"Dulcie, Dulcie... come on, love," he put his arms around her and held her firm, "pull yourself together, love." He couldn't for the life of him think of what could possibly have been revealed by Jess's exercise book to cause such anguish. "Come on, love. Jess and Jilly are up yonder," he waved an arm in the direction of the top south paddock, "I saw them not ten, fifteen minutes ago, just before I spotted yellow flag, so there's nothing to worry about this minute," he paused, feeling the tremors running through her body. "Tell me what's on your mind love, for Pete's sake. Give me something I can do something about for crying out loud, or I'll blow a gasket!"

"She's been up there, up there with him," Dulcie said, forcing it out.

"She's what?"

"Up there in that humpy with Old Bronc, that's where and who with. And it's just not healthy, them being together like that, unaccompanied," she pushed him away in her agitation and looked towards the offending abode as if it was a threat to their very existence.

The penny dropped loud and clear.

"Hey, hey, hold your horses darling. You're right about Jess going up there......"

"You mean you knew about it?" Dulcie's incredulity resounded in the pitch of her question.

196

"Let me finish darling, let me finish. She wasn't unaccompanied. She was with me darling. We went up there together. I'm sorry love, maybe I should have told you but I just didn't think anything of it. It happened ages ago, when you were in hospital with young Johnny."

She wilted as the worry that had fueled her tension evaporated. She returned to his embrace. He felt the return of her equanimity.

"Come on, let's go in and have a cup of tea, darling, and talk about it. I'm sorry darling. I'm sorry. I should've told you. You've nothing to worry about sweetheart. Nothing bad has happened to Jess. You'd know if it had, wouldn't you? She's not exactly shy about getting things off her chest. Think about it."

His words gentled her. She felt her inner wobbliness stiffen, in the way that happened when a body pulled itself together.

"I'm sorry, darling, you're right," she said.................

"I'd no idea you knew..........

Assumed you didn't in fact.

I'm sorry.

It gave me such a shock.

Yes, let's go in and I'll just put the kettle on.

It would be good to have your company for a bit."

- 0 -

They sat side by side at the table, Jess's exercise book in front of them, open at her composition about their eccentric neighbour. While Dulcie had made the tea he had quickly ducked out the back and lowered the yellow flag, a signal to Curly that everything was under control.

"It was mention of the pictures of pretty girls keeping him warm that really spooked me," said Dulcie, "with unwholesome connotations and all that goes with 'em, you know. That and the................."

"And the what, love?"

"................well, that and how much she seems to know about him."

"Ee up, love. I think it'd stick in your imagination too if you went up to Athol's place. He's no ordinary person, as you well know darling, and his home is no ordinary home; that's what makes it memorable; and no more so, I imagine, than to someone young and impressionable like Jess. But he's a gentle man, Dulcie; he's no threat to the girls. I'm sure of it," he paused, drank some tea, "and about the pretty girls. Well they're just from Pix and People magazines, some pin ups, a lot of society pages and fashion plates, and they're there to keep him warm, love, literally. He's papered the walls to keep out wind 'n rain apart from jollifying the place up, as Athol calls it."

He smiled encouragingly at her.

"Main thing is you sound confident of his decency, lack of any unsavoury intentions like."

"Aye, I am that, darling," he nodded reflectively as he said it. He took more tea, her earlier words resounding in his head. "And, by the way, as far as Athol's age goes, he's only a year or two older than me, believe it or not. Terrible what the demon drink can do to a man."

"Yea, verily," she shook her head in sad acknowledgement, buried memories stirring.

As they sat companionably drinking their tea, the heat leached out of Dulcie, her equilibrium restored.

"I'm a daft aputh, I am," self-deprecation reflected in her apologetic expression.

"I tell you what, darling," Bill had an idea, "Next time we have use of one or the other of the utes, I'll take you for a drive along Foresters Track. I've only done it the once but there's something I'd like to show you; tell you the story behind it, what I've gleaned. The track runs past Athol's place, on the other side so if he's at home we could drop in for a visit – I'd forewarn him of our intention to do so of course, darling. You'd neither of you be embarrassed."

"You'll not catch me passing up the chance to get out for a bit, that's for sure, love. Seems odd that I haven't got to meet the old codger properly," Dulcie replied, "we've been here gone six month after all."

"I think he's actually quite shy of the ladies, is Athol," said Bill just as an extraordinarily disheveled Jilly appeared in the laundry, hair matted with twigs and paspalum seed, bright green skid marks on the torn sleeve of her blouse below which red welts were forming on her arm, and covered in the ubiquitous red mud with which they had all grown complacently familiar. She rushed up the back steps trilling, "Mummy, Mummy, come and see what we found."

She was almost leaping out of her skin with excitement.

"Ee up! Ee up, love, easy on," said Bill, "We're coming, we're coming," with which he ushered Dulcie out of the laundry in Jilly's wake to find Jess in the garden squatted beside a large elephant's ear over which she was plainly keeping watch.

"What's this then?" asked Dulcie as she peered into what she called an 'umbrella' leaf to see some watercress leaves scattered around a rock with unusual markings on it.

"Can I tell, Jess, pleeeeeeze?" Jilly jumped in quickly, jumping up and down.

"Alright then, I s'pose," said Jess, grinning, "but then we've all got to be really quiet, or you'll never see what we're talking about."

"It's a real, live, living rock," cried Jilly, dancing a little jig.

"Well I never," said Dulcie as Bill chuckled, sneaking a wink at her.

Heeding Jess's exhortation, they attended the rock in intent silence. Though it obviously seemed an eternity to Jilly, it wasn't really that long before their patience was rewarded and their living rock produced a head followed by four stumpy legs.

"Well, look at that," said Bill, "that's a very special rock that is, girls." He bent down to get a closer look, "That's a tortoise."

"Can we keep it, Mummy, puleeeeeeze?" they beseeched in unison.

"Not in your bedroom you can't, and that's for sure," said Dulcie, hands on hips, decided by visions of its reptilian head scaring the living daylights out of her. "But we might be able to rig up some sort of home for it out here. What do you think, darling?"

"I'm not sure what this little fellow needs to survive. Maybe you girls will just have to keep an eye on him until I ask Curly and the boys about it. Be sure to keep that leaf it's on nice and wet and maybe give it some of the chooks vegie leftovers. Not a lot mind, just a bit. And don't interfere with it too much or you'll make it anxious."

The girls were ecstatically beside themselves.

Bill headed for the top north paddock in a totally reconstructed frame of mind to the one he'd borne down the hill.

Dulcie organised good wash downs in the laundry tubs, lavished the girls with love and calamine lotion and mercurochrome.

The tortoise laid low.

- 0 -

Dulcie felt a tremendous sense of wellbeing as they settled Johnny's basket between them in the ute and Bill started her up. They'd dropped Jilly off with Mavis before having fish and chips at the café for lunch washed down with a good strong brew served in heavy duty china cups which would do British Railway proud. She sniffed the light scent of lavender water on her wrists. It was a beautiful day in late May and Bill had turned the promised trip out along the Foresters Track into a late birthday celebration for Dulcie. They'd done well out of the sale of the pigs, managed to put away the money they'd borrowed from Don and Ruth on the trip out from their share of the proceeds and now had the beginnings of a nest egg. Today's treat was long overdue though the lack of it never complained about.

Bill drove down past the hotel, turned left and then right up Mary Street and past the school. Beyond that it was all new to Dulcie, and most of it empty save the animals, grazing cows, tails swishing, cows lying down chewing their cud, others standing motionless under the willows by the creek beds. The road was plainly not much used and in places the long grass and saplings seemed intent on reclaiming lost territory. Dulcie didn't think she'd ever get used to this country's sheer lack of human presence for mile after mile. They passed an intersection with another road of sorts and soon afterwards the track turned sharply to the left.

"We're on the Foresters Track now, love. It started back at that intersection," said Bill, "and we are now surprisingly close to home as you'll soon see," he nodded over to the left as he spoke. They clattered over a small

200

wooden bridge. "This is the rill that comes into top south paddock, so as you can imagine, we'd see the house if it weren't for those trees."

"Well, I'll be," said Dulcie.

The track turned lazily towards the left and the roadside cleared. Bill pulled over to the side of the road, "Let's get out and stretch our legs," he said, "take in the view."

He went around and opened her door, helped her down, closing the door gently so as not to disturb his sleeping son. She leaned back in the window to get her hat which she pulled firmly on as she joined him at the front of the ute to inspect the scene stretching out beneath them. It was strange having this eagle's eye view of the farm. That was their washing she could see on the line, those were their cows she saw in the lower paddock and this newly tilled soil just below them was the result of weeks of Bill and sundry boys' hard labour. It struck her that their existence was the only existence visible from this vantage point, until she looked off to the right, down the road, where Old Bronc's pineapple plantation was clearly visible.

"It's a lot bigger than I thought, his place," she said.

"Ten acres I think he has," said Bill, "which is enough for one man, the way he does things. You'll see what I wanted to show you just a little further on. I'll tell you the story behind it this evening, after the girls have gone down."

Young Johnny woke up and interrupted proceedings with the singular selfishness of the extremely young.

"Well at least he won't be making demands when we pop in to see Athol," said Dulcie as she changed his nappy. They sat in the ute whilst she fed him, looking out over the farm. Dulcie found the thin ribbon of smoke rising from Old Bronc's place strangely reassuring.

- 0 -

"Ee, you could have knocked me down with a feather," said Dulcie. "I can't say as what I were expecting, but it certainly weren't that. Whatever made him do that?"

Bill remembered the look on her face when she first spotted Old Bronc's gate and chuckled. It was a one piece, double gate with which Old

Bronc had gone to considerable trouble: firstly, to paint it as the Union Jack and secondly, to maintain the national emblem in pristine condition.

"Well, it wasn't patriotism, darling," Bill paused. "He's actually just keeping a promise and sadly, the longer he does it the less likely he is to gain from it."

"Why's that?" asked Dulcie as she poured the tea.

"It goes back quite a while and it's a longer story than I know but what I've managed to piece together is this. As you can no doubt tell from his accent love, Athol Bernard Wadkins hails from Wiltshire. He's a West Country boy who grew up not far from Salisbury. By all accounts his relationship with the demon drink started early and his family got fed up with his drunken ways, ended up kicking him out. He's what they call a remittance man."

"What do you mean?"

"Well, they weren't short of a penny by all accounts, the Wadkins, and they packed him off here with a sum of money to set himself up. For a time they also sent him regular money, his remittance."

"Ah," said Dulcie, "I see."

"I don't know what his side of the bargain was, other than to stay here, but he either reneged on it or his family's fortunes may have changed because according to him, he's on his Pat Malone now, so far as looking after himself."

"He doesn't seem to be making a bad fist of that," said Dulcie who had been surprised, impressed in fact, by her neighbour's resourcefulness and industry, "but where does the gate come into all this?"

"They're good these," said Bill helping himself to another biscuit. "Well, like all good stories, darling, there is a love interest. There was a girl back home, a girl called Elizabeth, to whom he was engaged. When his family packed him off her family wouldn't hear of her coming out here. They agreed that she would come out when he had set himself up, had a home to offer her; seems he made her a solemn promise that he'd paint the Union Jack on his front door so that she'd be sure to find him when she got here."

"Ye Gods, can you imagine the poor girl's face if she turned up to a humpy and a smokehouse in the middle of nowhere? To say nothing of her future."

"I don't think there's much chance of that, darling. By my estimation it's nigh on fifteen years ago that he left the old country. She stopped writing to him quite a while back."

"Do you think all this has anything to do with us ending up here?"

"It may well do, darling. It may well do," said Bill, "it's easy to see how a man would be lonely out here without a mate and not a neighbour in sight."

"And I agree with what you said, about him being woman shy. It's a pity he lost his chance, but I couldn't wish that sort of life on anyone as didn't choose it. At least he chose it, didn't he?"

"Can't argue with that, Dulcie," Bill said as he got up from the table to peer out the window. "It looks like a lovely night out there. Go and put a cardigan on love, and let's go out for some air before we turn in."

She did as bade and they walked out together into the pristine light of the Milky Way within which, high in the sky, the Southern Cross glowed brightly, outdone only by Alpha Centauri.

The haunting cry of a lone curlew broke the silence.

Chapter Seven

Matters of life and death............

Marge Watson died in the middle of June to the relief of her loving family. She had lingered on with that perverse stubbornness of those whose bodies won't set them free of mortal suffering. Soon after the family had laid her to rest, high up on the property in a spot she had chosen herself, Gladys came to see Dulcie with more on her mind than a shopping expedition or an inspection of current farm work in progress. They'd grown close, the pair of them in the past seven months, and Dulcie was quick to notice Glad's awkwardness.

"How're things at home, Glad? Dad alright, is he?"

"He's lonely, bound to be, but it's a relief to him that she's succumbed at last. He's a farmer, Dulcie. He'd have shot an animal in such a state. It might sound harsh, but it's not. In her case he would have done it out of love, and with our blessing."

Cold as it was becoming through the night, the days were perfect. The two of them were sitting out the front nursing their tea and enjoying the winter benefits of a north-facing log.

"So what's on your mind then, Glad? You're not at all yourself today. Is there something I can do?"

"Denis and I are going to get married, Dulcie. Dad's agreed. He says to do it how I want, but to be honest I'm not sure quite what to do, how to go about it, you know."

It took a minute for the news to sink in.

"Oh Glad, this is wonderful," Dulcie leapt to her feet in excitement, grabbing Glad by the hand and pulling her to her feet before throwing her arms around her.

"Come with me," she said when she'd calmed down, "it's time to write lists."

The ice broken, they headed to the engine room where they tore paper from the middle of Dulcie's exercise book and sat down at the kitchen table, their mission clear. They happily acknowledged the 'why' of the matter as they got themselves organised, fresh pot of tea made, biscuit jar on table.

"So," said Dulcie, "It's the how, where and when we need to sort out." She resisted the urge to chew the end of her pencil, "So 'how' would you like to be married, Glad?"

"By the local priest at St. Matthews," said Glad without hesitation.

"That probably comes more under 'where' than 'how'," said Dulcie, writing St. Matthews down under the section of the page she'd marked WHERE. "That's the Anglican Church, isn't it? Jess has spoken of it - often."

Glad was busy pouring the tea, nodded her agreement.

"Mmm," Dulcie continued, "I think under 'how' we should concentrate on the occasion itself; how big, how formal," she paused, "how soon?" she looked up to catch Glad's eye. "Although that comes under 'when' really," she added as an afterthought.

Gladys laughed, "Well there's certainly no particular urgency about it Dulce, other than the fact that we're dead keen to get on with it now we've decided."

"Right," said Dulcie, that hurdle cleared, "Good. So, going back to the hows, you need to think about the bridal party, how many, who you would like in attendance, colour scheme, your bridal gown and who'll make it — or maybe there's a family heirloom in moth balls awaiting this very occasion?"

Gladys shook her head, "Hard to keep such things in this climate, Dulcie. Mum gave up on it, though that could have had as much to do with the fact that it was obvious from the start apparently that I'd inherited Dad's big frame."

"Righto, so the gown stays in. Now where are we? There's your means of transport, the guest list, how you intend to celebrate after the ceremony, how you're going to accommodate those who have to travel, those sorts of things, you know. Get together like that with a bit of convivial drinking and no one is going to want to go home, much less be in any shape for it, some of them." The pencil was flying.

"You're right, Dulce. Some of them will stay longer than just the one night too, I imagine; too far for them to come for just one night. I can see I'd better have a serious chat with Denis and Dad; time to get cracking."

Much had been achieved by the time Glad headed for home to help bring in the cows. Jess was to be flower girl and a young cousin of hers, Kenny Watson, page boy, subject of course to his personal agreement and the consent of her aunt and uncle. According to Glad he was about nine, not big though, for his age. She left with copious notes, determined to set the date first,

"Sometime in October after the winter corn harvest and before the rain sets in, I'd say,"

And the time,

"Early afternoon would be nice, don't you think? It'd give the local denizens comfortable time to do the morning chores and travel in to Malanda on the day, and we could have a proper sit down meal at around 2:30, so those who have to go and do the evening milking won't miss out. What do you think, Dulce?"

"I think you're a natural at this planning lark Glad, that's what I think. Good luck with everything, and let me know as soon as you've decided on Jess and Kenny's outfits so we can go looking for some nice pieces of material, set about making them."

Dulcie stood in the turnabout waving Glad goodbye. Bill and Old Bronc were in the bottom paddock rounding up the cows, and the girls would be in soon to listen to today's episode of Jason and The Argonauts. She went back indoors to set about their evening meal, busting for Bill to come in so she could tell him the news.

- 0 -

Dulcie wiped the corners of her mouth with her napkin, Mavis always paid such attention to the niceties, and sighed with utter satisfaction.

"Thank you Mavis. That were absolutely delicious - second to none," she pushed the plate, emptied of her second helping of Pavlova, slightly to one side and pulled her tea cup towards her, relishing the lingering tang of passion fruit on her palate. Jilly and Johnny were both having their afternoon nap and the two friends were settling down for a long overdue chat.

"Now, enough of Glad's wedding for today, I wanted to ask you about your news, how things are going?"

"Come on, Dulcie, bring your tea out to the back verandah, I'll bring the pot. It's lovely out there at this time of day and we'll hear the kids if either of them yells for attention."

Dulcie did as bidden and they were soon seated, looking out over the garden where they had indeed first met.

"I do so like it here," said Dulcie taking in the attractively ordered surroundings. "But come on Mavis, put me out of suspense love, and tell me how are things going?"

Mavis smiled at her friend. Taking a deep breath she said, "Well as far as the adoption goes, Dr. Rankin says it is only a matter of weeks now and there is no change on the part of the mother. Meaning, you know, that she still intends to have the child adopted out immediately."

"You're nervous about her changing her mind, aren't you?" said Dulcie, perceiving the worry in her friend's eyes.

Mavis's intended smile slid sideways from her face.

"Don't be nervous about it Mavis," Dulcie paused, searching for the right words, "Que sera, sera, lovey. It may seem easy for me to say, I know, but I firmly believe that these things, these really important things that happen in our lives happen for a reason. So, if it doesn't work out this time you can rest assured that there is a reason."

"I think I think the same thing, Dulce, but it just seems that this course of action has proven every bit as uncertain as the other. You know, the actual possibility that I might, just might one day conceive. Oh, Lord, how I would like to be a 'fallen woman' in that respect!"

"Well at least you can still joke about it, bless you," Dulcie freshened their tea cups and helped herself to a little milk before proffering the jug, handle first, to Mavis.

"What do you know about the woman, Mavis, the child's mother? We've never really spoken about it, have we?"

"Well, I don't really know too many specifics. I believe she's younger than me, quite young in fact. I know she's white skinned, and Dr. Rankin says she lives in Cairns, comes from a good family, though to be honest, I don't rightly know what to make of that. He's not said a dickybird about the father. You don't have to be a genius to work out the circumstances; now do you?"

"I know what you're thinking," Dulcie said, "but appearances can be deceiving. And whoever she is, she has my admiration for carrying the bairn to full term in such circumstances as you imagine," Dulcie drew a quick, deep breath, "There are many who don't," she finished, and it was clear from the look on her face what she thought about that.

"Yes, so I hear, and in many cases nor should they," Mavis paused, sorting out her thoughts, not necessarily in tune with Dulcie, "It's a difficult question, I know, with many sides to it," she said, straightening up, the gravity of their conversation bringing her to attention.

"I'm not religious, Mavis. I was brought up a Lutheran but the war knocked any belief in an Almighty God right out of me, and many others alongside," Dulcie was uncharacteristically emphatic. "It's life I believe in, and the right to life of living things for as long as is naturally possible." She paused, looking out over the carefully tended rows of Mavis's fruitful winter garden, "It's why Bill and I came here, to Australia I mean. We wanted a place where our family could grow up safe and healthy without the constant threat of war, all the death and suffering it brings, their death maybe." She stopped. "I'm sorry Mavis, enough of such depressing talk. It rises to the surface sometimes and I just blurt it out. But I meant what I said about respecting the mother's decision to bear the child. She's a good girl I say."

"And another thing; I've just remembered," said Mavis, "Dr. Rankin says she's booked into a private hospital for her confinement. How could I have forgotten that? That's where we're to pick the baby up. That's a sure indication of the goodness of her, and her family's intentions towards the child if ever there was one."

"Hear, hear," said Dulcie, a warm smile transforming the drawn face of moments ago. "If there are only weeks to go, that's not a lot of time. How are preparations for baby's arrival coming along?"

211

"Oh, I've done a lot of things," Mavis said with animation, her earlier lack of faith dissipating, "Come inside and I'll show you, I need your advice about a couple of things."

- 0 -

"What do you think of this then, Dulcie?" Bill asked as she came down into the kitchen from the sitting room where young Johnny now slept in his cot. He was a robust baby as Dulcie proudly pointed out on a regular basis, and had quickly outgrown his basket. They'd been right pleased to find the cot, serviceable, complete with fitted mattress, drop side, legs on castors, etcetera, at a new place called St. Vincent de Paul in Mareeba. None of the assorted goods in the little shop carried a very big price tag so the cot was perfectly suited to both their needs and their means. They'd made the purchase the day they'd delivered pigs to the bacon factory with the use of Curly's ute; one of Dulcie's rare outings. Trip home had been peaceful. Jilly had spent the day with Nancy and the boys.

She peered over his shoulder. He pushed the exercise book forward on the table so it was well lit by the lamp, sat back, inviting her to sit by him on the bench.

"That's right nice, that is," she said, "I think Glad would be very happy with that. I must say, putting a body in there like that makes it much easier to visualise."

"That was the idea, love."

"So, what do we have here?" she asked herself out loud, "Mm, semi-circular yoke extending just beyond shoulders, plain round neckline and outer edges of yoke trimmed with a narrow ruffle," she traced the outline on his sketch with her forefinger as she spoke, " Is that right?"

"I had the idea that it might be a, um, well a collar I suppose you'd call it, rather than a yoke."

"Oh, I see. Well, that'd be alright; easier, probably, to make like. I could just attach it with a facing, couldn't I?"

He nodded.

"Fitted bodice," she continued, "that could be a bit tricky; we'd best make it a bit on the loose side, and long in the waist maybe. Mm, the skirt

212

looks quite full, gathered from the waist and, 'Tra la'," she almost clouted him with an expansive theatrical gesture, "Falls full length to the ankle." She paused, catching his eye, "That could be tricky too at the rate she's shooting up, I don't know whether it's the grub or the sunshine, but there's no stopping any of them, have you noticed darling?"

They surveyed the sketch.

"I was a bit concerned when Glad said it was to be sleeveless but didn't like to say anything."

"Mm, I thought of that Dulce, but days will be a lot warmer by late October. Jess'll be plenty warm enough, wedding being at 1:30 in the afternoon. The boys give me to understand that evenings will still be a bit parky; it'd probably be a good idea to have a cardigan on the ready if Glad's intent on having her reception in a marquee," he raised a quizzical eyebrow.

"Intent, marquee?" Dulcie looked at him, shook her head, but refused to run with it, "I was actually thinking of sun love, but they'll be under cover for a lot of the time, one way or t'other won't they?"

Dulcie had developed early a healthy respect for the ferocity of the Australian sun of which she'd not seen the likes before. She insisted on the girls wearing clothes with sleeves at least to their elbows though it was a losing battle trying to keep hats on their heads. Without exception the family soaked up the Nivea Cream. She bought lashings of it to meet the demands of unstinting after-bath application to all the bits of them that got exposed to the sun and wind; hands, arms, feet, legs, face, neck, shoulders. It was one of the few things she drummed into them, insisted upon.

"You'll like this, Dulce," Bill said as he turned a page in the exercise book to reveal a sketch of Jess wearing headwear very much a la Jane Austen bonnet.

"Oh, that's a lovely likeness of our Jess, darling, what a shame it's on lined paper, it'd look right nice in a frame," she studied his illustration. "Glad'll like that, but it's a relief you're making the pattern it is. I don't think I'd rightly know how to go about cutting it, or how to assemble it, come to think of it."

"We'll manage, love. We'll do a trial run, or as many as we need, with newspaper and sticky tape first, that'll give us a few clues."

213

"Real value for money, the North Queensland Register," said Dulcie, "from fire lighting and bum wiping, to toile making; fingers crossed for a few bumper issues in the near future is what I say."

"Twarl?"

"Aye, love, toile. The first version of a garment, or item of costume, made out of something cheap as a trial run, to get the pattern right like."

"It's a new one on me; you live and learn, eh,"

"My Aunt Dora taught me that," said Dulcie, proud to be his source of learning for a change, "Same Aunt Dora who passed on to me most of my sewing kit. She was a beautiful seamstress she was, satisfied with nothing less than perfection. Patience of Job she had. You've seen all those things she gave me haven't you, darling; the tape measures, lovely thimbles, cards of embroidery silk, hooks-and-eyes, press-studs, needles, buttons of every description; ah, what a boon. I've brought them all with me; I could never have left them behind; they're in trunk in bedroom, what's not in sewing tin."

Dulcie got up and went to the stove to stoke the fire, add some more wood. She'd bring Johnny in here to feed him in the warm before she put him down for the night. Unconsciously weighing up the kettle for content before pulling it back onto the hob, she set about making tea. "Glad and I are going shopping over in Atherton day after tomorrow," she said, "so we'd better measure Jess up tomorrow and try to work out how much fabric I should get."

"Right you are, darling, how about tomorrow night, when I've finished milking?"

He was the pattern maker.

"There's only three month to get everything ready…." ….. '*And there seems such a lot to do,*' thought Dulcie.

He pumped up the mantle lamp, got up to get his book.

Dulcie pulled the bag of scrap clothing to her and took up where she'd left off last time, tearing it into strips on the road to becoming stuffing for pillows and cushions.

- 0 -

Jess was down by the creek running down the back of the Coughlin's place, near the fallen trees they used as a bridge on their short cut to school, they being her and the Coughlin boys. When she was on her own at the weekend, usually because Jilly was having a rest, she would either go up to her special place on the hillside above the wind mill, near where the corn had been planted, or down here to see if any other kids were here checking the yabby traps, or having a swim, or just hanging around because they liked it down here. It was nice to spend time with other kids. It was different to being with Jilly that was for sure.

It was a lovely warm day, even though it was almost the end of July and near the middle of winter, and Graham and Michael Coughlin were there with some other kids she knew from school. Graham and a couple of the others were draped on their tummies over the trunk of the big fallen tree with their heels tucked up behind the smaller, slightly higher one to hold them in place as they peered down into the trap hanging below, checking it for spoils, or any hint of activity. There was obviously nothing in the trap. When Jess arrived Graham was loudly reckoning they were wasting their time because his dad said the yabbies wouldn't be around for a while, until it was nearly summer again.

There were only two traps, both made out of kerosene cans. Someone had cut the tops off the cans and a window in one of their bigger sides. Graham reckoned it was him but Jess didn't think so though she didn't say anything. Whoever it was, they'd bodged several small holes in the bottoms, and a hole in each skinny side of the cans roughly in line with the middle of the windows. A straightened out wire coat hanger was threaded through the holes at the sides and pulled through the can and twisted together at the open top of the can which was covered over with chicken wire. They tied the rope to the coat hanger wire to lower the trap into the creek, having first weighed it down with a rock and baited it with a bit of meat tied with string to the wire running across the inside of the trap so that it hung just below the window. Jess liked seeing the water cascading like a fountain out of the holes in the can when the boys pulled it up to bait it or, if they were really lucky, to retrieve their catch.

Graham had told Jess that the idea was that once a yabby was lured into the trap by the smell of the bait it wouldn't be clever enough to find its way out. She thought it made sense, but sometimes it was days before they checked the traps and if the meat stayed there untouched all that time, and it mostly did lately, it didn't half pong when they pulled the trap up. Other times the meat just vanished with nothing left to show for it, yabby or otherwise. It had been ages since they'd caught anything and two yabbies was their biggest catch in one trap that she could remember. As to what happened to the captives, she had no idea except that there was usually a lot of argument amongst the boys as to who got them.

She quickly lost interest in the traps and went down to the water to wade across to the other side, wondering if anyone was down round the bend near the swimming hole. She loved it down by the creek here; the sound of the water washing over the rocks, the wetness of everything, the soft green growth clinging to logs and rocks, the water so clear that you could see the bed of the creek clearer than the other side until you stepped in and the dirt clouded up as the velvety bottom squelched silkily between your toes. Although this wasn't exactly out of bounds, Jess knew that that was really because Mummy and Daddy didn't know about it. She knew instinctively that they would have forbidden it if they had known. It was part of the thrill of being here. She waded across the creek and headed down round the bend whence, after only a short walk, she could hear the peals of laughter issuing forth like a magnet.

Impatient to join in the fun she lost no time, pulling her wellies off as soon as she got to the top of the bank above the pool, followed quickly by her skirt and blouse, and leaving them there in a pile along with the other kids' stuff. Most of them swam in their knickers and singlet; there was nothing unusual about it. They found their own ways to explain the state they were in when they got home; she'd heard them talk about it. She hurried down the side of the bank, half sliding, using the gnarled roots of the big tree as footholds to slow her descent. This was one of her favourite places and it looked beautiful today with the sun shining brightly over the wide, open section where the boys jumped in from the rope tied to the overhanging branch of a big tree a bit further downstream. There was no activity down

216

there at the moment, but over time so many kids had done this that there were deep grooves in the branch, worn there by the rope now hanging over the water and others before it. She couldn't swim and always stayed in the shallow part of the creek, where she headed now to join the others already there. This shallow bit had been formed by the hard packed buildup of earth and rock and natural detritus against the trunks of two big trees of which there was no evidence above the surface at all, so long ago had they come down. It was always shallow here, so shallow you could pretend to swim by touching the bottom with your hands, keeping yourself afloat as you mimicked the strokes of the swimmers.

After wading in a couple of feet she flopped down into the water, only to spring up again, loudly gulping in air to replenish lungs emptied by the biting grip of cold water. Her exaggerated antics drew squeals of laughter from the rest of them who'd gone through the same initiation but now lolled about, happily accustomed to the creek's cool waters. She adjusted quickly and joined in the fun. It was a day much like any other she had come to join them. A few of them, Jess in their number, got carried away having a pretend swimming race and it was a real shock to her when her hands found no supporting creek bed below them and she suddenly realized how very close she was to the big pool. She put her legs down to stand up, found the edge of the big log under the water awkwardly, and in her anxiety pushed herself off it and out into the big pool.

She went down. Her feet threshed, as if to gain a foothold in the water as she tried instinctively to climb up and out of it. She came up, broke the surface, blurted something, frantically beating the surface of the water with the palms of her hands, but it didn't work and she went down again. The sun shone brightly. From under the water it looked like a luminous lamp, lighting up the bubbles she could see streaming to the surface from her clothes, from her activity, from her. It was cold here, very cold. She wasn't sure whether she was upside down or the right way up, she was confused, she couldn't think, her chest started to hurt, gripped by invisible bands getting tighter and tighter. The futile threshing of her limbs served only to stir up the silty creek bed and the light was being sucked into a deepening silence. She was beginning to acquiesce, the silence becoming her friend when she felt

217

herself grabbed by the hair, dragged through the water, and bursting in a spray of water and glistening leaves into the day, the light and the air where she could breathe. But she couldn't breathe. She had seized up, paralysed by relief and fear. The silent darkness claimed her.

- 0 -

When Chris Hammond heard the shouting and loud cries coming from the direction of the creek he felt a frisson of alarm, his instincts telling him with absolute certainty that something was going seriously wrong down there. He called to his group quickly explaining his intentions and ran along the bank of the creek towards the din. The lantana thinned out as he ran and he came upon the swimming hole on the high side, where the kids climbed the tree to launch themselves into the pool from the rope. He saw the turbulence below the surface, caught a glimpse of white amid the murky clouded water. Skittering unchecked down the bank he waded in without hesitation, took a deep breath and dived down under the water. Through the gloom he was still able to see the child and thanked his lucky stars when he clutched at first go a hand full of thick hair, *a girl*, he thought. He struck out with his legs and swam quickly to the surface, pulling her high and clear as he reached it. Cupping her chin in his hand, he held her head high out of the water and side stroked to the bank where he lost no time in dragging her out. She was unconscious but her eyelids appeared to flicker. He rolled her onto her stomach, laying her head gently on one side before straddling her prone body and exerting a firm pressure on her back, his palms between her shoulder blades. Barely had he started when she squirmed beneath him, coughing before taking a deep, rasping breath and starting to whimper, wriggling now to release herself and get up. Releasing her quickly he helped her to sit up, watching intently as she gasped noisily for air, her chest heaving inside her muddy vest.

They were surrounded by youngsters, among them his group of Cub Scouts, wide eyed at having seen an unscheduled piece of real life saving. Having set off to do some fairly routine exercises in tracking and woodcraft from Part II of their handbook they'd found their activities rapidly promoted to Part V, chapter VIII *Saving life, or how to deal with accidents.* Two of them

218

were quick to volunteer to fetch his horse when requested, and someone else found Jess's clothes and helped her to put them on. They were all very subdued, having learnt what a lucky escape really was, and touched still by the thwarted spectre of death which seemed to linger on.

- 0 -

Taking a breather from chopping wood out the back, Dulcie looked across the south paddock as she wiped the perspiration from her brow. She was startled to see a stranger riding purposefully up the rise; a big man, his horse moving with a slow, deliberate gait, heading straight for the house. Of that she was certain. She swung the axe down into one of the unsplit logs, left it there, and went quickly through the house and across the turnabout to the milking shed. Empty. To no avail she urgently scanned the surrounding paddocks. Going back indoors, she found the blue flag and ran it up the flag pole. Even at that slow pace she knew their visitor wouldn't take long to reach the house. She didn't rightly know what she should do but closed the front door and went into the bedroom to watch his steady approach surreptitiously through the half closed shutter. He was definitely unknown to her. As he drew nearer it was his garb which first grabbed her attention. It looked like a uniform, though not one she recognised at once. Then she saw that he had a passenger, and the more she looked the more sure she was that it was Jess. Her concern suddenly flared, and she rushed out of the house and into the turnabout to greet the stranger, in need of immediate enlightenment.

- 0 -

Bill and George were working on the far fence of the pig enclosure when Bill saw the blue flag. "Looks like unexpected visitors," he said.

"That what the blue flag means is it?"

"Aye," said Bill, "and seeing as how there's nowt come by here they must be coming cross country."

"Well, it's not Curly or Nancy. They were going to Atherton today, according to Curly in the pub last night."

"Dulcie wouldn't run the blue flag up for them any road, George. Last time she ran up blue flag she needed help dislodging that Jo McIntyre, Fire Officer's missus. Know her?"

"Impossible to avoid," said George with a grin.

"Only bloody woman I've met who went to the lavatory and relieved everyone else in so doing."

George laughed at the sentiment.

"Can't be her though, she'd have come by here. I'd best get over there, make sure nothing's amiss. If I leave flag flying you'll know I've got a problem," Bill finished as he mounted Big Red and headed around the perimeter of the pig pen on the shortest unimpeded way home. It was a large pen and he turned into the homeward track just as a big fellow rode into view in the south paddock, headed for the turnabout. Dulcie came out the front gate, saw him and waved in acknowledgment before turning to greet the arrival of the stranger. She seemed anxious. Bill dug his heels in to encourage a more enthusiastic commitment from his mount and rode into the turnabout as the big man dismounted, turning to take Jess down from his saddle and pass her to Dulcie where she clung like a limpet.

"*What the plurry hell,*" Bill thought as he reined the horse in. Dismounting quickly he tethered Big Red to the rail by the milking shed with a quick hitch, and walked over to introduce himself, find out what was going on.

"I'll just take her inside, darling," Dulcie said as he approached, "Rug her up, get her warm."

"Bill Johnson," he said as he thrust his hand towards their unexpected visitor, whose clothes he noticed, were sodden.

"Chris Hammond," the stranger said, reciprocating the gesture. "She's had a very nasty fright. I thought it best to bring her home; you never know how a youngster might react to such an experience. Bit of a shock really. But I think she'll be alright. I don't think she'll be any the worse for wear."

"What happened?" Bill asked, and the Scout Leader told his story, finishing up by stressing that her lungs hadn't yet taken in water when he'd pulled her out, and she'd recovered quickly once he'd "got her going, again."

220

"I don't know what to say, can't thank you enough. What might have happened just doesn't bear thinking of," Bill said, running a hand through his hair.

"There is a way you can thank me, Bill, as it happens," Chris Hammond sounded a bit sheepish, said it nevertheless.

"How's that?" Bill was pulled up short.

"Well, I'm afraid my watch is ruined. I noticed it as we were riding up the hill. I didn't even think about it when I dived into the water, but look at it, it's obviously not water proof, eh?" he said, undoing the strap and offering the watch to Bill for inspection.

- 0 -

After Chris Hammond had left, Dulcie railed vehemently against the instinctive urge Bill expressed to teach Jess a lesson she wouldn't forget. "Do you not think she's learnt a lesson? You can't take the strap to her in her condition. I'll not allow it," she said. "Nor would you Bill Johnson, I know you," she finished, "and there's no point in reading me the Riot Act either," said Dulcie, sticking her chin out, exasperated even though she knew that his angry tirade stemmed as much from deep relief as anything else. "We can't lock her or any of them up just so that I can watch over them every minute. They have a life to live, and besides, we both know Jess is never willfully naughty. She's just high spirited sometimes. It was our ignorance as much as hers that caused this, and we've got off lightly. Just be thankful Bill, just you be thankful!"

Strong though his feelings were, Bill wilted before the strength of her motherly defence, aided and abetted, as it happened, by George's arrival on the scene in response to the still-fluttering blue flag. Bill whipped out back to lower the flag. It gave him a change of pace and space, a brief respite in which to reflect. He concluded that if he were to take a strap to Jess now there was no doubt it would certainly hurt him more than it hurt her. He went back indoors, resolved to spare himself and leave Dulcie to her ministrations.

They got through the rest of the day as best they could, each trying to quell a rising tide of guilt about the part they might have inadvertently played in the near catastrophe. But they had their work to do, and they did it. Later, that evening, they talked. The pale blue organza bridesmaids dress did not surface. The wireless was silent. There was no homework being done, or books being read. Jilly had eaten her baked beans on toast in bed with Jess earlier, totally flummoxed, and still privately wondering how the world could have changed so much between going for an after lunch nap and waking up just a couple of hours later in time to play. That it had changed was patently obvious. It was quite clear no one was going out to play, and she stayed in bed with Jess to keep her company, knowing somehow that she should but having no real idea why.

"She's alright then, love?"

"She seems fine physically," said Dulcie, pouring their tea, "but she's not her usual self. She looks a bit peaky, obviously had a serious fright. We'll have to keep an eye on her, make sure she's not ailing, one way or another."

"That chap Chris Hammond was pretty certain she didn't take in any water, love. She'll be right, you wait and see. He made a suggestion, Dulce; something we should probably investigate possibilities of. He reckons we should try to get Jess into the Brownies, which I gather is the equivalent in the Girl Guides to a Cub Scout in the Boy Scouts. He reckons she's about the right age and would learn a lot about self-reliance and survival if she joined up, become more aware of her surroundings generally. He was a bit embarrassed he didn't know too much about the situation here, but said we should talk to the locals; reckons anyone with kids would know."

Dulcie sipped her tea, looking at him above the rim of her pannikin.

"I was never in the Scouts back home but my brother Doug was and he loved it. Learned a lot of things Mum and Dad couldn't have taught him; nor me, for that matter. War effort ended up benefiting most, of course, at the time."

Breaking the ensuing silence, Dulcie said, "I could ask Glad, you never know. But I've got the feeling she would have mentioned such a thing well before now if they did that sort of thing round here; not short of common sense is Glad. And I'm surprised neither Nancy nor Curley has said anything."

222

She finished her tea and asked, "Where's this Chris's outfit based? Did he say?"

"Over in Atherton," said Bill, "where he lives. If your intuition is right and the Brownies haven't spread this wide, we couldn't do it, it's as simple as that, not without a motor."

"Well there're other things we could probably do."

She paused, before continuing through Bill's silence, "Teaching them all to swim would be a start, wouldn't it? I'm not very good, but I do breast stroke well enough to get myself to where I can climb out of a pool..........thanks to Dad," she added grudgingly.

"Aye, you're right, darling. With all these creeks around there'll be plenty of opportunities for them to come to grief if they can't swim. I'll have a chat with Neville about how their boys learnt. I think there's a swimming pool down at the falls, you know, the Malanda Falls, but I don't know much about use of it."

He finished his tea, pushed his pannikin away from him, "I know there's been a lot to think of, things to pull together, but I should really have thought of this aspect before." He paused, lost in his thoughts, "Never went swimming when I was a kid, not something we did."

He looked at her, saw the tired lines in her drawn face, and suggested they pack it in for the day, offering to tidy up before joining her in bed himself.

"I'll just look in on them all," she said, getting up quickly, her gratitude for having her family intact washing over her.

He quickly put things in order in the kitchen and went outside, through the laundry, needing a moment to himself, space in which to revel privately in the good fortune which had befallen him. He was consciously thankful for being spared the deep and eradicable pain of losing Jess. He let the love he had for his children surge through him, revitalised by the narrowness of this latest escape, which he felt his own. It was a strange affirmation of something he intuitively believed; what, exactly, evaded him? Fate? And, if so, whose?

He went in to lie beside Dulcie, held her close as much for solace as to give comfort.

Their combined diligence soon revealed the absence of Boy Scout or Girl Guide organisations in town but they were determined to better equip the girls for their new habitat, "Starting with teaching them how to swim," said Dulcie to Glad, seeking her advice as to how best achieve this aim. They had naturally taken the step of banning Jess from the swimming hole; well from going into the water anywhere in fact whilst they sorted out their dilemma.

For her part Jess didn't attract any extra teasing from the kids at school; she was surprised when a few of them were, if anything, friendlier than before. Her biggest problem turned out to be the change in the way her Daddy spoke to her, and acted towards her. She could tell she had upset him "well and truly" as her Mum used to say. She knew it had been wrong to go down to the creek without telling them but her Mum seemed to see it differently than her Dad did and to forgive her outright. Jess knew she had to make it up to him somehow, mostly because she missed the bit of him that seemed to have gone away. One evening she overheard them when they were talking about the cost of giving a watch to the man who had pulled her out of the creek and brought her home. It couldn't have been a present because it was very plain that her Dad wasn't very happy about it at all.

She found it hard to say anything. There was always someone else around. Even at night when she did her homework at the kitchen table, if Johnny needing feeding her Mum brought him into the kitchen to feed him, where it was warm, instead of sitting in the rocking chair in the front room. It wasn't on her mind every minute but her need to say something, to make things go back to the way they were before, stayed with her, and when she did have the opportunity, quite unexpectedly one day, she just blurted out, "I'm sorry, Daddy," at which her mouth dried up and all the moisture that had been there just a moment ago seemed to well up in her eyes.

They were in the milking shed. Bill was sitting on the milking stool filling the family milk churn and Jilly had gone back indoors to get warm. The momentary stillness, the silent bubble they shared was an illusion created by a sudden acute awareness of one another to the exclusion of all else. He let go of the cow's udder and turned to behold eyes brimming over with tears washing zig zag tracks down dirty cheeks to a quivering mouth.

"I wasn't show… hic… showing off, Daddy… hic," her shoulders heaved, "it was an axe…hic… accident." She gulped, "Hic… it really was, Daddy."

"Come here, lovey," he said, putting his arms around her and pulling her to his chest for consolation. He patted her back unconsciously in an attempt to comfort her, "Don't cry kiddiewinks."

She rested her head on his shoulder, and her crying, punctuated by the occasional hiccup, soon ceased.

"You're forgiven, lovey, but we can have no more such accidents. You understand me?" He released her.

"Yes, Daddy; I haven't been back since that time, Daddy."

"So your Mam says, Jess. Good girl," he said, "and I want it to stay that way until I know you can swim young lady." She nodded vigorously as he continued, "I've got to finish off with the milking now, but we'll talk about you learning to swim in the next few days, alright?" She nodded eagerly again. "Now go on, off you go. Your Mam will be getting your bath ready soon and by the looks of you lovey, you need it."

"Thank you Daddy," she said, and raced out of the shed across the turnabout through the gate through the front door through the house and into the laundry where Dulcie was indeed preparing their tub, and her feet didn't touch the ground once.

- 0 -

"Oh, Dulcie," Glad laughed, "if only. But you obviously don't know how the Range Road works; nor would you, without experience of it; you came up on the train from Cairns, didn't you? Let me explain, and then we can try to nut out the best way to ensure everyone gets here on time."

They were sitting out on the front log on another beautiful winter's afternoon. Jilly was playing with young Johnny in the front room. These days he propelled himself to prevailing points of interest energetically for about half an hour at a time between sleeps and feeds and baths and generally just kicking his heels up; hence the special 'gates' on the front door and at the top

225

of the steps down to the kitchen. The shiny lino was his Godsend. He wasn't exactly crawling, but moving "like a tadpole on its back," as Jilly reckoned. She was warming to him. The room was less sparsely furnished than it had been, having now, as well as the table by the door, Johnny's cot and the rocking chair, a roll top desk in the corner near the kitchen steps, another irresistible find at the St. Vincent de Paul's in Mareeba. It was used to store Jess's projects and the farm accounts and the letter writing paraphernalia. Along the wall to the right of the front door was a set of kerosene case bookshelves, the top of which was beautified by an impressive array of natural treasures collected mainly by the girls whose constant contributions necessitated frequent rearrangement to better show off their latest prize; downy feathers and sleek quill-like feathers, patterned stones of all shapes and sizes, dried seed pods, the carapace of an elephant beetle, the skin of a carpet snake, a bunch of dried berries, a myriad brittle empty shells of cicadas carefully prised from the trunks of trees, the lid of a jam jar with shiny dead flies in it, snail shells, a birds nest, the bleached skull of a small creature, maybe a mouse, a curl of brittle rusty-red paper-like bark, a piece of green broken glass worn smooth around the edges by the rub of time. On the middle shelf there were a few framed photographs, of people Jess could hardly remember, Jilly couldn't remember at all and Johnny had never met at all. Of books there were few, but the number was growing. There were also a couple of records, in paper sleeves, not that they were any use without a gramophone. Now that Johnny was getting about, the bottom shelf which was on the floor, had been emptied.

"It's no ordinary road, the Gillies Range Road, Dulcie, there's a real treat in store for you there alright," said Glad. "Good head for heights have you? Because for starters, the road's very steep; I think it goes down some 2500 feet to sea level in just 12 miles and in order to do so it has in excess of 600 bends in it; not sure of the exact number, changing all the time, but it's a pretty hair-raising ride, that's for sure. It's an absolute marvel that it got built at all in my opinion, which I caught off me Dad's. You just wait 'til you see it. Apparently Queensland Main Roads built it on a pretty tight budget which is why it has so many sharp bends in it; they couldn't afford to cut through more of the heavy rock formations than absolute necessary, simple as that;

they're granite and slate those mountains, must have been really tough going for the road builders. Makes you wonder how the trees on those slopes manage to grow at all, let alone to such enormous size, doesn't it?" Glad paused to sip from her pannikin, joined by Dulcie who was privately beginning to think the Gillies might just be a treat she could happily do without.

"Apart from being precipitous, it's also quite narrow so it is in fact a one-way road," continued Glad, at which Dulcie's mind was made up, definitely not her idea of treat.

"What use is it if it's only one way," she asked, intent on taking an interest.

Her effort was unrewarded as Glad continued without breaking stride, "It was opened a few years before I was born and at that time they just had the times during which you could travel up or down posted on notice boards at the top and the bottom."

"Ah, I understand," Dulcie said.

"That didn't work," Glad shook her head, and laughed ruefully, "What were they thinking? There were fatalities – people coming and going. Dad reckons he wouldn't touch it with a barge pole in those days, but they soon installed a top gate and a bottom gate with a gate-keeper at each end linked by telephone. That's how they still do it and there are a couple of emergency telephone's at the roadside now. Jack Savage is our friendly top gate-keeper, poor bugger."

"Poor bugger? Why's that?" asked Dulcie.

"Worse than farming I'd reckon," said Glad. "They have to be available on a 24 hours a day basis, seven days of the week. Jack's got a good missus, everyone says she does a lot to make the job manageable but it's his job, and he knows he'd be held responsible if anything were to happen. Word has it that he's fighting through available channels for better conditions. Good luck to him, I say," she turned her attention back to her tea.

Dulcie had been mulling over what Glad had said which prompted her to ask, "So you need to know when the bottom gate is open on the day in question so that you can let your guests know, I suppose?"

"You're on the right track Dulcie, but there's actually a set time-table and that's the problem. It could be difficult to fit in with, especially for people who can only come up on the day," Dulcie looked at her expectantly, "the Bottom Gate opens between 9:00am and 9:30am and then it doesn't open again until 1:30pm – same time as wedding so that's no use. The gate's open earlier of course, between 3:30 and 4:30 but it's a tricky enough road in the daylight for anyone, let alone those who are new to it. I'd not like to think of anyone doing it in the dark for the first time, and anyway," she paused in exasperation, "earlier is not what we need."

"You could get a good few cars through the gate in half an hour, couldn't you Glad?"

"Course you could, Dulce, but numbers aren't the problem. Some of the family will be coming up to Cairns on the Sunlander, from Brisbane. They'll be picked up from the station to travel up for the wedding with local family members. If the train's on time there shouldn't be a problem…. it's due in early enough, 7:30 I think, and it's fairly reliable so that lot should be OK. No, I'm more concerned about friends coming from Mission Beach. It's a fair way south and they're driving up to meet with other friends in Innisfail to travel up with them, to save on fuel costs and give Mary a break."

"Well, if they're late, how late are they likely to be, and how flexible are the gate-keepers with the time-table for the gates, Glad? You'd think if they knew early enough exactly who to expect they could extend gate opening time a little to accommodate someone's special need."

"You know, Dulcie, I remember about ten years ago, when this whole area seemed to be taken over by the military,"

"What, around 1943 you mean?" remembering a conversation with Mavis.

"43 – 44, one of those years; there was a day when the Gillies was taken up for a whole day by a convoy of Australian Army vehicles, over 600 of 'em, all taking soldiers and their war equipment down to the Cairns wharves en route to the battlefields of New Guinea. Mervyn and I rode our horses up to watch from the high ground where Mum is now buried, and the road from Atherton was filled with them as far as the eye could see. They turned off just up the way," she pointed in the direction of Old Bronc's place, "and took the road through Yungaburra."

"Well, I'm not sure that you would have quite that clout, Glad, but then you'd probably only need an extra half an hour, wouldn't you?"

Glad burst into laughter.

"Thanks Dulcie, but all jokes aside, I thought that might be the thing to do and you've just given me the gumption to do it. I'll explain the problem to Jack, give him everyone's details on a piece of paper and ask him if he could have a word with Bottom Gate, pass the details on. There's no harm in trying, certainly nothing to lose, eh?"

They looked up in unison as the telltale thrumming of the cattle grid alerted them to Bill's return. Dulcie slipped indoors via the laundry to pull the kettle onto the hob before she and Glad wandered out into the turnabout. Bill pulled up outside the milking shed and Jess leapt out trilling, "Mummy, Mummy, guess what we did?" as she raced over towards them.

"What did you do, lovey?"

"We drove through a dirty big tree that was growing over the road," Jess announced breathlessly, "Didn't we Daddy?"

Bill kissed Dulcie on the cheek and smiled a greeting at Glad. "Aye, we did love. We did at that," he agreed.

"And look what I got," Jess said, pulling a bunch of bubbly looking material out of its wrapping.

"Whatever's that?" Dulcie asked.

Jess looked at it, looked at them, took a deep breath and said, "It's a wigwam for a gooses bridle!" at which they all burst out laughing, attracting the attention of Jilly who yelled out from the front door to find out what was so funny.

"In you go, you cheeky monkey," Dulcie said to Jess, "You can show me your surprise later. And don't you go showing off and upsetting Jilly now, alright?"

"Alright, Mummy," she said as she raced to clamber over Johnny's 'safety gate' at the front door, her high spirits undampened.

"I've put the kettle on, darling; time for a cuppa before you get cows in?"

Bill nodded and the three of them went round to the kitchen via the laundry, still chuckling.

"So you found her a bathing costume then," said Dulcie.

- 0 -

It was half way through August and the days were getting longer. Dulcie was relieved; it meant she could sew for longer in natural light, tackling the tricky bits of Jess's bridesmaid's costume which she couldn't manage in lamplight. She was sitting by the window in the kitchen one afternoon, thimbles on her right little pinky and its neighbour, struggling with her implements to join the crown of the bonnet to its stiffened brim. Young Johnny was sleeping; Jess and Jilly were outside playing. Bill had not long since started milking. So engrossed was she in her task that it was a while before she realized the persistent lowing she could hear was very close. She lifted her head to listen, conscious immediately that the animal was in distress. She quickly placed her needlework on the sheet spread over the table and looked out of the kitchen window, taking the thimbles off as she did so, dropping them into her sewing tin. There was nothing to be seen out there. She went down into the laundry and saw the cow at once, on the other side of the fence at the foot of Mervyn's two Cherry Penda trees. The animal was clearly in the throes of travail. She withdrew and went to look in on Johnny. *"He'd sleep through World War III, he would,"* she thought as she left, pulling the bedroom door to.

"There's a cow calving over by the house," she said in response to Bill's enquiring look as she entered the milking shed. "Have you seen the girls?"

"Jilly's over by the cream house," he said, "jumping up and down on that spongy bit they like so much."

"And Jess?"

"Haven't seen her darling, but she can't be far off."

"I'll just go and see Jilly, maybe she knows."

Bill was right as it happened; Jess wasn't far off at all. She was up the Cherry Pendas near where the first branches sprouted from the trunks, about in line with the guttering around the roof of the house. The idea of climbing

230

these two trees in a crabwise fashion had come to her whilst sitting on the concrete slab of the laundry one day, on her own, looking out at them, banned from going down to the swimming hole, feeling a bit bored with everything else she could think of doing. Since then she had put quite a bit of time into perfecting her climbing technique which involved first exerting pressure with the palms of her hands on each of the trunks to take her weight, hold herself in position whilst she lifted her legs and pushed with the soles of her feet to hold herself in a crablike crouch from which she straightened up, allowing her hands to take over again further up the trees. She'd discovered it didn't take too many repetitions of this hands-then-feet manoeuvre before she was right up there where the branches started growing. She also discovered to her chagrin, that it was a lot easier to climb up than it was to come down and she'd nearly come a cropper a couple of times.

At this very moment she had her knees locked to brace the soles of her feet against the two trunks and peered down upon the labouring cow. She'd been stuck up there for some time but coming back down was the last thing she had in mind. Although inconvenienced she was fascinated by the cow and its antics. At first it had just stood there, bellowing in complaint, its eyes rolling in its head which it tossed up and down and from side to side. At first she thought the cow really angry about something, but as it just stood its ground without butting the trees or ramming the fence she changed her mind and thought maybe it was in pain. When the animal went down on its front knees, and then rolled onto its side she knew right away something was wrong; a big, dark, shiny thing started coming out of its bottom. 'Boy, that cow's really constipated,' she thought, watching as the cow pushed this big poo out, bellowing loudly without pause.

And then, all at once, in the silence which came with the cow's successful evacuation, Jess became aware of voices calling to her. She looked up and saw Mummy over by the cream shed with Jilly. Mummy had her hands cupped around her mouth as she called out across the south paddock. Jilly was just jumping up and down and yelling, "Jess, where are you?" She called out to them and waved. They didn't hear or see her the first time so she gave it another go, suddenly acutely aware that she was getting really tired. This time Mummy turned and waved back, and she looked back down

231

at the now silent cow. She was so astounded by what was happening below she almost fell. The cow was on its feet again and licking away at the dark, shiny mound on the grass and it wasn't a big poo at all. The head was the first thing she saw, just lying there, all bedraggled. But then, as the shiny stuff was licked away, she saw its body and legs, and the shiny stuff was left to one side like a glistening puddle as the cow nudged its baby into life, pushing it unceremoniously into its first, spindly, wonky steps. When Daddy rode up on one of the horses she could hardly speak, partly from tiredness and partly because of the event she had just witnessed. He stood in his stirrups, and with a smile and a "Come on lovey, come to me," he reached up to grip her under the arms and bring her down onto the saddle in front of him where he settled her comfortably so that she could still see to watch what was taking place. They sat there in silence, inveigled by this timeless ritual of mother introducing her newborn to the demands of the wide open world, to food. The calf grew stronger by the minute and was soon using the knowledge with which it had been born to suck instinctively, if clumsily at first, at its mother's udder. That was when Bill decided to turn the horse that few steps towards the laundry where Dulcie and Jilly had been watching proceedings with equal interest. He dropped Jess off into her Mam's care.

"Did you lick us when you borned us, Mummy?"

"No darling," Dulcie smiled, as she ruffled Jess's hair, "Human beings are a little bit different to cows, lovey, but we do show our young uns where to get their tucker quick smart, just like that cow did."

"Yeah, like Johnny does," said Jilly, very matter-of-factly.

- 0 -

September arrived and Dulcie expected Mavis and Reg would soon pay one of their Saturday visits. There was a lot happening and timing was of the essence. She said as much to Bill one evening, as she was putting the finishing touches to Jess's wedding bonnet. Glad had been on a shopping expedition to Cairns with her Dad and come back with some lovely pieces of trim, amongst which was satin ribbon of the perfect blue for Jess's outfit.

"I had a perfectly marvelous time Dulcie, with a Miss Myrtle Lavern in the *Millinery, Haberdashery, and Drapery* department at Armstrong, Ledlie and

Stillman's; couldn't have managed without her. You must have seen it Dulcie, in Lake Street, next to the Hides Hotel?" Glad said when she delivered the bounty to Dulcie, "And I took the opportunity to tell Jack Savage at the top gate about the possible difficulties for guests on the day of the wedding." Dulcie had smiled at Glad's rampant exuberance, a side of her she'd not seen before.

Tonight Dulcie hoped to finish securing the narrower ribbon to each side of the bonnet to be tied under the chin, and to sew the wider bands into the side seams of the gown to be tied at the waist at the back. She would use enough ribbon for a double bow and long tails.

"I thought Mavis and Reg might drop in one Saturday soon, darling. Have you heard owt?"

Bill looked up from the paper in which he had been engrossed, "Sorry love, what was that?" He put the paper on the table and flexed his shoulders, rotating them backwards and then forwards. He'd been up in the corn field for most of the day, "hilling" the plants which were coming on "pretty good" according to George who'd added, "Another month she'll be ready to harvest." The physical demands of the day were taking their toll, and he stifled a yawn as his eyes met Dulcie's.

"I just wondered whether you'd seen Reg or Mavis, and whether they might be planning a visit soon," Dulcie repeated. She had little regular contact with anyone really, beyond Bill and her clutch of children to whose daily needs her time was devoted.

"No, love, I haven't. I rarely see Mavis any road, and Reg wasn't about when I went in to the butter factory the other day. As you know, I'd not a lot of time to go looking for him, Curly needing ute in a hurry. I'll make time to ride over in next few days and see how they're placed, if you like. There's something he brought up last time he was here I wouldn't mind the opportunity to discuss with him further now I come to think of it."

"Right; well, I remember Mavis saying September was an important month in the garden, love, for some reason. Can't afford to miss the boat, can we?" she said.

Bill rose to stoke the fire and put the kettle on, "You won't be long with that will you, darling? Cup of tea and bed is all I'm good for."

"You look all in, love. I saw you and George up in the corn field. Hard work was it?"

"Aye, love, it was, and George tells me that overhauling the hammer mill, that's next on the agenda apparently, will be, in his words, a bit of a mongrel which doesn't rightly inspire one with enthusiasm for the task."

"What on earth is 'ammer mill? Windmill is what I thought we 'ad," said Dulcie, cutting the thread and securing the needle in her pin cushion with finality.

"You'll bloody well know about it when we get it going, I can tell you love," Bill poured boiling water over the tealeaves, "it's over in grain shed, purpose being to turn the corn harvest into feed for pigs."

At the sound of those two words, corn harvest, she forgot to chastise his cursing and Glad's words when setting the date for the wedding came flooding back …….. *Sometime in October after the winter corn harvest* ……….. it was a rum country, and no mistake, and the wedding was almost upon them. She stood up and went to the pantry to get the biscuit jar as Bill poured. They enjoyed a nice biscuit for supper.

The next morning Curly came over with a message from Reg Johnston. Dulcie invited him in for a cuppa but he declined, "Got to get back to factory," he said, "what with Reg being away. He wanted me to let you know he and Mavis have gone down to Cairns," he said, "should be back next week some time. He said you'd understand, and that they'll pop in on Saturday week, orright."

Dulcie thanked him for his trouble and smiled, nothing more.

"Say G'Day to Bill for me, Dulce," he said as he hopped behind the steering wheel of the ute. She stood in the turnabout and waved him farewell, as was their custom.

- 0 -

Just as the 'homestead', and the farm environment generally bore no resemblance to those bucolic idylls reproduced in all their pastel glory on a plethora of "Ye Olde" calendars back home, neither did the spring harvest of the corn invoke visions of pastoral bliss. From Bill's point of view it was plain hard work and not without its share of unpleasant surprises. Dulcie, to her repugnance, shared in the first of these when Bill came in for lunch after his first morning's harvesting. After hanging his machete high on a nail in the laundry he was about to wrestle his gumboots off when Dulcie greeted him from the back door, "You're late coming in for lunch, love. Come in here and I'll help you off with those boots before you scrub up. I've had my lunch, too hungry to wait I was."

Having come into the kitchen and sitting himself down on the end of the bench he held one leg out before him, supported behind the knee by his intertwined hands. Dulcie gripped the gumboot at the back of his ankle with her right hand and pulled it towards her while pushing the sole away from her at the top with her left hand. After a little bit of jiggling the boot slid off in one fluid movement to reveal a blood streaked leg, clinging to which were several slimy black, "Aaaaggghhhhh, leeches!" she cried, leaping back, repulsed.

"Bloody hell, so that's what he was talking about. Salt, Dulcie, salt — quick, get the salt love."

Dulcie fled to the pantry and returned armed with a blue container of salt. She pulled out the pouring spout and handed it to him. He wasted no time in sprinkling it lavishly on the leeches clinging to the front of his lower leg. They immediately shriveled and dropped off, onto the lino.

"See how they run, alright," said Bill with satisfaction.

"Thank goodness for that. It works."

They worked feverishly together to get the other boot off followed by every last stitch of his clothing so he ended up in the bollocky buff while Dulcie administered liberal sprinklings of salt to every last slug that clung to his body. Getting rid of the leeches was one thing, but stopping the bleeding was quite another. Ignoring that fact he scrubbed up in the laundry before standing in front of the stove to keep warm while Dulcie went to get fresh clothes, not trusting the ones now tossed onto the laundry floor to be free of the parasites.

"How long is this going to go on for?" Dulcie asked as he sat eating his lunch, "You're not going up there again today, surely?" The leeches had all been swept up into the dustpan and thrown into the fire and she was just finishing mopping the floor.

"Don't worry, Dulcie, plurry leeches are just a fact of life around here apparently. I don't understand what George says to me half the time, as you know, and it wasn't until we saw the little bleeders clinging to my leg that the penny dropped – he warned me about them this morning; that's how I knew about using salt. Salt or the tip of a burning cigarette's what he said. And they're insidious little sods, I didn't feel a thing you know, not a thing; except disgust at the sight 'em gorging on my body." He shook off a shudder and took another mouthful of his sandwich, "Anyway, we'll not be cropping this afternoon, just bringing today's harvest down to the barn; George says we'll be done by end of week, sooner if Bruce can help out one morning."

"Thank heavens for small mercies, I suppose," said Dulcie. "Speaking of which, I'm glad Jilly didn't wake up during that performance love. Bit of a shock to the system that would have been, seeing you with blood streaming from your body like that." She took the bucket down to the laundry, washed her hands before coming back. She turned the teapot three times, absent-mindedly, before pouring their tea, "I wonder how come the girls haven't come across 'em," she said, hoping it would stay that way.

A couple of days later, Bill was standing on the sheets of newspaper Dulcie now laid on the laundry floor for the de-leeching ritual and recounting to her the highlight of his morning.

"Well, I'm really getting the hang of it now, Dulce; getting into the rhythm, so to speak, and concentrating on my technique to improve my yield from a single cropping spot."

"Oh, aye," said Dulcie, sprinkling salt liberally on the only daily crop she had anything to do with.

"Aye, and I'm improving all the time. This morning I must have reaped nigh on forty ear of corn from same spot when, blow me down, the earth moved beneath me."

"Give over," said Dulcie, "what on earth are you on about? I think this regular loss of blood is affecting your senses, Bill Johnson. That I do."

"I kid you not, Dulce. Except of course it wasn't the earth at all. I'd stood for a good ten minutes or more on a plurry carpet snake."

"Bloody Nora," Dulcie exclaimed, to his obvious amusement.

"That's not like you, Dulcie."

"Ye gods! Some things'd make a saint swear, they would; it would have scared me out my wits, poisonous or not," Dulcie retorted.

"I wasn't exactly calm at the time mysel', believe you me, it were a right big booger," he said, chuckling. "State I was in, I'd no idea it was only a carpet snake, not right away. George and Bruce wondered what the plurry hell was going on, I can tell you. I'm surprised you didn't hear the commotion yourself, love."

"I've been out back most of the morning; washing, chopping wood. Whatever next," she said as she went in to put the salt back in the pantry. "So, what on earth did you do about it?" she asked as she came back to put his morning's clothes into the water simmering in the copper.

"Well, they identified it right off but Bruce still found it hard to overcome his natural desire to shoot it," Bill said, bending to prod the newspaper parcel containing the detritus of the de-leeching operation into the fire under the copper. "George's inclination was to sic one of the dogs onto it, shepherd it down to the barn where it could do some good he reckoned," he stood up, "but by the time they'd made up their minds to just let it be, it had vanished anyway and we got back to work."

They turned towards the kitchen together, "We were all plurry careful where we put our feet after that I can tell you, but we got on with it; we'll be finished tomorrow according to George and I can't say as I'll be sorry to see the back of it."

- 0 -

Saturday was a day made in heaven. It was bitterly cold when Bill and Dulcie rose to perform their ablutions in the lamp-lit kitchen while the fire in the stove got going and the water in the kettle came to the boil sending Jilly's 'dogs' of steam rushing from the spout to disintegrate slowly as they drifted lazily upwards. They sat together sharing a pot of tea until Old Bronc's swaying lantern appeared off in the distance through the kitchen window signifying time to round up the cows. They embraced lightly before he set off and Dulcie turned her attention to preparing for the ritual of Johnny's early morning feed. The day before, Old Bronc had given Bill a nice bit of ham and she looked forward to preparing ham and eggs for them all for breakfast,

237

a rare treat since they had decided to tighten the belt in order to get a bit of money put aside. It was a challenge that, something always seemed to need doing for farm's upkeep and it always cost money.

Breakfast was but a memory and a fresh batch of scones were cooling nicely on the work bench when the unmistakable thrumming of the cattle grid sent the girls rushing out of the front door, squealing in eager anticipation of Mavis's arrival. Bill rode into the turnabout from the south paddock just ahead of their visitors and tethered Big Red to the rail by the milking shed. There were big smiles and greetings all round but when Reg went round to help Mavis down and leaned back to bring out the basket the girls were suddenly tongue-tied. This wasn't the first time they'd seen such a basket.

"So who have we here?" asked Dulcie as she peered in at the sleeping child.

"This is Roger girls," said Mavis, smiling as Reg held the basket lower for Jess and Jilly to have a look, "he was two weeks old yesterday."

"Come on, let's get him indoors out of this sun or he'll wake up and start demanding attention," said Reg, and they each took something to help Mavis with the rest of her paraphernalia and went back inside.

"There's a bottle of beer in amongst that lot, Bill," said Reg, "thought we should maybe wet the baby's head once the sun is over the yard arm. Not had the opportunity to do that as yet; what do you say?"

And so, after a nice morning tea in the warmth of the kitchen, Bill and Reg sat out on the log out front and enjoyed a beer and the long overdue chat they'd promised themselves on a previous encounter. Jess and Jilly soon grew tired of admiring baby Roger and retired to their room to munch through their bounty of Redskins and Choo Choo Bars and discuss this sudden, and not entirely welcome turn of events – "Aunty Mavis didn't even get fat," observed Jess around the top end of a Choo Choo Bar which was resisting her vigorous efforts to separate it into more 'choo'-able pieces. In the kitchen, Mavis covered the events of the past few weeks in the detail required to satisfy Dulcie's avid thirst for news. Her subsequent inspection of progress in the garden earned their efforts a high commendation.

"You're looking marvelous, Mavis," Dulcie said as they came in from the garden, "having a family suits you, make no mistake."

It was over all too soon for Dulcie but they'd see one another soon enough this time, and a lot of others besides.

"See you at the wedding," were their parting words as Reg drove the Model T out of the turnabout and down the track towards Old Bronc's place on the way out.

- 0 -

The day of the wedding was an absolute purler, a real knockout, bit of a stunner.

"Smarvelous day; knew what she was doing when she set date for wedding, did Glad, eh," Dulcie said as they all tucked in to their porridge that morning.

She'd spent best part of the week preparing their outfits, sorting through the trunk for hers and Bills glad rags, much steaming, airing and pressing; hanging them in neat batches on coat-hangers from the line Bill had put up across the corner in the front room, near Johnny's cot. Jess's outfit, which included a brand new pair of pale blue patent leather shoes and matching socks from Glad, was up at Glad's place. Curly would come by to take her there at around ten o'clock, to get ready with the rest of the bridal party. Jilly was to wear a lovely frock which Jess had only worn once or twice to her dancing classes back in Birmingham, and Jess's white sandals which now fitted her perfectly. Dulcie had found a clean almost new pair of white socks, set them across the sandals in readiness.

The girls raced off after breakfast to do their chores and Dulcie prepared a tub for them, knowing she'd be a lot happier when their hair was not only clean, which it usually was, but also tangle free which it usually wasn't, especially Jess's which was so thick and curly combing it didn't seem to make a blind bit of difference and therefore wasn't worth the aggravation. Nevertheless, she didn't want any daughter of hers being shown up, well aware as she was, of the importance of appearances in the social scheme of things. She needn't have worried. The buzz of excitement with which they'd all woken remained with them, and carried the girls through their rigorous grooming entirely without complaint.

The day passed in a blur of activity, leaving each of them with indelible relics in their minds eye. The sight of Glad emerging on the hand of Ray Watson from the back of an elegant white automobile which Bill was quick to identify as a Studebaker, cream of the Cairns Tableland Motor Service fleet; "She's a beauty," he'd said as Dulcie tugged on his sleeve to motivate him towards the church as the rest of the bridal party was assisted from the back seat; the familiarity of the ceremony which bound Glad to her beloved Denis til death would them part, conducted before family and friends close in number to the population of the town. The part they had been invited to play in proceedings, and the consideration with which they found themselves treated, brought home with vivid simplicity to Bill and Dulcie how different was the world they now inhabited; the readiness with which they had been accepted being no small part of that difference, though it did not go unnoticed that those who chose to really befriend them were relative newcomers to the town themselves, except of course for the Watsons, whose conscientious recognition of the obligation imposed on them by Old Bronc's guile had laid the very foundation of their new life. By the time the happy couple left the church there wasn't a dry eye in the house; the high emotion occasioned for many by the memory of Marge Watson's burial earlier in the year.

After the service everyone made their way, some by car or ute, others by horseback, dray or sulky, to the big marquee set up in the front garden of the Watson homestead. A hearty lunch, of ham and chicken pie with new potatoes and a big salad of mixed variety, was washed down with copious jugs of beer which flowed freely from the barrel set up on a trestle in the corner, transported from the pub and set up by Old Bronc though he was no longer to be seen. There was sherry for the ladies for the toast, and lemonade for the children. For pudding they had individual homemade cocktail fruit jelly and custard trifle and after the cutting of the cake, the kids all went out for an organised game of hide and seek and tea was dispensed from enormous teapots, and the adults settled in for a good chin wag.

Bill and Dulcie found themselves in the immediate company of Reg and Mavis, George Kinnear and his wife, and Mary and David Baxter, Glad's friends from Mission Beach. David Baxter's blindness was immediately evident. It was also clear that he and Reg knew one another well.

Dulcie recalled, with a new understanding, Glad's earlier concern for their travel arrangements. "Good to see you and your friends made it to the Bottom Gate in time," she said to Mary.

"Oh, but we didn't," said Mary, "we had to stop twice to put water in the radiator. Muriel and Ernest were so apologetic. We were a good fifteen minutes late by Ernest's watch so we really thought we'd missed everything. It was a close thing though. Although the chap at the Bottom Gate was expecting us, he said five more minutes and he'd simply have had to close the gate and signal through to Top Gate as we'd not shown up."

"Did I just hear you say they kept the Bottom Gate open for you, Mary?" a fellow sitting a bit further along enquired, leaning forward to engage Mary's attention.

"You don't miss much, do you Harry?" said Reg, "Have you met everyone here mate?"

"Yeah, I have," said Harry, smiling now at Dulcie and Bill, "You might not remember me, but I was on the job when youse came in from Tolga last year."

"Dulcie and Bill, meet Harry Melvern," said Reg, "one of the stokers on the local rail line."

Amid murmurs of acknowledgement Mary said, "You heard right enough, Harry. A good fifteen minutes I reckon he gave us."

"Well I know Glad spoke to Jack Savage, Top Gate keeper, a while back and he'd given her the nod, so to speak, about coming up with suitable arrangements for possible latecomers," said Dulcie.

"That's bloody marvelous, that is," said Harry, "and I mean that sincerely." He laughed, "Ha! Same Jack Savage as accommodated your tardiness gets a big kick out of relating with great satisfaction how he refused entry to the highway to none other than the Bishop of North Queensland; and he was only fifteen minutes late, as I recall."

"Give over," said Dulcie, "did he really?"

"Yeah," said Harry, "according to Jack, this geyser just turned up, said who he was and demanded access to the highway, pontificating about the importance of presenting himself at some meeting down the hill. God knows whether Jack could have assisted; but the bishop certainly didn't and his bombast got him nowhere."

"So, there but for the grace of Glad, you reckon, eh Harry?" said David.

"Ha, ha! Too right mate," said Harry, "that's what it's all about, eh? Bishop Shawl, I think the bloke's name was. Talk about no idea. During the two and three quarter hours he had to kill he decided to settle in at the Lake Barrine Guesthouse from which he rang the Queensland Main Roads Office and reported Jack for insolence. Jack knows this because Mrs. Curry, who runs the guesthouse, rang him and reported the conversation."

"So what did he do," asked Mary, cheerfully expectant.

"According to Jack, the Bishop was at head of the queue when time came to open the gates and he took particular pleasure in getting through the formalities, you know all that stuff they have to record about road usage, as slowly as reasonably possible; ha ha …….. Revenge is sweet, eh."

"Well, I'm pleased it's not just about Who you know," said Mary, casting her eyes to the heavens, and they all laughed.

Bill and George polished off their beer as the laughter died down and excused themselves from the table. It was time to round the cows up for milking and the dynamic in the marquee was changing. People not on the milking detail decided to disperse for a while, stretch their legs, all the better to enjoy the planned evening festivities – there was to be music and dancing, singing around the campfire, a bush poet to entertain them.

"This is what makes the world go round," thought Dulcie as she and Mavis headed for the house where a temporary crèche had been set up, knowing full well they would find hungry mouths to feed. "We'll be back to old clothes and porridge on the morrow."

– 0 –

"Beneath the trees where nobody sees
They'll hide and seek as long as they please

242

Cause that's the way the teddy bears have their picnic."

Jess was singing as she made her way up the rise behind the windmill to her special cubby house which was really just a bush which hid her from the world but still let her see everything around her. Although she could swim now and was allowed to go down to the creek with the other kids, she didn't feel like it today. It had rained during the week and the water in the creek had still looked muddy when she came home from school. Jilly was playing with Johnny and she didn't have much homework so she thought she'd just come up here and have a bit of a think. She crawled inside and lay on her tummy, briefly fascinated by the pattern cut into her forearms by sharp blades of sunlight. A raucous squawking of cockatoos passed low overhead and she wondered idly what would happen if one of them were to suddenly die. Would it just drop out of sky? She didn't think so; she'd never seen one plummeting to earth, or just lying around, dead. So what happened to them? Her attention now drawn skywards she saw clouds drifting steadily overhead and rolled onto her back to see if they were making faces. She had just spotted a dog floating by when she heard the thrumming of the cattle grid and turned her head to see Curly's ute advancing slowly past Old Bronc's place. "Probably Daddy," she thought, looking back up to the sky. The dog had quite gone.

Images in the scudding clouds completely eluded her and she was tiring of the pastime when a loud noise rent the air. Just like that cow when it was having its calf. The hair on her arms stood on end as she rolled over to peer in the direction from which it had come. She saw Daddy standing in the turnabout with his arms around Mummy but she seemed to be fighting him off, trying to get away from him. The sound came up to her again and she saw in the hand Daddy put around Mummy's shoulders a piece of yellow paper, fluttering in the breeze. Scrambling out from under her bush she ran down the hill as fast as she could.

- 0 -

His stomach clenched when the eye-shaded clerk in the Post Office handed him the TELEGRAM. He walked outside to hide in the bright

243

sunshine, braced himself for bad news about his father as he opened it. The utterly unexpected news it contained however shocked him to the core and he carried it home like a dull ache, a precursor to the terrible pain he knew it would inflict.

Dulcie came through the front gate to meet him as usual but her welcoming smile slipped sideways as she beheld the pinched pallor beneath the tan she had become so accustomed to, the trembling lopsided lips over which he so obviously sought control. "Whatever is it, darling? Is everything alright?" she asked as she reached for him.

"Ah Dulcie, I'm sorry darling," he put his arms about her, "There's no easy way to tell you. It's your Mom, love. She took poorly and died on Monday."

Chapter Eight

The eye of the beholder ....

*J*ess gazed at him fixedly, her large, solemn eyes swimming with the mellow yellow light of the Tilley lamp. Jilly had dozed off to sleep but he sensed in Jess's alertness something other than interest or absorption in the tale he had been telling them of the three little English boys who went on an adventure to Abergavenny, a Welsh town down in the West Country, as their family called it. A town with no factories, but with a splendid castle alongside which ran a brook whose waters worked the watermill down in Mill Street, tripping busily through the huge waterwheel on the side of the mill and providing hours of fascination from their favourite vantage point on the bridge. It was a town with clean, fresh air where they climbed the big apple tree in their front yard for fun as well as for the fruit it bore, where they went clot fishing in Spring and caught eels the size of a man's arm, where they learned to swim in the River Usk, where they were scared, at first, of the sheep being driven up the main street by whistling farmers and their canny dogs, and where they sometimes hid underneath the kitchen table to keep an eye on their 'new' Mom as she sat crying, unaware of their presence and grieving the absence of her own son, her own son who had left home and gone with all his mates to serve his King and country and who had gone missing, which meant no-one knew where he was any more.

He had just got to the bit where the boys were going to bed, in a big bed like Jess and Jilly shared, in a room high in the house with a tiny window high above their bed through which they could sometimes see the moon and wonder if Mom, their real Mom that is, could see it too.

"Will Mommy be alright, Daddy?" Jess interrupted the story.

"Of course she will kiddiewinks, don't you worry about that," he said, patting the back of her hand, "she just needs a bit of time to adjust."

"What do you mean, ajust?"

249

"Just to get used to things, that's all lovey, just to get used to things the way they are now like. Come on now," he drew the covers up high around her chin, "shut those peepers. I'll finish the story some other time. Time for sleep or you'll be late getting up for school in the morning." They kissed one another on the cheek before Bill picked up the Tilley lamp and left, pulling the door gently to behind him.

He went down into the kitchen to put the kettle on. Looking back he saw the strip of light under the door to his own bedroom, a room where he found himself awkward, ill at ease, uncomfortable with the stranger Dulcie had become these past two weeks. He took her a cup of tea before going back out to set things in order in the milking shed and found her suckling the babe. He felt, not for the first time, genuine gratitude for the care and attention she continued to give the lad.

He had witnessed Dulcie's grief when they'd lost their third child. At that time, out of their shared sorrow, he had found the means to comfort her, but nothing could have prepared him for the vehemence with which she had reacted when she learned of Edith's death; so much grief, and something else in abundance besides, was it anger? Was it guilt? She had pummeled him unknowingly, unseeingly, unaware that he had put himself between her and the iron walls of the milking shed, finally ceasing only when utterly spent, hardly able to hold herself upright. How they had managed to get through the first night and day he couldn't recall, but thereafter he had found himself a stranger, cut off by Dulcie from all but the polite communication demanded by ingrained good manners in those who shared the same table, if share it she did. In bed a no man's land yawned between them and he felt bitter pangs of loneliness and rejection to which she had never before subjected him. His impotency to offer her succour weighed heavily on him.

- 0 -

Dulcie sat next morning on the end of the tousled bed with the baby to her breast, unkempt, numbed by the grief that had consumed her since Bill had brought her news of her mother's death. She cast a baleful eye over the scene revealed beneath the corrugated iron awning and recoiled from the barren wasteland before her, not a living soul in sight, nothing to divert her

250

from her vile misery, no kin with whom to share the burden of her loss; nothing. The void reminded her with a poignant clarity of all that she had forsaken, family and friends gone, maybe forever. During the last couple of weeks, enervated by her condition, she had sought solitude, welcomed it, but now as she succumbed to loneliness, depression settled upon her, absorbed all that was once good in her, sucking her dry. Chores took such a gargantuan effort she did a bare minimum. She met young Johnny's needs instinctively. Providing food for the family was a different matter, often more than she could manage. As a result they had more than their fair share of porridge or bread and vegemite for tea. Bill took Jilly out with him in the mornings and the girls whispered to one another in their bedroom when Jess got home from school, their customary playfulness having deserted them. As Dulcie retreated into herself, the simplicity of her existence made daily survival possible but she found herself spiraling down, sucked into the self-perpetuating emotional deprivation of utter solitude from which escape grew increasingly less desirable, increasingly difficult. Only the needs of her baby bound her to the outside world.

Then fate took yet another hand.

She was out the back chopping kindling, intent on the task, oblivious of what day of the week it was, and aware only vaguely that it was afternoon. A shrill scream rent the air followed quickly by a second and the cocoon into which she had meticulously woven herself was pierced, letting in a suddenly frightening reality. She lifted her head as a frisson of alarm slithered up her forearms raising goose bumps. Further screams came from the direction of Old Bronc's place. "That's Jess," she breathed, and was galvanised into action. Gripping the axe tightly in her right hand, she raced around the side of the house and through the front gate. Jess's cries got clearer and from the turnabout Dulcie could see her, waving both arms and running for all her might along the track towards home. Letting out a bloodcurdling yell Dulcie waved the axe in the air and took off towards her.

"Jess, Jess," she called out as she ran, "It's alright lovey, I'm coming."

Dulcie threw the axe on the ground as they reached one another, stretched her arms out and gathered her daughter up into her arms.

"Whatever is it, lovely? What's happened? Are you hurt? Have you been bitten? What is it?"

Jess's chest was heaving but she shook her head and managed to get out between sobs, "It was a man, Mummy...... in the trees up near Old Bronc's place," she pointed and paused. "He had nothing on." She was again wracked by sobs and Dulcie hugged her to her chest and patted her back, "There, there, darling. There, there."

"He called out to me Mummy and when I looked I could see he was bare and he had a big willy with a safety pin right through it and it looked horrible, and I felt scared so I just started running as fast as I could."

"You're a good girl Jess. You did the right thing, love. He didn't get anywhere near you did he darling?"

"No Mummy, I ran away as fast as I could."

"Good girl," Dulcie balanced Jess on her hip and jiggled her up and down and patted her back rhythmically as she peered towards Old Bronc's place, scrutinising the copse of trees but seeing nothing out of the ordinary. "Come on then, darling. Let's get you inside. I'll make you some nice warm milk and then we'll find Daddy. He'll take care of things. Do you think you can walk, darling? You're a bit heavy for me to carry all that way."

Dulcie put Jess down, stooped to pick up the axe and they turned towards home just as Bill crossed the turnabout with Jilly running on ahead of him.

Once the bush telegraph kicked into operation, the upshot of this frightening, though blessedly passive ambush was a visit from the local copper to get a description of the man and the exact nature of the incident. He left with information almost as scanty as the miscreant's attire but reported back the following day that a worker from the abattoir at Mareeba had been apprehended over in Tumoulin the previous evening after having exposed his person to a young girl on a property just out of the township, similarly secured, not skewered as medical examination of the offending appendage had revealed, by a large safety pin. The girl's mother was the proud owner of a recently installed telephone and had been quick to report the incident. As a result, the perpetrator was waylaid on the edge of the property by the police, in one of the abattoir's delivery vehicles. His lack of a credible reason for being there led police to search the vehicle, and a plentiful supply of his favoured ligature was discovered on the dashboard. It was all it took to convince the local constabulary to take him in for questioning.

Although they were all shaken by the experience, it actually brought Dulcie back whence she had withdrawn; a return accepted by them all without comment or question though a collective sigh of relief stole through the house as they once more felt the warmth of her love. They each welcomed it back silently; as if any utterance would scare it off again.

This triumph of good over evil conspired to Dulcie's good in other ways too; though one only called a win by the coppers 'good' in sympathetic company, and 'evil' was rather too strong a word for the perpetrator who, after copious interviews and, finally, an examination by a psychologist brought up from Cairns, was deemed, according to Curly, "just that bit short of the full quid," or as George put it, "a roo loose in the top paddock." On hearing the news Dulcie just shook her head and asserted that he'd no place carrying on like that regardless and summat would have to be done about him.

Incidents of the sort were rare in the area and news of the "Safety-Pin Flasher", and his subsequent capture, was quick to get around, the latter making ribald parody of the former possible amongst workers at the butter factory and the saw mill, especially among those to whom the pub was the first port of call after work. At the outset however, for purposes quite different, Curly was quick to tell Reg who mentioned it to Mavis who immediately dispatched, via Curly, a message to Dulcie not to worry too much about things, that she would come to visit just as soon as she could. It had been too long.

If Jess's ordeal had served to bring Dulcie back to the present, dispelling the jaundiced view which had danced attendance on her grief, Mavis's note opened her eyes to the sorry state into which she had let their home fall and she set about making reparations. Her efforts restored more than domestic order. She felt the lingering vestiges of her inner gloom dissipate with the dust and cobwebs, the activity replenishing rather than draining her. It took her a good couple of days and when she finished she surveyed her handiwork with a critical eye. Satisfied that 'appearances' would be 'kept up', she made a fresh pot of tea and took her cup out the front to sit on the log and take in the warmth of another beautiful day. It had been an early, solid downpour which had forced Jess to take the long way home on the day of her misadventure and as Dulcie now observed, the silver filigree of winter grass had vanished beneath the lush green of resurgent pasture. The bright, light sunshine lifted her spirits. For a brief moment the smoking factory chimneys of home came to mind, renewing her pleasure in being right here, where she was.

If only it wasn't so very far away ….. "*but that was part of its original attraction, after all,*" she thought with a deep sigh.

- 0 -

Reg drove Mavis over on the Monday morning, and did more than a couple of runs from the car to get Roger indoors with all of his paraphernalia; treats for the girls, "Just some milk bottles and false teeth," said Mavis, "We'll keep those for later, when Jess gets home," said Dulcie taking advantage of Jilly's preoccupation with Roger in the front room to stash the lollies in the larder. Mavis, bountiful as ever, unpacked loaves of bread, peas and beans from the garden, a pot of jam, a handsome piece of matured cheddar cheese, "Reg bought that for you when we were down in Cairns the other week Dulce. He knows how you like your cheese! I do so like having a refrigerator, Dulce; what a difference, eh?" and so on. Reg drove back via Foresters Track to pass the time of day with Bill and George before setting off back to work, "For a rest!" saying he'd be back around three to pick Mavis up.

After lunch, Jilly went down for her nap, and Bill rejoined George in the top paddock where they were working on the perimeter fence. Dulcie put the kettle on to make a fresh pot of tea.

"I'm worried about you, Dulcie," Mavis came straight out with it, "and it's not just this business with Jess that concerns me either, though I know it must have given you a nasty scare. I bumped into Nancy in town the other day and she says you haven't been down to play cards with them since the wedding and it's not for lack of invites or reminders. According to her Bill's gotten uncharacteristically vague lately which is never a good omen as far as she's concerned, and she said Jess was looking a bit peaky before all

254

this business with that wretched loony happened." Mavis paused for breath, unconsciously gripping the edge of the table, watching Dulcie intently.

Dulcie remained silent; her hand trembled slightly as she poured hot water into the pot to warm it.

"And I wouldn't be saying any of this except you're looking more than a bit peaky yourself, Dulce. You've lost weight, I can see it. I don't mean to be a busybody but if there's anything wrong that I could help with I do so hope you'd tell me, Dulcie. Your friendship has been such a comfort to me."

Dulcie turned from the basin where she had emptied the hot water from the teapot, "Thank you, Mavis, I appreciate your concern. I, er," her lips trembled and a large tear rolled down her cheek; she caught it with her tongue at the corner of her mouth. "I'm sorry, Mavis. I'll be alright. It's just," she snuffled an errant gobbet back into her nostril and wiped the end of her nose with the back of her hand, "I just need a," she dug her hanky out of her skirt pocket and blew hard into it. "I'm sorry Mavis, but my Mom died and it was such a shock and I miss her so much just knowing that she's gone, and….."

Mavis leapt up and hugged Dulcie to her, "Oh, Dulcie. Oh, my. Oh my Goodness. Oh God, I'm so sorry. You poor love," she said, all in a rush, rubbing and patting Dulcie's back the while, rocking them both to and fro.

After a time Dulcie cleared her throat and straightened up, saying, "Thank you, lovey, but if you don't stop that you'll have me puking up my lunch all over you," and they giggled soggily. "I'm on the mend Mavis, believe you me. I've been through a bad patch, that much is true but that loony, as you call him, helped bring me round, no mistake. You just let me make the tea now and pull myself together. I've been so looking forward to seeing you."

A short while later they sat opposite one another at the table, nursing their pannikins of tea.

"I knew when I left that it would be a long time before I might see her again." Dulcie paused to steady herself. "But I didn't consider that I would never see her again; no, not for a moment did I think that."

They drank.

"Coming out here was a hard decision, Mavis, but we believed then and we believe now that it is for the best. It's not that I have regrets, not at all. But all the same, it's hard. It's nothing like I imagined and there's a lot I miss, and …." She quelled the quaver in her voice with a cough.

"I'm sure there is, Dulcie." Mavis was quick to respond, squeezing Dulcie's hand gently as she continued, "Would it help to talk about it, love? You've never really said much about your family or your life back in England. I'd be interested to hear, really I would. My life has been so ordinary compared with yours. You grew up in Manchester, didn't you?"

"Aye, in Oldham," pronouncing it All-dom. "Owdom, as my Aunt Dora used to say. But it's part of Greater Manchester, you're right love," Dulcie paused in reflection. "Why they called the household linen section of these department stores Manchester we could never work out. Cotton industry started in Oldham it did, and it's still strongest there. But might is right, I suppose, and we not going to change that in a hurry are we?"

"You were born there then?"

"Aye, I was love. First house I remember was at 244 West Street right in middle of Oldham. It was right near Featherstall Road where all the big bus stations were and I remember it were dead opposite a pub called The Globe. Nothing like the Malanda Hotel, Mavis. It were a small brick building and there was no drinking on the footpath outside of there I can tell you. Men were pleased to drink their ale indoors, have a good yarn without fear of interruption by the fairer sex; though they seemed to tolerate the floosies who frequented such places alright. Them's not my thoughts though love. They're me Mom's, and not shared directly with me either. Funny what a kid remembers, isn't it?"

Mavis had risen from the table and was in the process of topping up the tea pot with hot water, "Don't stop, Dulcie. I'm listening, love."

"What I remember about that house mostly was that it had a coach house, so it really must have had quite a history. Of course, we didn't have coach and horses. Dad used to stow his bike in there, and that's where the coal was kept and it was our favourite place to play when the weather was poorly which was a lot of the time, I can tell you. And another thing was, even though house was so old, it had a proper bathroom, indoors like. It

256

were in the corner of Harvey's and my bedroom, making the bedroom a sort of L-shape. It didn't mean much to me as a little 'un. You know what it's like, if you've got something you just take it for granted; it's just the way things are. But when I went to school I soon discovered that most of the other kids didn't have such luxuries."

"You mean someone once lived there who'd had a horse drawn coach? Like gentry, you mean?"

"Must have," said Dulcie. "No point in a coach house otherwise."

"How terribly posh," said Mavis, "what a shame you had to move."

"You know, I've no idea why we left there. Neither Harvey nor me was very keen at the time. At that stage I think there were just the two of us though I could be wrong; Harvey was a couple of years younger than me. We got along did Harvey and me, when we were little, and we both especially liked the day trips we used to go on from the bus station around the corner. I think we both thought that would come to an end when we left, but we didn't really move that far and of course most things stayed the same, or actually got better. I remember I had to change school and I didn't like that at first but now I can hardly remember my first school at all."

"It's hard to imagine how you ended up here, Dulcie, honest it is."

"Well, that's another story altogether, Mavis."

"Yes, I suppose it is. Go on Dulce, I didn't mean to interrupt. So where did you go on your day trips?"

"Few different places but our very favourite place to go was Blackpool, on the Irish Sea. They had a big fun fair there, you know, with rides 'n sideshows 'n things. I've got a photograph somewhere of Harvey and me with our sticks of Blackpool Rock. Mom gave it to me when we left. On Blackpool Pier we are, with the tower in the background, Harvey all done up in his little sailor suit. He were that proud of that outfit. We looked forward to those outings for weeks so we were nearly sick with excitement before we left. You can imagine the state we were in by the time we got home after a day of high activity and a good hour or two on the bus, polishing off our Blackpool Rock while the grownups had a good old sing song and smoked their heads off. They were usually a bit on the well-oiled side by then, the male half of them any road. Talk about getting a fug up – you could cut the air with a knife on those journeys home – by the end of the journey we'd have sick tummies and sore eyes but we loved it. I remember George Formby getting a good airing on those trips home from Blackpool. Harvey and me had a few favourites. One of 'em went like this,"

Dulcie jumped up, went to the door and swaggered back strumming an imaginary ukulele as she sang very softly,

"Every year when summer comes round, off to the sea I go.
I don't care if I do spend a pound, I'm rather rash I know.
See me dressed like all the sports, in my blazer and a pair of shorts.
With my little stick of Blackpool Rock, along the promenade I stroll.
It may be sticky but I never complain, it's nice to have a nibble at it now and again
Every day wherever I stray the kids all round me flock……."

………reaching the end of the table she flopped back down onto the bench, "There's a lot more to it than that," she said, "if I could but remember it." Her cheeks were flushed both with the exertion and the wave of shyness that suddenly washed over her.

"I didn't know you were a performer, Dulcie," said Mavis with a broad smile. "The ladies of St. Matthews' Drama Society would love to get their claws into you. They need an injection of new blood from what I hear."

Mavis laughed at the look on Dulcie's face, "It's alright love, I'll leave introductions entirely up to you. Come on, don't let me distract you from your story. I'm enjoying it I am."

They both drank their tea and Dulcie regrouped during a trip to the larder to get the biscuits she had made especially for Mavis's visit.

"We had some good times before the war," she resumed her narrative as she sat down again. "We were lucky." She stopped, taken aback by a sudden memory, "You know I'd nearly forgotten, but there was a workhouse just up the road from us back then. I used to be quite scared of it, or its inhabitants more like," she shook her head, "you couldn't get a more grim reminder of just how lucky you were than that."

"You mean one of those poor house places? You had a poor house right by you, you with your coach house and all?"

"I don't think there was any connection, but the rich and the poor do seem to have an odd sort of affinity for one another in certain circumstances, don't they? They were hard times, the thirties, Mavis, and they reckoned the further north you went the worse it got; and we were pretty far north I can tell you, just shy of the Lake District. But give Dad his due, he was always in work, do anything to put food on table he would, and always did better than the bare minimum – he delivered coal at one time and I remember him working in a bakery too. Only difference to me was the colour he were when he come home; but not Mom. You could see she worried about him. By the time we moved he'd got a job as a factory hand with AV Rose Aeronautical. I remember Mom saying as how it were a good job, that one, and he had it a good long time. Things would probably have been very different if it hadn't been for the war."

"For all of us," murmured Mavis in agreement. "So why did you leave a nice big house like that; where did you go?"

"Well, as I said, I don't rightly know why we left," said Dulcie, "but I do know there's a big new road through there now. Most of West Street has gone. The pub's gone, workhouse, everything. Plans for that road had summat to do with it like as not. I took Bill there to show him but you wouldn't know as how it had been there at all. He was surprised how close it were to where Mom and Dad live now but as a kid it felt like a long way away to me."

She paused, gulped, "where Dad lives now," she said.

"And where's that," asked Mavis gently.

"Chadderton. We moved to Chadderton and that's where they stayed. Number 390 Chadderton Park Road. That's really where I grew up. It's just an ordinary residential street. Nothing like streets here though, I can tell you. It has a long line of working men's houses all joined up with their front doors opening onto cobbled road like, no garden to speak of, just enough space out back for the toilet and the dustbins and coal shed, you know; and Mom's Mom lives just a couple of doors down road. Mom was right happy about that as you'd imagine. Maybe that's why they moved; never occurred to me before. You just don't think about some things do you, when you're a kid?"

Mavis offered Dulcie a biscuit and asked, as she helped herself, "So, where did you kids play?" She was having trouble envisaging life in a house that was joined to a long line of others and opened right onto the road itself.

"Well Chadderton Hall Park's right close. Us kids used to spend a lot of time in the park, just mucking about the way kids do you know, and Dad would sometimes take us boating on the river. River Irk it was called. We used to laugh about that, called it Irky-Pirky when we were skylarking about. Dad said as how it was once a lovely river that used to fair gurgle along but the cotton industry drew so much on its waters that it had grown heavy and sluggish, dirty, even in Chadderton which wasn't that far from its source up by Royton. Lord knows what it was like downstream. Terrible shame," Dulcie sighed, "I think I'll make a fresh pot of tea, Mavis. All this talking is making me thirsty."

"I'd love another one, Dulce. You make the tea and I'll just pop out to make room for it."

While Mavis was outside Dulcie made a fresh pot of tea and decided to start preparations for dinner. They were going to have a stew, thanks to Mavis for picking up the beef, and boiled potatoes. It'd been a good while since they'd had a nice bit of beef, for more reasons than the one, and she assembled the ingredients with pleasure. When Mavis came back she went straight through to the front room mouthing to Dulcie in transit that she was going to check on young Roger.

"Here, give me a knife and another board and I'll help you with the vegies, love," she said as she came back into the kitchen.

Dulcie obliged, "I didn't think you'd mind me doing this, Mavis. You know how much better a stew is if it's cooked on low heat for a long time. I thought we'd have it with some of those lovely beans you've brought and some boiled potatoes. The potatoes we planted have been ever so good, love; there's still plenty of 'em and very tasty, never had a spud like it before these. Bill was saying t'other night it's time to be replanting."

"He's right; you can have fresh spuds from garden all year round up here if you plan properly," Mavis said, "and of course I don't mind you preparing evening meal now, Dulce, you know me well enough by now surely. I checked up on all of 'em by the way," she tilted her head in the direction of the front room, "they're all still sound asleep. So where were we?"

"You're sure you're not bored? You'll let me know when you've had enough, won't you, love?"

"I'm enjoying it, Dulce. I've never spoken to anyone about life somewhere else, in some other country. It's fascinating, if a bit hard to imagine in parts."

"Aye, I don't doubt it is. It's certainly very different to life here, I can tell you. I've still not entirely come to grips with this way of living, the way you do things here, especially not on the land, in middle of nowhere like," said Dulcie, "but where were we? Chadderton Hall Park wasn't it?"

Mavis nodded as she started to peel the carrots.

"Aye, well, as you'd imagine, we ended up spending a lot of time in the park and we visited the Hall too. I remember Dad took Harvey and me there soon after we moved to Chadderton. At that time Hall and grounds were a Pleasure Garden. There were a boating lake and a menagerie as had a boxing kangaroo....... well I'll be," Mavis peered at Dulcie and swore later that she could see the penny dropping, "a kangaroo; 'a roo loose in the top paddock.' That's what George said about that loony. It was easy enough to follow what he was getting at but I couldn't for the life of me figure out what a roo was. I'd forgotten all about that creature at Chadderton Hall. Ee, fancy that."

Mavis chuckled as she scraped a pile of chopped carrot off the board into the pot.

"Well we only went there that once," said Dulcie by way of excusing her errant memory, "the Pleasure Garden didn't last for very long after we arrived which is probably just as well for us. You had to pay to go through turnstiles to get in to Pleasure Garden, but the new people who leased the place only used the Hall. Park were open to public gratis. They were pickle manufacturers. Lived in one part of hall and converted rest into a factory," Dulcie giggled, "bit of a come down from the early days of manorial splendour. You can see Geoffrey de Chadderton spinning in his grave, eh.

261

He was first Lord of the Manor back in the 13th Century if my memory serves me right."

"The 13th Century?" Mavis was flabbergasted, "I can't even imagine being in a place that's been around for all that time."

"It has a history does Lancashire, love," said Dulcie, "Goes back well before Domesday Book though it weren't always called Lancashire. I think it's one of the so-called historical counties of England, for what that's worth."

"The Domesday Book?" asked Mavis.

"You haven't heard of it?" Dulcie looked up in surprise. She shrugged, "Well, maybe such history is not so important over here. It goes back to the middle ages does the Domesday Book. It were put together for William the Conqueror after he invaded England, the Norman conquest, Battle of Hastings, all that. He was William I of England by this and the book listed the vital statistics of all the settlements, thousands and thousands of them, in the English counties. It was in the late 11th Century, can't remember exactly when but well after 1066 for sure."

"I remember 1066. That was the Battle of Hastings, wasn't it?"

"That's it," agreed Dulcie. "As you might imagine, the book, or books, I think there might be two of them, has a lot of information that's very interesting to historians now but I think at the time it was just an enormous ledger really, to make sure as no one got away without paying their taxes in full to fund William's battles."

Mavis's head was reeling. England was just a vague concept to her, created mainly by a largely unremembered list of the Kings and Queens and a similarly largely unremembered list of important historical events from her school days, plus a few romantic novels and the odd newsreel since. It was somewhere the Queen lived when she wasn't visiting far flung parts of her empire, shaking hands with jet black people with her pristine white gloves; where Winston Churchill had chewed his way through the war years on a seemingly endless supply of big fat cigars, where people all talked funny, some funnier than others; and you couldn't forget that it was somewhere where they had punished a man for stealing a loaf of bread by sending him to live his life in shackles in the penal colony that had become Australia. She

262

had a sudden notion of history as a real, live, human experience. She scraped the last of the carrot into the pan and started on the onions. "You must have done other things, apart from going to the park," she said, bent on dragging the conversation back to the twentieth century.

"Oh, aye, we did," said Dulcie as she started dusting the cubed meat with flour. "The moors were but a cock's pace away. Borough of Oldham were right on border with Yorkshire and Chadderton; seemed more in touch with the moors somehow than the other place we lived. It were nice that. Harvey and me, and the boys as they got older, we used to love going for picnics on the moors, so long as Mom had money for bus fares and we were in her good books. We'd get the bus right near the big iron gates of the park and it would take us past the school, up Mill Brow and Streetbridge Road before turning left into Cinder Lane. I loved Cinder Lane," Dulcie lifted her head from her task and gazed through the window off into the distance.

"It winds its way up Cinder Hill through a number of small farms, some of the farmhouses right by road like. The view out over Royton were ever so pretty if it were clear, with the moors just beyond, where we were headed. From Cinder Lane bus turned into Oozewood Road which ran through more open country with Tandle Hill up on left all the way to the other side of Royton. I think that were part of Crompton Moor, Saddleworth were further south, but I can't be sure; you know how it is, you forget such things as names with familiarity. We used to get off where the bus terminated and head out onto the moors. We had some lovely times. We always took a cut lunch and Mom nearly always put in a good sized bag of broken biscuits, 'under the counter' as it were called because that's as where it were kept. Now that were a real assortment that were, and cheap as chips."

Dulcie smiled as she turned back to her task. "The moors were lovely," she continued, "but not at all like the countryside around here. There were no trees to speak of, just purplish grass and lots of heather, little streams and lakes I remember, when we went further out with Mom and Dad on a day trip. When we went on our own we had to promise Mom to stay where the good paths were and not lark about too much, get oursel' into bother. It could be very boggy in places, which I wouldn't know for a fact if we'd always done exactly as we were told," she chuckled.

"The moors make me think of Jane Eyre and Wuthering Heights," said Mavis. "They don't conjure up a convivial place at all. They rather make me think of wind and rain, and freezing cold…."

"….. And wraiths and witches and warlocks, if you've read your Bill Shookledagger," finished Dulcie, and they nodded at one another in agreement.

"These onions are getting to your eyes too, I can see," said Mavis, sniffing as she scraped the last of them into the pot.

"I'll have this on the stove in no time," said Dulcie. She placed the floured beef into the pot with the vegies, added salt and pepper and poured water in to just cover the contents before carrying the pot to the stove. "Long slow simmer and that'll do us nicely," she said as she rubbed her hands together vigorously over the board to remove the flour from her hands before rinsing them.

"Well, moors could be like that too but they weren't always so inhospitable," Dulcie continued as she started to clear the table, "We had great fun out there, but I'll be honest with you Mavis, the air were bad for the most part, nothing like it is here. Looking back towards home from moors, there was a forest of chimneys with black smoke pouring out, billowing and flowing in the wind across the landscape so you couldn't see very far at all, distance were quite close, you might say. There were times Mom kept us in at home, if it were a pea-souper. We didn't even go to school."

"A pea-souper?"

"Aye, love, a pea-souper; air so thick you could practically cut it, not quite up to pease pudding but getting there. If you went out in it you'd be black before you'd got to corner, believe you me, black with soot. It was disgusting. No wonder so many of the kids were poorly. We used to play the pease pudding game when we were cooped up indoors. You know the one?"

Mavis shook her head, not having the least idea what Dulcie was talking about. "Of course you don't, whatever am I thinking?" Dulcie beckoned Mavis out from behind the table and proceeded to demonstrate how it went, saying, "you just copy the clapping with me," before chanting the words:

Pease Pudding hot,
Pease Pudding cold,
Pease Pudding in the Pot
Nine Days old
Some like it Hot
Some like it Cold
Some like it in the Pot
Nine Days old

They did it a couple of times before packing it in and sitting down opposite one another at the table again, giggling.

"If anyone walked in they'd think us a right couple of daft 'apuths," said Dulcie. "We used to play that for hours on end when we were kids, trying to get faster and faster to catch one another out."

"What on earth is pease pudding anyway?" asked Mavis.

"It's like the dollop of peas you have on pie 'n' peas, love. Stodgy peas you might say. In our 'ouse it were pea soup after two or three days reheating with no extra water added; I certainly don't remember it lasting nine days."

"There's a bakery in Cairns sells pies 'n' peas," said Mavis, "Ray loves 'em."

Dulcie got up to stir the pot which was just starting to come to the simmer.

"But the collieries and cotton mills were our livelihood," she said, getting serious again as she pulled the pot to one side of the hob, "so you just put up with such things; no point in griping, though there was plenty as did and they did get somewhere eventually, though not far. Conditions never changed much while I was still there. I worked in mill after I left school. There were good money to be made in the mills there were. They used to say *'England's bread hangs by Lancashire's thread'*, and I believe it were so though you can see things are starting to change now."

"I thought you were a nurse, Dulcie."

"I am love, double certificate at that, but I worked in mill for a good twelve month before I decided to take up nursing. I was a winder by the time

265

I finished up there. It were good money alright but you worked hard for long hours to get it. Winders were responsible for keeping the looms running properly, you know, no broken yarns or anything; we had three looms each which kept you on your toes it did. Egad I used to look forward to the break signaled by Harvey's running footsteps coming up stairs. He were grand he were, always brought me an 'ot dinner and it were still right 'ot when I got it, not like some had to put up with. I think he liked the extra pocket money, but he earnt it." Dulcie grinned, "It were the most oft repeated chastisement I 'eard in them days. 'You're too slow to carry 'ot dinners you are!' If I heard it once, I heard it a hundred times."

There was a wail from the front room, which rapidly blossomed into a duet as the sleeping boys surfaced and demanded attention with characteristically uninhibited gusto. They smiled at one another across the table.

"To be continued, by the sound of it," said Mavis.

"It'll keep love," Dulcie replied, "so long as I remember it. Nothing can change the past."

They headed towards the door together.

"Hopefully we can at least bring some influence to bear on the future, eh, if we play our cards right," Dulcie added before they started clucking esoteric greetings to their respective offspring.

- 0 -

Mavis's parting words for Bill out in the turnabout as he helped to stow young Roger's paraphernalia in the Model T were, "She'll be alright, Bill. She just needs time to heal." Her words reminded him of the natural instinct he'd previously observed in women, for charting the territory inhabited by births and deaths. It was something he knew he lacked. He knew with gratitude what a comfort the afternoon with Mavis would have been to Dulcie. After waving the Johnstons goodbye, and promising to bring Dulcie into town for a visit soon, he went straight back up to top paddock without going into the house, thinking to give Dulcie a bit of time to herself to reflect on whatever had taken place between the two of them.

266

To reflect on such an afternoon was natural but after Mavis left, Dulcie's reflection didn't initially yield the comfort Bill foresaw. After settling Johnny and Jilly down to amuse themselves in the front room, she topped, tailed and stringed the beans and set them aside, went and dug up some potatoes, and scrubbed them before dropping them into a pot of water on back of the hob, tidied the kitchen, set the table, and prepared the copper for the night's batch of washing, all of these chores punctuated with searching inspections of the bottom paddock, looking out for Jess coming home from school.

Of all the things she and Mavis had talked about during the afternoon, Nancy's observation that "Jess was looking a bit peaky before all this business with that wretched loony happened" would not leave her be. Try as she might to shake it off, her mind kept at it, like a dog with a bone. She felt strangely ashamed, not so much to have been the probable cause of Jess's distress, but to have not noticed what an outsider had so clearly observed. When Jess arrived home she did so to a more overtly affectionate welcome than she was accustomed to. It didn't go altogether unnoticed and her perception of this curious state of grace was somehow strengthened by the two milk bottles and false teeth Dulcie dished up apiece after the girls had had their glass of milk and vegemite butty. Dulcie's surreptitious scrutiny of her daughter throughout these homecoming rituals reassured her that there really seemed little to worry about, the smudges under Jess's eyes being belied by her usual sunny disposition; nothing a couple of good sound sleeps wouldn't fix.

Part of their normal routine, which was slowly reestablishing itself, was for Jess to sit at the kitchen table and do her homework after Jilly had gone to bed but after they had finished dinner that night Dulcie stroked the back of Jess's hand as she said, "You look tired, lovey. I'll do the washing up tonight; you go to bed with Jilly, an early night will do you the world of good. I'll give you a note for the teacher if there's any homework you've not finished."

Jess actually liked doing her homework, added to which she thought going to bed early was a punishment rather than any sort of privilege but her memory of recent events was still strong and she was also intuitively aware that she was still very much in her Mom's favour. She acquiesced without demur but was quick nevertheless, to seize upon a possible advantage in the situation, "Can we have another story then, Daddy, like the ones you told us before Mommy got ajusted?"

"Yes please," chimed in Jilly.

Bill winked quickly as he caught Dulcie's eye, "If you are both ready and in bed in fifteen minutes when I get back you get a story, alright? And I mean in bed; no mucking about, no shenanigans; understood?"

"And can we have another lolly for pudding? Pleeeeeeze?" said Jess with Jilly helping out in the pleading department.

"You don't miss a trick, do you?" said Dulcie as she went to the larder.

That was the night Bill told them the story of Oscar, just as it had been told to him in a letter from his young brother Doug during the war, not that he told them that.

"You remember them boys who went down to Abergavenny, down in the West Country?" All he got were blank looks. "With a castle and an apple tree…."

"…and they caught some big eels," said Jess.

"Right, that's them," said Bill, "well, you'll remember they were sent down there so they'd be safe from all the bombs the enemy might drop on their home town."

The girls nodded.

"Well, as it happened, after some time when no bombs had been dropped at all, them same boys were sent back home. You can imagine how happy they were to be back with their proper Mom again."

The girls smiled.

"Trouble was, they hadn't been back home long when the enemy did start dropping bombs. They were alright because their Dad and their big brother had built what they called an air raid shelter in their back yard so they had somewhere to go when air raid siren went off and the bombs came falling down out of the sky, but one of the boys, whose name was Walter, was really scared when all the noise and shuddering and flashing lights of the bombing were going on, and he imagined terrible things happening to them all. But then something happened that made him, and the others, feel much better. He wrote a letter about it to his big brother, a letter I was lucky enough to see,"

"Did you know his brother, Daddy?"

"Oh aye, you could say I knew him very well Jilly," Bill answered. He paused, "and this is what he said.

Dear Bernard,

I just thought I would write to let you know how we are all doing now that we are all back home again. Since you're in the army I suppose you know that, right when we thought it was safe, the enemy has started dropping bombs on us.

I was really frightened at first, and I think the others were too, but then suddenly we had Oscar. Oscar is Dick's pet flea. We don't know where he got him but he is our saviour. When we go down into the shelter Dick holds his thumbs in the air and says, "do a double somersault, Oscar," then he watches as Oscar does this trick, following it with his eyes, then he strokes his thumb and says, "good on ya Oscar!" Oscar can do anything asked of him. If Dick's going to send Oscar out on a mission, he flies him around the shelter just for a warm up, and if He, [Oscar] gets carried away with the mission, Dick catches him in a paper bag. We all hear it when he flies into the bag at the end of the warm up. That's when the mission begins.

If we can hear a plane going over and no sirens have sounded, Dick sends Oscar to investigate, and if the sirens need to go off, Oscar is the one to wake the sirens up. Sure enough he always makes the sirens sound. If the sirens go off and no guns are fired, then Dick sends Oscar off to liven up the gun crews. Then we all say "On ya Oscar!" when the guns start firing. When it's all quiet after the sirens sound, Oscar is sent to find out the news. On a bright moonlight night, Oscar reports "all clear on the western front"; which means we can all get some sleep, but if we've heard on the news that Hamburg, or Bremen has been bombed by the Allies, then we know we are in for the same treatment ourselves.

The other night the sirens sounded, and we couldn't hear anything above the din we were making. So Mom shouted – "QUIET!" – and everything went quiet. Not a bad result was it, for someone only five feet tall and six stone wringing wet? Then we heard it, that horrible urgh, urgh, urgh of an aircraft engine. That is the sound we know. It's the sound I hate most – enemy aircraft, "Dick," said Mom, "Send Oscar to see if those gunners are awake." A couple of minutes went by, nothing, a couple more and just then the guns started firing. Oscar returned. Dick said, "Good on ya Oscar" and stroked his

269

thumb. We knew then that Oscar was still looking after us. And the sun would rise in the morning.

I know you helped Dad to build the Anderson shelter so I thought I'd let you know how it is doing. Firstly you will be happy to know we are all safe, Mom says to tell you no injuries to report. The sleeping arrangements are. All the kids lie across the shelter in a line, Mom and Clare plus the baby Helen, sleep on a camp bed over our feet. Dick has started to complain that he can't lie straight; he's getting too tall for the shelter. He's tried all sorts of positions. He's tried sitting up to sleep, and sleeping in a ball but he can't settle properly. So Mom's promised him she'll try to work out another way, in the hope this will shut his whinging for a while. I don't know what we will do if you and Dad come home for a visit.

I can't think of anything else to write this time. I hope more than anything that you are safe and send you all of our love. Mom says she will write you in a couple of days.

Your brother, Walter."

– 0 –

"I think you were right to get Jess off to bed early, Dulce," said Bill as he came down the stairs into the kitchen, "they're out like lights, both of 'em." He lowered the wick of the Tilley lamp as he spoke, hung it on its nail on the wall by door. "I told them about Oscar. You know, I remember that bloody letter near word perfect. Read it often enough, I suppose. Young John was with 'em then, you know?"

"Aye, I know he was, darling," Dulcie could see the emotion that had stirred in him through the telling of the story. "*Some things never go away,*" she thought as she changed the subject, "do you think Jess is OK darling? You don't think she's fretting about that wretched fellow exposing hisself, do you?"

"No," he said. "No," more emphatically and shaking his head, "I think she was more concerned about you when you were poorly than she's been over him. I think we explained things pretty well, and we're lucky we know he's been picked up by the plod. I think that's the main thing. She's not scared of him coming back. No, she seems fine to me, just a bit tired, as you thought," he topped up the kettle and put it on the hob to boil while Dulcie finished the wiping up and put things away.

His words had struck a chord. "I'm sorry I let myself go like that, Bill, really I am. I think it was a lot of things all got on top of me because I felt so low. I'll be alright now, love, now that I've 'ajusted' as Jess so aptly put it."

Bill turned from the stove and caught Dulcie's eye, "I didn't want to tell them about your Mom, love. I didn't know how to and I couldn't see what good it would do, so I just told them you'd had bad news, that you needed to adjust to."

"You were right love," she turned and walked into his arms, "and Jess was right too, the cheeky monkey. I have adjusted," she paused and rested her head on his chest, "as much as one can. It was so good to see Mavis this afternoon. I've come to realise as how I need more company, or at least company more often if you know what I mean. A person can get maudlin left to their own thoughts for too long." She sighed. "We're going to have to try and do summat about it you know, love."

Bill held her gently and stroked her back absentmindedly as the kettle started sending its dogs to the ceiling behind them. She was telling him nothing he hadn't thought, nothing he wasn't trying to put to rights, but tonight he had other things on his mind. He hugged her in tacit agreement and kissed her on the cheek before turning back to make the tea.

"Let's have of a couple of those biscuits you made for Mavis with our tea, love. There's summat I need to talk to you about. Well a couple of things, truth be known."

He was not normally one to make such pronouncements so he had her full attention. She quickly took off her apron and hung it up, and draped the tea towel over the pots still draining on the tray by the basin to give it some air. Fetching the jar of biscuits from the larder she sat opposite him at the table. As he poured tea it dawned on her as how out of touch she had become, not having the slightest notion what might be on his mind. She was shocked inwardly at how quickly this had happened.

"You're looking better, Dulcie, this past week," he said, "It's a relief I must say, love. You had me worried."

271

"Aye, and I'm feeling better, darling, really I am, and it's good to have things more ship shape around the house, like. I'm sorry it were such a mess, love," she paused briefly before finishing on a positive note, "and weather's been well-nigh perfect this past week."

"I thought so myself until George gave me the gen today."

She sat up in surprise, "What gen?"

"Well, apparently weather's been well-nigh perfect for summat else as well, and he's worried. Farmers are all worried."

"Whatever for?"

"Conditions at moment are perfect, according to George, for a plague of locusts."

"Grasshoppers like?" She'd read about them back home, though they weren't a feature of the landscape there. She'd a vague notion they had them in Egypt, where Harvey had been.

"Aye. We've eggs in scattered patches up in top paddock but it seems the threat is more from up Mareeba way and over towards Ravenshoe where there are real infestations, if that's the word. It's been really dry their way for a good while but weather reports say as how they got their share of that rain we had last week."

"So what are they worried about here then?"

"Well might you ask Dulce, well might you ask," Bill paused. "Though to be honest, George reckons we'll likely come out of it alright here, on farm. Pastures should restore quickly, he says, so we shouldn't have to get feed in for cows for long. No, it's farmers as have crops coming through as have most to lose."

"I don't follow you at all Bill. I thought you just said…"

"Sorry love, just getting ahead of myself," Bill cut her short. "Thing is, locusts swarm, and if they're around in big numbers they just mow their way through thick and thin, eating all before 'em, forever pushing on to fresh pastures as it were. Relentless, George says."

"Is there owt we can do?"

"Nowt anyone can do, love, according to George, except be prepared for it."

272

"And how, exactly, is one supposed to do that?" said Dulcie, wrestling to imagine the form and features of such a phenomenon. A plague of locusts; it had a nasty ring to it whatever way you said it.

"Good question, love," Bill said, standing up as he did so, patting the pockets of his shorts and finding nothing. "I've got something to show you," he said as he went down into the laundry. When he came back he was carefully unfolding a wad of paper, "George gave me this today," he said, "it was in my shirt pocket. He said one of the CWA ladies typed it up after a locust plague a few years back and it's been floating around ever since." He sat back down and started to scan the top page.

"I'll go and put the copper on while you read that, love," Dulcie said as she left.

When she returned Bill suggested that she come and sit beside him. In her absence he'd freshened the tea pot and pumped up the lamp so there was good light to read by. "It's a poem," he said to her surprise, "but I think I get the point."

Centred at the top of the first page, in capital letters and underlined was the title A BALLAD OF DUCKS. She sipped her tea and followed the words to the poem as Bill read them out loud:

The railway rattled and roared and swung
With jolting and bumping trucks.
The sun, like a billiard red ball, hung
In the Western sky: and the tireless tongue
Of the wild-eyed man in the corner told
This terrible tale of the days of old,
And the party that ought to have kept the ducks.
'Well, it ain't all joy bein' on the land
With an overdraft that'd knock you flat;
And the rabbits have pretty well took command;
But the hardest thing for a man to stand
Is the feller who says 'Well I told you so!
You should ha' done this way, don't you know!' –
I could lay a bait for a man like that.

They were at the end of the first verse and Bill paused, catching Dulcie's eye, "Mmm," she said, and sipped her tea.

"*The grasshoppers struck us in ninety-one*

"Ahh," said Dulcie.

And what they leave – well, it ain't de luxe.
But a growlin' fault-findin' son of a gun
Who'd lent some money to stock our run –
I said they'd eaten what grass we had –
Says he, 'Your management's very bad;
You had a right to have kept some ducks!'

"*To have kept some ducks! And the place was white!*
Wherever you went you had to tread
On grasshoppers guzzlin' day and night;
And then with a swoosh they rose in flight,
If you didn't look out for yourself they'd fly
Like bullets into your open eye
And knock it out of the back of your head.

"*There isn't a turkey or goose or swan,*
Or a duck that quacks, or a hen that clucks,
Can make a difference on a run
When a grasshopper plague has once begun;
'If you'd finance us,' I says, 'I'd buy
Ten thousand emus and have a try;
The job,' I says, 'is too big for ducks!

"*You must fetch a duck when you come to stay;*
A great big duck – a Muscovy toff –
Ready and fit,' I says, 'for the fray;
And if the grasshoppers come our way

274

You turn your duck into the lucerne patch,
And I'd be ready to make a match
That the grasshoppers eat his feathers off!"

"He came to visit us by and by,
And it just so happened one day in spring
A kind of cloud came over the sky —
A wall of grasshoppers nine miles high,
And nine miles thick, and nine hundred wide,
Flyin' in regiments, side by side,
And eatin' up every living thing.

"All day long, like a shower of rain,
You'd hear 'em smackin' again the wall,
Tap, tap, tap, on the window pane,
And they'd rise and jump at the house again
Till their crippled carcasses piled outside.
But what did it matter if thousands died —
A million wouldn't be missed at all.

"We were drinkin' grasshoppers — so to speak —
Till we skimmed their carcasses off the spring;
And they fell so thick in the station creek
They choked the waterholes all the week.

"A week!" cried Dulcie.

There was scarcely room for a trout to rise,
And they'd only take artificial flies —
They got so sick of the real thing.

Bill laughed.

"An Arctic snowstorm was beat to rags

When the hoppers rose for their morning flight
With the flapping noise like a million flags:
And the kitchen chimney was stuffed with bags
For they'd fall right into the fire, and fry
Till the cook sat down and began to cry –
And never a duck or fowl in sight.

"We strolled across to the railroad track –
Under a cover beneath some trucks,
I sees a feather and hears a quack;
I stoops and I pulls the tarpaulin back –
Every duck in the place was there,
No good to them was the open air.
'Mister,' I says, 'There's your blanky ducks!"

"Bit of a character, whoever wrote that, do you think he knows what he's talking about," said Dulcie.

"A.B. Banjo Paterson," said Bill. "Probably."

"Do you really think they'll come down chimney?" asked Dulcie, wrinkling her nose, "It sounds as if we'll have to keep shutters down."

"I wonder if the chooks will be alright?"

"Jess won't be able to go to school if it's anything like that, you know."

"Milking's not going to be any fun."

"What about laundry? Do you think they'll eat clothes, like goats?"

"We'll be lucky to get feed for cows with everyone wanting it at same time?"

"Bloody Nora, the garden!"

"It's going to cost this is, I can tell."

"They might be wrong, do you think?"

"Slim chance from what George says."

"I hope the girls aren't frightened."

"One of the reasons I told them about Oscar; thought it might help if we really do come under siege."

"I hope I'm not frightened."

Bill put his arm around her shoulders and pulled her to him, "We'll be right, Dulce. They're only grasshoppers love, they won't go off with a bloody bang, but we should make a list of things to do just in case, eh; things could get awkward."

"It's a rum country this is," Dulcie commented as she got up to get her exercise book, "turns that saying about clouds and silver linings upside down a bit, doesn't it, perfect weather having its dark side 'n all!"

She sat down again, opposite him, "But you said as how there were a couple of things on your mind, darling."

"Aye, there is something else Dulcie," he looked at his watch, "but it's getting late and we should try to come up with some sort of a plan in case we really are invaded by grasshoppers en masse. It'll keep love. We'll talk about it soon. I won't forget."

She licked the end of the pencil to get it going............

- 0 -

It was late morning a couple of days later that Dulcie heard a thrumming of the cattle grid following which she heard Bill calling to her from the turnabout. By the time she reached the front gate the ute was vanishing back up the track and Bill was saddling up Big Red, a sure sign something was up.

"Word is they're on their way love. I'm going to get Jess. You know what to do. I'll be back fast as I can."

Her heart fluttered in her chest as she waved him off. She went quickly indoors where Jilly was lying on the floor in the front room playing with Johnny. Starting with the girls' room she let down the shutters. When the house was all closed up save the front and back doors she went down into the laundry and pulled on the ropes holding up the tarpaulin across the entrance to the garden and it clattered down into position. It wasn't quite wide enough but had been all they could find out in the shed and they hoped it might help prevent a wholesale invasion of the laundry where a temporary privy had once more been installed.

277

"What are you doing Mommy?" Jilly was clearly unsettled by this odd behaviour.

"Do you remember Mommy and Daddy telling you about the grasshoppers, darling?"

"No."

"Yes you do," she challenged Jilly's memory. "Well George says they'll be here soon. It might get noisy but all you need to remember is that there's nothing to worry about. Daddy's gone to get Jess so we'll all be here together, alright, including Daddy, so whatever happens there's nothing to worry about."

Mollified if a bit mystified by this Jilly, thankfully, went back to take charge once again of her game with Johnny. Dulcie hung a Tilley lamp in the front room. It was all quiet. Closing the front door quietly behind her, she went outside and found the clothes on the line to be blessedly dry, folded them quickly into the clothes basket and brought them in through the laundry. "*Gawd, I'm a daft aputh I am. I should have done this before letting the flipping tarpaulin down,*" she thought as she battled with it to get back in.

Bill had sat with a map the night before and worked out that through the window in the kitchen one looked roughly towards Mareeba and the window in the laundry faced towards Ravenshoe. She peered through both at mocking blue skies before setting about making lunch. The sandwiches were stacked on a large plate under a tea towel and she was just putting the kettle on when she heard the first pinging sound from the laundry. Almost instantaneously she heard the front door open and Jess was calling loudly for help from the front room. She hurried in to find her eldest struggling to get something out of her hair. "It's all right darling, show me. I'll get it, just relax," she reassured her daughter whilst she wrestled with a strange stick-like creature with big strong back legs and tenacious, claw-like feet firmly entangled in Jess's hair. It felt horrible in her hands but she set about the task of removing it calmly, denying the panic which hovered at the edges of her consciousness, increasingly aware of the noise building up to a steady tattoo on the iron walls about them. At last the stick insect came away and she went swiftly to the laundry to throw it away. She vaguely heard the front door again above the staccato pinging of the house as she went down the laundry steps. It was as though night had descended. The light of day through the laundry window had been extinguished, save odd flickering shards piercing the churning gloom. Bill came down the steps behind her plucking several of the insects from his clothing, "Christ Dulcie, get inside love, and shut this door, the air's thick with 'em out there."

As she closed the back door behind her she heard young Johnny's screams above the now relentless bombardment, joined by the girls' shrill cries for help. "*Whatever next*," she thought. "I'm coming," she called as she hurried through to the front room.

Chapter Nine

That's another story altogether ....

*M*r. A.B. Banjo Paterson had known what he was talking about when he wrote The Ballad of Ducks; such was their shared opinion after nigh on three days under siege. From where he now stood, high in the top paddock, Bill surveyed the aftermath, recalled his initial loss of composure when that strange host had risen out of the west, blocking out the sun as it swarmed towards them. He and Jess had been making their way up through the south paddock, having taken a short cut which would soon be denied them, when the big wet arrived. The magnitude of the host had sent shivers down his spine as it had pushed night towards them, the brittle sound of their progress that of wind rushing unchecked through myriad dry twigs; but from the onset, he and Dulcie had rallied with such determination to reassure the girls, they had succeeded in reassuring themselves in the process.

It had been both a surprise and a relief when Glad had come by earlier this morning, to take Dulcie and the little ones into town for a welcome airing. With Jess back at school and George working over at Ray Watson's place, he found himself alone. Just the other week, worried about Old Bronc's prolonged and unexplained absence they'd learnt, upon asking around, that he was visiting a sister who lived over Millaa Millaa way. The news had been a revelation, shedding a somewhat different light on Athol's circumstances, but even so, Bill had simply commented, "Well, a man's business is his own and if he doesn't want to share it then that's his business too."

He gazed up at a sky the intense blue of his Mam's Wedgwood clock which it now brought to mind. They'd all gone hungry, at one time or another, to save that clock from a one way trip to the pop shop. Below him the rill slowly flushed itself of countless locust carcasses, disgorging them into the creek flowing under Skennar Bridge to join the undulating raft of bodies already stretching the full breadth of the creek. The south paddock had been ravaged, the rill now a jagged scar in the bare earth, the girls' elephant ears, spared, the only green relief. He'd moved the cows over to the paddock abutting the pig pen, between the house and the road, where big patches of grass had survived. There'd been talk before their invasion about the erratic migratory patterns and activity of swarming locusts and he was grateful to benefit from proof of it. Maybe such proximity to the pigs had offended their olfactory receptors, if a locust had such things. Maybe the greater abundance of trees over there explained it. Who knew? His first cursory inspection of the property had revealed very little tree damage anywhere. He looked now over towards Jess's bush. He'd seen her heading up towards it from time to time, watched her settling herself under it. After the first time and during her absence, he'd gone up from the milking shed to give it the once over, make sure nothing inhospitable lurked there, not that he'd mentioned it to anyone. It was Jess's little bolt hole, and he was pleased now to see that it appeared, at least from this distance, to be relatively unscathed. He'd go over there later and have a closer look, check that everything was alright at Athol's place while he was at it.

This serendipitous solitude sat well with him, time to reflect scarce as hens' teeth in the daily grind. Sitting down on the uneven ground, he drew up his good leg and leaned back on his elbows. Though pleased to be alone, he felt Dulcie's absence and a shimmering desire for her return washed over him, like a momentary itch. He collected his thoughts, lay back with his hands under his head. They had come here nigh on a year ago now, worked hard. The physical evidence of their achievement gave him a certain pride, though, even before this extraordinary plague, he had fathomed, and faced up to the fact, that the farming life, on this farm or any other, was not going to provide that to which they aspired, independence, a place of their own, in which they would be secure. Any real benefit from his achievements here would go, he knew, to someone else. Additionally, and even more importantly, he felt hampered by this style of life; the subsistence living of a tenant farmer. The constant lack of any real money to call one's own made it impossible to plan for, work towards, the situation they hoped for. Life back home had been hard, no doubt about that, but he had grown accustomed to having his own purse, solid if modest, with which to plan. He'd been on a good wicket, as foreman at the factory.

He had yet to share these thoughts with Dulcie but he didn't expect they would come as any great surprise to her.

As she entered his mind he lifted his head, looked over towards the township whereto she had gone. There had been other achievements too these past months, he thought, changes wrought. From the moment he had been caught by those mesmerising eyes in the photograph displayed with such pride on the mantelpiece at Frank's place, he had seen her kindness, felt intuitively the love and warmth she would have for her children. His instincts had served him well, he hadn't been wrong about that. He remembered writing his first letter to her, enclosing a small photograph of himself, head and shoulders, in his service uniform. Fancied himself, he had, in uniform, not afraid to say so, amongst mates. In time he'd received a letter from her, accompanied by a different photograph to the one he'd already seen. She was dressed, in this photograph, in the tailored suit of a military nurse off duty, at least that's what he'd presumed it was. Her eyes had met his fair and square every time he'd looked at it, which had been often during his free time, when he thought of home, the family he was part of and parted from, the family he wanted to have. When he'd been demobbed and left Frank in India, their cards having fallen differently on that occasion, she and Merry had come to meet him in Southampton. It had been June 1946. He still remembered being utterly taken aback by the physical reality of her. When he married her just a few months later, Jess on the way, he was proud to do so, pleased in his choice of mother for the family he was impatient to have, but, much as he was drawn by her sensuality, her mother earth being, he had not considered himself to truly love, or to be in love with her.

He gazed up at the pristine sky, took a deep breath. His world now spun in a different orbit. He had learnt succinctly, when she had withdrawn to her own, sad centre, mourning her mother's death, that without her he was diminished. He felt, in his new, conscious need of her, a vulnerability he had never before experienced. He marveled at this reality, a reality immeasurably better than anything he had ever imagined. Only with her was he whole. From unrecognized seeds his love had grown to full blown splendour, nurtured daily by the simple acts through which they shared their lives, spawned their family. He smiled as he allowed himself the private joy of inspecting this new treasure, turning it in his mind's eye, seeing the light streaming from it, like the sunshine glowing at the heart of one of those luminous trees, Robinia pseudo acacia, wasn't it, that they called the Black Locust? His mind ranged free.

A raucous gobbling of turkeys cut into his brown study. He stirred, briefly pondered the cause of their disturbance; probably just feeling frisky after three days cooped up in the farrowing shed with the ducks. The day's unblemished canopy harboured no promise of the rain needed to regenerate stripped pastures. Back now to earth, he spared a thought for others, how they had fared these last few days. Some badly he'd heard. He stood up and brushed the earth from his elbows, the seat of his pants, then made his way down to the house, the crunch of dead locusts beneath his feet. He would put the kettle on and settle down to bring the books up to date, plot a course to the future, plot also the manner in which he would recruit Dulcie once more to his cause. He glanced over towards Jess's bolt hole, Athol's place. They would keep.

- 0 -

When Glad and Dulcie set off for town that morning, the manner of each other's endurance and survival of the past few days was uppermost in their minds but, as usual, their deference to small ears had them teasing the subject, like fish nibbling coyly on the bait before darting off, instinctively seeking safe waters. Jilly soon put them right, chipping in with the observation, "We had lots of grasshoppers, Aunty Glad; hundreds and hundreds that were coming and coming and bashing into the walls outside and making a big mess of the window, and getting into the laundry......" She slumped back in the seat, her animation waning momentarily, but promptly sat up, taking a deep breath, "And Daddy didn't like them one bit. He said so.

286

He told Mummy they were horrible little blighters. Didn't he, Mummy? Jess and I heard him."

"You're right, lovey. He didn't like them at all, certainly not in those numbers," Dulcie patted Jilly's knee, "But they're all gone now aren't they?"

"'Cept the dead ones," said Jilly, "They're everywhere."

"They'll soon be gone too," Glad said. "They'll be eaten by ants, or trodden into the dirt. By us or by cows, horses, you'll see."

"Good," said Jilly with finality and settled back into the seat.

Dulcie caught Glad's eye and winked. They turned their attention to the landscape through which they travelled. Dulcie was keen to ask Glad about her honeymoon but now wasn't the time for that either. Her chance came soon however, and in quite a different circumstance to that she'd imagined.

When they got to Mavis's place, Mavis talked Dulcie into leaving Jilly and Johnny whilst she did the bit of shopping she wanted to do. Then, back in the ute, while she was still waving ta-ta from the window, Glad suggested they go to the café for morning tea before they did their chores. They'd never done that before.

"We've a lot of catching up to do, Dulce," she said.

Within minutes Glad was parking the ute by side of the road under a tree. She turned off the engine. "Come on, tea and scones are on me," she said as she jumped down.

"Sounds right nice to me, it does," exclaimed Dulcie as she climbed down from the cabin, deliciously unencumbered, "I'll not play hard to get, lovey. Are you sure you've got the time?"

There was a slight awkwardness in Glad's affirmative response, a discomfort all the more noticeable to Dulcie through never before having been witnessed, well not in Gladys any road. A flickering notion that it may augur something not altogether palatable went almost unnoticed. Then they were walking across the road together towards the café.

When their eyes became accustomed to the inner gloom they found themselves alone. Glad gave the bell on the counter a rap and they settled into one of the dark wooden booths along the side wall. Although they knew exactly what they wanted they peered intently at the simple bill of fare which was stuck to the wall beside them, neatly typed, some in red, such as "SCRAMBLED eggs only with sausages" in the BREAKFAST section. Its slightly fly-blown condition was testament to the time it had spent there, as were the curling corners of the tea coloured paper.

"Bill brought me here for lunch for my birthday, a while back," said Dulcie. "I had the fish and chips," Dulcie smiled, "it were right nice. We went the long way home for a drive, by Foresters Track, past Athol's place."

"Surprised you could get through," commented Glad, "It's not much used these days."

"Aye, you could see that," Dulcie agreed.

The distraction of ordering tea and scones was brief, the proprietor being a reserved man, not prone to wasting his time with small talk. After he'd left, Glad smiled at Dulcie, "So, you've survived the locusts alright, I can see. Jilly seemed more put out about them than anything else." She chuckled, "Jess alright?"

"Well, we were forewarned, thankfully, and therefore forearmed, at least to the degree our understanding allowed. After the initial shock we just had to get on with it. Bill had to go out of course, tend to cows. Jilly was right, he didn't like the little blighters one bit; gave him the creeps. I rigged him up a cover for his head, over his hat you know, out of some pink tulle I had in the trunk, left over from one of Jess's old dancing costumes. He didn't half look a sight I can tell you," Dulcie giggled. "No, it were more a matter of what to do with the kids, cooped up indoors for all that time. The cribbage board got a good airing, it did. Wonder there's any spots left on the cards. I'm glad to see the back of it but we're none the worse for wear, Glad. As Bill said, they don't go off with a bang!"

Their tea and scones arrived and Dulcie asked Glad when she and Denis had arrived back,

"Last Friday."

And how their trip had been..........

"It was a long journey, Dulcie - I'd no idea - but once we changed at Albury we were almost there; four or so hours to Melbourne. It was a relief, honestly, to be finally there. It was the first time for me but not for Den. He reckons it used to take even longer." They'd traveled by train to Melbourne, setting off on the Sunlander and arriving at Spencer Street Station on the Spirit of Progress.

"Why ever change? I thought you were going straight to Melbourne, to meet up with Denis's uncle," as was her habit Dulcie turned the tea pots three times before she carefully poured through the strainer, first Glad's and then her tea.

A frown, signaling Glad's momentary confusion, vanished, "Oh, that's right, I forgot. You came as far as Brisbane on the boat, didn't you? You didn't travel by train from Melbourne at all."

"Aye," said Dulcie, lifting her cup with a firm wrist, sipping gingerly at the piping hot tea. "That's right. Egad, but these could be straight from British Rail caff, these could Glad, no mistake," raising the thick china cup higher to signify her meaning. "Made me quite homesick last time I was here. I'd forgotten all about 'em. Sorry, love, didn't mean to interrupt. As you were saying…"

"You're right, Dulce, we did go straight to Melbourne," Gladys put down her cup and helped herself to one of the scones, "You just can't do it on one train from here. State railway lines are different widths."

"Different widths?"

"Further apart, you know what I mean, or closer together whichever way you look at it, or wherever you are."

"What are?"

"The lines are, you know, the rails, the tracks."

"Oh."

"So that means the trains are, their wheels, you know."

"Ah."

Dulcie had a sudden sense of the enormity of this country; the difficulties of settlement, establishment, and connection touched the edges of her mind. '*Back home you'd be anywhere you wanted within a day, comfortably. There and back, like as not, unless you were going from Lands' End to John o' Groats,*' she thought, '*and even then……..*'

Glad filled Dulcie's nonplussed silence, "Albury's the border town, between New South Wales and Victoria. From there it was eventually straight to Melbourne. Den could hardly sit still by the time we got there. I'd no idea he'd been so looking forward to seeing them. I knew he'd been born down there, but it wasn't until I met them that I'd any idea of how close they are. Bob, that's his uncle, was at the station, as was arranged. Den was right after that," she paused, sipping her tea. "We had a lovely time. They made me very welcome, and I liked their place, good land, well established homestead. Closest town for them is Tatura, nice place, small, just the basics, bit like here, but Shepparton is only nine, ten miles away. Bit like having Cairns right on your doorstep, Dulce, as far as shopping, things to do, though it's inland of course, on the river."

"That's nice," said Dulcie, envious of such ready society of people, "So how did you spend your time?"

"Bob gave us use of one of the farm utes when we wanted so it was easy getting around. We went camping for a couple of days on the Goulburn River, fishing, walking. Den potted a couple of rabbits one day. We cooked up a rabbit stew on the camp fire. Not a soul around. It was wonderful, but crikey it was cold, morning and night, freezing - days not much better. You'd think it would be warming up by now, wouldn't you? I can understand why Den's old man moved up here. His Mum's got a weak chest," she added by way of explanation. "At least we warm up during the day here, eh? Mostly," Gladys paused, added a dollop of jam to a piece of scone and popped it into her mouth.

"Mmm," Dulcie agreed, stuck for words, her knowledge of Denis's family slim, what was their name? That's right, the Campbell's. She was presently taking tea with Mrs. Gladys Campbell. She smiled at the thought.

"One thing I'll not forget," Glad continued after washing the scone down with a sip of tea, "and that's the Number One Internment Camp. Government built it right by one of their perimeter fences. Bob took us over to have a look one day. He was obviously relieved about it being put to a different use now than that it was built for. Even so, that it was purpose built for incarceration is obvious; so out of place in those lovely surroundings."

"Internment Camp? Down there? Give over, whatever for?" Before coming to Australia, it could have been on the moon for all Dulcie knew or cared but since arriving in the country she'd heard plenty about its wartime tribulations. The bombing of Darwin, Japanese subs in Sydney Harbour, and from Glad and Mavis she had learned much about the local military activity, here, up north, a well-worn launching pad for combat in New Guinea and the Asia Pacific Theatre as the strategists called it; but the deep south of the country seemed an odd place to find an internment camp.

"I was just as mystified as you, Dulcie."

Glad had Dulcie's undivided attention.

"First off, from what Bob says, it was for men of German origin who'd settled here before the war, and then, later on, men of Italian origin were included too. The government didn't take the loyalty of these people for granted; suspicious of its very existence apparently. Saw them as potential, if not likely, security risks, and locked them up. Unfortunately for Bob they started right on his doorstep, but there must have been a lot of these so-called enemy alien civilians, because, from what he said, there ended up being several internment camps just around there, and they only put the men away. Can't say as I knew about it happening at the time; just a kid, too busy paying attention to my life, what was going on around here. Sure I never heard anything about it on the news, not that that means much," she concluded.

Dulcie had been attending to the remnants of scone on her plate, bound them together with a morsel of cream and a morsel of jam, posted them neatly to her mouth on the tip of her right index finger.

"I must confess my ignorance, Glad. Beyond *toorali-oorali-addity* I didn't know much about Australia before Bill started talking about it. They must have been adventurous types who came of their own free will before the war, eh? Either that or spreading the word of God maybe," Dulcie had been brought up to Lutheranism. "Though there's never been a shortage of things to escape for some poor souls," Dulcie shook her head as she thought on it.

"As you might imagine, there were a lot as fell into that category back home, Glad, you know, enemy alien civilians; authorities took similar precautions 'n all, though it can't have been easy. There were those as changed their names to escape imprisonment, enlisted, went to fight, hid. No doubt there were those who did become spies too, or who did find their way back to their own country, but you'd be unlikely to do either from here, wouldn't you. Aye, all sorts went on during wartime. I don't think we know

291

the half of it, and we've certainly not heard the last of it, mark my words," she paused. "But I always thought what an awful dilemma it must have been for them, you know, those so-called enemy aliens. Can't have been easy to have family and friends who were now considered our enemies, and, by association, theirs. Hardly likely is it that anyone would simply turn on loved ones? Left authorities twixt a rock and a hard place if you ask me," Dulcie paused, took a deep, audible breath, "And what about the families of these men who were interned, eh? They weren't half on the end of some rough treatment back home. No different here I bet. And the kids; can you imagine? Children can be very cruel."

"Yeah, well kids are not the only ones. According to Bob, some of the poor buggers were there in Number One Internment Camp for the duration; didn't get out until about five, six years ago, 1947 it closed apparently, more than two years after war ended. Now it houses some of these immigrant boys arriving out from Britain, so let's hope there's some benefit in that."

Glad freshened their cups, shrugging off the topic, sorry now that she'd brought it up, sensing Dulcie's disquiet, "Ah well," she lifted her cup and took a sip of tea, "enough of all that. I haven't told you about the highlight of our holiday yet, Dulce."

"Come on then, out with it?"

"We managed to get in touch with Mervyn, met up with him in Echuca."

"But Glad, that's marvelous, I'm so pleased for you lovey. He must have been pleased as Punch to see you. And how is he then?"

Echuca could have been Timbuktu for all Dulcie knew, but her animation was rekindled.

"It's a matter of how THEY are, Dulcie. He's about to get married. Cheryl – remember me telling you about her? The girl he met in the Philippines? Well, she is obviously good for him, he was in great form, really come out of himself he has. Her father, Ron, has an interest in the gee gees, horse racing you know; took them all to Flemington for the Melbourne Cup, Tuesday before we saw him. Call it beginner's luck, call it what you will, but Mervyn backed the 14 to 1 winner so he was still pretty cock-a-hoop."

"Good on 'im, who wouldn't be, eh? 14 to 1 – them's good odds. Bill's Mom and Dad liked a bit of a flutter. We lived with them for three years so I learnt a bit about it. I remember Dad having an omen bet once, I think that's what he called it," Dulcie giggled. "It was a Saturday morning and young Jess, she was only a bab then, well she got out from under our guard and crawled into coal cupboard under stairs. We were on the verge of sending out search parties, took so long to find her, so you can imagine the state of her when I eventually fished her out. Black as the Ace of Spades she were. Well there was a horse running that afternoon called Black Jess. Dad couldn't get down to his bookie quick enough to put his money on. It won and all, and at very good odds. Cause for celebration that were," said Dulcie, bending her elbow.

"A good win has the same effect over here too by all accounts, Dulce."

They laughed.

"So," Glad returned to the subject of Mervyn, "To answer your question properly Dulcie, he seems really happy, but somehow I got the feeling he's homesick too," she paused, "Wouldn't surprise me one bit if they showed up here after the wedding."

Dulcie knew immediately that this was what Glad had brought her here for, the implications of the news not lost on her. "That's great news, Glad. Your Dad must be right chuffed. So, when is the wedding to be? Have they set the date?"

"It's not set in stone yet, Dulce, but they're talking about a January wedding."

"Lovely, during the wet season, eh," said Dulcie, "They say a marriage made on a rainy day leads to a fruitful union." She smiled and wiped her mouth with her handkerchief. "Thanks for the morning tea, love, it was a rare treat. It's grand having you back, and I appreciated our talk but I think I should be getting back to young Johnny. I'll have him weaned soon but in the meantime he doesn't take kindly to me keeping him waiting for his feed, not at all, and it's due soon. I've not much to get really. I can walk back to Mavis's after I've been to the butcher; see you there later if you like."

Glad smiled in agreement as she got up, grateful for Dulcie's understanding and forbearance. She rang the bell on the counter, keen to settle up now that her mission had been accomplished. She had a lot to do, things that had been neglected during her absence. Dulcie waved from the doorway as she headed across the road, fading into the brilliant sunshine before vanishing suddenly, snatched from view as the door to the establishment of Mr. Arthur Grubb, Butcher, closed behind her, enveloping her in his world of chopping block and cleaver where carcasses on hooks waited to ooze their metallic, blood-red smell under the keen skill of the hammer-thumbed butcher, once rasp of blade on stone was stilled. Dulcie was shored up by the unchanging familiarity of it all. The sawdust on the floor, the mounds of meat neatly trimmed and labelled, awaiting selection in a shroud of condensation, the freshly made sausages spilling from hooks in festive self-advertisement, strung out like the pinkly bulging gut of some sated mythical creature. Restored by this comforting constancy and Arthur Grubb's perennial good humour she purchased four fat pork sausages - two for Bill, one for herself and a half each for the girls - and a pound of chuck to make a beef pudding, before bidding the butcher goodbye with more robust cheer than she had greeted him.

The distraction of the social intercourse necessary to effect her purchases, and the instinctive sense of wellbeing occasioned by the procurement for her family of good food, worked their simple but powerful magic. When she came out Glad's ute had gone. She walked up English Street, turned left into Catherine and stepped out lightly for Mavis's, taking pleasure in a spring day all the more beautiful after the ugliness and discomfort of the plague locusts, "*Like heaven is to hell*," she mused. As she pressed on, her course of action took form almost subconsciously. For the time being she would keep her own counsel. She would give herself time to think on it, work out how best to tell Bill; how best and when. That it had been a warning she had no doubt, nor did she doubt the expectation on Glad's part that she would share the news, prepare the way; went without saying.

"Here I am," she called as she slowly climbed the back steps.

"Mummy, Mummy" called Jilly, jumping up from the verandah floor and appearing at the top of the stairs as Mavis came to the back door.

"There you are, Dulcie. Shopping all done then?"

"I hope I've not been too long," Dulcie patted Jilly's head and bent to kiss her cheek as she reached the top of the stairs, the comment meant for both of them.

"Did you get me something?" Jilly asked, grabbing Dulcie's hand and swinging from it on her arm.

"I got you your favourite," said Dulcie, joining in the game, "nice fat sausages for your tea tonight, Jilly, to have with baked beans. That's what I got you."

Jilly was clearly less than impressed by this news. Though she forbore to say so, her ardor in their game ran suddenly cold.

"You'd better give me those then, Dulcie, and I'll pop them in the fridge love," said Mavis, taking Dulcie's packages from her. "And as for you, young lady," turning to Jilly and chucking her affectionately under the chin, "there'll be apple pie and ice cream after lunch if you eat your sandwich, crusts and all."

Jilly grinned, the perfection of her world restored.

"But we'd best see to the boys first. They're awake; they were quite happy just burbling at one another when I poked my head in, not ten minutes ago," Mavis smiled at Dulcie, "don't think it'll last much longer somehow."

"They've done well," said Dulcie, drawn to the ritual of meeting her son's simple needs. The two of them headed indoors. Jilly returned to her colouring-in book.

- 0 -

"I think you were right in the thick of it, Dulcie," said Mavis in response to her friend's compliments on the garden's state of preservation and orderliness, "It wasn't near as bad here, and we have done a lot of cleaning up; but see that wire netting?" she turned and pointed to several rolls protruding from under the end of the verandah, by the far fence. "One of the men at the factory suggested covering the garden beds with it. Reg

295

only took his advice when we knew we were in for it. It wasn't as easy as it sounds to be honest, but I'm sure it helped. The peas are a bit ravaged, and the beans; too hard to cover them properly. But they'll come back, early days yet."

Mavis gave the teapot a twist, poured their tea, "Is your place alright, Dulce. You certainly seem to have taken it all in your stride, and Jilly is definitely none the worse for wear."

Dulcie nodded, shrugged, smiled, all at once. *"Our place?"* she thought.

"Not one of Nature's more pleasant gifts, plague locusts," Mavis's words hung in the air behind her as she popped back into the kitchen to get the apple pie.

"But, tell me how you are Dulcie. How you've been," placing the pie on the table, sitting down, "you still look a bit pale," she said, evidently concerned.

"I'm much better thank you Mavis," Dulcie took a spoonful of the pie. "I haven't heard from home, it's too early yet. I expect I will soon," she paused. "I'm fine, really. There's nothing quite like a locust plague to take your mind off things," she smiled, the irony not lost on her. She thought of Jess, that strange fellow, "Funny the way new threats to a peaceful existence can make existing ones seem more bearable."

"I know what you mean, Dulce."

"Still, she comes to me at all sorts of odd times, Mum does. There's no preparing for it. I see her suddenly, in her apron, in the kitchen or pegging out the clothes," she steadied herself, "Or sometimes sitting at the dining table playing cards or just listening to the wireless. Not a vision, not really, but an overpowering presence that seems almost tangible. When it happens, I remember afresh that she's gone, it knocks the wind out me, takes time to recover, get my breath back."

They drank their tea, sat in silence.

"You're eating properly then?"

"Oh aye, Mavis, we all are. I'm thankful for that," Dulcie drew tall, "I enjoy cooking love, you know that, and keeping busy is good for me. I don't know how Bill managed, those first weeks like. I can't properly remember them, but he's not complained. He's grateful to you, he is Mavis. For coming to my rescue like you did. He hasn't said as much but I know he is."

"I'm only sorry I didn't know sooner, Dulcie. You have to promise you'll tell me in future, if you need help, love, even just a shoulder. It's what friends are for. No-one else to turn to, is there?"

A poignant truth for none more so than Dulcie, was that. She finished her pie. Her present dilemma stirred, she pushed it back down, nodded absently as Mavis offered more pie.

"I enjoyed our chat last time, Dulcie. Think of it a lot. To be honest I still find it hard to believe you'd want to come all that way over here, leaving so much behind."

"Well, as I said, that's another story, love. Things change, we change. Everything was changed after the war."

Dulcie inadvertently emptied the cream over her pie, apologised as she saw what she'd done. Mavis patted her hand as she rose from the table.

"It were Bill who'd set his mind on coming out here. When I said I would follow him to the end of the earth I'd no idea he'd actually ask me to do it."

Mavis joined in her laughter as she went to get more cream from the fridge. "So, come on Dulce," she said, coming through the back door, "You were going to tell me about doing nursing. I was attracted by the idea of nursing myself once, but it came to nothing."

"It wasn't just nursing I was interested in, Mavis. I really wanted to be a midwife. I qualified alright which was a real achievement for me; never very good at exams, and you have to become an S.R.N. before you can do your midwifery. I did my S.R.N. training at the Lake Hospital in Ashton, not far from Oldham, lived in Nurses Quarters as was usual when you were in training."

"S.R.N.?"

"State Registered Nurse, love."

"Ah, right."

They finished their second helping of pie. "That was definitely superfluous to requirements, that were," said Dulcie, "but ever so good." She gently pushed the bowl away, sighing as she patted her stomach and gazed out over the garden. It was a lovely spot here on the verandah, shaded from the afternoon sun.

"I really have Plumfritt to thank for getting me through the first couple of years"

"Plumfritt?"

"Another trainee; started her nursing the same time as me and we hit it off right away. Wonderful friend was Plumfritt but an incorrigible practical joker. She helped get me through, no doubt of that, but she was almost the undoing of me a couple of times. I'll never forget one night, Mavis. It were before the war started, this were. We were both rostered on what we all called the mortuary detail. Oh Gawd, how I hated it. It gave me the willies, it did, which fact was well known to Plumfritt, in whom I confided many things."

Dulcie pressed on the rim of her empty bowl with her fingertips, tilted it slightly, let it lower again to the table; a nervous distraction.

"We had preliminary paperwork to do, transit and delivery responsibilities, had to witness a proper handover of the body like, which in itself was not troublesome, but at the Lake Hospital you had to accompany the gurney from the hospital proper through a long tunnel and then across a good 20 yards of open courtyard to get to the entrance of the mortuary. The night time shift was always the worst, weather was often bad."

Dulcie paused in her storytelling, "Now what was that orderly's name. I can't believe I've forgotten. Him and Plumfritt were thick as thieves, they were."

Mavis smiled.

"Any road, Mavis, the night in question was particularly foul. Wind blowing a gale, sleet like needles in your face. I remember the light over mortuary door rippling greenly onto the wet paving stones, feeling the same colour inside I was 'n all. Well, we'd come out of the tunnel, pushing on against the elements, when the corpse on the gurney suddenly sat up, moaning. Ye Gods, I shot so far off the ground in fright I nearly joined moon in orbit; took me two days to get my voice back it did!"

Mavis looked at her, eyes like saucers.

298

"It were no corpse at all were it; it was Plumfritt! Just another of her plurry pranks, in collusion with her orderly friend."

"Oh Dulcie, how could anyone…...?"

"She was just a practical joker, love, but she were well and truly hauled over the coals for that one, I can tell you, and not because I dobbed her in because I didn't, but because it put me right out of action and she had no option other than to explain. I think she was genuinely sorry afterwards, when she saw the state I was in. But I must confess, Mavis, most of the time she made those macabre surroundings bearable with her skylarking about. She were no different to the rest of us really. We all took the mickey out of our worst fears like, one way or another; stiff upper lip 'n all that. I must confess I really missed her when I moved on to do my midwifery."

Mavis smiled, settled back down.

"As it turned out I did midwifery to intermediate level at the Boundary Park Hospital. Lived in there 'n all, though it were only just out of Oldham too, in the outskirts bordering Royton. There was still plenty of opportunity to visit the family, it being so close to home like. They changed its name to Oldham Municipal Hospital just before I left to go to Stepping Hill Hospital in Stockport. Looking back on it, it were only then that I felt as if I'd actually left home."

"So how old were you then?" Mavis had left her family home when she married Reg, moving from beneath the family umbrella to the space beneath another, not like her Mum who'd gone into service in Sydney at the tender age of 12. The idea of 'leaving' home seemed strangely exotic though she knew a lot of young Australian women had done it well and truly, like nurses, going to serve in places like New Guinea.

"Stepping Hill? Mmm, first birthday I had there was my twentieth, love. Talk of war had been rife before I started training back at the Lake Hospital. All I'd ever really wanted to do was help bring babies safely into the world but by the time I finished my midwifery war was so far upon us it should have been over. But it wasn't, so I went into the QAs didn't I? No choice really; had to. It was what one did, though it were a passport to hell in many ways."

"QAs?" Mavis didn't want anything to do with hell!

"Aye, well, all the letters are a bit of a mouthful, Mavis, so it's generally referred to as just the QAs. Its full name was Queen Alexandra's Imperial Military Nursing Service, the QAIMNS, see what I mean; changed its name since then. Any road, I ended up at the Macclesfield District General which had been commandeered by the Army. Fat lot of midwifery I ended up doing there, I can tell you; wouldn't have turned a hair at one of Plumfritt's pranks after a week there, you mark my words. More like a slaughterhouse than an 'ospital, it was. You get inured to it you know, death and dismemberment," Dulcie paused, "until it comes back to haunt you."

"So you were in the Army then?" Mavis didn't want anything to do with death and dismemberment, nor haunting neither.

"You know, I don't think I was at first. I was there until the end of the war. I was Senior Sister by then; had an equivalent Army ranking of Captain which might sound grand but is actually well down the military pecking order. Only one rung below Matron though," Dulcie's smile revealed her personal satisfaction in that achievement. "I remember being issued with service dress uniform to wear off duty. I can't remember exactly when but what a boon. Clothes were desperate hard to come by. Can't imagine how the women kept their growing children decently clothed all those years. Bill's Mom had eleven, you know; her youngest is only a couple of year older than our Jess. Only five foot and a tealeaf she was, and she never stopped."

"So is that where you met Bill, Dulcie, in hospital, when he was injured?"

"No, no, no, lovey," Dulcie shook her head. "I didn't meet Bill till well after the end of the war."

"But I thought......."

"Well I got to know him before I met him in a way. It was Merry told me about him first. My little sister Meredith, you know. I think she was sweet on him herself - schoolgirl's crush. He was Frank's friend, that's one of my brothers. They met up at training camp in Yorkshire before being posted to India in Royal Signals in '44. I was in Macclesfield by then. Anyway, before they left Frank invited him home and, well, to make a long story short, Bill saw a photograph of me in nurse's uniform Dad had on the mantelpiece in front room." Dulcie paused and shook her head, "Why Bill was taken with that I will never understand, I take a terrible photo. But he was; taken enough to write to me. Merry gave him the address like. Well, I wrote back and as a result we corresponded regularly until he eventually came back home in '46."

"Dulcie, I had no idea. But how romantic! Come on," Mavis stood up and started gathering things from the table, "I'm going to make another pot of tea. Come with me, I'm dying to hear more."

"Sorry Mavis, call of nature, love; back in a minute," and Dulcie headed down the back stairs, for the privy.

When she came back up the stairs she could hear Mavis in the kitchen, humming, preparing further refreshment. Clean cups and saucers graced a table freshly dusted down, tidied. Her natural inclination to help was ambushed by the peripheral turmoil of past and present vying for her attention. She sat down abruptly, turned towards Mavis's garden, Glad's earlier warning suddenly uppermost in her mind. Bathed in sunlight, the garden was the epitome of life and fertility, seemingly undiminished by the visitation of ravening locusts. How unnatural it seemed that someone with this extraordinary ability to bring forth such fruitfulness should be herself, infertile, denied motherhood. It seemed unjust – unkind even. Dulcie took a deep breath. As her composure returned she saw with startling clarity the good fortune with which she had been blessed and although Glad's warning stayed with her, her fear of it vanished like a pocket of mist in bright sunshine. She had her Bill and they had their brood. The fear and the hunger were behind them, lost to a different world. They had moved on. It had been hard work but this country had been good to them. It wouldn't stop now, not if they had anything to do with it. She'd tell Bill right away, this evening. They'd need to make plans.

"There you are," said Mavis, coming out the back door with a fresh pot of tea and a plate of Anzac biscuits, "I thought you'd fallen in. You alright then, are you?" she looked closely at Dulcie as she put the tray down on the table.

"Oh, aye, Mavis, much better now thank you lovey."

"Good," said Mavis, "They're all a picture of innocence, they are," she nodded towards the nursery, lifting her eyebrows, "So come on, at least tell me how you two eventually met."

301

Dulcie smiled. "You're an incorrigible romantic, you are," she said as she helped herself to a biscuit whilst Mavis poured tea. "Well," she nibbled reflectively around the edge of her biscuit, "letter writing was not such an easy or rewarding pastime back then, Mavis, I can tell you. It took us a while to get into the swing of it."

"Reg never went overseas," said Mavis, "but I wrote to him in Townsville for a bit. He always said how surprised he was to hear from me. Not because I'd written, you know," she giggled, "but that the letters actually got to him."

"Well he had a very good point," said Dulcie. "Imagine what it was like when letters had to find their way from India to England via a censor. Egad, you'd go weeks with nowt and suddenly a whole bundle of letters would arrive all at once. What with not knowing which one was first, or what the bits with a blue line through 'em might be, it could all be a bit frustrating. You soon learned to put the date on each page, and that was just for starters. Weren't too long before you learnt to censor your own letters too, and just hope your style of prose didn't meet with censor's contempt!"

They laughed.

"But really, Mavis," Dulcie went on, as she turned to gaze over the garden, "It's amazing how much you can get to know someone through correspondence," she sighed, "though none of it prepared me for meeting him."

Mavis held her breath.

"Writing to him had become a sort of ritual well before then. I used to take his photo out of my handbag and prop it up against the lamp stand. I'd glance through his latest letter as I wrote but mostly I looked at him, he not smiling, but looking at me intently, his gaze unwavering. It was clear from his letters that he was homesick, but I could also sense that part of him was revelling in being in a different country. He met Australian soldiers, became friendly with some of them. His eyes were being opened to a world he'd not imagined before. Their stories of life back home fascinated him. I didn't know it at the time, but he was, and still is, an incurable romantic, reading those Zane Grey stories about the early white settlers in America. Really gets a kick out of the pioneering sagas of the Wild West where the main battle always seems to be winning the hand of the pretty girl and carving a homestead out of the wilderness."

"Reg likes a good Western too, at the pictures. Only time I don't have any trouble talking him into going, when I come to think of it," Mavis interjected.

"Men; they're not likely to do owt they don't want to, are they?" Dulcie commiserated, "We just need to work on keeping their ulterior motives alive and well, lovey!"

Mavis nodded in agreement, giggling, "So, how did you meet eventually, Dulce?" as her patience ran out.

Dulcie sighed, remembered the butterflies fluttering up against the walls of her chest as she and Merry had travelled in the train to Southampton, buoyed by Merry's irrepressible excitement. She had recognised him immediately, looking, as she recounted later to a girlfriend, for all the world like Robert Taylor in *Stand by for Action*. He had greeted Merry first with a resounding kiss on the cheek before acknowledging her directly, administering the same greeting with an accompanying hug. Her knees had gone to water at the very sight of him but with his arms around her she was light as a cork, bobbing on a chaos of potentialities, defenseless against the tide of feelings, emotions, sensations which suddenly assailed her … "She's got the bug bad, Mom, you can see it; totally smitten!" Merry had asserted, not without a hint of chagrin, on her arrival back home.

"….. We were married within six month, Mavis," Dulcie said, "and we've never looked back. I could see from the start he was intent on finding a way to get to Australia; land of opportunity he called it, opportunity to do a lot of things he saw little chance of doing back home. Determined he was, and when he sets his mind to something he doesn't give up easily. I remember him saying to me one day, 'Dulce,' he said, 'we can go on living like this or we can go to Australia and make a real life for ourselves and the kids.' We didn't have any at the time though Jess was on the way. He's always wanted a big family has Bill. 'I'm for going to Australia, darling,' he said. 'Come on, I'll toss you for it – heads I win, tails you lose.' Well, I heard him with my heart not my head and he got me, didn't he, not that I minded – I just wanted to be with him."

303

Mavis laughed.

"Next thing I know he was off down to London in search of the Good Cobber's Society to make enquiries about finding a sponsor, and well the rest is history, though it was three years before we got news. They were hard years, Mavis, very hard; served only to strengthen our resolve to seek opportunity elsewhere."

"Do you still have the photo? The one Bill sent with his first letter?"

"Oh, aye; I could never part with that, love, though I don't carry it with me now, not needing an 'andbag like."

"Could I see it some time, Dulcie? And the picture he had of you?"

"Of course you can, lovey, though I'm not sure where the one of me is. Just remind me next time you visit. Oh, he were beautiful, he were; so handsome."

"Still is Dulcie."

"Aye," Dulcie agreed, "looks better now than ever!"

"Can I go for a wee wee, please Mummy?" Jilly asked sleepily from the doorway.

- 0 -

On the drive home Glad and Dulcie were subdued, each wrapped up in her own thoughts, the instinctive care of the children undertaken on a different plane. As they entered the stretch of road above the pig pen, before the turn off at the cattle grid, Dulcie saw the farm with eyes newly opened by the affirmed transiency of their tenure here. She thought back to their arrival. "It's a different place; even the house looks like a proper home," she thought, a poignant edge to her satisfaction. It was later than they had expected to be. The milking was underway and Jess came to the door of the milking shed to greet them, Bill close behind her, intent on helping Dulcie indoors, thanking Glad who didn't stay but promised to drop in soon.

That night, after the girls had gone to bed and young Johnny's demands had been satisfied, Bill and Dulcie sat with their pannikins of tea, Bill not reading, Dulcie not sewing. Gently Bentley was on the radio, which normally had their full and animated attention but now it merely provided a

304

background to their thoughts, each wondering how to best broach the revelations of their day. Dulcie was the first to find her voice.

"I'm not sure we're going to be able to stay here you know, darling?"

"How did you know?"

"Well, who told you?"

"What do you mean?"

"Glad said Mervyn might be coming back… would probably be coming back." There, it was out.

"Ye what? Well I'll be," Bill put his pannikin down with deliberate care though it was empty, and clapped his hands together before beating a tattoo on the kitchen table, "And he will probably want to take back what is his, is that it? And that doesn't bother you, darling?" he asked.

"Well, it rattled me at first; not any more though. We've come this far. There'll be summat else to do, no doubt," Dulcie said, "but you seem positively pleased about it. I thought you liked it here, love, this life?"

"I do, love, I do."

"Well I don't understand. What was it you were meaning?"

Bill stood up, went to get the exercise book with Ledger printed neatly on the front cover. "Well, much as we all like it love, it's not without some significant faults, a big one being that it could always be taken off us. It's that 'something else' I've wanted to talk with you about. You only have to look in here to see that this occupation is not going to provide the future we want, darling. We've been here nigh on a year now and the farm's much improved. You only have to look around to see it, but it's very high maintenance what with one thing and another and we're no better off than when we arrived."

"We've the money to repay Do….,"

"Aye, love. We've managed to hang on to that alright, but it's not been easy and there's precious little else in kitty. It's all in here," he patted the ledger, "makes it clear, love, if we want to get on we need to seek other avenues." He pulled the kettle back onto the hob and went to empty the leaves into the slop bucket. "So, what did Glad say? How long do you think we've got?" he asked as he came back indoors.

"A couple of months, I'd say. Glad said Mervyn is getting married to that girl, the one he went off to find. No dates set or anything, but she suggested they'll tie the knot in January some time."

"So soon," said Bill, a frisson of anticipation sending a shiver up his back.

Dulcie rose to fetch the biscuit jar from the pantry, suddenly aware of the opportunities presented by this new situation. She resolved to raise her wish for the greater accessibility of others, and recreational activity beyond the occasional picnics they had up in top paddock which really only meant taking their sandwiches up there with a Thermos of tea to sit on a rug to eat, instead of sitting at kitchen table. Truth was she felt safer at kitchen table!

That night they discussed a great deal. They drank a lot of tea, taking it in turns to 'do the honours'. They shared anew their dreams for the future, how they could work best together to achieve them. They dared to look one another in the eye and acknowledge with happy acceptance the rightness of their being here, the goodness of the life they had found. And then, before they were utterly depleted by the day's demands, they retired to bed and made the most of young Johnny's newly found ability to sleep for eight hours straight.

The last thing they heard on the fringe of consciousness was the plaintive cry of a curlew mourning the passing of yet another day.

- 0 -

Don't regret and vex for the past.
Bide by the true things to nurture.
Determine to hold to these fast,
And avoid to fear the future.

Chapter Ten

Transients [sic]

*T*he grey predawn light billowed softly into the bedroom under the shutter Bill opened on waking. Dulcie stretched, yawning as he went down into the laundry to set light to the fire under the copper, give the clothes a cursory prod with the copper stick. After lighting one of the Tilley lamps he cleared the detritus of yesterday's fuel from the stove, and quickly set and lit today's fire using kindling and newspaper from the nearby box. Dulcie would replenish the box during the day; keep the fire going until they retired after supper, if only smouldering at times. Maintenance of this rudimentary energy supply was part of life's daily domestic ritual. He took the remains of yesterday's fire out to the privy and emptied them in the bin, walking gingerly, barefooted, on his circular-slabs-of-penda path. On the way back, he collected an armful of firewood from the stack by the fence, something he did with circumspection, ever wary of the wild life that might have made it home.

Among the snakes and withered timber,
Some dead branches often drop.
My life's exposed to constant danger,
It is suicide to stop.

Before stacking the wood behind the stove he put a couple of pieces on the fire, and then went for another load. After adding another piece to the fire under the copper and stowing the rest, he washed his hands in the laundry, filled the kettle. With the kettle and a big pan of water on the hob, and tealeaves in the pot in readiness he opened the front door quietly, careful not to disturb his sleeping children, as he went out to saddle up the horse, tether him to the front fence. Dulcie rose soon after he returned and they performed their ablutions together in the kitchen, a ritual both practical and

311

pleasurable, before taking their tea out the front, to sit on the log, and listen to night chirrup into day.

Their mornings were always busy, what with cows to be milked, bread to be made, breakfast to be had, animals to be fed and watered, eggs to be collected, washing to be got on line, Jess to be got off to school, wood to be chopped, housework to be done. It was a routine they had become accustomed to but today there were letters to be written, important letters which couldn't wait. 'Housework will just have to wait,' thought Dulcie, after straightening up the beds, 'no time for hospital corners this morning,' she thought.

After Bill had set Big Red in the direction of town she sat to catch her breath, think about what lay ahead, what they must do and the order of doing it. By then it was early afternoon and, though tired, she knew if she didn't put the kids' napping time to good use she would end up in a pickle. Thinking was what she needed to do. She fetched her exercise book from the bureau, pulled the kettle back onto the hob and sat down at the kitchen table. 'This wouldn't half tell a story, this would,' she thought as she opened the exercise book, passed Bill's sketch of Jess in her wedding bonnet on the way to fresh page.

First thing she wrote down was FOOD, and underneath it the sub-heading Pantry. She then chewed on the end of the pencil, contrary to her constant advice to the girls, before leaving a few lines and writing, Garden: 'Depleted though it is we've still got spuds and cabbages,' she thought. She pondered further, took a few sips of tea, left a few lines before writing Farm Produce, and below that, Old Bronc, whose contributions of ham or bacon were regular if not often, and enormously appreciated, especially since their economy drive didn't allow for such treats. On a fresh page all of its own she wrote SHOPPING LIST and underlined it purposefully.

After a couple of false starts, she decided on doing things chronologically and wrote CHRISTMAS at top of next page. Having Christmas here was one thing they could rely on, but visions of a treasury bereft of funds stemmed the flow of potential plans. Momentarily stalled she drank tea and looked out the window, before rallying to her cause and writing beside CHRISTMAS: to be discussed.

312

Sitting, thinking about things it suddenly dawned on her how little they had. Leaving a few lines to record their Christmas decisions, she wrote down KITCHEN EQUIPMENT with a sense of urgency, closely followed, halfway down the page by FURNITURE. Given the dire pecuniary straits in which they found themselves she wondered where these things might come from and was simultaneously aware of the extent of the Watson's patronage. Determined to think her way through things and come up with some practical solutions, she poured herself another cup of tea and looked back through what she had written down, each heading a conundrum in itself under the circumstances, but her jottings would keep her on track, give her something she could work through to fulfill her end of the bargain.

Looking out the window, she judged from the angle of the shadows falling across the pig pen that it was time to bring the washing in, think about getting dinner. Jess would be home soon. 'My brain hurts,' she thought, putting the exercise book back in the bureau, escaping to the humdrum of getting the clothes in off the line before Jilly and Johnny woke up to demand her attention.

- 0 -

"Oh, yuckie poo, yyyyyuuuuuuucccccckkkkkk!!"

"Bloody 'ell!!!"

Jilly and Jess ran out of the kitchen down through the laundry and out into the garden, shrieking and yucking their heads off whilst Dulcie stood dumbfounded, gazing at the horrible green mess dripping from the eggshell in her fingers, spattered on the wall, some even on the ceiling. She almost gagged as the breathtaking stench of rotten egg enveloped her. Young Johnny, who'd been standing holding onto the gate at the top of the steps, sat down smartly on his bottom and started bawling his lungs out. By the time Dulcie had gathered her wits, and young Johnny, to rush out the front door for fresh air, Bill was running across the turnabout seeking an explanation for all the fuss.

"Everything alright, Dulcie? Egad, what's that pong?" he said as they met by front gate.

313

"Rotten egg," she said, "all over kitchen. Here you take him. I'm going to wash my hands," dumping Johnny unceremoniously into Bill's hands and going over to the hose as Jess and Jilly came around the corner, looking sheepish.

"So where did rotten egg come from then, eh, you two?" Bill asked.

"Jilly found one yesterday, under one of the little bushes in the corner. We meant to tell Mummy when we brought it in but she was out the back and we just left it there and went out to play and then I was running late for school and we just forgot." Jess's explanation tumbled out with guilty breathlessness.

"Well, you'll not be collecting eggs from under any bush again will you? Next time there'll be hell to pay. You understand?"

"Yes, Daddy," they replied in unison.

"Right, there's no point in crying over spilt milk," he said. "We'd best get kitchen cleaned up before dark or we'll all be camping out here for the night. Place'd go up in smoke if I tried to light Tilley lamp in there at the moment, like as not. Here Jess, take your brother while your Mom and I go and sort out mess."

Jilly wondered where spilt milk came into it but forbore to ask, intuitively aware that she was in the poo in more ways than one. She didn't even mention it to Jess when they were left out the front, sitting on the log trying to keep Johnny's mind off food. Eventually they had bacon and egg pie for their tea, eating it picnic style out the front whilst in the kitchen the lingering pungency of rotten egg gained occasional ascendancy over the stringent smell of Dettol. But it was a balmy evening and a freshening breeze tripped unhampered in the front door and carried the last vestiges of decay out the back. By the time Jilly and Johnny went to bed, Dulcie had declared the kitchen suitable once more for habitation. She gave silent thanks that 'big wet' had not yet arrived.

- 0 -

The RSL Club in town was a modest weatherboard structure. Two steps led up to the central front door which opened straight into a room with a bar along the back wall and a few laminated tables scattered about. A doorway to the left of the bar led to the only other room which was furnished with plump stuffed armchairs, a couple of occasional tables and a long, low table holding an assortment of periodicals and magazines. Newspapers, none of them current, were stacked in a corner. The furniture had obviously come from different sources. Nothing matched, not even the cushions or antimacassars on the armchairs. It gave the room a nice homey feel, abetted by the slightly threadbare charm of a carpet which covered much of the wooden floor. Bill had first been here back in April, on ANZAC day, at the invitation of Reg Johnston. Yesterday his delivery to Reg of Dulcie's note for Mavis had been timely, and he came now to meet with David Baxter who, according to Reg, not only had 'news' for him but was in town to impart it himself.

Entering the club, he found David already sitting over by the louvres, a small beer before him, his cane resting against the corner of the table. Bill greeted him on the way to the bar where he ordered a small beer for himself before joining the man. "Bill Johnson, Dave," he said as he eased himself into the seat on opposite side of table.

"I'm aware of that, Bill," a wry smile crossed the returned soldier's face, "no one else round here sounds even remotely like you, mate." He paused, turned as if to look Bill in the eye, "So, how are you doing? Bad leg giving you trouble?" he asked.

"Well, how the...."

"Ears mate."

Bill looked at the damaged head before him, waited.

"You've an uneven gait, Bill, resounds off floorboards. The relief you got from taking the weight off your feet was plain too. Expulsion of breath as was almost a grunt, dare I say. I'm right," another pause, "Aren't I?"

"Aye, you are," Bill conceded, "and there are plenty as can see don't notice."

"Maybe rain is on the way after all," another wry smile.

"Well I hope you're right about that mate," said Bill, and then, "Good health," raising his glass before taking a sip.

315

"Got that leg injury in India?" David Baxter enquired. In the absence of an immediate answer he went on to say, "Mary said as how your wife had mentioned that you'd been posted there."

"Ah," acknowledged Bill, who had been reassuring himself that he hadn't uttered a peep which could have revealed any connection with India. He relaxed, comfortable in the other man's company. "No Dave, no; I had a couple of near misses in India but got off scot free; had a wartime accident back home, before being posted to India. Dispatch rider at the time."

The blind man found his glass with a steady and unerring hand, took a sip and replaced it carefully on the table, "My older brother spent some time in India. Fought with you lot, with the 77 (Indian) Infantry Brigade in Burma; flew to Burma in 1944 in the 1st Battalion the South Staffordshire Regiment; eventually came out through India."

"Bloody hell!" exclaimed Bill, on a surge of adrenalin, "the Chindits! 2nd Expedition! '44 was the year I was mobilised, Dave; with Kings Signals by then, New Delhi. What was his name, your brother?"

"Peter," was the response; a pause, "Neville Peter Harry Baxter, to be completely correct. Still is his name. He's alive and well, Chief Accountant for a thriving furniture manufacturing company in Britain last I heard."

"Good news is that. Name rings no bells. Would have been monumentally coincidental if it had, eh, though I met up with a few Aussies; sowed seeds for me being here, they did."

Perusals of inner landscapes took place; beer sipped.

"When I set off for India I thought I was headed for Easy Street, Dave, a bit of an adventure. To my mind disseminating information, intelligence if you like, was hardly likely to be the stuff of which heroes were made. I weren't light infantry at front line, shitting myself most of the time for one reason or another like a lot of other poor sods. I soon learnt different; wrong in many ways." He paused, suddenly and vividly immersed in what he thought a closed chapter of his life, parts of which would remain private forever. "New Delhi itself was a revelation. Part we were in were beautiful, elegant even; wide boulevards, beautiful flowering trees. Mosquitoes as big as buffaloes, mind you. Bred in the Yamuna and wafted in through Delhi Gate they reckoned."

316

"Not unknown to me mate, mozzies like that."

"Place had been under strict blackout for a good while when I arrived. Not that inhabitants were dug in, like, living in fear of losing their lives in cramped Anderson shelters if their luck ran out. Not like back home," he paused, stopped by the unexpected assault of images of the bombardment his Mom and the young uns had endured, thankfully survived. As if sensing Bill's need to continue, David Baxter waited, took another sip of his beer.

"As a posting it weren't bad really. Copped a couple of field trips, though neither into Burma; spared a taste of hell from what we heard; a bloody, muddy, vicious death-trap was putting it mildly, ask me. They were all heroes those lads, every last one of them."

"Yeah, well Peter lived to gain recognition for his efforts. One of the lucky ones," he laughed grimly, pulled himself together before continuing, "Yeah, he was awarded the Military Cross for action took place in 1944. Main task the 1SSR had, I only know this from his subsequent accounts of course, was to cut the lines of communication serving the Japanese Army. They set up base at Henu, near Mawlu, in the Mogaung-Indaw Valley."

"White City!"

"Yeah, I believe they called it that because of all the parachutes hanging from the trees."

"Aye, that's right. Egad, he were right in the thick of it, no mistake," Bill paused, his memory rampant, "Communications, intelligence if you will, was paramount to success of those operations – responsibility weighed heavy on us lot, and it were often not possible to come up with goods; casualties were high. We all felt it. Americans flew their Dakotas in and out delivering equipment, personnel, supplies, bringing casualties out as could be helped. Wasn't easy that, place came under very heavy Jap bombardment. They sent in their carrier-based Mitsubishi Zeros in force. Seen 'em?"

"Yeah, I've seen 'em alright, Bill. One of the things I'll never forget. Bastards dropping bombs to the accompaniment of machine gun fire from wings and cowlings."

"Aye, I've often wondered what life would be like now if our ack-ack bulldogs with their Bofors auto-cannons hadn't proved superior," Bill paused, wet his lips. Since demobilisation opportunities to talk man to man about these experiences had been rare. Whenever he did his mouth ran dry. He sipped his drink, "Chindits' job was to 'rattle' the Japs apparently. They did that alright; surprisingly little heard of them now in my opinion, they deserve better. Or of Wingate; man was a bloody genius for my money. "

"So legend amongst men has it. Lentaigne had taken over command by time 1SSR arrived. Different kettle o' fish altogether by all accounts," Dave responded.

"Seems an odd place for an Aussie to end up," Bill remarked.

"Yeah, well he was born here same as me but Peter was the brainy one Bill. We both went to the Shore School in Sydney, boarders. Church of England Grammar School, strong academic record, etcetera, etcetera."

Bill listened intently, the social standing of his companion becoming clearer by the minute, though he'd noticed long ago that the locals didn't stand much on ceremony as such things went.

"Peter always had an interest in figures, money – Finance they call it; expressed a strong desire to find his roots too. Well, he did well enough at Shore to get into Cheltenham College in England. Dad still had family over there which probably worked in Peter's favour. Agricultural College was where I was headed. Fact that I always wanted to come back up here, work the land, take over the farm when the time came probably worked in his favour too. Well, he was over there when war broke out, was commissioned into the South Staffordshire Regiment. Rest you know."

"What about you, David, where did you see action?"

"Papua New Guinea, mate," David said, "with Australian 39th Battalion fighting Japanese invading from north. Yanks helped, for which we were all very grateful, I can tell you," he paused. "In some ways I can understand the complaints – you know, over sexed, over paid and over here."

"Aye, much the same sentiments expressed back home."

"Reckon we would have been up Shit Creek without 'em all the same," David took a sip of his beer before continuing. "Conditions in PNG were much as Peter described in Burma. We've talked about it. Was a time we shared the same nightmares. Japs overhead spitting bullets at you, Jap snipers, Jap bombs, Jap ambushes, Jap grenades – Jap painap to the locals in PNG or Janpani finafur, if you were a black African soja, I understand," he drew a

318

deep breath, "but warfare itself was just a part of it. Peter had Burma itself to contend with. In PNG we had Kokoda."

"Kokoda Trail?"

"Bloody lie of land was almost our biggest enemy. Could only be travelled on foot, torrential rains, so bloody high in the Owen Stanleys you had hot humid days followed by freezing nights. Suffered as many casualties, if not more, from their vile tropical diseases – malaria, typhus, trench foot; some there's no name for, made their presence known by burning, itching, tingling sensations all over the body."

"Allergies, insects maybe," Bill interjected with a shudder, always having had a dread of such maladies, something to do with having had a neighbour with psoriasis when he was a kid.

"Yeah, who knows?" David said and continued his litany of ills as though it were a roll call, "Swollen tongues, dysentery as made a man weak as a kitten – saw the lot, had a few; and as for the reptilian life. There were times Japs presented a healthy distraction, no kidding."

He paused, reached for his beer.

"Owe my life to a local man, only a boy really. Didn't even know his name; still don't. But I'll never forget his last words. He yelled 'Painap ikam!' as he caught the bloody thing, Jap grenade, lobbed it up and away from us. Flash as it exploded was last thing I ever saw." They sat in silence, any useful purpose in verbal expression escaping them for a time. "I learnt later he lost his life."

"I'm sorry to hear that, Dave," Bill said quietly. "Finish your beer and I'll get us another seeing as you got the last."

When he came back from the bar Bill sat down in deliberate silence, privately amused that his companion's acute hearing had made him self-conscious. His contrivance didn't go unnoticed. David exercised his wry smile before taking a draught of his fresh beer. "Fuzzy wuzzy angels, we called them," he continued, "the locals. I'm one of many to owe them my life, mate. Good people they are, gentle, caring, in my experience. Eight of 'em carried me out of there on a stretcher contrived by slinging blanket between two poles with spreaders at each end. I'd seen 'em do it heaps of times. Carried me out well past nearest ADS and on to Owers' Corner where I could be airlifted to Port Moresby."

"ADS?" Bill asked, unable to find meaning in the acronym.

"Advanced Dressing Station"

"Right, like our Casualty Clearing Stations"

"I dare say. I'll never know how much time I lost but when I came to I was in the 2/9th Australian General Hospital in Port Moresby under the cool and gentle hands of Phyllis Knightman. Still corresponds with Mary, she does, from back home in Tasmania; started off with her penning my letters to Mary, before they could repatriate me. She was a good sort was Phyl, bit of a character; had what you might call a robust sense of humour; pretty handy in ugly circumstances, eh?"

"Aye," Bill agreed, an image of what Dulcie had had to withstand coming to mind.

"I don't know what Phyl's rank was, if any. She was a member of the Voluntary Aid Detachment, a VA. In hindsight, it was about to become the Australian Army Medical Women's Service at that time. Anyway, she hadn't been in PNG long, keen as mustard to fit in, do a good job. As she told it, she'd heard various people, blokes, using the word 'Tufutma' pretty much the same as you'd say, 'see you later'."

"Ta ta for now, like."

"Yeah. So anyway, thinking to fit in with local custom, become one of the lads, she started using it to sign off on all her notes, memos, correspondence generally. Made quite a name for herself as it happened. She'd been doing it for a month or so before someone took it upon hisself to let her know it was an acronym invented by ranks to disparage brass; stood for 'Tell Um Fuck Um They're Mad Anyway'!"

Emotions heightened by their shared reminiscences were suddenly released, bouncing off the walls in laughter, long and loud.

They were still chuckling when Bill asked, "How did poor girl get out of gaffe like that then?"

"No dummy, Phyl, even if she was just a bit too eager to please. It was actually brass who tipped her off," David Baxter paused to get a grip on mirth rising in his throat, "and as she said to me, what was done was done,

320

last thing she wanted was to show herself up for a fool so she kept up use of the salutation and just enjoyed the reputation it'd got her. Only change she made was to print it in capitals, like an acronym should be but without any full stops. She reckoned it did her a lot more good than harm."

They burst out laughing again.

"Anyhow," said David eventually, wiping his face with a handkerchief he'd fished out of his trouser pocket, "about this news I have for you."

"Reg mentioned something about a vehicle," Bill responded, sliding back into the present.

"Yeah, it's nothing too flash at the moment, but it's going for the right price. All you have to do is to get it to your place; doesn't go. Needs some work, but they reckon you know your way around a motor, Bill."

"What is it?" Bill asked as he tried to absorb import of David's news.

"A Willys 77, 4-Door Sedan, Bill. 1936 but well kept. It's a handsome looking motor."

"I know it," he now had Bill's undivided attention. "Why would anyone want to let one of those go if it still has life in it?"

"It's been under wraps for four or five years I'd reckon, since Bert's missus passed away; holds too many memories for him. Reckons the ute's all he needs."

"So what's the asking price then," Bill asked, to leave no room for misunderstanding, excitement mounting from the pit of his stomach.

"Well it'll probably set you back a set of tyres, few parts, nothing serious. You'd probably want to contribute to petrol, maybe a couple of beers for Curly to cover towing costs. Apart from that, she's all yours."

"Hells bells, you mean it! He's a generous man, your mate Bert. That's bloody marvelous, what can I say? I'm delighted; dead chuffed to be honest."

"So I can hear, mate."

Bill took a sip of his beer, and subsided like a recalcitrant soufflé as his current circumstances flooded back.

"What is it?" It was as if Dave had heard the wind leave his sails.

"I was getting carried away with the idea but things aren't that cut and dried at the moment, Dave. They've changed since we last spoke. To be honest I was right pleased to hear you were up here. I thought you might have advice as to best course of action."

David Baxter picked up his near empty glass and drained it.

"What's the time?" he asked.

"Plurry hell, it's after three," Bill said, "I'll have to be getting back mate – milking."

"Right, well, time's escaped us. Mary will be picking me up any minute, but we're back up here, me and the family, for the next few months, Bill, so you and I could get together again any time. When suits you? Friday sound alright? Here again, around 1 o'clock," he'd sensed an urgency in Bill's appeal.

"That'd be grand," said Bill, "outside of milking time anytime is good for me, and thanks mate. Thanks for everything. I've enjoyed talking with you. And I'd like to think on the car; maybe there is a way. It's a smashing offer."

"Friday then," they said in unison, shaking hands.

- 0 -

Fuzzy Wuzzy Angels

Many a mother in Australia
when the busy day is done
Sends a prayer to the Almighty
for the keeping of her son
Asking that an angel guide him
and bring him safely back
Now we see those prayers are answered
on the Owen Stanley Track

For they haven't any halos
only holes slashed in their ears
And their faces worked by tattoos
with scratch pins in their hair
Bringing back the badly wounded
just as steady as a horse

322

Using leaves to keep the rain off
and as gentle as a nurse

Slow and careful in the bad places
on the awful mountain track
The look upon their faces
would make you think Christ was black
Not a move to hurt the wounded
as they treat him like a saint
It's a picture worth recording
that an artist's yet to paint

Many a lad will see his mother
and husbands see their wives
Just because the fuzzy wuzzy
carried them to save their lives
From mortar bombs and machine gun fire
or chance surprise attacks
To the safety and the care of doctors
at the bottom of the track

May the mothers of Australia
when they offer up a prayer
Mention those impromptu angels
with their fuzzy wuzzy hair.

By Sapper Bert Beros

- 0 -

He picked Jess up near the ford, found in her exuberant chatter a welcome distraction from serious thought, knowing his subconscious would carry on in the background anyway, needless of his interference. As they came up the rise of the south paddock towards home he saw with pleasure smoke rising from Athol's campfire. The wanderer had returned; to the satisfaction, Bill thought, of those looking forward to Christmas hams from his neighbour's renowned smokehouse. Beyond the thin scribble of wood smoke above the humpy there was no sign of life. It was too late to pay a visit; milking to be done. Hardly likely that Athol would turn up for that, and if not he would drop in to see him tomorrow. Setting Jess down at the house, he reassured Dulcie that he'd had a good afternoon and exchanged the Thermos of tea she had awaiting him for the mail, letters from Merry and Harvey at last. She clutched them to her bosom with a smile saying nevertheless, to reassure him, "Don't worry, darling. I'll read them later, when kids are all in bed, asleep."

Since then he'd brought the cows in, gone through the motions of milking whilst his mind did battle with a ragtag of thoughts about life past, present and future, and dispatched the herd back to the depleted pasture. They'd had one of Dulcie's famous beef puddings for tea, with potatoes and cabbage; the girls loved it. Nothing did him better than to see his family eat a hearty meal. Young Johnny sat in his high chair bashing out a staccato tattoo with a spoon and spraying sieved vegies over all and sundry. It was hard to maintain the rule of silence during meals under the circumstances. Dulcie had looked calm throughout, resolute. His newly recognised love beat powerfully in his chest.

Now he stood at the front door, seeing his surroundings with the hungry eyes of one soon to be dispossessed of all before him. He had grown fond of this place with which his sweat and blood had mingled. The jacaranda tree whose every leaf had reflected the play of sunlight a few hours earlier, now stood black against the darkness, the purple carpet from which it had risen this morning a shimmering stain at its feet. A single star twinkled in the reddish, closing sky. One of the cats walked from the windmill to the milking shed with cautious steps and crawled into a space between the corrugated iron wall and the concrete slab. There was a gentle breeze on which rode the earthy pungency of pigs and cows, crushed grain, cut grass, rich red dirt, the life with which he had grown so familiar. He headed back over to the milking shed, pigs to feed, apparatus to be sterilized and stowed in readiness for morning milking.

Night had descended in pristine spring splendour and he had nearly finished up when he heard Dulcie calling him softly but urgently from the entrance. He quickly turned the water off before hurrying out to meet her. She stood by the entrance, glimmering palely in the starlight, looking for all the world as if she were waving a white flag. Of one thing he was certain; it wasn't bad news that had brought her here. He could feel the energy of her excitement as he approached, "It's Harvey, darling," she whispered frantically, "He's coming out, love; coming here, like right here I mean, love, to see us. Coming to stay like! I couldn't wait to tell you."

She was beside herself. He hadn't seen her so happy in a long time, couldn't really remember seeing her so at all. He took her in his arms and stepped her into the turnabout where they danced a lively jig, sending up puffs of red dirt beneath the Milky Way which blazed above them. Bill called a halt up by the barn, gasping, "Bloody wellies weren't made for this, darlin'," as he let go of her, bent over with his hands on his knees, gulping for air. "That's grand news, that is, darlin'," he rasped, "but it could take a while you know, depending on which course of action he chooses to embark on. Best not get your hopes up too much, for seeing him soon, I mean."

Dulcie brought her giggling under control, she too panting, though less raggedly, "I think it's been on his agenda awhile, love; he says he could be here as soon as April, May next year. He'll inform us when his passage is confirmed. Oh, it will be wonderful to see him," her face glowed with pleasure.

"Well he's certainly put my news in the shade, love," Bill smiled, put his arms around her shoulders. "Come on, let's get in, have a cuppa. All that cavorting has made me thirsty."

Jess opened the front door as they went through the gate, "There you are," she said, "Something woke me up and I couldn't find you!"

"Sorry darling, I didn't mean to wake you. I just went over to milking shed to see your Dad about something that's all," said Dulcie.

"Come here love," Bill put his hand out to Jess, "as you're up, come and I'll show you something special, something you can only see at night time, while your Mom goes and puts the kettle on."

"Hang on a minute, love. She'll need her wellies, won't you darling? I'll just pop in and get them."

Beyond the front door Jess was accustomed to the sight of the milking shed and cream house, the jacaranda tree over by where Dad had moved the big log, the green fields, barn and windmill beyond, but tonight she was faced with a chimerical landscape of a quite frightening kind. It was a world without colour, just different shades of black. The strange night light kneaded the familiar shapes she knew into grotesque blobs, giants and monsters with palpably malignant intentions. The jacaranda loomed overhead like a bogey man and she took comfort from the warmth and firmness of her Dad's hold on her hand. Dulcie came and left, closing the front door behind her after putting Jess's wellies on.

"You'll be right in a minute, love," Bill said as if sensing her discomfort, "when your eyes adjust," he led her across the turnabout to the stump by the molasses tank. He brushed the top of the stump with his free hand and picked her up, sat her on it, "You sit here love, I'll be back in a minute."

Jess only remembered being out at night once before and that was at Aunty Glad's wedding party. Then she had been busy running around with all the other kids, playing tag or hide and seek, or seeing who could twirl around the fastest before falling over in a dizzy swoon; everything had been lit up by lanterns and campfires and she'd been much too busy to take any notice of what was going on up in the night sky. Even now she was allowed to stay up later than Jilly, once they'd had their bath they had to stay indoors on pain of going to bed early if they got dirty again. By the time they'd listened to Jason and the Argonauts and The Muddle-Headed Wombat and had their tea it was usually time for Jilly to go to bed anyway, and she really only stayed up to do her homework or, if there was none, to read or work on one of her projects.

She looked back towards the house, was surprised to see it quite clearly. The jacaranda tree was still black though easily recognised. To her surprise, deliberate inspections, first down towards the Coughlin's place and then up towards Old Bronc's, revealed their objectives in remarkable detail and, drawn to the source of this amazing light, she looked up. It was as if the sun was shining brightly through hundreds of tiny higgledy piggledy holes in a black curtain.

Bill came back, one of the horse blankets slung over his shoulder.

"It's much lighter now Daddy."

"Aye, that's just your clever eyes, love. Light's not changed, your eyes have adjusted to it," he helped her down and led the way to the edge of the south paddock. They climbed through the fence instead of opening the gate

326

which was a bit rusty and squeaked loudly; he threw the horse blanket down on the ground. Signaling Jess to join him he lay on his back on one side of the rug and put his hands behind his head. They lay there looking up at the sky.

"What do you think of that, eh, Jess? That's the Milky Way."

"It's making me giddy Daddy."

Bill chuckled. "I know what you mean, love. It's like being on the edge of a big black hole, but you're all right. You won't fall. You're lying flat on your back, remember."

Jess giggled. "That's a funny name, the Milky Way, but it's pretty; like the diamonds in my black velvet dancing costume, remember it? They twinkle just the same. It's beautiful."

"That's outer space, Jess. Those diamonds are stars."

"It's as if the sun has exploded into lots of tiny pieces."

"No, no, don't you worry, that's no super-duper-nova," he chuckled. "Sun will come up in the morning, lovey. It's shining on the other side of the world at the moment, lighting up someone else's day while we have a sleep. That's the way it works."

"Where do they come from? Looks like there's zillions of them."

"Zillions, eh?"

"Yeah, at school the kids reckon there are millions and billions and trillions and squillions and zillions. I think zillions is the biggest, hugest number. Kids use it to really show off about something."

Bill chuckled. "Notice how some of them are brighter than others? Like that one over there, see, that very bright one. That one's probably Deneb, low like that in the northerly sky at this time of year." They had both raised their heads to look where he pointed, to a spot just above Old Bronc's place.

"Have they all got names?" she asked in astonishment.

"No, lovey, no; I don't think they ever will. That's a job for astronomers for time immemorial I should think. One thing I do know though, there's more up there than meets the eye and a lot of what we see now is not there anymore."

"What's a stronomus, Daddy?" not having understood a word of what he said. Mummy would have called it double Dutch for sure and certain.

Bill chuckled again.

"We'll be here all night if you start asking questions, love."

"Sorry, Daddy," Jess held her tongue. The sky was a magical thing she wanted to keep looking at. Then she had a sudden thought and before she knew it another question popped out, "Are the stars only like this here? You know, in Malanda?"

"That's a bigger question than you know, Jess. You remind me and I'll tell you the answer as best I can after tea one night at the weekend, and to your other question about astronomers. You just remember, alright," he said, pushing himself up into a sitting position before standing and offering her his hand. "Come on, let's get you back to bed." He saw her to the front gate, put his index finger to his lips and whispered, "Close door behind you quietly love, we don't want to wake the others up, do we. Say goodnight to your Mom and tell her I'll be in in a minute."

- 0 -

From where they had camped under Skennar's Bridge, Jenkin Evans and David Davies were unaware of the long shadows cast by the westering sun into the south paddock, jagged black brushstrokes in the vivid red dirt. A billy of tea mashed over their campfire, their swags already rolled out in readiness for the early sleep needed by those who've to rise and be on the road before sun-up; Evans to walk north to a farm he'd worked on before, clearing land, splitting wood, carrying out repairs and maintenance; Davies to head into town where he expected a lift to a loggers camp out past Peeramon. They'd both been in this vicinity before, were known to be good workers. They'd met before too, more than once, rubbed along quite comfortably together. Maybe their Welsh roots had something to do with it. This year they'd met by chance in Innisfail, made their way to Malanda together, the destination each had been bound for.

"Did you see Old Bronc this afternoon, Davey?"

"Yeah, I did as it turned out. He came into the pub to pick up supplies; says he got back a few days ago, busy smoking his Christmas hams."

"Aye, I stopped in at Post Office this morning, saw him there. Told me same story, said we were welcome if rains come before we're fixed up with something; said he'd manage to put us up somehow. A superfluous invitation for my part, but much appreciated all the same."

"You be right at the May's place til you get the job done then?"

"Aye, settle into the barn up there, and the missus is not stingy with the tucker. I could have done a lot worse. Pay's fair. How about you Davey, fared well yourself have you?"

"Yeah, pretty good. I'm gunna be blue-tonguing, take over from Bogga Jack. Know him? Apparently he's gone walkabout again. Suit me if he isn't in too much of a bloody hurry to get back."

"Heard of him," Jenkin nodded, "So you're working with that young Godfrey bloke eh? Heard he broke his leg. He'd be needing help. What about when big wet arrives?"

"Phil's a good bloke mate, smart too. When logging's not possible he reckons he'll invest in veneer logs condemned by Forestry, maple, walnut stumps and we'll get the best out of 'em we can with axes. Do the same thing with the crutches in the heads of the big maple trees if they have good figure in 'em. He knows the market. There's them as want that sort of timber."

"Sounds like you've done it before; should keep you going, you reckon?" Jenkin leaned over towards the billy, using a big handkerchief to protect his fingers from the heat of its handle. He was suddenly distracted by a commotion up stream. They turned as one and observed a disturbance on the northern bank reveal itself to be a couple of youngsters who'd taken a spill at the top and tumbled down into the drift of leaves by the side of the creek.

The bigger of the two was quick to recover, help the other one up, give it a bit of a looking over before they both leaned on a branch which seemed to rest on the bank along the water's edge, a vantage point from which they peered out into the stream, intently scanning back and forth across the surface of the water and along the banks.

The two men froze, as did their conversation. Nevertheless, their presence was soon discovered as the youngsters' quest carried their visual investigation downstream. For a moment in time old eyes locked with young before the two 'drop-ins' scarpered in another flurry of leaves, leaving in their wake a ribbon of childlike shrilling which fluttered down from the south paddock, the only remnant of their passing presence.

"There it is," said Jenkin, breaking their silence, "reckon that's what they were after."

"What?" Davies stood up, turning to follow the direction indicated by Jenkin's pointing finger. Then he saw it, "Platypus!" he exclaimed in disgust, "bloody vermin."

"Aye, well that's as may be," it wasn't the first time Jenkin had listened to such sentiments from David Davies, "miracle more like to them," nodding his head in the direction of their escape. "It's a pity we scared them off. I think they were daughters of the Englishman living on Mervyn Watson's farm. Creek runs down the western side of the property. They'll not have seen anything like that where they come from," with which Jenkin turned his attention back to replenishing their tea.

"You know a lot for someone who's only been in town as long as me," Davies accepted his replenished pannikin, added a good tot of rum and sank back down on his bed roll.

"Aye, well I spend my time differently to you, as you well know. Maybe it's just different 'stuff' I know."

Their conversation dwindled.

"Anything for you at the Post Office?" Davies broke the silence.

"There was; letter from Margaret, eldest daughter. Letter she wrote in April."

"Taken it's time then."

"Been on the move."

"What's news?"

"My father-in-law has died, 94 year old he was. Three others have gone too, one of 'em my brother-in-law, of Pontfaen. He was a distinguished sea-captain was Dewydd. Fell from his horse and was killed on the 15th February last, on the road between Llanrhystyd and Llanon, when returning

330

from Aberystwyth market. News as provokes the thought that I should think of getting back home."

A useful word didn't come to Davies' mind so he settled back, pannikin held like a friend to his bosom. They sat in silence for a long time until the closing day immersed them in the quotidian stridency of cicadas.

Jenkin Evans placed more wood on the fire, drew closer to the resulting light with a pencil and paper and set about making the notes which would assist him in keeping a full and correct record of the day's activities in his diary when he once again had the requisites for the activity, ink, light, and a level writing surface. His eighteenth Australian diary awaited his attention amongst his scanty belongings. The previous seventeen languished in his eldest daughter Margaret's Welsh attic with the unknown number he had written of his life before his departure.

Time goes, You say? Ah No!
Alas, Time stays, We go.

- 0 -

A thought buzzed around the edge of Jess's mind, a thought she couldn't quite bring into focus. She had the vague feeling it had something to do with Mummy. Unsettling forces were at work. Although she had obviously adjusted, as Daddy put it, Mummy now seemed to be happy and sad at the same time. Added to this, Daddy had picked her up from school again today, on Big Red. In all the ages and ages they had been here he had only picked her up once before and that had been in Curly's ute. She knew he only rode into town for especially important things which couldn't wait, so what was so especially important twice in the one week. They had arrived home earlier still today which is why she and Jilly had had plenty of time to go exploring around the rill down by the creek. As the heat of the day pushed on relentlessly into the late afternoon, they'd been splashing their feet in the cold clear water of the rill when Jilly had wondered out loud whether the locusts had all washed down the creek yet. It was when they went to investigate that they saw the platypus sliding into the water on the other side, swimming off downstream. No conference had been necessary; their pursuit of the creature had been pure instinct. So intent had they been on their quarry neither of them noticed the bank's sudden steep descent and they tumbled down in a flurry of arms and legs.

"Ow, that hurt," Jilly said as they came to rest in a drift of leaves by the edge of the creek.

"Lucky there's no rocks here. Are you alright? Let me look at you."

"I'm alright Jess, but we probably scared it off," Jilly had her miffed look on.

Jess took her hand and together they leaned on a tired old branch lying down by the water's edge and peered into the water, looking carefully downstream where the cynosure of their searching eyes had seemed to be heading. The bridge came into view at the same time as the smell of wood smoke reached their nostrils. They gasped in unison as they saw the two men looking directly at them from under the bridge.

"Come on, Jilly. Let's go!"

And they were off, scrabbling their way back up the bank as best they could, startled rather than scared, and spurred to greater exertion than usual by the definite feeling that they had been caught out doing something that would have been denied approval had they taken the trouble to ask. They went back the way they had come, through the opening where the lantana was thin and they could push it aside out of the way. When they got back to the south paddock Jess was surprised at how late it was. She could see her Dad was busy in the milking shed. "I hope we haven't missed The Muddle-Headed Wombat," she said to Jilly.

"Me too."

"And I think we shouldn't say anything about going down the creek," added Jess, "just in case."

"Just in case what?"

"Just in case, that's all, silly. Alright?"

"Alright, I won't say anything about the creek but what about the platypus?"

"Jilly," Jess was clearly exasperated, "how can you tell about the platypus without saying anything about the creek? That's stupid."

"Alright, I won't say anything. Race you up the hill!"

Jilly took off as fast as she could. Jess made a strategic decision to let her win, but not by so much as to spoil the victory. Their adventure had quite dispelled her disquiet about the forces at work around her.

- 0 -

Dulcie carried the two pannikins of tea out to the shed, was pleased to step into the light cast through the open doorway by the bright mantle lamp illuminating Bill's work. She had developed a prudent need to see clearly the creatures with which she might inadvertently share her personal space; it was a need left wanting by the starlight, however luminous. A naked plastic doll smiled at her lopsidedly as she put the tea down on the work bench. "We'll need to fix her lippy up," she said, "a bit of nail polish should do the trick. How's it going darling?"

"Here, have a look love. I think this was left over from the wood Mervyn used for the larder, plenty of suitable off cuts. I've cut all pieces. Putting the holes for screws in the ends will take a bit of work but there's plenty of time. I thought I'd just paint a simple design on each end, here," pointing to the illustration he'd stuck to the bench, "a Fleur de Lis maybe, in red, and then give the whole thing several coats of what I think is a nice honey-coloured shellac. See, over there. I've a lot of time for a man as doesn't throw things away."

"Mervyn you mean?"

"Aye, we've everything we need except red paint. What do you think?"

"Sounds lovely; they'll be tickled pink they will," she leaned on the bench drinking her tea, taking pleasure in watching his capable, well-shaped hands at work sanding the raw edges of the pieces he'd cut. He was making a cradle for the doll which he'd picked up from St. Vinny's in Mareeba months ago, smuggled into the shed and promptly forgotten until his memory had been jogged by Dulcie's question earlier in the week about plans for Christmas. They'd decided that he would make the cradle and she would make the bedding and a couple of sets of clothes as a shared present for the girls. Individually they would each be given a book. Jess would have one to

333

read, Jilly one to colour in. Johnny's development of such expectations would be actively discouraged for as long as possible.

"I can take her inside now then, can I, get on with my end of the bargain?" He grunted in the affirmative. Dulcie finished her tea, picked up the doll, pushed its arms and legs down into the standing-at-attention position and tucked it under her arm. Gathering the pannikins she made a move to go back indoors, "You won't be long will you darling?"

"No love. I'll just tidy up here and be right with you. I know we've things to talk about."

She pulled kettle back onto hob when she heard him running water in laundry to wash his hands. By the time he came in a fresh pot of tea was ready and the crochet hook was busily at work. He went to the pantry and fetched the jar of biscuits; he'd earlier welcomed the mouthwatering aroma of baking as a further sign of Dulcie's recovery – her adjustment – to say nothing of looking forward to a nice biscuit for supper.

"The girls alright then," he asked as he poured the tea, "they seemed a bit quiet at teatime. Nothing happened I need to know about?"

"Not so far as I know, love. I think they just wore themselves out, playing, what with Jess getting home so early like, and it was a hot day darling, hotter than it's been. Didn't you notice?"

"Was hot."

"I was right pleased to have hand with chopping wood, I can tell you," she poked the crochet hook well through the loop and held it in place with her left thumb and index finger, reached for her tea, took a sip. "I was right surprised when Athol turned up with that old geezer, swag on his back 'n' all, but honestly darling, you could have knocked me down with a feather when they made purpose of their visit clear. I hope I didn't do the wrong thing, love, but I told them straight up as how I couldn't offer more than a ploughman's lunch and chopping wood was all I could think of. Jenkin Evans seemed well satisfied with that, complimented me on bread he did. He was full of surprises, he was. Did far more than I imagined he might, better at it than I." She took another sip of tea, took up her crocheting, "Never been in that sort of rum position before, finding tasks for the hired help."

"Did Athol tell you I saw them in town?"

334

"Aye, he said as much, in Post Office."

"I asked him to mention it."

"Thanks love, certainly made me more amenable to situation."

"I think providing Jenkin Evans' services was Athol's idea, his way of making up for going off without a word, leaving everything to us; and I could see he and Evans were more than passing acquaintances."

"That's funny. I had same thought, they were very comfortable together."

"Aye, well, I mentioned him to David Baxter. Way he tells it, Evans was a successful farmer, left a thriving farm at Trecefel in Wales to come here, left a wife and grown family 'n all. Bloody long time ago, he reckons. Nigh on 18 years."

"Deep in depression that was," Dulcie mused.

"I doubt a successful farmer's Depression would have been quite the same as ours, love." Tightened belts, his Mom's pain at parting with yet another family treasure to afford the prices asked for small part of an illegal catch, her pleasure in seeing her family eat a half decent meal; vivid images assailed him like the fleeting pain of an exposed nerve in a decaying tooth.

"I suppose you're right, when you think about it. Large part of job is putting food on the table, when you're living off the land like. It takes enough of one's time."

"Aye, Dulcie, but at least you eat well. According to David, the man wasn't absconding from any financial responsibilities; he had no financial stringency from which to escape. Apparently Evans has firmly laid reason for his leaving at the door of his spouse, a woman some ten years younger than him; according to him their marriage was sorely blemished by discord and disaffection. One day, he reached the end of his tether, his offspring had grown up and he decided to emigrate to Australia. He just upped and off."

"That seems a bit harsh. You wouldn't just up and leave me like that would you love?"

"Come on, Dulcie. What a thing to say. You'd never give me reason to darling," he leaned across and stroked her cheek, "besides, we've already emigrated love, together like," he smiled broadly.

335

She returned his smile, commented, "You seem to know an awful lot about this Jenkin Evans."

"Aye, well," he continued, offering Dulcie a biscuit before helping himself, "his story interested me and David likes a chat. Chance has it that Trecefel, where Evans is from, is not so far from Athol's family home. They've both been out here about the same amount of time, so even if they didn't know one another back in the Old Dart they'd find plenty to talk about."

"Like as not," agreed Dulcie. "Good to be able to share your memories," she added, "can act like the glue in a friendship they can."

"Whatever the reason, they hit it off apparently right from start and over the years Evans has kept coming back. Spends most of his time in Victoria but comes north most years to escape their bushfire season."

"Rum, if you ask me, floods at one end of the land and bushfires at t'other."

"Aye, Dulcie," he acknowledged, "it is that. Anyway, he's obviously become well known to a good few people around here, and David Baxter's one such," Bill paused, prepared himself to broach the subject they really needed to talk about. "Athol mentioned earlier he's got himself work up on the Mays farm, Evans has, on Atherton road, not all that unexpectedly it seems."

"Well, that's good news then, but tell me about your day, darling. I'm busting to know what David Baxter had to say when you told him our news."

"Weren't really news to him as it turned out Dulce. He'd made a few enquiries since we last spoke, but he was pleased all the same to have the informed version and to discuss the situation it puts us in. If it's within his power, and I think it is, I'm confident he'll help. There's no doubt that he has connections and he and I have developed a mutual respect, one for t'other. We have things in common, glue as you put it."

Dulcie concentrated on her crocheting. The sentiments seemed, indeed were, important but where was the substance in all this? Where was it leading? Her hitherto unacknowledged anxiety was in sudden need of a solution.

336

Bill stood, freshened the teapot, still not sure quite how much he should reveal to Dulcie of his activities, conversations, investigations. He told himself the purpose of any omission on his part would be purely to spare her disappointment, but he also owned that sown expectations could weigh heavily on him.

"Well, you were right, Dulce, about Glad's warning. Word is out there's every chance Mervyn will be back, sooner rather than later it's thought," he paused, "though nothing specific. Even so David was adamant that, regardless of when it happens, Watsons will do right thing by us. I told him we both took comfort from the same belief."

"I appreciate his affirmation all same," said Dulcie, crocheting ever more swiftly, the activity a by-product of her mounting nervous energy.

"I thought it best to tell him quite honestly how I've been, well how 'we've' been feeling about our situation regardless of young Mervyn's intentions; fact that we're not really getting anywhere, like."

"I'm glad you did darling. No point in hiding truth about your aims if it's assistance you're seeking in achieving 'em."

"Aye, well, as a result, we had a good long chat about local labour market," he paused. "For crying out loud, Dulce, you're making me nervous. Slow down, darling, slow down."

"Sorry, love," Dulcie stopped abruptly, put her work to one side and stood up, "I'm one as is nervous. Things just get on top of me sometimes. I think I'll make a fresh pot of tea darling; this has lost all flavour. You keep going; I'm listening, no mistake."

"Well, seems labour market's not so organised here as it was back home, not the numbers to warrant the activity. Job opportunities are a lot fewer, but apparently suitably qualified people to fill some positions are fewer still. Means finding opportunity to do summat as might get you where you want to be could be more likely. It's really a matter of working out what that summat is exactly, and of finding an opening."

Dulcie was mystified. It showed. Bill caught her bemused expression and chuckled quietly.

"Sorry darling, just thinking out loud, giving you final summing up first; I'll go long way round, make things a bit plainer," he paused, took time

337

to put his thoughts in order. "Situation we've found ourselves in on farm here, love, is not likely to be repeated. It's a one-off according to David, brought about by a unique set of circumstances starting off with Athol's subterfuge and us turning up unexpected like, plus fact that Mervyn had left and Marg Watson's being so poorly. I don't think there's any revelation in that, love, is there, and besides we've already decided it's not a situation as will get us anywhere."

"No love, you're right, but there's no disputing our good fortune that it were so. When I hear of work some of these migrants are being co-opted into down south, Snowy Mountains Scheme and such, I'm right relieved we come to rest here believe you me. Two more men died last week in another tunnelling accident," Dulcie put the rinsed pannikins back on the table, added milk and sugar.

"Aye, sad business for their families," said Bill before firmly steering the conversation back on course, "Around here, Dulcie, most of the land, the farms and forestry blocks are owned and run by families, or the odd individual who had a bit of money and chose this place to put their faith in, one way or another. Didn't need David to point that out; I mean we see it for ourselves, don't we. When there's any real work to be done they bring contract labour in."

"Mmmm," Dulcie began the ritual turning of the teapot, looking thoughtful, "Most of shops are same, and the odd café I've been into. Family concerns, run by owners. There aren't many as employ people."

"Aye, work that is available is seasonal like. Cane harvest has been in full swing down the range these past five month but cutters are all heading south now, to spend their hard earned. The big wet brings a halt to a lot of activity. Logging will cease when roads become impassable by bullock teams. We don't notice it being so far out, but population of town dwindles severely once the rain comes and loggers move out of the pub and nearby camps."

"Not a good time to be looking for work, darling," Dulcie poured tea. "So where are positions for suitable, qualified people you mentioned?"

"Ah," Bill took a circumspect sip of hot tea, "Industry," he said, "which is not so different to back home except of course industries are different. Some we know, like butter factory, sawmills, there's a few of those,

338

bacon factory in Mareeba. Tobacco cultivation's big in Mareeba too but the leaf goes to Ayr for processing apparently. Oh, aye, and there's the Tinaroo Dam project as might provide opportunities."

"I don't like the sound of that, love, Tinaroo I mean; it's a big undertaking, too dangerous for my liking."

"Don't worry darling, I had same thought. No, David's connections are confined to butter factories, there's one over in Ravenshoe too he tells me, and a couple of sawmills, Rankin's at Peeramon was one he mentioned. He'll put out feelers, see if anything is in the offing, and I'll ask around myself once I've had a chat with Ray Watson. But whatever comes up it'll likely only be a short term solution."

"Why's that, love?"

"Well Dave brought up fact that seeing as how I don't have any formal qualifications I'll probably have to do manual work of some kind which might not be most suitable long term occupation for man in my condition. I tell you, Dulcie, he sees a lot for man as is blind, and he's right on that score. We both know he is."

"It worries me now sometimes, to be honest love, seeing the work you have to do around farm. What about your experience as foreman at factory back home? It were a right good job that, doesn't that count for summat?"

"Interesting you should raise that. We talked about that at some length, what job had actually entailed like, and David struck upon an idea. It'd require a bit of time to bring to fruition which means of course, I'll have to do something in the meantime, but it's a good idea, summat I'd like."

"This one of those good news, bad news conversations, is it?" she smiled.

"No love, not at all. All good news," he paused, "in long run. He suggested as how I should get a qualification by correspondence, in accounting or something like that, something I've actually a good bit of practical experience in. I'd stand chance of getting work down in Cairns with qualification like that and pay would be good apparently. You'd like that wouldn't you?"

"Oh, Bill. You know as how I would like it, darling, but how long do you think it would take?"

"I've no idea to be honest, but I'll certainly waste no time in looking into it. Paper's out tomorrow. I'll ride into town and get one."

The idea stirred in him a sense of mission, it appealed to his strong streak of auto-didacticism and promised future prosperity sufficient to obviate the fear of poverty he'd disliked so much in England. They went to bed that night with rekindled optimism, enjoyed a vivid renewal of their commitment to one another. The mournful cry of the curlew fell on deaf ears in the slumberous depths of their stygian bed.

- 0 -

"Daddy?" asked Jess.

Mummy was writing letters and she and Daddy had just had a long talk about astronomers with strange names like Ptolemy, Copernicus, Galileo, and Huygens and it all sounded very complicated. Not just what they did but the fact that everyone hated them and thought they were bad people just because they thought the earth was round which she thought everybody knew anyway because she did. She couldn't understand at all that light took so long to travel that what she saw in the sky wasn't actually there any more. It seemed to her that light was just light, like air was air and water was water but according to Daddy a lot of what you could see was just something that had been there a long time ago. What was the use of that? She understood the bit about not being able to see the stars in the daytime because the sunlight was too bright, that was easy, and after Daddy had shown her with the orange turning on a pencil around the saucer in the middle of the table, she thought she understood about how night and day worked and a bit about the differences between the top half, above the black line he'd drawn called the equator, where they used to live, and the bottom half, where they lived now. She could see too that the part you could see of the universe, which was the kitchen and beyond, depended on where on the orange you lived. Her head had never been so full of questions but she couldn't find space in her head for any more answers, in fact she'd already forgotten a lot. There was however, something else she wanted to know.

340

"Yes, love?"

"What's a peer?"

"Well, that depends. How do you spell it?"

"P-E-E-R, I think."

"And it's definitely 'a' peer?"

"Yes."

"Well, in England it might mean a nobleman, but I think here it would probably mean someone same as you like, your equal so to speak."

"That doesn't sound right."

"You sure it isn't spelt P-I-E-R? That is a jetty or wharf, which is where boats come in to take on passengers or cargo."

"That doesn't sound right either, Daddy."

"Come on then, did you hear it or read it? Give me example."

"Well. We were talking in class about the sounds animals make and the way they write it down in stories and the teacher said it was a peer on a mat."

Bill gave her a puzzled look.

"Well she actually said, on a mat a peer, back to front," Jess clarified, "and I want to know what a peer is because I think they get it wrong a lot, the sounds I mean, and they should find a better way."

"Ah," said Bill keeping a straight face, "now I understand." He put his book back on table untouched. "It's same problem you had with thinking astronomers were a stronomus," he picked up the list of questions she had written down as a reminder for herself, "except this time there's a bit more to it. Seems a big word for teacher to be using, ask me, but what she said was onomatopoeia, all one word and not so easy to spell, Greek, means words which mimic sounds." A regular grab bag of odd pieces of knowledge and information was Bill, result of his endless reading.

"Ohhh, that's a funny word," said Jess, "but a lot of the words are wrong, they don't get the sounds right at all. Our pigs never go 'Oink', they grunt and snuffle and squeal and make all sorts of sounds but never 'Oink', and Jilly and I have listened to the chooks over and over again. They don't go 'cluck, cluck, cluck,' they go 'book, book, book'. They can't cluck. They can't say their 'L's'."

Dulcie looked up, laughing at the observation.

"It's true Mummy. You just ask Jilly. She'll tell you."

Bill chuckled, "I'm sure you're right love, I don't suppose it's such an easy thing to do when you come to think of it. You should try giving it a go. Come on, leave that piece of paper here and I'll write the word down for you. I'll have to think about it though, and it's already past your bedtime. Off you go, give your Mom and I bit of peace before our bedtime, eh?"

"Anyway, I knew Graham Coughlin was wrong," said Jess packing up her things, "he said Geoffrey Gates in Fourth Grade was the World Champion Peer at school because he can pee over 5 feet nearly up the back wall of the dunny."

"Jessica!" exclaimed Dulcie.

"I can see boys haven't changed much since I went to school," Bill said, "but your Mum's right love, it's hardly a proper topic of conversation for a young lady to be having with a boy." He couldn't help but smile nevertheless, offered his cheek for a good night kiss.

After Jess had gone to bed, Dulcie observed, "I sometimes wonder what keeps them occupied for hours on end; would never have dreamt deciphering animal noises was one of their diversions." Avoiding any mention of boys peeing up walls, she bustled about making a fresh pot of tea, brought out her crocheting, and was finally prepared to hear the day's developments. Bill fetched biscuit jar from larder, yawned long and loud as he sat down.

"You're tired aren't you, darling," said Dulcie as she poured their tea, "big day?"

"Aye, but a good one, love," he responded, "Ray Watson was in. We had a good long chat. Things are pretty much as we'd taken 'em to be. He did, however, voice his appreciation for our achievements here, offered financial recognition I'd not expected, as a parting gesture, like."

"He what?" Dulcie gasped. "You're a wily bird, Bill Johnson, fancy sitting on news like that all night, cool as a cucumber."

Bill laughed, "Easy on, Dulce. I haven't exactly been inundated with opportunities for a quiet word love."

"Well now's your chance. Come on, love, put me out of me misery then."

- 0 -

Jess knew exactly what she had to do. Daddy had made it quite clear the night before. She didn't understand why she was to do it, but she was glad to be asked to help. This morning she'd woken up very early, as if something inside her had known that she had to get up. After having a glass of milk and some toast and vegemite with Mummy she'd gone to help with the milking, like Daddy had said, giving cows their ration of molasses to lick on while they were in the stalls. She liked that rhyme Daddy had told her about cows:

Cows are of the bovine ilk,
One end moo, the other milk.

It was second line she really liked, couldn't understand the first but she liked the sound of it anyway.

They were going down to the Coughlins to play later, Mummy and Johnny too, it was a special treat. Jilly was going to collect the eggs so they'd be leaving as soon as she'd finished helping Daddy and they'd all had their porridge. Nancy Coughlin had invited them for a picnic down by the creek. When she'd asked why they were going so early Mummy had said, "Because y's a crooked letter, and z's no better. That's why." It was her Mum's way of closing a conversation, that much Jess'd learnt.

The last of the cows was now in the bails. She'd given them their helping of molasses and checked to make sure the tap on the molasses tank was firmly off. Dad talked often enough about how much money it cost; not to be wasted, like a lot of other things besides. He'd shown her the particular calf he wanted her to bring out to the turnabout; "As soon as milking is finished," he'd said, "before we open gate out to pasture. And stay with it love, keep it company 'til I get back."

She called that calf Toffee, not that anyone else knew that. It wasn't her favourite but she liked him well enough. Taking the molasses pail with her, she went over to the big water tank by the windmill where he was

343

drinking. She patted his neck as she slipped the rope over his head, talked to him as she offered him the pail in her outstretched hand, like a carrot on a stick. He came eagerly. She knew he would. They loved molasses, calves did. He followed her out into the turnabout where she tethered him to the hitching rail by the shed and put the molasses bucket on the tree stump, right under his nose. At this early hour the calf stood in the shadow of the milking shed. She held the bucket firmly, watched him lick it clean, fascinated by his long, silky eyelashes. The sunlight splashed all over her where she stood. All at once the animal raised its head, and to her astonishment she found, in the ebon orb of its eye, her own golden reflection, from head to foot, close and clear, and in the background, equally clear, the house; all around them, glittering in the early morning sun, was reflected a breathtaking view of the land right to the horizon in all directions. Then Toffee looked away, taking the image with him, attracted to the noise of Daddy's boots on the concrete as he came down from the separator room. The fleeting thought that she had seen the world the way cows did passed through her mind. She marveled that so much fitted so beautifully into such a small space though the image was not at all what she saw when she looked around. Daddy beckoned to her, and the notion fled as she unhitched the calf and led it towards him.

After they all crossed the rill on the way to the Coughlins, Jess and Jilly ran on ahead a little way, skylarking about, in high spirits and looking forward to the day's activity. Mummy was taking it nice and slowly. "You're a big lump, you are," she said to Johnny more than once, smiling and bouncing him on her hip all the same. "What was that?" yelled Jess as the air was rent by a loud explosion which bounced off the slopes all around them. A vivid remembrance of snakes and hail assailed Dulcie as she glanced back up the hill towards the homestead. "I don't know," she said, "but don't worry. I'm sure Daddy can take care of it; watch where you're going now, the two of you. Come on, we don't want to keep Nancy waiting."

On the way home that afternoon, the echo of that loud noise reverberated in Jess's mind, arriving in the company of several unanswered, indeed as yet unasked questions. Questions whose shape she couldn't fashion but which hovered nonetheless, refusing to fade into forgetfulness. She and Jilly trudged up the hill, worn out by the picnic and all the running around, the games and the competitions, the squabbles and the arguments, arguments in which she naturally engaged, the resolution of which decided who was in charge of this game or that. Milking was well under way when they got back and tired though she was, she was drawn towards the separator room; not, on this occasion, by her endless fascination with the hypnotic whine of the machine, but rather in search of Toffee who'd been in there last time she'd seen him and was now nowhere in sight.

"Bill, Bill," Old Bronc got Bill's attention with his second call, "Young Jess has just scarpered up past mill, in a hurry, seemed upset. Any chance she could have seen yon hide?" He nodded towards separator room.

"Bloody hell, I should have known better," Bill was well taken aback, immediately regretting having hung the rack holding the stretched hide in that room to air. "That's last thing I wished to happen." He finished cupping the udder of the cow in the bails, stood up and faced Old Bronc, "Any chance you could finish up, just to get 'em back out to pasture, if need be Athol? I'll go and tell Dulcie what's happened, what we assume has happened any road, then I'll go straight out and speak with her. I've an idea where she might be."

The sound of her sobbing carried to him on the evening breeze as he made his way towards the bush, her secret hideaway, cubby house, whatever she called it. Under the circumstances her knowing that he knew her secret was unimportant, more important by far that she be given comfort. The intensity of her anguish told him that she knew. It was only natural that she should be grieved, feel sorrow, but he wanted her to know that her unknowing complicity in the act had been for the good, made a necessary situation better, been good for the animal. His fatigue, the aftermath of the day's work, descended like a dead weight on his shoulders; the kill, with its adrenalin rush, the heightened emotions attendant upon butchering the animal, the sheer physical labour occasioned by his determination to respect the carcass as he had the animal, use its remains for all they could provide. Grubb had warned him, and he had been mentally prepared for it. He was not new to the physical chemistry of violent death and he now recognised its toll.

"Jess, it's Daddy, love."

"Go away, I hate you!"

"I need to talk to you. There's something you need to know."

"What?"

He stood beside the bush.

"Should I come in, or are you going to come out?"

"I'm not, hic, not coming out! You're horrible. How could you do that? Why?"

"It's not what I did. It's what you did I want to talk to you about," he paused.

Silence.

"You did a good thing, Jess. I want you to know that," he paused again, waited, in silence broken only by her continued sobbing.

"It's important we talk about it, love. I'm not going before we do."

He sat down on the ground, careful not to crowd her.

After a time, a disturbance under the bush and sounds of a runny nose being brought under control preceded her emergence, but she still kept her distance, regarding him with a suspicion to which he'd never been subjected, not ever, by anyone. It moved him strangely.

"So how was it good then," she asked, "what I did? I brought him to you like you said and you killed him." She made fists and pressed her knuckles into her eyes as if to rid them of what they'd seen. Tears threatened. Bill knew what he wanted to tell her but found himself bereft of words to deliver the lesson gently. A sudden attack of common sense led him to simply answer her question.

"The good you did, love, was to make the end of that calf's life peaceful and contented. I saw you gave him some extra molasses. He would have liked that. He didn't suffer any pain or anxiety, love," he paused, giving her time, "Most cattle don't have that privilege of a peaceful death."

"Most of what cattle?"

"The cattle that are killed so butchers have meat to sell to their hungry customers, love. Like your Mom, for one, so she can make us one of her famous beef puddings," he paused as she came closer. "Some animals are bred especially for that purpose Jess. It's why you should always eat

346

everything on your plate; out of respect for the animal which gave its life to help sustain yourn."

She came and sat down beside him, sniffing.

"I called him Toffee," she said after a time.

Bill was taken unawares, his response caught in his throat.

"But he wasn't my favourite."

They sat in silence.

"Will we eat him then?" Jess asked quietly.

"Aye, love, there'd be no point otherwise, would there? We're to have half and the butcher will have half. The meat needs to hang for a time and it's much too hot here so Mr. Grubb is looking after things. He'll have half as payment for his services. When it's ready he'll tell your Mom and she'll let him know each week which parts we'll have. There will be lots of things to choose from. Nothing will be wasted, love."

As they walked hand in hand down towards the house Bill reflected on a day which seemed to stretch as long behind him as his shadow now stretched before him. Although a practical man, well able to do as was necessary for the wellbeing of his family, he would never, could never be indifferent to death. To his mind the smugness with which some did to other species as they pleased exemplified the principle that might is right, the evil ends of which the world, his world, had just witnessed. He was grateful for the love which shone in Dulcie's eyes when they walked into the kitchen together in time for tea.

Chapter Eleven

Blackbird's bend ....

*I*sa pot stick is my name.............. '*Poking clothes is my game,*' thought Dulcie, though she could now barely discern the words carved into the copper stick, worn white with use and hairy as an old man's chin. She stood beside the copper, looking out over the south paddock at another pristine blue sky. No sign of rain. A cackle of jackasses sent jocular messages to kith and kin, a crescendo of enthusiastic amusement undulating through the gums down by the creek. She smiled; kookaburras always made her smile. Hanging the copper stick on its hook, she returned to the kitchen to make a pot of tea, write a letter to Merry.

Merry my dear, Christmas will be well gone by the time you receive this. I hope you managed some good cheer though I imagine it will have been very hard without Mam in your midst. Even here, so far away from you all, I feel her absence from mortal coil. Miss her something terrible but not, any longer, for every waking moment. I hope you too are becoming more accustomed, if not reconciled, to life without her. I am pleased to report that we have not had, as yet(!), any serious natural incident following the locust plague, except lateness of the 'big wet' which everyone seems of a sudden to pine for. It has become clear that there is no opening for Bill in this area and he therefore looks further afield. I see this landscape with a different eye now Merry, now that I know we must leave it. It is a beautiful place and I won't ever forget it, but, and I know I can say this to you in confidence, I am pleased to be moving on and truly hope to find a more peopled place, wherever it is, though I will certainly miss Mavis and Glad a good deal. I sense an excitement in Bill, too, to be getting on with things like.

A fly droned laboriously in through the kitchen door sounding sated, gluttonous in its continuing quest for food. Dulcie looked up, distracted by the sudden frenzied buzzing of its agitated attempts to free itself from the fly paper strip hanging from the ceiling by the pantry door. Her nose turned up in distaste at the sight. Dashed strip only remained in place because the abhorrence she had for it was ever so slightly outweighed by that she harboured for the pestilence it trapped, particularly of the current victim's kind. Perspiration trickled slowly down between her breasts; she patted the front of her shift to stem the flow, mopped her brow with her handkerchief, and wiped her hands on her apron before resuming her letter.

Since I last wrote, most exciting news is that Joe paid us a visit, remember the chap at the hotel in Cairns I told you about. He drove up from Edmonton with his girlfriend, Sophia, who he blamed entirely for not having come up to see us before now. He met her not long after we came up here, nigh on a year ago now. He even lets her drive the car. Wedding bells in the air, you ask me. Honestly Merry, you will remember me telling you about his car, the FX Holden Bill was so besotted by. Well you can't imagine the stir it caused in town, still looks as though it's just been driven out of show room it does – cynosure of all eyes Joe were, like some famous film star or something. Town folk will be talking about it for months according to Bill. He was right quick to change his plans for day when Joe turned up, Bill was, and we all ended up going for a drive over to Yungaburra, a small town not that far away. I'd not been there before. The men are marvelous how they find their way about with whatever map is at hand. As you know, my navigational skills exist entirely on remembering which number bus to catch – and a fat lot of good that is here! Turned out it was there, in Yungaburra, Bill bought Jess's bathing costume. To get there we had to drive through Jess's 'dirty big' tree growing over the road. Well that is something, that is, Merry. No wonder she were so full of it at the time. Fig it is, the tree, defies description it does love, you really do have to drive right through it. I do wish we'd had camera with us. Bill says it's very like the Banyan tree they have in India but he never saw a specimen quite like this one. It were a lovely outing, a real pick-me-up. Our preparations for Christmas progress in ever hotter temperatures. It does seem rum, it does, I don't think I'll ever get used to it. School is breaking up for Jess end of next week. She's not been her normal self lately, very touchy, easily upset. We decided to kill one of the calves a couple of weeks ago, in the interest of self-sufficiency, part of the new regime aimed at boosting our bit of a nest egg in readiness for the move. Unfortunately Jess found out. Bill assures me she understands. I daren't tell him as how she's suddenly changed so, he'd be that upset. Just noticed the time, Bill will be in for his lunch soon so I'll finish this tomorrow, with love, Dulcie.

- 0 -

"Stop squabbling, Jessica. What on earth has got into you?"

"She's been mean to me all afternoon Mummy," Jilly felt hard done by and was quick to garner Dulcie's support.

Jess remained silent, sulking, but her heart didn't really seem to be in it.

"Look at me, Jess," said Dulcie, "when I speak to you."

The girls were in the tub in the laundry and Dulcie was preparing a load of washing to soak overnight. Jess looked up. Dulcie could see immediately that something was wrong. She went over and put the back of her hand against Jess's burning forehead.

"Why didn't you tell me you weren't feeling well, darling?" she asked. "Come on love, let's have you out of there," she gave Jess a quick wash over before helping her out and wrapping the towel around her. In the kitchen, after telling Jess to look the other way, she moved the lantern closer so that she could inspect her daughter's head, neck and ears more closely. "How long have you been feeling poorly, love?" she asked as she started putting on Jess's nightgown.

"I can't remember," said Jess, "but I only started feeling all hot today and now my eyes feel sore."

"I'm not surprised, darling. It's measles you've got if I'm not mistaken. I'm going to pop you into bed and put a nice damp cloth on your forehead lovey. Your eyes will feel better in the dim light. You can have your tea in bed tonight, alright?"

"I'm not hungry," Jess said and a tear escaped her strangely pink right eye, "Will I be all better in the morning, Mummy?"

"Don't cry darling, you'll only make your eyes worse. You might feel a bit better tomorrow love, but sometimes it takes a bit longer to be fully back to being your old self. We'll just keep you in bed and make sure you're nice and comfortable and get plenty of liquids. You just sit there a minute love. I'd best get Jilly out of tub first."

Before going back down to tend to Jilly, Dulcie brought her medicine chest from the larder, took the thermometer out of its casing, shook down the mercury and popped it under Jess's tongue. She checked the contents of the wooden chest, was silently pleased to see they had aspirin and there was still plenty of calamine lotion in the bottle. Jess's temperature was quite alarmingly high. In the absence of a doctor to prescribe same, Dulcie took out the packet of aspirin and gave Jess half a tablet with a glass of water. "I won't be long love. Don't go looking at lamp, will you, bad for your eyes, it'll only make 'em hurt more."

Johnny had been standing, clinging to the slats in the safety gate at top of the steps, watching proceedings with keen interest, rattling the gate vigorously from time to time to gain attention and crying out in high pitched indignation when the ploy failed. Dulcie quickly made sure Jilly was clean, dried her on a fresh towel and got her ready for bed, exhorting her to look after her brother whilst she went to break news of what was happening to Daddy. "*Egad,*" she thought as she eventually hurried over to milking shed, "*Keeping them apart is going to be the hard part and it is probably too late anyway. If there were a doctor nearby I'd just lump them all in together and be done with it.*"

"Her temperature's over 102 darling, rash has just started coming out around her ears, back of the neck. Oddly enough her chest seems to be quite clear. She's no cough. Let's hope it stays that way, though it's unlikely. Most important thing is to get her temperature down, try to keep it down. I've given her half an aspirin and popped her into bed. We might just have to have Jilly in with us for a few nights love. I can't see me getting much chance to lie down any road, best that I keep an eye on her, rash is likely to get much worse in next 24 hours but active phase is a relatively short one, thankfully."

Old Bronc was quick to interject, "You can have one of the beds from yon smoke house for the wee lass, don't you worry about that Dulcie. I'll go for it now, Bill; we're all but finished up here."

"What about the others, Dulcie? Do you think they'll be alright?" asked Bill after Athol had left.

"Only time will tell, love. Them as have it are usually infectious for three or four days before rash comes out and then four or five days after it goes so Jilly and Johnny could have it already, darling. We'll just have to keep a close eye on them. I'll mark days off on calendar so we can monitor their progress properly. I'd best get back love," said Dulcie, turning to go. "You'll have to go to school tomorrow, darling, and let them know. They'll all be at risk, you know, unless they've either had it or had contact with disease before. No telling where it started."

When Bill visited the school the following day he carried a concise, hand-written description of the disease, its usual cycle of symptoms, a neat list of the basic steps in its treatment, and a few hints for managing potential crises, produced by Dulcie during her long night's vigil. Strict instructions rang in his ear, to bring a copy back with him. He was to insist on it, even if someone had to write it out by hand for her. Back at home, the rituals and routines of nursing returned to Dulcie as if she had never left them. During the first couple of nights her visits to the bedroom were frequent, during which she monitored Jess's temperature and the advancing rash, applied cold compresses to her brow and calamine lotion to ever larger areas of Jess's back and chest. She administered aspirin and generous quantities of boiled, sometimes sweetened water, recording her activities and findings throughout on a chart she kept on the kitchen table beside the Tilley lamp whose glow accompanied her through her nightlong watches. In the intervals between tending her patient she prepared cold compresses, chilling them in the icebox, boiled water and consigned to the flames in the stove the detritus of treatment, consisting mainly of the wads of cotton wool used to apply calamine lotion. Unfortunately for Dulcie, her experience as a nurse had brought her into contact only with the most serious cases of the disease, cases in which emergencies, some of them life threatening, had occurred. Hence her single-minded devotion to Jess's welfare, activity which helped to keep at bay spectral visions of the many potential complications of the disease as it ran its course; visions of pneumonia or worse still, meningitis, would only serve to drain her reserves. *"A tragedy foreseen is one twice suffered,"* she thought on one occasion, as she reclined in the rocking chair on the edge of sleep, comforted by the easy breathing of her other children. *"Who was it said that,"* she wondered fuzzily, rocking absentmindedly to and fro. The door to their bedroom was closed. At night Bill slept. She had insisted on it. Nursing was woman's work. Besides cows need him, she was drifting off. *"Their udders and our livelihood will both dry up if he neglects them,"* she thought, *"Can't have that."* She dozed fitfully that night, was once again tending Jess when Bill rose at 4.30. The words of her song carried to him softly as he listened by door to the girls' room.

Weeping willow tree
Weeping sympathy
Bend your branches down along the ground
and cover me
Listen to my plea
Hear me willow and weep for me
Willow, willow, weep for me

Dulcie paused, murmuring to Jess as she turned the sheet, applied a new cold compress, took up the same refrain as she prepared to leave.

During those first couple of days, the family unit assumed a curiously atomic structure with Jess and Dulcie at the nucleus, patient and nurse masquerading as proton and neutron, and everyone else, faithful electrons, maintaining orbit, accommodating the imposition of sudden orderliness, reacting instinctively to the gravity of events that had overtaken them. Bill was moved to remark later that young Johnny had remained voluble as ever throughout the ordeal but as if by magic his baby talk dropped by several decibels, "as if someone had turned his volume down, like." After morning milking Bill took over day time care of the little ones and kept an eye on the patient, waking Dulcie, if she slept, at various appointed hours throughout the day to tend Jess, until it was time to round up the herd for evening milking. Having become accustomed years ago to sleeping in shifts, Dulcie was grateful her ability to catnap had not forsaken her.

Then, in the middle of the third night, Jess called out to Dulcie.

"I'm hungry," she said as Dulcie entered the bedroom, signalling the end of the critical phase and the return of the household to a semblance of normality though Jess's isolation was enforced for a good four more days. With neither Jilly nor Johnny exhibiting any of the classic symptoms Dulcie chose to err on the side of caution when determining the quarantine period, not at all keen to undertake back to back bouts of such intensive nursing. Released at last from solitary confinement, Jess was volubly relieved at 'getting out', having latterly become a less than perfect inmate. Dulcie's caution was vindicated, however, when neither Jilly nor young Johnny contracted the disease. Her subsequent relief made Jess's impatient irritability

356

a small cross to bear. Ten kids at school had come down with it. Only one had needed hospitalisation after developing pneumonia and six of the others wouldn't be back to school until next year.

It was plain to see that Jess considered herself one of the lucky ones to make it back to school, even if it was just for the two days before break up. Having forgotten all about it, she was happily surprised when the teacher gave her the class photo taken in the week before she became poorly. Little did she know what an important memento it would become, that one day she'd have a daughter of her own to whom she would pass on this remnant of her past; but for now it was Dulcie who got most pleasure from it, drawing comfort from the fact that Jess, who was sitting in the front row on the grass with her legs crossed, right next to the child holding the slate with "Grade 2 – Malanda" chalked on it, was not the only one with bare feet; in fact, quite a number of children had no shoes. The family spent a lot of time poring over the picture and Jilly was curious to know the names of all the other kids, especially those whom Jess called her friends. Eventually, when Dulcie remembered the silver frame in the trunk, the photograph was proudly displayed on the top ledge of the desk beside the lamp. Before that though, indeed almost before they could blink, school holidays were upon them and Christmas not a stone's throw away.

After tea one night, kids all sleeping, Bill suddenly lifted his head from scouring the paper for a sign of suitable work as might have escaped his previous notice and asked, "What was that song you were singing to Jess, darling, when she was in throes of fever. I know I know it but I can't for the life of me think of name." The melody had been haunting him for days.

Dulcie, who was putting the finishing touches to one of the doll's outfits, lifted her head, looked at him vaguely.

"The one about the willow," Bill prompted.

"Willow Weep For Me? Eric Child has played it a few times lately, love. It's on Frank Sinatra's latest recording I think; words are a bit melancholic but it's the melody I like, can't get it out of my mind," Dulcie put her work down, looked up at him, clearly in thought. "There were no particular significance like. It was a matter of thought association as brought it on really, I suppose. I don't know whether you're aware darling, but aspirin is a salicylate drug, from the Latin *salix* I think, which is willow tree, from the bark of which salicylic acid is produced, you get my drift. Treatment of measles was summat we devoted quite some time to when I did my first certificate, on account of there being no vaccine like. Still isn't as far as I know. I really ought to check. Nancy should know."

"Ah, so it was tennis, elbow, foot," Bill responded, making light though inwardly impressed by Dulcie's knowledge, "how song came to mind."

"Aye, it was love. Now how about tea, bed, cuddle?"

He was even more impressed with that.

- 0 -

When Bill had broached with Ray Watson the subject of the potential need for them to move on in the relatively near future, the farmer had asked if he could have the farm ledger for a few days to give it a "good looking at", something he'd not got around to doing properly before now, what with one thing and another. The outcome of his inspection was that he moved many of the items Bill had listed as maintenance, or day to day running costs, to a new column he'd headed *Capital Expense/Improvements*, "to get a better idea of farm's performance," he said. Ray Watson left it to Bill to work out the new position. He didn't need asking twice. The task was attended to as a matter of priority. Finally downing his pen one night, an uncharacteristically jubilant Bill, he being of a generally more reserved nature, gave Dulcie his news. She was flabbergasted. In truth, they both were. The picture now painted was a rosy one by comparison to previous results, and, based on the simple division of profits agreed with the farmer, indicated the farm's indebtedness to them of close to two months' pay. In addition to which they were yet to work out their share of the money realised from the pre-Christmas sale of stock, the pigs and turkeys, which they had thought would represent the entire financial resource with which to embark on the next leg of this Antipodean journey. Dulcie was pleased to have sherry as hadn't yet been used to lace their Christmas pudding with which to enjoy a celebratory tipple with supper that night, before retiring to the bedroom and a more intimate celebration wherein murmurous moans cleft the nocturnal silence.

From the back door she watched the sinuous curtain of rain billowing into the laundry where it disintegrated on the sodden concrete floor, sending up a fine mist to envelop and refresh her. The thunderous din on the tin roof of these teeming tropical storms was rendered marginally more tolerable by their reliable evanescence, but its physical discomfort was unquestionable. At least Glad's early advice to stand by an open door for relief, if only that of distraction, held true. Today's rain had come much earlier than usual and she hoped it would be similarly premature in passing. "*Jess will be drenched,*" she thought, glancing at the clock on the workbench, "*like as not caught in this lot on her way home.*"

Not that Jess would mind. The girls loved running about in the rain, in the altogether as a rule. Even took young Johnny with them for a lark sometimes, if rain weren't too heavy. To the vocal relief of local farmers the big wet had arrived in the few days before Christmas, manna from heaven for many. By then their pasture had already grown back luxuriantly, especially in the south paddock, testament to the richness of the soil and the closeness to the surface of the subterranean reservoir from which the rill sprung.

If Bill were lucky this deluge would ease off before milking time which was nearly upon them. "I'm glad that shed's waterproof," she thought as she went to the stove to put the kettle on, prepare his Thermos of tea, "he spends enough of his time over there." It was the farrowing shed she had in mind, in which Bill was sequestered with the Willys as he lately was at every opportunity. His decision to take up David Baxter's offer of the motor was made without hesitation, the moment the extent of their unexpected windfall had been revealed. It put a certain spring back into his step, as remarked by Dave before he'd even broken news of his decision on the occasion of their next get-together in the louvred cool of the RSL Club. These meetings had become a fortnightly occurrence, established out of the commitment and friendship which had grown between them. Saying nothing to Dulcie he made plans with Curly to pick up the motor from David Baxter's friend's place, on the Malanda side of Tarzali. To his mind, the big wet couldn't have timed its entrance better. A couple of days earlier and all his plans might have come to naught. As it turned out, once he'd got the motor home persistent rain had conspired to force him off the land and into the farrowing shed where he tinkered to his heart's content. Methodically learning every facet of her make-up, he was determined, once having her measure in full, to have her ready for the road by the time the roads were once again ready for them.

Challenging as it was to make a grand entrance at the end of a tow rope, the Willys, whose aged beauty spake of a rigorous regime of loving attention, created quite a stir on her arrival. Dulcie was speechless. Not so the girls who leapt up on the running boards, chanting a myriad purposes for which this splendid motor car could be used. Things other kids at school did, that Jess had told Jilly about many times, stimulating lively debate as to the extent of their missed opportunities for fun; things like going to rodeos, and going fishing and going to church, to name a few. As if by magic, in their unselfconsciously selfish view, all of these highly desirable activities had, surely, entered the realm of genuine possibility. Probability was all they now needed to work on. When she regained her equilibrium something stirred in Dulcie's breast too, something akin to the call that had interrupted Mole's spring cleaning in *Wind in the Willows;* a sort of wanderlust, a pull towards adventure in the outside world, adventure in which she would join with, and be joined by, others.

Having been successfully diverted, not to say bribed, with the promise of a fishing expedition at the first opportunity, the girls exercised great patience while Bill toiled week after week to restore the Willys's life and vitality. During the first week of Jess's holidays, persistence and perseverance had rewarded them with the discovery of the platypus burrow down in the creek bank, and they had taken to visiting the site daily, were frequently rewarded with more than a mere glimpse of the mystifying creature. As a result of their success, creek adventures loomed high on their current list of favourite pastimes and one night, in response to their concerted pleas, Bill allowed himself to be cajoled into retelling them the 'clot fishing' story.

"Right, so where to begin?" he asked as they settled themselves in bed, Jilly a bit late, Jess a bit early, both drowsy.

"With the worms," said Jilly.

"Ey up, clever girl, Jilly; every successful fishing trip depends on having right bait, as any fisherman will tell you, eh," he paused, "So . . . .

Down in Abergavenny, after a very, very cold winter the weather started to get warmer at last. Spring arrived and the countryside took on an aspect the boys had never seen, them being from the city like. Flowers were in bloom everywhere and the lads they were living with decided to organise a fishing expedition. Clot fishing. They'd never heard the word used like that before. The older boys explained that the 'clot' was a heap of worms tied to a pole so the first thing they needed were….."Bill paused expectantly,

"Worms," they both chanted loudly.

"*Right. First thing they had to do, was get hold of a wooden box with a lid which they found easily enough at the market. Then they went around the countryside collecting moss, from around the rabbit holes dotted around in the local fields, walking for miles and miles and for hours and hours. When the box was half filled with moss, the next step was worms, and plenty of them. They waited for the full moon to do this, remember?*"

The girls nodded vigorously.

"*Walter had always thought that worms were slow-moving wriggly things found in the garden but he was in for a big surprise. The night of the full moon they went to bed as usual but at about half past ten, the big boys came and woke them up. Although it was spring it was still cold at night so they put their trousers and jackets on over their jamas, and the four of them went out scouting the hedgerows for worms. Finding them was the easy part. The older boys showed them how to catch the worms, by creeping up on them, then grabbing for the middle of the shiny straw, because a straw is what they looked like in the moonlight. It took them a long time to catch their first worm. At the slightest sound or movement worms were gone, back into their hole. Result was they all had to go out on safari two nights in a row before they managed to get a good enough supply of long worms to put in the box of moss which would keep them fed and cool.*

The next thing they had to do was to thread the worms onto a length of string about 10 feet long and really fine. For this they used an eight inch long needle on which they threaded the worms lengthwise."

"Oh yuck," said Jilly while Jess turned her nose up.

"*Aye, it was a yucky job, Jilly, by all accounts, but when they'd finished they went on to prepare the fishing pole which weren't so bad. The pole was a piece of bamboo about 10 feet long and just over half an inch thick. Around the top they tied a length of light cord*

361

about same length as the pole. Then the worms were folded into a big blob of live bait. After weighting the end of the cord with a large lead weight they hung the worm ball under it."

At this stage Jess was having second thoughts about the attraction of fishing but listened intently all the same.

"So at last, after three weeks of exhausting preparation the fishing trip was a goer. Armed with their worm pole and an army style kit bag off they set for the river Usk. Terry, one of the older boys, was the first to try it. After about five minutes he hauled in the rod and swung it onto the bank; hanging off it were two eels. With a whoop they dived onto the fish, grabbing them with great difficulty, juggling them, would be more the word, into the waiting kit bag. Well, this went on all afternoon; on one occasion they pulled three eels in at once. They lost one in the long grass, and though they searched high and low they couldn't find it anywhere. Still they were having a high old time of it and carried on with great success. About ten minutes later Walter saw the grass part and the eel's head appear and he grabbed it, right on the edge of the riverbank. By the time all of them had had a go with the pole the kit bag was squirming with eels and they'd all had great fun, especially trying to hang onto the eels that didn't want to go into the kit bag.

This sounded like fun, enthusiasm returned.

When they got home their new Mom made them all hang their clothes up outside and climb into the bath. The older boys said there'd be a great feast of eels the next day once they were all skinned, and gutted and cut up. This was quite a different matter to the fun of catching them but Terry said as how they must learn to do it as it was all part of a fisherman's responsibility. Up til now tiddlers in a duck pond were all the fish they were used to, so they'd not been introduced to this practical aspect of making a catch table-worthy. Luckily their new Mom, Mrs. Fields, was a good cook and the yummy smell that rose from her cooking pot soon overcame their memory of all the blood and guts. It was good appetites they took to the table that night to tuck into the feast she prepared. They'd never had owt like this at home."

On the other hand……..

- 0 -

Their Christmas had been a quiet one. Glad was already firmly ensconced with the Campbells and Ray Watson had joined them over in Atherton for a family celebration spanning a few days. The Coughlins had all come over again on Christmas Day and they'd enjoyed a most agreeable afternoon and evening together but Mavis and Reg were down in Cairns and didn't visit, weren't expected. The outbreak of measles had sent Mavis ducking for the cover of Cairns, determined to protect young Roger from infection and loath to risk prolonged isolation at her Mum and Dad's if the big wet arrived before it was safe to return. In the past she'd been prepared to do the trip on horseback with Reg when the road became impassable, but he'd not found the words to talk her into attempting the same journey with the baby. When Curly told them that Reg had gone to join his family down the hill over Christmas, Dulcie had not been at all surprised. On the other hand, when Mavis had still not returned towards the end of January she thought her friend a trifle over cautious and was saddened as opportunities to spend time together slipped away as inexorably as the tide of change broke over them.

The long summer holiday had come to an end and Jess was back at school when Bill's correspondence course turned up in the mail. He'd been shocked, though stoically undaunted, on discovering it would take three years to complete all aspects of the course but he determined to put his back into it and meet the prescribed milestones, finish earlier if at all possible. In his experience three years would be gone in a flash anyway though when Dulcie heard same news she felt moved to share her unwillingness to endure prolonged social isolation, and aired her private dreams of an actively more companionable environment.

Jilly discovered, when Jess returned to school, that she was still not allowed to go, a situation with which she was properly miffed, and initially most vocally so. Young Johnny was walking by then though, and devoting his every waking moment to the infinitely thorough investigation of every aspect of the newly accessible stratosphere to which he had become privy; what was a voyage of discovery for him became a full time job for Jilly, and 'keeping her eye on him' denied her any decent opportunity to feel sorry for herself. For a time she and Jess continued their weekend forays to the creek to check on the platypus, but after a while they stopped, acknowledging that it seemed to have gone away, "and taken its babies too," observed Jilly with disappointed resignation when they eventually agreed that the animal had absconded. Even at her tender age she was beginning to realise that nothing ever seemed to stay the same.

Yesterday, gladness; today sadness.
Disappointment, but no bitterness.

- 0 -

In February, Mervyn Watson brought his new bride to Malanda. They heard about it soon enough from Old Bronc, but the manner of his return to the farm took them entirely by surprise. Having taken their tea out the front one morning to escape the cloying atmosphere of a kitchen strung to capacity with drying clothes, they were standing by the log which was still sodden from the night's rain. Their quiet conversation ceased as Dulcie pointed towards the approaching light of a lantern, swaying rhythmically on the end of pole as was Old Bronc's habit.

"He's a bit keen, isn't he? Or in his cups and not made it to bed yet," commented Dulcie. It wouldn't be the first time. Bill turned to observe his neighbour's approach and in the ensuing silence the distinct sound of two sets of hooves cleft the early morning air.

"Well, who could that be then?" murmured Dulcie, not so sure any more.

"Friend, not foe, I'll be bound," Bill reassured her, his own curiosity piqued.

They watched with interest as the duo drew close enough to reveal in the golden halo of Old Bronc's lantern his companion, a young man whose appearance and demeanour bore unmistakable witness to his lineage and heritage. When he quickly dismounted and reached over the front fence to shake Bill's hand, saying, "G'day Bill, Mervyn Watson," the introduction was entirely superfluous. When Bill commented to Dulcie later, that the confidence and ease emanating, plain as pikestaff, from young Mervyn were born of rights of ownership, Bill felt with equal plainness their tacit recognition of the embodiment of the very status to which they themselves ultimately aspired.

364

"Bill Johnson, Mervyn. Heard you were back. Couldn't stay away, eh?" Bill reciprocated, taking the proffered hand, shaking it warmly, his smile genuine at finally meeting the man of whose land he'd become the accidental caretaker. "It's good to meet you, Mervyn. This is my wife, Dulcie," at which Dulcie's greeting too reflected pleasure in the occasion.

"I'll just go and make another Thermos. You'd like a cuppa before you set off? It'll only take a minute," and she returned carefully to the house to fulfil her mission.

Whilst right about Mervyn's eagerness to tread his own soil again, Bill learned before milking was finished that day that underlying the visit was an ulterior motive. Having bumped into David Baxter in town the previous afternoon, Mervyn bore news of a job going at the butter factory over in Ravenshoe. During the course of their morning's work, he managed, with typical Australian brevity, to impart the personal message too, that he would be happy to take over farm duties forthwith, give Bill chance to follow up on the opportunity. "Good for both of us," he'd said, "It's a pretty full day, Ravenshoe and back with a bit of time in between to do something. You need the time. And like you said, I would find it hard to keep away. I've really missed this place. It's good to be back. I can see the work you've done. I'm grateful to find her looking this good mate."

- 0 -

"Ravenshoe? Blackbird's bend, eh? There's a raven in family crest of one of my dim distant antecedents as I recall," said Dulcie, lost in thought. Reining in her thoughts, she pulled herself back to the present, "You've mentioned it before, love, but never said owt about it."

"The little I know Dulcie is that they have butter factory and sawmill, and, at the moment, butter factory is looking for a cream carrier to service farms on the Herberton run. Truck comes with the job. David's put a word in for me but he reckons sooner I get myself over there to show willing, the better."

"Like chap who comes to collect churns from here, like?"

"Exactly so; I'm afraid I'll still have to be up at sparrers' love, and according to David, winters are a different kettle of fish over there. Highest

365

town in Queensland he says, 3,000 odd feet up; windy 'n all, but good little township, prosperous, nice land. I'll have more to report after I've been to see 'em, won't I?"

"So it's further inland then," Dulcie remarked, "How are you going to get there? I thought roads were well-nigh impassable."

"Aye, as crow flies Millaa Millaa Road is way to go but you're right, love, it's closed, or good as. Curly says best bet is to drive to Atherton and take train, says I can have the ute on Wednesday if I just drop Nancy back to work. David reckons it makes sense. He'll talk to his contact to tee it up. I'm to meet him tomorrow to get details."

Things were advancing on all fronts. In the last week they'd had two letters as had caused a stir, one more so than the other. The one from Mavis had rendered Dulcie more mystified than ever about her friend's prolonged absence, but the one from Harvey held no such conundrum. After getting it open with trembling fingers and hungrily devouring its every word, she had exhorted Bill's keen attention before commencing to read out in a voice shaking with excitement, *"So there you have it Dulcie. After departing Southampton in early March we shall take our bearings via azimuth south with a view to coming to rest in the good township of Cairns, North Queensland no later than end of April, last leg of journey to be by train. I will be in communication from Cairns before departure if you could just leave news at the GPO as to how I would best get in touch. I am looking very much forward to seeing you, TTFN, love, H"*

"Well that's all very plain, isn't it love?" she said, beaming. "Except this business about azimuth south; what on earth does he mean by that, *we shall take our bearings via azimuth south?*" she finished.

"That's just Harvey's sense of adventure getting best of him, love. With his Air Force background, I'd say he's referring to taking a reading off an Azimuth Compass to plot his course. Pilots had 'em up in cockpit during war; used 'em to plot the coordinates at which to launch certain bombs to have them land in desired spot."

"Ah," understanding dawned.

"If he'd been a naval man, his meaning would have been otherwise, referring to an aid of different sort, navigational like. James Cook, the same as made voyages to these shores on more than one occasion...."

366

"In the Endeavour?"

"Aye, love, one and same. During his voyages in Southern Seas he referred many times to taking a reading by south azimuth, recorded it in his ship's log. I've seen extracts. I'm not hundred percent sure he would have had benefit of Azimuth Compass back then, I'm of the mind mariner's accomplished the task using their sextant but I'd be willing to stand corrected."

"Well I never, trust Harvey to come up with summat like that."

Harvey's letter added a real dimension of urgency to their plans. As Dulcie pointed out it really was time to make their move if they were to settle in, be prepared for this imminent and most auspicious arrival.

"All in the fullness of time, Dulcie," said Bill.

To which she responded, "Aye, patience is a virtue, I know!"

- 0 -

"Righto, mate, she's in neutral is she?"

"Yeah," Curly yelled, jiggling the loose gear lever audibly for Bill's benefit.

"Foot on the brake?"

"Yeah, mate."

"Switched on?"

"Yeah, yeah, yeah!"

"Righto, I'll give her a turn or two so be ready with the accelerator," Bill caught Curly's eye, braced himself, then leaned hard on the crank handle to push it through a full turn. "Bloody hell, but that's heavy," he grunted as perspiration started beading his forehead. He gave it another go. "*That's a bit better*," he thought, putting all his weight into the third turn which rewarded him with a vague splutter of life from the old girl. "Now we're getting somewhere," he muttered, before his next turn brought them closer to the result they were after.

Responding to the engine's experimental cough, Curly started giving her 'a bit of juice,' cautiously pumping the accelerator as Bill almost danced a jig with excitement, all the while exhorting 'easy does it, mate, easy, don't want to drown her!' Though she didn't come to full blown life immediately, the Willys had obviously coughed with sufficient oomph to clear all its vital passages and the engine roared into life with next turn of the crank.

"Ey up, we're in business. Thanks mate," Bill grinned as he climbed in behind the wheel, tossing the crank on the floor on the passenger side, over where Curly had slid having got the old girl going. "Here we go, moment of truth, eh?" Bill said, engaging first gear and giving the motor a couple of experimental revs before slowly releasing clutch and edging forward to a round of applause from Dulcie, who stood in the turnabout, pleased to witness what all the fuss was about. Curly leaned out the window, whooping it up and waving energetically as they drove towards her. Retreating to the front garden, she watched in delight as Bill drove the car into the turnabout and did indeed, turn about before stopping and calling out to her to hop in and come for a spin while Curly climbed out and held the door open for her.

With Dulcie safely installed in the middle, Bill took off nice and slowly, proceeding cautiously, nursing the Willys along the high side of the muddy track like a newborn. After easing her over the cattle grid he turned right onto the tarmac, in the direction of Atherton, and an explosion of spent breath filled the cabin, collective relief at the success of the journey thus far. The road climbed gently to the Watson's place after which the land levelled out and the Willys started picking up speed. Just as Bill slipped her smoothly into top gear Dulcie burst into song, giving vent to the extraordinary exhilaration suddenly pulsing through her.

Me and me wife and me family three
Went down Royton by the sea
We watched the clog dancers and
We listened to the band
And then we went on Royton sands

"Come on, darling, join in the chorus," she encouraged Bill.

And we kept on eating parkin
We kept on eating parkin

368

We kept on eating parkin
That's why we are so brown.

She settled back, and they all laughed as they continued up the road in high spirits.

"You'll have to excuse Dulcie, Curly. She's a female ham as can't be cured, she is," Bill said with a chuckle, grinning at Dulcie the while.

"Give over, love. It were just a bit of fun," Dulcie smiled. "We used to sing that on the bus coming back from a day's outing when I were a kid. Being able to drive around for the sheer pleasure of it, as we are at this very minute doing," she smiled broadly, "made me think of holidays and that song just came to mind out of nowhere. Daft thing is, Neville, Royton is actually on edge of moors between Oldham, my home town, and Rochdale, in Yorkshire. It'd have to be a good 40 odd mile from coast. Only sand as you'd find would be in bunker on golf course like. Song's really just a bit of a joke of local cotton workers as couldn't afford holidays by seaside."

"And what's 'parkin' then?" asked Curly,

"Oh, that's the local oatmeal gingerbread made with black treacle, very dark in colour as a rule. Idea was if you ate enough of it you'd end up with turning brown, go home with holiday suntan anyway."

"You really will be able to go for seaside holidays now," Curly said. "Now you've got the Willys," Curly patted the outside of the door with his left hand and smiled, "and you'll not be tied to milking twice a day Bill."

"Aye, and I'll get some real time off once I've put in 12 months 'n all," said Bill. "David and Mary have extended invitation to go down to their place at Mission Beach once we settle into new routine."

"I've gotta say, you've got the old girl going real smooth, mate," commented Curly, patting exterior of passenger door again.

"Knows her inside out by now, I shouldn't wonder, amount of time he's spent with her," said Dulcie, "Different attitude and aptitude to his brother Dick, Curly. Dick adhered to the naval school dictum 'if it moves oil it, if it doesn't paint it'."

"Lot of good that would have done," Bill chipped in, laughing at the veracity of Dulcie's words all the same. Seeing a signpost up ahead, he turned to Curly observing, "That's Yungaburra turn off up ahead, isn't it Curly?"

"Yeah mate."

"Right, well I'm just going to turn around at intersection and head back home. Judging by them clouds, evening storm is right on time and I'm not sure how well these wipers work, if at all."

"Aye, and I'd best get on with it 'n all," said Dulcie, "It's been a godsend Nancy having kids for the day, Curly. I've got ever such a lot done. Just over a week now until we leave," she was stopped from further comment by the lump she suddenly found in her throat, tried in vain to hide her emotion with a smile.

No-one said anything. Bill reached for her hand and gave it a squeeze. After turning at the T-junction up ahead he put his foot down, managed to stay just ahead of the storm chasing them home from the north.

- 0 -

In consultation with various others, including Mervyn, Curly and David Baxter who, although no longer sighted, maintained through his contacts as up-to-date an idea of local developments as any, Bill had decided to take the family to Ravenshoe in the Willys. There would be plenty of room, having precious little by way of goods and chattels to take, and although it had been less costly for him to do the trip by train, it would represent no saving, indeed cost significantly more, if all of them were to do it. Besides, he had to get the motor there somehow and he'd no intention of having Dulcie travel on her own with kids on the train. He'd noticed the extent of improvement on the road to Atherton when he'd gone for his interview, told Dulcie as much when he got back. Most of road had been tarred, and he'd had no trouble from that as hadn't.

To go to Ravenshoe they'd turn south onto the Kennedy Highway at the big T-junction where they would ordinarily turn north to go to Atherton. David Baxter was in no doubt the highway to Ravenshoe was well maintained bitumen all the way, it being a main thoroughfare between Smithfield in Cairns to Mt. Garnet and, to a lesser degree, beyond. The stretch they would travel was a good clear run too, avoiding townships like Herberton and Tumoulin which would only slow them down. When Bill showed Dulcie on the map she couldn't help but notice just how good and clear the run would be, there being no sign of habitation on the road at all, though it cheered her considerably to see a number of towns just a bit further west. On arrival they were to stay at The Top Pub for a week as guests of the Ravenshoe Butter Factory whilst they sorted out permanent accommodation. "It's at the opposite end of town to The Bottom Pub apparently, but it's not called The Top Pub for that alone, Dulce. Curly reckons it's the highest pub in the state, highest above sea level like."

The two days before they were due to leave were sunny and dry, not that they were concerned about rain affecting their travel plans, but it did give them an unexpected chance to bid the farm a private farewell. On the second day, around mid-morning, Bill came in from tinkering with the Willys in the farrowing shed and suggested a picnic lunch, up by the rill where it flowed into the south paddock near Forester's Track. "It's gorgeous out, darling, blue skies, sunshine, gentle breeze. It'll be a bit damp up there but it'll be good as gold with a tarpaulin to put rug on." Not only had he checked and double checked both the car's performance and his preparations for the trip, but he also knew that Dulcie was as prepared for departure as she could be, save things as could only be done at last minute. The spontaneous enthusiasm with which she agreed revealed the relief she too felt, to have an unforeseen outlet for the nervous energy fuelled by excited anticipation of departure.

Perched beside the rill, high on the eastern perimeter of the farm, they enjoyed a bird's-eye view of the farm bounded on the north by Old Bronc's place whence the wood smoke from his camp fire dissipated quickly in the lively breeze. To the south they could see the track into the Coughlin's place which was itself obscured by the stand of hoop pines. Opposite, to the west, the blue line of mountains beyond the immediate landscape now bore the added significance of housing, in its highest reaches, their next destination. After lunch, Jilly and young Johnny, happy as, and looking not unlike, Mudlarks, played a game of seemingly endless fascination, requiring no props other than those provided by nature. Bill and Dulcie sat surveying

371

the farm and its surroundings with the individually selective perception of people having different vested interests, her eyes drawn to the 'homestead', his further afield.

"It's served us well, Dulcie, don't you think?" Bill asked, recognising in her keen inspection of the scene a desire akin to his own to impress the image on his mind forever.

"It has, darling, and none more so than the kids. I can't believe how strong and straight and true they're growing, and how independent. They'll be leaving us early, darling, you mark my words."

"Well, it was our main reason for coming here, love, to see as kids had a good life. Weren't it? But don't go getting maudlin on me now, will you. There's plenty of time to be spent with 'em before they go leaving home, however independent they might become."

Dulcie smiled at him reassuringly, "No, no, darling, I'm not getting maudlin. Good as it's been, and I really do agree wholeheartedly about that, in many respects I'm actually looking forward to getting on with things. Still, goodbyes always have their sadness."

They sat in companionable silence, watching Jilly and Johnny playing.

"Do you think if we took some cuttings from the hydrangeas, they would survive the trip, love?"

"We can always give it a go, Dulce, put them in a jar of water, keep it topped up until we've somewhere to plant them. They might be alright; worth a try."

"Of course, if Mavis were here she would know what to do for best. It's a pity she's not back yet," she sighed, "would have been nice to see her again."

"Well, as she said in her letter love, they'll come over to visit as soon as rains stop, when we're properly settled in. So you will see her again, just later rather than sooner."

"Are you picking Jess up from school?" asked Dulcie, changing the subject.

"Aye, love, I think I might ride over to fetch her, seeing it's such a nice day, give the horse a run, save on petrol too."

"We'd best be getting on then love. These two must be just about ready for an afternoon nap and they're both in need of a good bath first," she laughed at the sight of them, made a move to pack up.

On that, their last night in Malanda, the last thing they heard on the fringe of consciousness was the plaintive cry of a curlew mourning the passing of yet another day, and with it another episode in life's enigmatic journey.

- 0 -

Just as the exhilaration and relief of arrival had disturbed his repose on the first night spent beneath this corrugated ceiling, so, on this, the last, his restless anticipation of departure conspired with the muted sounds of nocturnal activity to wake him long before there could be any benefit in rising. He lay in the inky darkness and gave himself up to a parade of random reflections. Dulcie's words, spoken this very afternoon, echoed in his mind ……. *"I can't believe how strong and straight and true they're growing, how independent."* He smiled, recognising the truth in it, savouring with pride the vindication of his decision to come to this far flung country. Since arriving, his confidence in the wisdom of the move had been growing, the fact of the family's removal from depredations of war, deprivations of poverty. To his mind, this country's wars would be fought on other shores for many generations to come; they'd not be laid waste here, none of 'em, though young Johnny might see service abroad. The deadly head of the recently created, newly unleashed nuclear monster rose in his imagination, but he shook off fruitless thought on it, *"What dictates of time will decree only time will tell,"* he thought, rolling over, moving deliberately to lighter reflections.

Pockets of need, remnants of the depression, still existed to sufficient extent even here to have come to his notice. The swaggies who returned for seasonal work, having become estranged from their families, whether here or back home, were misfits some of them, eccentrics others. Still, there were those that came simply for work as couldn't be found elsewhere, wired money home, what they kept out of clutches of local publican. He remembered songs sung by the travelling entertainer at Glad's wedding, bush poet they called him; songs he'd sung later in the evening, when alcohol

373

fuelled nostalgia, and most felt gratitude for their current good fortune, though capable, at same time, of lachrymose lament of a less fortunate past. Snatches of them hovered fleetingly in his mind's eye like will-o'-the-wisps over songs bogged down by subsequent memories; fragments which spake of *soup queues* and *potato peelings, tightened belts* and *lack of work,* leaving no doubt of the depths of this country's suffering, its peoples' hardship. Still, all that was now relegated to history, same as war; blind Freddy could see the country was on the up and up, and two of the three big government projects he knew of were being undertaken right here, on their doorstep; Tinaroo and Koombooloomba, not that he'd have to resort to the dangerous work they offered a man for his living. There was no doubt Lady Luck had favoured him, in the connections she had provided. They were an enterprising lot these farmers; he'd be first to admit he'd landed on his feet in that respect. Fact that English was his language was added insurance against such misfortune.

"*Some of these foreigners are having a hard time of it,*" he thought, turning towards Dulcie, resting his hand on her hip, his thoughts gravitating similarly towards her. "*Things will be different now, with the Willys,*" he thought, "*though it's company of others she needs.*" Jess's clamourous exhortations to go to church because *everyone goes to Evensong on Sunday night and the kids are all allowed to play together afterwards* came to mind, along with something about parents enjoying cups of tea in church hall. He'd long ago recognised religions as instruments of social control, regardless of which faith they espoused. Like many he remained, had become, more like, detached from any credo, save, in his case, his abiding belief in the simple fact that life was a miracle deserving of the utmost respect, no matter whose, or what's, though "*Egads, even that much isn't simple!*" He lay for a time in quiet meditation. "*Still, can't be any harm in a bit of a sing song and a cup of tea afterwards where you can get to know neighbours,*" he mused. A song came to him as he drifted away, another of the bush poet's songs. How could he have forgotten it, sung, as it was, to the tune of 'It's A Long Way To Tipperary.'

> *It's a long way down the soup-line,*
> *It's a long way to go.*

374

It's a long way down the soup-line,
And the soup is thin, I know.
Goodbye, dear old pork chop,
Farewell beefsteak rare;
It's a long way down the soup-line,
But my soup is there.

He woke suddenly, as though disturbed by some outside agency, and climbed out of bed wondering how long he had actually slept. Pushing out one of the shutters, he secured it and leaned out to breathe in the freshness of the day's air. Across the paddocks night did battle for supremacy with day. Clouds sprawled on the horizon. The rooster crowed, cutting through the maniacal laughter of jackasses floating up from the direction of Curly and Nancy's. A morning like many others, a morning like none other, a morning in which they experienced, suspended dreamlike above real time, effectively removed from 'now', a heightened awareness of every nuance of every action, however simple, ever aware of time's relentless march, time spent. Bill went out with Old Bronc and Mervyn to round up. Glad turned up early with the makings of a big breakfast. George and Bruce came over to tuck in, say their farewells, though not so's you'd notice. The Willys was packed and they teetered on the verge of departure when a thrumming of the cattle grid drew their attention to the unmistakable arrival of the Model T.

"Didn't think Reg was due back 'til later in the week," Glad said as they all peered out of the kitchen window.

"He's got someone with him," observed George and they all made a move.

By the time Dulcie made it to the front gate, Mavis was striding across the turnabout, young Roger on her hip, laughing and crying at the same time. "Oh Dulcie, I'm so glad we made it before you'd left, love," she said, throwing her spare arm around Dulcie's neck. "I'm sorry I've been gone so long without much of a word, love, but I'm sure you'll understand. I couldn't say anything before I knew for sure in case I was mistaken," it was all pouring out in such a rush Dulcie couldn't understand half of it.

"Mavis, Mavis, take it easy love, whatever is it?"

"Oh Dulcie, I'm pregnant!"

ACKNOWLEDGEMENTS

Having now written a 'book', I can understand the many acknowledgements I have read which give first place to family members. I must now do the same and thank Samala and Laurie for putting up with me, and for doing without me during the process, for being prepared to join me in my 'created' world when I needed to share it, and most of all for their undiminished love and continuing encouragement even though I may not have met their every expectation.

I want to thank the JJ Manuscript Club who gave unstintingly of their time in reading the manuscript in draft form and providing considerate and constructive feedback. Thank you Danny Ward, Gail Ferguson, Irene Parker, Jill Knoblauch, Karl Jensen, Katrina Gaitero, Laurie Wharton, Samala Dewe-Mathews and Tessa Qua – much appreciated.

I would also like to record my gratitude for the courage and determination of my parents, who did migrate to Australia in 1952, and so laid the foundation for a wonderful life. To my 'Aussie' Uncles, Harry Howlett for sharing copious reminiscences of early times with me and the many trips he made with me in search of the 'real' Malanda – its people; and Douglas Walter Jones for his memoir, *The Corrugated Ceiling,* a valuable source of information and inspiration, certain 'bits' of which I have, with his blessing, borrowed.

Finally, my great thanks go to Peter Jones. Without his IT and self-publishing savvy, his enthusiastic commitment to the entire publication process, and his special brand of creativity, this book would not exist.

Whilst the basis for certain aspects of this story is provided by my forebears, all of the people within these pages are works of fiction.

www.ingramcontent.com/pod-product-compliance
Lightning Source LLC
Chambersburg PA
CBHW022139010726
47493CB00002B/272